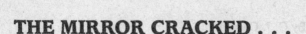

THE MIRROR CRACKED . . .

The amulet in Ela's hands began softly to glow and cast a light on her face—a mirror it was, a simple mirror. Tamas remembered the goblin saying that Ela's mistress would not touch what Ela had taken up. Tamas looked into the mirror.

The dark around them receded. They stood beneath the ghostly lamps and hangings of a great hall, and all around them men and women fled in fear. Suddenly a veiled woman stood in this thundering chaos. She looked full at them, at *him*, and pointed her finger, crying into the gale— "One and the same . . . remember that. There is always a flaw!"

The image shattered, with a sound of breaking glass. Shocking quiet followed, ordinary night around them.

By C. J. Cherryh
Published by Ballantine Books:

RUSALKA
CHERNEVOG
YVGENIE

THE GOBLIN MIRROR

THE GOBLIN MIRROR

C. J. Cherryh

A Del Rey Book
BALLANTINE BOOKS • NEW YORK

A Del Rey Book
Published by Ballantine Books

Library of Congress Catalog Card Number: 92-53171

ISBN 0-345-38476-8

Printed in Canada

First Hardcover Edition: October 1992
First Mass Market Edition: January 1994

THE GOBLIN MIRROR

1

A WITCH WIND, COUNTRY FOLK CALLED THE SUDDEN STORM that plunged Maggiar from autumn into winter, that stripped the colored leaves from forest and orchard all in a night. Behind it came an ice wind, edged with sleet and bitter cold— but that same winter brought a wealth of game the like of which the old folk had never seen. Hunters trekked home over the drifts with their pack ponies laden with meat and furs to keep old and young well-fed and warm; and with ample stock besides for trade to the west: deer and badger skins, marten and fox and ermine, from a plenitude of game that never seemed diminished. By midwinter deer had stripped the forest branches low enough to reach, foxes raided middens and storehouses, and the hunters could not shoot or trap them fast enough. Deer took to farmers' fruit trees. Boar rooted after winter stores, and marten and ermine hunted right up under the porches of Maggiar's isolated steadings. The old folk said: It was never like this before.

Behind the deer and the marten came the wolves, well-fed, content, inclined to lie about at first, but more and more of their voices sang in the mountain heights, songs cold and keen as the winter wind, that set folk looking anxiously toward the shutters at night and asking themselves was the door latch snug enough and had they barred all the sheds?

At last and as suddenly came the melting wind, a dark nighttime storm that rattled doors and windows, pelted the trodden snow with mingled sleet and rain, and turned the fields overnight to hedge-rimmed lakes. Farmers slogged about their spring chores in mud-weighted boots, attempted

1

planting in the high spots, and swore that they had never seen so quick a thaw or so much flooding.

In that season hunters began to find strange tracks in the woods, and spied shadowy movements flitting at the edge of the eye—a creature that left bearlike prints, walking upright.

The forest took on a dangerous feeling then, and the Old Folk whispered that a troll might have moved in. As yet no one had seen it, but the woodcutters and the charcoal burners cast anxious looks over their shoulders as they worked; while in lord Stani's keep, hunters old and young gathered and whispered in somber tones. Lord Stani's wizard, Karoly, wore a longer and longer look, casting the bones often and listening with his ear to the stone of the walls and the earth of the courtyard. Lord Stani asked Karoly what he heard in the earth, and the hunters asked. At one such asking, Karoly only muttered that many things seemed blessings that were not, and that father Sun and mother Earth never gave so liberally without a cost.

A deer was found at the forest edge totally blind and thin as a wraith—hunters killed it out of pity and let it lie and rot. That, too, they whispered about, unsure why that single death so disturbed them—but the truth was, once pity had afflicted them, a sense of guilt crept in, and made them think twice about the pelts stacked so high in the storehouses. It made them wonder for the first time whether luck that came so easily could be wholesome, or whether there might be something wrong in what they had gained too cheaply—as if they had plundered what was sound and left what was lame to breed and increase.

Master Karoly waked the watch one midnight swearing that he smelled something burning—not cookfires or rush-lights, but something like old straw set ablaze. The watch failed to smell it, the night scullions failed to find it in the kitchens, and no more discriminating nose they roused could smell it at all. Still, when a wizard insisted, it seemed only prudent to wake the lord and lady, so before all was done, lord Stani had his men and lady Agnieszka her women searching the keep from tower to deepest cellars, while servants scoured every outbuilding and haystack inside the walls and nearby for any hint of smoke.

But nothing turned up, after the hold had been in uproar half the night. There was bleary-eyed grumbling among the people at breakfast that their wizard might be confused in his old age—complaint that fell silent once Karoly came draggling into the hall, haggard and worried, and begging their pardons for his foolishness. Somber looks followed his distracted passage through the room, and folk whispered how wizards sometimes had the Sight, though Karoly had never had it: the bones gave him merest hints about the future.

In one rainy mid-afternoon soon after, Karoly asked a passing serving maid what child was hurt; but the maid heard no crying child at all. Karoly stopped more than one servant, upstairs and down, distressedly asking did they not hear some child? And that report sent more chills through the keep. A ghost, some muttered. Ill luck, the servants began to say. The cooks obsessively feared fire, and parents kept an anxious eye to their children.

"What do you see?" lord Stani asked Karoly that night. "Is there some danger—of fire? Of flood? Or is it some other thing?" There had been peace in lord Stani's land for all his lifetime, except the ordinary bear trundling out of the forest after easier pickings, and once, twenty years ago, an incursion of bandits. So lord Stani asked the questions the hunters had asked, as a man who had known peace all his life, and feared now, as the hunters feared, that his run of luck might have been too much and too long. "I need leave," Karoly said for reply, "to visit my sister over the mountains, and ask her what she sees. My dreams worry me."

Lord Stani (the servants who witnessed it reported so) asked very cautiously, "So what *do* you dream, Karoly?"

Karoly was silent a moment, gazing at the wall. Finally he said, "Wizards' dreams are all true and all treacherous; and if we knew always what we dreamed, we'd be no wiser. I put no trust in my dreams. I beg you, let me go."

No one had known Karoly had a sister—that news flew quickly about the halls, likewise Karoly's saying that,

"Something drove the deer." The rumor of the hour said that lord Stani was reluctant for his old tutor to leave, especially now, but saw no way of stopping him, none, at least, that Karoly would regard. It was foolhardy to ignore Karoly's advice, that was the consensus on the scullery stairs and in the smithy: some disaster boded, that Karoly sought to head off at its source.

So Stani called his two elder sons, Bogdan and Tamas, and bade them take Karoly through the mountains and bring him home again as soon as possible.

"It may be an old man's notion," lord Stani told them, "or it may be foresight—he always was wise before. Don't let his horse throw him, don't let him go cold or hungry— and above all bring him back in one piece. Woodcraft was never his best point; and he has no seat at all. If his horse so much as caught wind of a bear, he'd be afoot with it."

The brothers laughed, restless with the spring rains and delighted with the proposal. Bogdan said, "So much worse for the bear," and Tamas, the younger, said, "We'll take good care of him, papa." No one of their generation had ever ventured over the mountains. They had distant cousins and uncles in that land, they supposed. They knew of places like Krukczy Straz and Hasel, Burdigen, and Albaz, where their grandmother had had brothers and sisters—a land, the gran had told them, of beautiful waterfalls and tall pine forests. They knew all the names of them: the land over-mountain was their own land of once upon a time, and to ride out on their father's orders, to find this unguessed and surely witchly sister of master Karoly's—for the rescue of Maggiar, if the rumors were true—all this, and to have a winter full of their own tales to tell when they got safely back again? This was the chance of their young lives.

Their mother took a far dimmer view of matters. Lady Agnieszka went storming to lord Stani's chambers and servants pressed ears against the doors and listened wide-eyed to the shouting inside for half an hour; while the youngest of lord Stani's three sons, Yuri, aged fourteen, declared to his friends that Bogdan as heir should by no means put himself in danger; *he* should be the one to ride with Tamas—which opinion he bore to lord Stani, himself, hard on his mother's icy retreat.

But to no avail. Lord Stani informed his youngest son in no uncertain terms he was the sacrifice to his mother's good graces, the piece held in reserve against fate and accident; lord Stani said no, and no, and no.

After which, Nikolai, the master huntsman, his feet propped in front of the kitchen fire, told the pastry cook, "Trolls, that's what it is. Truth is, I'd rather not have the boys along. And come to that, I'd rather not have the old man. Send us up in the mountains and let us singe a few hides, I'd say, and leave the youngsters out of it. But the boy's of that age. . . ."

Bogdan, he meant. Bogdan, who was lord Stani's own image, dark haired and broad shouldered, the first in every game and every hunt; lord Stani foresaw the day Bogdan would be in his place, and wanted his heir to gain the level-headedness and the experience of border keeping a lord ought to have. Bogdan should see the land over-mountain and maybe, lord Stani had confided it to Nikolai in private, come back with a grown man's sober sense, less temper, and less interest in girls and hunting.

As for the younger son, Tamas, just past his seventeenth winter—shy, too-gentle Tamas, prettier than any girl in the keep—the boy was a fine hunter, if he could hit anything he'd tracked; a fine bowman, against straw targets; a serious, silent lad who would sit for an hour contemplating an antheap or picking a flower apart to find out what was inside. A little slow-witted, Nikolai summed him up, a little girlish, decidedly different from Bogdan's headlong rush at life. And this was the boy lord Stani sent in his charge, likely to hunt trolls?

Because that was what was really behind this flood of game, lord Stani himself had said as much to Nikolai when he had charged him pick the men for the escort and see that both the boys and the wizard got back with a whole skin.

"Don't speak of trolls," the pretty cook said, making an averting sign.

"I'll bring you a tail," Nikolai said. He was courting the cook. And not lying: a troll-tail he had taken, once upon a time, and given it to a silly maid he had been courting then. But Zofia was horrified. The kneading of bread had grown furious.

"You keep those boys safe," Zofia said.

"Keep Tamas safe. That's why m'lord sent young wander-wits: to put a rein on master head-foremost Bogdan."

Zofia frowned. The dough changed shape and folded again, in Zofia's strong, floury hands, a fascinating process. "The scullions heard a thing in the eaves last night," Zofia said. "Skritching and scratching and beating with its wings. And master Karoly said yesterday—he was sitting just where you are, having a sip of tea—he said we should do without mushroom picking, not send the lasses out, not go in the woods. And I says, Why? What's out there? and he says, Just don't be sending the youngsters beneath the shade of the trees. Why? I says again. Is it trolls? And he says—he takes this long sip of tea, like he's thinking—but he says something odd, then, like: There might be a troll, but it didn't *want* to come here.—That's just the way he said it. What do you make of it?"

"That it's exactly what I said to m'lord upstairs, a fat summer in the high country. A fat summer, a bad winter, too many deer. They strip the woods and they're straight for the orchards, it's as simple as that."

"And the trolls?"

"The wolves and the trolls, they go where the pickings are. But now that the bears are waked up—" Nikolai re-crossed his feet on the bench, so the fire warmth reached the sole of his other foot. "*They'll* put master troll back up the mountain in short order. Then *they'll* be rattling the shed doors and sifting the midden heaps—so you can look to hear trolls under every haystack, half of them with cubs and all in a bad humor."

"It's not lucky to make fun." Zofia licked a floury thumb and made a gesture toward the witch-knot on the rafters, garlic and barley stalks. "You watch those two boys, you hear, don't you be letting them do something foolish, and don't you and Karoly do it, or the lord and lady won't let you back again.—You!'' Thump of the dough on the table, and a scullion froze in his tracks. "Fetch the milk upstairs, and don't be slopping half of it.—I swear, the help is all scatter-wits this evening.''

But Nikolai, thinking about the lord's two sons, said, half to himself, "The boys with trolls is one thing. Over-mountain is another. See his sister, the old man says. Why hasn't he seen his sister before this, is what I'd like to know, and where did he get a sister and what's he to do with her of a sudden? He's never been back over-mountain that I know. And I ask lord Stani about this sister business and he says Karoly insists and we should go.''

"Old Jan says he'd come and go over-mountain.''

"Upon a time, you mean.''

"When he and the *old* lord was pups, long before you or I was born.'' Another folding in, another cloud of flour. "Old Jan was saying how Karoly was always out and around, in those days, off in the woods, up in the hills . . . the old lord, too—or least as far as old Jan remembers. So there could be a sister over-mountain, could be a horde of sisters, for all anybody knows. And how did the old lord find the lady gran? We all know she at least come from there.'' The dough thumped down onto the table, whump. "Lady gran used to come down here and stir the pots herself. 'More salt,' she'd say, and me mum and she'd be going round and round about the pepper and the spice. . . .'' Whack. "She used to get herbs from Karoly. Karoly'd go pick at the right of the moon and the old lady'd say, Which side of the tree did you dig it from? And Karoly would say, snippishlike, The *right* one. I 'member that, plain as plain, I'd be stirring the pot, me standing on a step stool, I was so little, and they'd be arguing. And me mum said I shouldn't listen, the old lady had strange practices, that was what me mum called it. 'Strange practices.' The lady gran died and they still hang charms on the grave. Don't they?''

It was true. And it was certainly not the first time Nikolai had heard witchery and the lady gran joined in one breath—along with the observation that Karoly had been the guiding hand behind the young lord, Stani having been about Yuri's age at the time the old lord went over his horse's neck and never walked again—and the lady gran had had her way with the land until lord Stani was toward twenty and nine, with the god only knew what arrangements (or doings) between her and Karoly.

"Don't they?"

"They do that," he said. Women's business and witches. It was bad enough Karoly wanted to consult a witch: Nikolai wanted no part of the lady gran's business. The lady was in her grave and stayed there, thank the god; trolls were enough trouble for any man.

Cook gave a shake of her head and mounded the dough into a bowl, threw a towel over it. "Over-mountain isn't where I'd like to be right now, with strange doings and things flying about a' night. Ask yourself what was trying to get in with the scullions last night, eh?"

The boy was clumping up the steps with the milk pail. He came in white faced and hasty, all ears. Nikolai looked at the boy, who set the pail down and said, "Is that all, dame Zofia?"

"Be off," cook said. And when the door was shut: "They don't want to go into the barn, don't want to go to the sheds in the dark. I don't rightly blame them."

"There's no troll in the courtyard. They don't go where there's this many people."

"If they eat them one by one there's not that many people, is there?" Cook's voice sank to a mutter. "I don't like the store room meself, and that's the truth. Karoly said keep all the latches tight. And what did he mean by that; and what was that smell of burning, I'd like to know. So he's running off to over-mountain, to the lady gran's relatives as well as his, if you ask me—and lord Stani sending the boys with him . . . at whose asking, I want to know. His lady certainly didn't want it; and lord Stani wasn't listening to her at all, that's what the maids heard come out of that room."

That was what the men were saying, too, down in the courtyard and in the stables and the barn. The grooms were saying other things, how the barley sheaves above the stable door had fallen down in the wind, the doors had come open, and something had scared the horses last night, the same maybe as had scared the scullions.

Or maybe the wind had been what had them all upset. The old man smelled smoke and heard lost babies, rumors of it traveled from village to farmstead, and you could stay in the kitchen listening to tales until all the world outside seemed dark and evil.

But Nikolai had a lonely walk out to the tower tonight to reach his quarters, and on the way up the twisty, narrow tower stairs, where the light he carried up from the doorway made rippling giant shadows on the stones, he found himself thinking about the upstairs shutters and wondering if he'd left them latched or open on the night.

Foolish notion. An open window had never bothered him before. There was nothing to fear—nothing that wouldn't have a better chance at him tomorrow night, when they were sleeping under the stars. But there was something about old piles of stone like this, that had seen lords and servants come and go, that they accumulated shadows and odd sounds, and creaks and sighs of wind; you could well expect to meet the lady gran or old lord Ladislaw on the stairs—and it was no good thing to think of, on the eve of going troll-hunting and wizard-shepherding: the lady gran might be safe in her grave these last ten years, but *he* had to open the door of his room and probe the shadows, a grown man, for shame! who did not like to find the shutters open on the night and the light blowing precariously in his hands.

He went and pulled the shutters closed. In that instant the lamp blew out and the door slammed shut, thump! plunging the room into dark and echoing through the tower like doom. It actually took courage to turn again and calmly latch the shutters, to remember his way blind through the dark of his own chambers, feel after the door, and open it.

A very little light came up from below, not enough to light

the steps. He found the lamp on the table and felt his way downstairs again to light it—not the first time the door had played that rotten trick, with the wind coming out of the south; not the first time he had trekked down the steps to relight the lamp—but he had never had a heart-thumping panic like this, god, not since he was nine years old, and he'd dared the bogle in the hay-loft that the neighbor boys refused to face.

It had known better than to meddle with him, and fled with a great rustling of straw and a clap of wings.

He lit the lamp. He climbed the stairs and on that last turn half-feared that the shutters in his room would be open again, or that something would be waiting in the shadows, or behind the door. That was the price of listening to stories, and he was a fool to think about them. Zofia was probably snug in her own bed, forgetful of all her notions.

But he thought not. He somehow thought not, tonight. And even with the shutters shut and the lamp burning bright, he longed for the morning, when they could be under the sky and out from under vaults of stone and memories.

Trolls and wolves isn't all that's wrong, he thought to himself, suddenly, for no good reason. He remembered over-mountain, at least the glimpse of it he had had from the heights, the year of the troll. He remembered a green land under a strangely golden sky, and a feeling he had had then of secrets beneath that green and witchcraft thick as leaves in that country. He had come from the north, followed the soldiers at fifteen, through wars and famine and the doings of wizards and witches—but that place had had a spooky feeling to it even that long ago. He had closed his mind to it, then: put away the memory until it was nudged by a rattling shutter and talk of the lady gran.

Karoly? Karoly was a dabbler, a pot-wizard, a weather-witcher. Think of Karoly and you thought of wheaten charms and jars and jars of powders for toothache and the gout. Karoly was sunny fields and winter firesides—

(But in the lady gran's day Karoly had gone off for days on end, that was so. One wondered where. Or why. Assignations with some sunburned country lass? Karoly was a man. And the lady gran—)

The lady on the stairs, dreadful in the lamplight—she had not been old. Her hair had been black. He remembered it as black, the year he had come to Maggiar. "Whose are you?" she had asked. "Whose are you, pretty? And what are you doing on my stairs?"

Shutters rattled with the wind. Forget the pretty cook, her pastries and her stories. Forget the lady gran, the stairs and the long-ago dark. Lord Stani's master huntsman longed for sky above him, for the sighing of leaves—the forest had no memory such as stones acquired, when men piled them up and dwelled in them and made walls and bolts to keep themselves safe from each other inside.

2

THE WHITE BITCH HAD WHELPED IN THE NIGHT—SOFT nosed, was nudging the newborn pups against her belly to nurse in the morning chill.

No few of them were yellow. Yuri was quick to point that out; and Tamas rubbed the ears of the gawky yellow hound that thrust its head under his arm to have a look at the puppies: Zadny, they called the ugly stray, who desperately wanted to please, who was good-tempered and keen to do what a body wanted. Somebody had lost a fine dog, in Tamas' estimation, the day Zadny had slipped his leash: he had arrived in the ice wind, starved and foot-sore, refusing every hand but Tamas' own, from which day he was Tamas' dog, and fastest of all the dogs Tamas used. In case wanderlust took him away this spring, Tamas was delighted to see the puppies.

But Tamas came to the kennel in armor this dawn, with grandfather's third best sword bumping at his side, breakfast uneasy in his stomach, and the stark realization in his mind that he could not be here, that Yuri must inherit the puppies—to see them walk, and tumble, and play. Yuri had run up looking for him and Bogdan as if nothing else were going on in the yard: Bogdan was busy at the stables, in the deepest throes of packing; but Tamas had excused himself and come for Yuri's sake; and, faced with changes that would pass without him, was suddenly beset with apprehensions.

Yuri lifted up a puppy and showed him the face. "It has to be his, doesn't it?"

"No question," Tamas said, rubbing the blunt puppy nose

that had Zadny's yellow fur. "Only lighter. But puppies are, you can't tell yet." He had come here to mollify Yuri's offended sense of importance; now he felt unease, and a sense of loss he could not define. It prompted him to say, "Take care of them. If anything should happen—"

"It won't happen!" Yuri scowled and set the puppy down against its mother. "No reason I can't go, I'm only two years behind you, but no one sees that."

It was three. But shading on two. " 'Anything can always happen,' " Tamas quoted Karoly, and reached out to squeeze Yuri's sullenly averted shoulder. "Maybe it's nothing, all this business, maybe it's just a bad year and it's a foolish goose chase, over-mountain. It might be. It's not what goes on there that I'm worried about, it's what happens here."

There was a wet-eyed angry look from Yuri. "Nothing happens here. Nothing ever happens here!"

"So it's your job to see it doesn't. Hear me?" His brother longed after importance. Tamas offered what romance he could. "Noises in the stables, scratches at the windows . . ."

"Birds," Yuri said sullenly. "That's all, it's birds. It's springtime, master Karoly says so, what do they expect?"

"Just take care. And don't go off alone in the woods and don't let your friends go. There *could* be a troll, and I don't want you to find it."

"I thought there *was* a troll. I thought you were supposed to kill it on your way."

"If we meet it on our way. We're supposed to ride over-mountain and back, that's all we're supposed to do. Master Karoly isn't happy with things *here*, that's why we're going to talk to his sister, isn't it? It's no good if we get there and something dreadful's happened back here, if the house has burned down or something. So watch out for things. Keep an eye on everything—don't let your friends be stupid, don't go into the woods. Don't let something go wrong. You're taking Bogdan's place in the house. —And take care of Zadny for me. All right? The houndsmaster doesn't like him; he threatens to lose him in the woods, and I want you to watch out for him and see he's all right while I'm gone. Promise me."

There was not much time. Men were mustering in the yard. And talk had only broken the dam: Yuri glared at him with tears brimming, temper and shame equally ruddy in his cheeks. "You get to do everything. Bogdan ignores me. It's not fair!"

"It's the first time, I promise you, it's the first time I've ever gone anywhere—and next time, you will go. You'll be tall as I am in another year."

"It won't do any good. The baby has to stay home if the rest of you get killed. For the rest of my life they'll say, 'Somebody has to stay home . . .' "

"Take care of Zadny. Keep out of trouble. Promise me?"

"I promise." Sullenly. Tearfully.

"Come on." He tousled Yuri's hair and Yuri batted at his hand.

"Don't treat me like a baby. Don't do that."

"I promise. Never again." This morning seemed an ominous time for Never Agains. He skirted around that thought, into irrevocable decision. "Come on. Walk me to the yard."

Yuri got up in glum silence and dusted himself off. Zadny came wagging up, brushed his cold nose against Tamas' hand, and got in his way—Zadny was roundly cursed for that habit, by cook, by Taddeuscz the houndsmaster, by Bogdan, especially since the day Zadny had gotten shut upstairs and chewed Bogdan's best boots. Zadny had a way of crossing one's path on stairs, or in doorways. Zadny chewed on things. He was lost, Tamas was wont to argue on his dog's behalf. —He likes to be close to people. He hasn't grown into his feet yet. He hasn't had anyone to teach him manners.

He thought of Zadny underfoot in the yard, with the horses, or the very likely chance of Zadny following them down the road. "Yuri," he said, "we have to tie him," and Yuri agreed and got a rope.

It was a betrayal. He got down on one knee and tied the knot tight, getting dog all over him in the process, and a wet kiss of forgiveness in the face. "Be good," he told Zadny.

"Stay, mind Yuri." After which he got up, wiped his face and his leather surcoat, and went with Yuri out of the kennels.

Barking pursued them through the gate, onto the trampled earth and flagstone of the larger courtyard, where horses and grooms mixed with stray goats and a handful of agile pigeons. The escort was gathering, with relatives and well-wishers, mothers and wives and younger brothers and sisters, uncles and aunts and cousins and grandparents, all weaving perilously in and out among the horses, all turned out in holiday best because it was no hunting party they were organizing, it was as bold and ambitious a setting-forth anyone had made for years in Maggiar, to legendary over-mountain, with the chance of trolls along the way—fifteen men, all told, with their horses and three pack ponies loaded with grain and canvas for the mountain passes. The commotion caught Tamas up, making his heart beat faster. Colors and edges seemed both bright and unreal this morning. Master Nikolai was shouting at the grooms. Jerzy was flirting with a knot of Zav's cousins. Bogdan, looking every bit a lord's son and a warrior, was taking his leave of their mother and father at the top of the steps.

Tamas eeled through the confusion, hurried up the few steps to the landing with Yuri in his wake. "Do you suppose you can get this lot away today?" their father asked Bogdan just then. Bogdan laughed and took his leave, clapping Tamas on the arm and ruffling Yuri's hair as he passed, with, "Be good, little brother."

Tamas went and kissed his mother—"Be careful," she said to him, straightened his cloak-pin and remarked how handsome he was, but she had said a great deal more than that last evening—about witches and trolls and the necessity of watching what he ate and what he drank and never, never, never believing something that looked too good to be true.

"We'll be back before high summer," he told her, seeing tears glistening—high summer was what master Nikolai had assured all of them; he kissed her a second time, guilty for her tears, then briskly hugged his father, who patted him on the shoulders, saying, dryly, "Tamas,—keep a leash on your brother."

"I will," he promised, startled: his father had never said such a thing before, never hinted in all their lives that he doubted Bogdan's leadership, and he was not sure it was not a joke, except his father was not laughing. Had there been some falling out this morning? Bogdan at least had been laughing as he left.

Their father hugged him a second time, closer, clapped him on the back and shoved him after Bogdan, as if that was after all his final judgment of the sons he was sending out into the world—but, lord Sun, he had no idea how he was supposed to restrain Bogdan's headlong rush at obstacles: master Karoly could hardly do that. He was the younger son, Bogdan was in command, and their father told him to keep Bogdan out of difficulties?

The clatter of horses racketed off the courtyard walls, drowning shouts and conversations as Tamas went down the steps, past master Karoly, in armor like the rest of them, who was on his way up to his father. He spotted his own horse in the milling yard: the grooms had brought him, and they had indeed tied his packs on for him as they had said. He headed that direction in relief, done with good-byes and parental tears. Now his only worry was not to look foolish among the older men—when out of nowhere a chubby girl ran up, pressed a heavy packet into his hands and fled.

He stopped, confused, as Yuri turned up at his elbow, breathlessly asking could he have use of his hunting bow while he was gone, his own was too short for him, and he needed a far heavier pull than Bogdan's old cast-off . . .

"Yes," Tamas said absently. The packet the girl had given him smelled wonderfully of cake and spice; and he wondered who she was, or what he had done to deserve her attention. Other girls were giving out gifts of cakes or garlands to their sweethearts—but he was notoriously, famously shy of girls— everyone teased him for it; she intended he give it to Bogdan, that was most probably the answer.

"Tamas? Can I?"

He remembered his promise not to ruffle Yuri's hair—just in time. Yuri stood looking up at him, promising fervently, "I'll take care of it," —meaning the bow, which would only gather dust this summer, and that was not good for a bow. Or for other things. "Use anything," he said. "Anything of mine you like." One did not hunt trolls and come back and play with kites and tops. The clothes, he would outgrow. The few things else . . . why detail a few sentimental trinkets? Yuri had the last of his boyhood to go, the exploring years, the hunting and the fishing out at distant farms a marvelous half day away from home and supper. . . .

Pottery crashed. Michal's horse, fighting the grooms to avoid a gaggle of girls, backed into stacks of baskets, then surged back toward the screaming girls, across a ruin of apples. Chaos spun through the yard, Michal and the grooms all cursing as they restrained the horse.

"All right, all right," the master huntsman shouted, "to horse, lord Sun, clear back, can we have less commotion and get us underway? Master Karoly? M'lord Tamas? Can we get to horse?"

His face went hot. He glanced back, where Karoly was still with their father, insisting, he suddenly realized, on rehearsing every detail he had gone over with their father last night—he knew Karoly and he could catch the gist of it from here. So he ran back up the steps, tugged master Karoly by the sleeve, with: "Master Karoly, we're leaving *right now*," and drew the old man down to the yard.

"The weather-glass," Karoly was calling over his shoulder as grooms at the foot of the steps were boosting his armored weight into the saddle. "Don't forget the weather-glass, I showed Yuri how to read it—"

Their father called back, "Be off or you'll be here for harvest. —And mind, *listen to advice*, master Karoly!"

"—have to keep the water up to level!" Karoly shouted back, while Tamas tucked his be-ribboned prize into his saddle pack before mounting. "Be careful!" Yuri wished him, with worry on his face.

"Use your heads!" their father bellowed across the yard.

Bogdan, ahorse, laughed and waved, already turning away; "Good-bye!" Yuri was shouting, and with his foot in the stirrup, Tamas had an overwhelming impulse to glance back toward his parents and his home as if—as if, it seemed, he had only this last moment to fix everything in memory, everything about this place . . .

But Bogdan was riding for the gate with Karoly and Nikolai, leaving no time for moon-gazing, and he hit the saddle as his horse joined the milling spill outward, overtaking Bogdan and the horse his own was most used to following. Hooves rumbled on the bridge, thumped onto the solid earth of the road, and the voices and the cheering grew faint. When he looked back a third time, home was gray, forbidding walls and a last pale glimpse of festive well-wishers within the gates, but no sight of Yuri, who was probably sulking. The day seemed perilous, full of omens; yet there was nothing he could put a thought around, as master Karoly would say. As if—

As if he were on the brink of his own forever after—or maybe only of growing up. It was a slice of his whole year this journey might take, bound where there might be bandits, or trolls. And he had given everything away.

He asked himself why now. Yuri would only lose the things—Yuri was fourteen, still careless, and could Yuri know the value of a broken toy horse and a bird's nest? Yuri would toss the keepsakes into the midden and use the painted box to hold his fishing weights.

But fields surrounded them now. The horses ran out their first wind and settled to a steady pace as friends sorted out their riding groups. In a little more there was no sign or sight of the keep at all, only orchards on either side, and a dark straggle of wild woods in front of them. The day had settled to a steady creaking of leather and jingling of harness and armor—as life would be for days and days, and probably more of that than of meeting bandits.

And they were not strangers he was riding with, they were mostly Bogdan's friends; and a few of his father's men. Bogdan might be in command for appearance's sake, but master

Nikolai was in charge where it came to trolls—not to mention master Karoly, who could tilt any odds to Nikolai.

As the day passed, it felt like any ordinary hunting-party, forgetting the armor and the swords and master Karoly's presence with them: the jokes and gibes were the same, older men testing the younger ones—in which, being youngest and a fair target, he made no jokes, only defended himself. He could trade gibes with his lord brother, if he chose, which the others only rarely dared—

But he would not do that in public. Not in front of Bogdan's friends. Bogdan was anxious about having him along: Bogdan was always anxious about his wit in front of witnesses, and generally left him alone: by Bogdan's example, he supposed, so did Bogdan's friends, although he was a fair target on certain points, like girls and hunting, and doubtless had a reputation for glum, dull silence.

'Keep a leash on Bogdan,' indeed. Only because he was a weight on his brother, and knew court proprieties and not to set his elbows on the table.

And maintaining Bogdan's good humor in this company meant calling down no untoward attention on himself, making no mistakes and not becoming the butt of jokes. Of Bogdan's friends, Filip was amiable enough. Of the grown men, master Karoly was safe, even master Nikolai. But Jerzy— lord Sun, who could deal with Jerzy, elegant master Barb-in-everything? Or Michal, who was still smarting about his horse and the apple baskets?

Apples, Jerzy recalled at every opportunity. Michal was frowning, dark as the thunderclouds that shaded their road, and making shorter and shorter retorts.

In that way they passed from fields to occasional thicket. It rained, a sudden downpour, and they rode under rain-dripping branches of the deeper woods—("Where's weather-witching?" the grumble was heard then in the ranks. "Our own wizard along, and we're soaked the first day out. Wake up, master Karoly!")

But the air held a clean fresh scent the rest of the day; Jerzy wearied of apples; and they camped in a charcoaler's clearance as the trail grew too dim for safety, with a fire of wood and leftover lumps of charcoal.

Then everyone broke out the drink and the packets of honeyed sweetmeats, fresh baked bread and cheese and sausages, all the rich food that was bound to go bad in a few days, and shared it around—"Oh, ho!" Bogdan said, as Tamas offered the cake, "that's not cook's work, is it?"

"I think she meant it for you," Tamas said, trying to hand it to him. But Bogdan waved it off—"I'm *sure* it's yours," Bogdan said. "Keeping secrets, are we, brother?"

"Many," he retorted shortly, and glanced down, for fear of the cake becoming as notorious as apples.

But in fact, the plump maid's spice cake was delightful, and, sharing it around, and with the men not too wickedly asking who the mysterious sweetheart was, he found himself thinking she *had* been somewhat pretty: the gatewarden's second daughter, if he had his girls sorted out.

And not even an impossible match for lord Stani's second son, although his mother would hold out for (he shuddered) Jerzy's hot-tempered younger sister, or lazy third-cousin Kataryzna, lord Sun save him. A wife was another prospect that came with growing up and riding with the men. All too soon, someone else's decision was going to arrive in his life with a clutter of baggage, disarranging his quarters, his habits, his days, his holidays, and his time to himself. And while spice cake was a benefit, the loss of privacy was not.

"Don't mind if I do," master Nikolai said, taking a chunk. "Mmm."

Master Karoly meanwhile had strayed off about the fringes of the clearing, among the trees. Nikolai's eyes were on him. So then were Bogdan's.

"Master Karoly," Bogdan called out as Karoly wandered further into shadow, but the old man showed no disposition to come back.

"It's going to be that way," Bogdan muttered, and elbowed Filip on his other side. "Filip, —god, —go watch him. Don't trouble him, but don't let him find a bear out there."

Filip swore wearily, got up and took his sword and his piece of cake with him, while master Nikolai washed his mouthful down with a long drink from his flask.

"Trolls aren't much for fires," Nikolai said, and finding every eye on him, went on with satisfaction: "They're not much for wizards either. The one I killed, now, that was the year a whole band of them came in on one of our farmers, killed the family, him, his wife, her brother, all the livestock. We found just the bones left of most of them. Dreadful winter. When we tracked them up into the mountains they charged right into the firelight and tried to make off with our horses. Either they thought we'd be easy as the farmers or they were that hungry. Trolls have a prodigious appetite."

"What did you do?" Jozef wanted to know. Jozef was new in the hold, an exchange from maternal uncle Ludwik's hold at Jazny-brook. Tamas and Bogdan and every youngster in the household had begged the tale every winter, how Nikolai had grabbed the chief troll's tail and cut it off, but Jozef was a new audience.

". . . bear-sized, these were. Big as a bear at least. You could take them for bears, except the faces, except the tail. It's long and naked as a rat's; and if you can grab that, you've got him. Except then you have to decide what to do with him."

Nikolai was joking with Jozef; the older men's eyes were sparkling with amusement. "So what did you do?" Jerzy asked, in the exact moment.

"Why," Nikolai said, "cut it off and ran like hell."

Laughter around the fire. Of course Nikolai could be talked into telling his story in detail, starting from the ruined farmhouse, and the dreadful find there.

Meanwhile Karoly came trailing back with Filip, sat down in silence and seemed to listen, hunched over with his arms about his knees. Nikolai told of the events near the cave, and how he had done for the king of the trolls, and him big as a bear and strong as two men.

The whole woods seemed full of sighs and whispers. An owl called. Jozef jumped, and laughed about it.

Karoly said, afterward, "I don't look for them here. Though it's possible. We should have a guard tonight."

"Jerzy," Bogdan said.

"A guard against *what*?" Jerzy protested. "That's what I'd like to know, if I'm going to sit up listening."

"Against whatever comes," Karoly murmured, staring abstractedly into the fire, and that was all subsequent questions could get out of him.

Jerzy, grumbling, dislodged Michal from the most comfortable spot near the fire, set his back against a tree and propped his sword across him, while the rest of them settled to sleep: Jerzy, and Michal, Filip, Pavel and Zev, that was the sequence of watch Bogdan set up, to take them to dawn; and Tamas loosened the belts and the straps of his armor and slid out of some of it, besides the boots—he watched what Nikolai and Bogdan did, to see how much comfort was prudent under the circumstances; and settled down with his saddle packs for a pillow, and Nikolai's story to darken his thoughts.

The newly leaved trees rustled and sighed over them. Night-creatures creaked and hooted through the woods around about. Their horses moved about their firelit grazing, bickered and shifted suddenly, rousing several heads from blankets, then quieted for a while. Nikolai had sat down near Jerzy, on watch, and the two of them talked in low voices, something to do with bear tracks in the woods: Tamas tried to hear, his mind too full, he feared, for sleep, and what regarded trolls or bears interested him. He shut his eyes to rest them while he listened; but he waked with the sun filtering through the trees, the whole camp stirring, and Bogdan calling him the family lay-about.

Things were immediately dull once Bogdan and Tamas had ridden away. Night was worse, with no brothers bickering down the hall. And breakfast was altogether glum and much too quiet. Yuri stirred his porridge about, with no appetite for it, slouched about his morning duties for Karoly, the slate-marking and the daily estimation of the weather-glass, then ghosted through their mother's sight, their mother moping and sewing and discussing with her audience of maids and matrons.

But he was too old to have to sit with that. He went down to their father's hearings of the farmers and tradesmen, but the only excitement there to be had was the story about farmer Padriaczw's bull and widow Miriam's cow, and once that was done, he slumped downstairs toward the yard to look for some of the other boys.

He was sure he would find them about the kitchens. But cook was making pastries, and said the boys had ridden out to Ambrozy's holdings to hunt rabbits.

That was completely unfair. Nobody had told *him*. Never mind he had slept late, and dallied about master Karoly's study, and lingered to hear about the bull and the widow's cow: one of them could at least have looked for him, and he was not now even interested to go and scare rabbits with a pack of boys too busy to come and find him.

So he collected a few special scraps for the white bitch and his brother's dog, deciding puppies were more fun than traitors, and that he and Zadny could go hunt rabbits around the orchard outside the wall.

So he flew down the scullery stairs, leaped puddles of wash water, and skipped down and around to the rickety kennel fence, near the stables. His father's dogs immediately set up a row, wanting what he had; Bogdan's six hurled themselves at their kennel gate and barked and yelped to attract his attention.

But the new mother, the white bitch, put her nose up to the gate and took her scraps with licks of gratitude, like the lady she was. He counted to see were the puppies all in their nest and they were. Then he went as far as Zadny's lonely and ramshackle pen, which Tamas had made doubly strong to keep the other dogs from fighting with him.

But no Zadny came up to the gate; and when Yuri lifted the latch and looked, there was the rope lying in the mud, chewed through.

He had let Zadny get away. Tamas would kill him.

No, Tamas would forgive him, and that was a thousand times worse.

"Where are you going?" the armorer asked. "Isn't that Tamas' bow you're taking?"

"He lent it to me," Yuri said. And never answered the first question, in his flight downstairs.

"Where are you going?" cook asked, when he begged a hamper of food.

"To find the boys," he lied—although it was not quite a lie, if one could count his brother and their friends. "Please could I have extra? They'll probably be starved."

"Where are you going?" the stablemaster asked, when he caught him saddling his pony, Gracja.

"Oh, cook gave me this for the boys." He showed the basket, but not what was in it.

"You mind don't break your neck," the stablemaster said. Yuri was sure the stablemaster was thinking mostly of the pony's neck and the pony's welfare, no matter Gracja was his pony and he had never brought her to harm.

"Where are you going, young lord?" the guard at the gate asked.

"Oh, out and about," he said, and rode through.

"When will you be back?" the guard called after him.

"When I find my brother's dog," he shouted back, and set Gracja to a brisk trot, because the guard was hard of hearing, and every boy knew it.

And because he knew what direction Zadny had gone, and how far he might go, and because that direction was (he would admit it to himself only for a moment or two) exactly the way his heart wanted to go, at least in his fondest imagination . . . only, in his pretending, he dreamed of overtaking Zadny just as Zadny reached the men on the mountainside, and hearing his eldest brother say, "Oh, let him come, he's already here."

But that was not what Bogdan would say. And he knew the look Tamas would give him if he could not even keep his dog safe in his pen.

He had some pride. And if he was out all night and if he came back with Zadny, maybe everybody including his traitor friends would have worried enough to realize they cared.

It was forest for the next whole day; and expecting trolls palled after a time, in Tamas' thinking. The land began to rise. They saw game, but never yet a sign of trolls, and made no diversion to hunt—Bogdan maintained that rabbit stew would be a fine supper and argued that they could spare the time; but Nikolai overruled him, as Nikolai had their father's instructions to do, saying they could enjoy that luxury on the way back: it was better they move along, until they knew for certain what weather they were facing in the mountains.

Besides, they had the remnant of the cakes and cheese and sausage from home; and they had to dispose of that before it went stale or spoiled—amazing, Tamas said to himself, how obsessively men's thoughts turned to their next meal, when there would be no kitchen to provide it; and how after two days of looking for trolls under every log and bush, the mind wandered and began to observe other detail for relief, the flight of birds, the sunlight on new leaves, and the quick scurrying of vermin in the undergrowth.

The damage of the winter past was everywhere evident, in bushes that should be budding, now attempting to come up from the root; in trees leafing only above the reach of deer. But deer left little sign, now; instead, there was a great busyness of small scavengers—at one days-old carcass, like a swarm of rats when the granary door was opened.

—The forest is wounded, Tamas thought, not to the death, yet, but wounded—when no one could imagine a forest this wide and healthy could take harm, even by fire. He would never have said there could ever be too many deer, or too many foxes, but seeing the damage here, considering scratchings at doors and desperate flutterings at the eaves of the keep itself, he began to believe it more than a mere omen of harm: the harm here might be subtle, but it was already begun, in a spring that would not come with its usual vigor, and in the abundance of carcasses that the wolves had not touched.

There were always deaths in winter, that the melting snow turned up—deaths culling the weak and the old and the lame: but these were too many, and too recent: animals that had survived the winter were dying of privation, one kind preying on the next. Undergrowth was less. Roots had washed bare in the rains. Berry-thickets were scant of leaves. The other men began to remark on it, and asked Karoly what he thought.

Karoly said, "One thing touches everything." But when Jerzy asked what he meant, Karoly only looked at the sky through the branches, gazing, it might be, toward the hills, and said, "That answer is over the mountains."

It was a good thing cook had put extra biscuits in the basket; and a bad one he had not managed to come away with but a light cloak—but, Yuri said to himself in the chill of the night, if he had gone out with a blanket and everything he needed he would never have gotten away.

And if he had been a little earlier going out to see to Zadny the way he had promised, he might have caught Zadny before he chewed through the rope.

But there was no use sleeping with might-have-beens, his father would say. He was in the woods. He had called after Zadny until every farmer in the valley and every deer in the forest must have heard him. It was only after the sun went down that he had begun to think overmuch about trolls, and wolves, and bears; and now in the dark it seemed scary to call out. This was the hour the four-footed hunters were out—and the time that trolls moved about, looking for boys and lost dogs to have for their suppers, if they could not catch a deer.

Or maybe they would rather catch boys and stupid dogs.

He had given up trying to start a fire. He had never been good at it. He wrapped himself in his cloak. Gracja's blanket was too sweaty and he had rubbed her down with it. And now he was acutely aware of the dark around about him, and the sighing of the leaves and the calling of night creatures he would swear he had never heard before in his life.

But then he had never been alone in the woods.

Perhaps he should give up and go home tomorrow morning. Surely they were searching the woods for him now, although he had not heard them, and whatever their opinion, he was not lost: he was absolutely confident of the general direction of home, and he had found what he was sure was Bogdan's party's trail through the woods, which was one of the usual ones. Zadny, with a hound's keen nose, had surely found it, too, and followed it.

And ever so much he wished that Zadny's keen nose could find him, because he could hear something moving about in the brush, and something was beginning to make Gracja very nervous.

He leapt up, the way he judged his brothers would, waved his cloaked arms and yelled, "Go away!" in his gruffest voice.

Whatever-it-was scampered away through the woods. Gracja jumped and almost broke her tether. Yuri sat down and tucked his cloak about him again, feeling better, at least.

Maybe even a wolf had been afraid of him. Maybe a bear. At best a deer or two.

God, he hoped that had not been Zadny.

"Zadny?" he called out into the dark. "Zadny? Here, boy—come here." It raised a dreadful noise in the night, and he imagined every bear and every troll within earshot pricking up its ears and saying, "Now there's a boy in the woods, isn't it?"

"Zadny?"

He heard a stirring in the brush. He imagined wolves and bears at least, took up Tamas' bow and nocked an arrow and waited.

"Zadny?" His arm trembled. He *wished* he had tried harder to start a fire.

But a pale starlit nose crept out from under the leaves, and ungainly large forefeet followed. "Zadny!" Yuri exclaimed, letting the string relax. "Lord Sun, I'm glad to see you! Come on, come on, boy!"

He had, he had realized it this morning, come away with no rope or leash, only Gracja's tether, and that was in essential use. So it had to be his belt. He laid the bow down as Zadny came out and regarded him in the dark, he talked gently to the hound the way Tamas would:

"Come on, come here, boy." He knelt down, delved into his pack and pulled out a biscuit. "Here, boy, cook sent it, come on, there's a lad . . ."

Zadny would not approach his hand. He broke off a bit and tossed it, but like a wild thing, Zadny took that and shied out of reach, and stood staring at him from a safer distance like a deer about to bolt.

"Oh, I'm not going to grab you. Here's a nice biscuit, *nice* dog, *good* dog, Zadny. You know me. I'm Tamas' brother. Tamas said to take care of you. The houndsmaster didn't hit you, did he? He surely didn't hit you. And you wouldn't run off from the puppies, would you? Tamas said you were to mind me while he was gone, and you're not to follow him, you hear? He won't like that."

Zadny might hear, but not for any coaxing would he let a hand near him. Offer a morsel of biscuit and Zadny would creep up, stretch as far as he could, snatch the bit and go; on the second such approach Yuri made a grab after him.

That was a mistake. Zadny shot off into the brush and vanished.

"Zadny?" Yuri called, over and over again, and apologized. "I'm sorry. I won't do it again, there's a good boy. . . ."

The nose came back, under the leaves. The forepaws did. But not a bit closer would Zadny come, not for any coaxing.

Yuri slept finally, exhausted; and waked with a sloppy wet tongue on his face. His eyes flashed open on dawn woods and a yellow hound's face, and he made a startled snatch after Zadny's collar.

And missed again.

"Zadny," he pleaded. "Zadny, come back here!"

But the dog simply stood out of reach while he saddled Gracja and climbed up.

Then the hound trotted off his own way, the way his master had gone.

The next day's ride was climbing. All the party bundled up in cloaks as soft-leaved trees gave way to cedar and to scrub pine. Snow patched the ground and fell in spits and fits from the gray overcast, until the horses went with beards of ice. High on the mountainside, they stretched their two canvasses between stout, uneven trees, in a wide spot in what Nikolai swore was the right trail. They shared a fireless supper, huddled in cloaks, with the wind roaring and thundering at their tents. Trolls could carry them all off tonight and welcome, Michal swore: slow roasting was preferable to freezing.

"Trolls wouldn't go out in this," Bogdan said, and more loudly: "I think a wizard's company ought to be worth better weather, don't you, master Karoly?"

"It could be worse," Karoly retorted, "and it could have been better, if we'd stopped where I said, an hour lower down."

They were at recriminations, now: things had devolved to that. Master Karoly had said wait, Bogdan had said go ahead, Nikolai had grudgingly admitted there was a stopping-place further on; and now they were all at odds, with the canvas snapping and thundering in the gusts.

With no warning then their canvas ripped, letting in a great gust of cold air, and Bogdan and master Karoly were shouting and swearing at each other, while Filip and Zev grabbed after the canvas and called for cord, shouting down all recriminations. Tamas hugged his cloak about him and buried his cold nose beneath its folds, lifting it only to say (but no one stopped arguing to listen) that if they used the sense the horses had and sat close against one another they would all be warmer.

"The storms aren't through," Nikolai said. "We should have waited."

But Bogdan said, "We're in it now. You say we're halfway. This is no time to talk about quitting."

Tamas agreed with Bogdan, though no one listened to his muttered opinion. Michal and Zev and Filip had patched the canvas with a rock and a wrap of cord, which stopped most of the wind; and in relative comfort he drowsed and waked to find the wind fallen and everything still. Filip was on watch, tucked up at the door with a dusting of snow on his knees—he moved his feet as Tamas got on his knees and looked out from under their shelter.

The dawn sky shone cold and clear and the horses were bunched in the shelter of the pines near the other tent. New snow made dusty blankets on their backs and in the hollow of the canvas. Like the mountain storms he had heard Nikolai tell of all his life, this one had been fast and bitter—but it had left the air clean and tingling with life.

Karoly was awake, too: Karoly got up from his place at the back of the shelter, and excused his way over sleepers, on business Tamas figured for urgent and private until Karoly failed to return in the usual time.

"He's been gone a while," Filip whispered, and got up; Tamas rose to go with him, stiff and sore in every joint, peered out and saw the old man standing out in the open, looking out off the cliff into the distances of a rose and shadow sky, where shone a few bright morning stars.

Maybe he's working magic, Tamas thought. He had never seen Karoly at work: master Karoly had taught him and Bogdan and Yuri what he called the principles of the arts, shown them the weather-glass and other such prognosticating devices; but the true magic master Karoly had never given them, nor ever worked in front of witnesses, unless one counted his communing with the walls of the keep and the earth of the fields.

"What's he doing out there?" Filip whispered distressedly at his shoulder.

"I don't know," he whispered back. Nikolai and Bogdan stirred, then, grumbled and swore they might as well be up and moving, there was no sleeping with all the whispering and the coming and going, and they'd made acquaintance with every rock under them.

"Why are we under snow?" Jerzy asked, punching the patched canvas, that sifted snow down on everyone. "If he's so great a wizard, why do we have such rotten luck?"

"Because he can't do everything at once," Tamas said under his breath; he had stopped expecting the men to listen to him. "We haven't met any trolls, we haven't lost anybody, we got to cover last night before the storm broke. . . ."

"I'd like to know what he *is* doing," Michal complained. "Standing on the edge like that—a wind could blow him right down the mountain."

He's listening, Tamas thought of a sudden, he had no idea why, but he thought of master Karoly listening to the stone of the hold, and thought, if those stones talk to him—what might a whole mountain sound like?

There had been a time he could have turned back, Yuri said to himself, wedged in behind Gracja, among pines, among rocks, and nursing his little fire into a dawn spitting and blustering with snow. The first night he could have come back and lied and said, well, he had not found the dog. But not after another day. Not after a third, Zadny always dancing out of arms' reach, accepting his charity and always, with a worried expression, looking off the way the men had gone, as if he would wait for a boy on a pony, but only just, only long enough; and he would stay for a boy and a pony to sleep, but never quite long enough.

If he had to go back now and claim he had outright lost the dog, he might have to maintain that lie between himself and his brother for ever, perhaps. And if he went back and told the truth, the other boys would say he had been outwitted by a mongrel stray, and that was a tag he would have to live with for the rest of his life. That he had hedged the truth with everyone, and that Zadny running away had given him a chance to do exactly what he wanted to do, did rub at his conscience—but there was actually no choice but to keep going now. They would forgive you if you were dead and they would forgive you if everything turned out all right (well, truth, papa would put him on bread and water for a week when he got home.) But when you got a reputation for lying or foolishness when you were fourteen, nobody ever forgot it, and your friends when they were grown men would never let you forget it—unless you were lord of Maggiar, which, being the youngest of lord Stani's sons, he never would be.

So he could not go back without the dog, who would not be caught, and very soon now, by tomorrow, he would be out of food and closer to over-mountain than he was to home, which meant he had to find Tamas and Bogdan. He certainly was not lost: Zadny gave every sign of knowing where he was going—and he could see the traces the horses had left, so he knew Zadny was not mistaken. They were going to be slower: Gracja was nothing for speed and he had had to camp early and hunt for food along the way; but eventually, on the other side of the mountains, he would catch up with Tamas and Bogdan and the rest of the men, in that country grandmother had told them about.

Or Zadny would run ahead and find them first, and while they were still wondering where Zadny had come from, he would come riding up on his pony and say blithely—he had this planned—Hello, brothers. And when Tamas called him a fool: You said I should watch your dog. Was I going to let him get eaten by bears?

No, it was Bogdan who would yell at him, first: Tamas would want to, but after Bogdan had vented his temper, Tamas would start defending him: that was the way he planned his reception.

And, after all, they could hardly send him home at that point: that was what he was sure master Karoly would answer to the men's objections to having him along. But he did not want to look at master Karoly until after his brothers had gotten to quarreling, because master Karoly would see through him otherwise and give him one of those soul-seeing looks Karoly could give . . .

In all versions, he had first to get there, and not to freeze before he got to the pass, which he had to reach today, if he was following master Nikolai's accounts. He had worked from dusk into full dark last night to get a smell of smoke out of the driest pine tinder he could manage—he had had it drying in his pocket all day, the way Nikolai had said one should in the mountains, where sudden showers and snowfalls were likely and the air was moist. He had cut pine boughs for a bed and for shelter to sleep under, and had Gracja's blanket under him and his cloak over him, besides. He had fed his fire dry tinder and pine needles before he offered it twigs and little branches and more tinder before solid wood, the way Nikolai had taught him in his ninth summer. The biscuits might have run out—he had shared the last one with Gracja and Zadny yesterday noon—but he had chopped and stuffed grass into Gracja's empty saddlebags and his empty food basket, so she had food for the climb, be it ever so little. Yesterday afternoon he had shot and cleaned a rabbit, that he had cooked last night, while Zadny had had the offal for his supper. This morning he peeled the red, soft lining out of cedar for tinder for his next fire. He would pack a fistful of that in his pocket, and as much dry wood, broken to lie flat, as he could tie to the saddle. All these things he had learned from master Nikolai in winter tales, how he had done when he had hunted trolls—and unlike some boys of his acquaintance, he *listened* when his teachers told stories, of which he was very glad this morning.

He was still reasonably warm in the shelter of the rocks, while the sleet skirled around the mountainside; and Zadny, the rascal, came almost but not quite within reach, seeking that warmth. He had not slept soundly last night. Keep the fire going: master Nikolai had said that was the most vital thing. People had died up here who had let their fires go out, frozen stiff by the time the searchers found them—and he had never kept an all night fire by himself.

That was the only truly scary part, knowing his life continually depended on things he had never done before—like getting a fire to take, like staying awake, with no older brothers to wake him if he nodded. But he had done it. He had not frozen last night. So he thought he could do the other things, and the next and the next.

He had a small bit of rabbit for breakfast, and gave the bone to Zadny, who came just close enough to nip it in his teeth. He thought if Zadny were truly clever he would find his own rabbit, but he did not think Zadny was thinking about being hungry right now until someone held food in front of him. Nikolai said it was four days from the start to the top of the mountain, he had tucked that away in his memory, too, so that was all the breakfast he afforded himself. He crawled out of his bed of pine boughs into the cruel wind, dusted the snow off Gracja, and put the warm blanket he had slept with on Gracja's back, before the saddle that had been his pillow.

Then he bundled up the wood he had had drying all night next the fire's heat, and tied it on with Gracja's saddle-strings. He had done everything Nikolai had taught him to do; his breath hissed with shivers as he climbed onto Gracja's back the hard way, with a great deal of squirming about to bring his leg over Gracja's neck, because of the wood; the cloak flapped in the wind, and half-blinded him—it was not a graceful mount, but he was up and on his way to the hardest part of the climb, with Zadny already leaving tracks in the new-fallen snow.

He would show up on the other side of the mountain with Gracja and Zadny and say, "Of course I made it. No, I didn't have any trouble—none at all . . ."

"Quiet everywhere," Nikolai remarked, riding closer to Tamas and Bogdan. "No sight nor sign of trolls."

"No sight nor sign of anything," Bogdan complained, with a gesture outward, toward the sky and the eagles that hunted above them, in the thin, cold air. "Except them. —Where are the trolls, master Karoly?"

"Minding their own business," master Karoly retorted.

Master Karoly meant they should ask him no more questions; but it was a half-hearted shot, as if he was thinking about something else entirely.

"Something's wrong with him," Nikolai muttered to Bogdan. "He hasn't complained once today."

It's true, Tamas kept thinking—he kept hearing that remark over and over in his head and it made him more and more uneasy about Karoly. Something was wrong, something that distracted the old man, as if he were hearing something distant and difficult.

Bogdan remarked finally, when they were riding side by side, "The old master's worried. Has he talked to you?"

Tamas shook his head. "No." He waited for Bogdan to confide further in him, the way Bogdan would if they were at home and without Bogdan's friends around. But that was all Bogdan said. He asked finally, to fill the silence, "How far are we from the top? Did Nikolai say?"

"We're past it, Nikolai says. We're through the pass and going around the mountain—Nikolai says. But he's never been farther than this."

The valley looked no different than the one they knew. There was nothing magical about it, nothing that gran had described, no sign of trolls or faery. Bogdan rode beside him a while more in silence, then fell back to talk with Filip, in words too low to hear, perhaps confiding his worries to his friend, since his brother was too young for his confidences.

The journey was not turning out as he had hoped. It was certainly something to see the mountains from up here. But what had seemed an adventure into once-upon-a-time at its outset, came down to ordinary, barren stone, with more spits of sleet to sting their faces. Karoly was not talking to any of them, the older men were not talking to the younger—they rode in their own small group, with Jerzy wondering aloud were they on the right trail; and *no* one was interested in Stani's second eldest's opinions or his presence.

But it did, thank the god, seem that the trail was slightly downward, now; and by afternoon, that pitch was unmistakable, even steep—all rocks and scrub pine, never yet a flat place and never yet a leaf the horses could use to fill their stomachs, but at least the wind was not so bitter cold, and even Jerzy grew more cheerful.

Now, Tamas thought, they would begin to see the landmarks their gran had described. A place called Krukczy Straz, that was the first—a tower in pine woods, that guarded the broad valley where the road went down to Hasel, where there might even be relatives, if grandmother's kin were alive. At Krukczy Straz they might find a warm gate-house to sleep in, at least, even if it was nothing but the defensive tower its name implied. There would be warm water for washing, and a good meal, and hay for the horses, and they might still get there tonight, if it was well up in the highlands, the way he recalled in gran's stories.

"Isn't there a tower?" he ventured, riding close to master Karoly. "Do you think we can reach it tonight?"

Everyone else was more cheerful. Master Karoly was not. Karoly took a glum moment about answering him. "It's possible. Or not. Let's not get ahead of ourselves, shall we?"

It was certainly not the forgiving master Karoly of the drafty tower study or the orchards around home. Tamas rode by him a moment more, wondering if Karoly would have more to say, or remember his presence—a lad could begin to wonder if he had not gone invisible to his companions, or whether Karoly saw him at all: Karoly did not so much as look at him again, or speak. He let his horse drift back to a slower walk, until it was him in the middle, between Nikolai's group; and Bogdan's group.

Tell Bogdan about it? Tamas wondered. What could I say? Master Karoly frowned at me?

The trail meandered along the mountain and then plunged steeply, wearingly downward, with never a sprig of grass for the horses, into a dead, skeletal ruin of pine and cedar. They had fed the horses the scant grain they were carrying, and pressed their journey late into the afternoon on a level road, with the mountains like a wall around them, unforgiving, sleet-dusted lumps of rock.

"This is madness," Jerzy said, as a sudden bitter wind howled out of the heights, whipping at their cloaks and the winter-coat of the horses. "Are we on the trail at all? I swear we're going up again."

"It is the road," master Karoly broke his silence to say. "It's illusion. We're still descending."

"I'm not sure you know where we are, old man. I'm not sure we didn't take a wrong turn on the mountain—"

"No," Karoly said shortly.

"Master Karoly," Bogdan said, "we're out of supplies; and if we come to green grass, or if things get better lower down, that's one thing: but it's far from encouraging, what we're seeing. We can't press on without limits: these horses can't do it, we can't do it—"

"We can't make it back over the pass," Nikolai said, "without supplies. There's no point arguing it. No matter where we are, we've got to go ahead. It is a road, it has to go somewhere, and somewhere has to be down from the heights. We should keep moving, past sunset tonight if need be."

"It is the right road," Karoly said under his breath.

Tamas said, "Grandmother mentioned—" and then held his peace, because what gran had said had no more currency than what Karoly knew.

"We're lost," Jerzy maintained; and Karoly only shook his head and looked away across the valley. Wisps of cloud veiled the depths. Birds circled far out across the gray expanse, eagles or carrion crows it was hard to say: size and color were illusory in this place. The birds made long shadows on the clouds.

Crows, Tamas decided, as they rode lower, through a foggy patch. Carrion crows and ravens fit everything they had seen so far; not only Maggiar had suffered a blight last winter. Trees on the mountains had died, leaving sticks of evergreens. The wind came out of the west, down the throat of the pass and against their backs, cold and damp off the patches of sleet on the slag-heap mountains. Instead of gran's waterfalls they found frozen, soot-stained ice; instead of the pine groves of her stories, charcoal stumps thrust up through sere, blackened brush.

Filip said, "The whole forest burned."

Master Nikolai said, with despair in his voice, "At least

we've passed well below the tree line now. Spring will bring out the green in the lowlands, no matter the fire. There's bound to be forage further down.''

Down was where they were surely going now, Karoly and Nikolai were right in that. The horses maintained a weary, jolting pace. The dusk between the mountains had closed about them, and since the foggy patch, cloud hung around the heights above their heads, gray and heavy with snow, casting everything in gloom.

Maybe Jerzy's right, Tamas thought: maybe we missed some turn of the trail on the heights and we've come down in the wrong valley—

But could master Karoly let us go astray? He's a wizard, Jerzy said it, persistently: Why don't we meet better luck?

Except if master Karoly could have cured what was wrong at home, wouldn't he have? And if he could have gotten us through the mountains without the storm, wouldn't he have? He's come here looking for his sister because things are happening he can't do anything about. Didn't he say to our father—I have bad dreams?

They passed into a defile of pale rock and a wide stream below the trail, that Karoly suddenly proclaimed was the road he remembered.

''Was it this grim?'' master Nikolai asked.

''No,'' master Karoly admitted, still riding.

The men said other things as the road wound around the barren hillside, a slip zone of rockfalls and a long slope of rubble and dead brush down to a barren streamside—an appalling place, deeply shadowed by mountain walls on either side, but the road was most definitely a road now, broad and well-defined. They came to a milestone of the Old Folk, which explained the stonework bracings along this stretch— such roads ran here and there in Maggiar, too, with similar milestones; but a grinning face was roughly painted on it.

''What's that?'' master Nikolai wanted to know.

''No good thing,'' Karoly said. Nikolai had reined to a stop at that find, so had they all, but Karoly passed it by with a look, as if it was part and parcel of everything in the land.

"What?" Bogdan called after him angrily. "Master Karoly, where are you leading us? What do you know, that you're not telling us?"

"That there's no way but this," master Karoly said over his shoulder. "That we've no choice but straight ahead. Come on!"

"Bogdan," Tamas began to say, with a strong feeling of misgiving about this road, but Bogdan set his horse to overtake Karoly's, saying something about keeping Karoly from breaking his neck; master Nikolai did the same, and the rest of them followed.

Tamas cast a second glance at the stone that seemed to mock any further venture down this road, wondering if the men all knew what that painted countenance signified, and he did not. He did not want to be a coward, and they would not regard his arguing. He worked his weary horse up to the head of the column with Bogdan and Nikolai and Karoly— easier on the overtaking just then as the road wound along the hillside to a steep descent.

But there they caught the first hopeful sight, a pale green vision of sunlight in the east, beyond the mountain shadow. Against that sunlight a dark tower loomed on the roadway, its foundations butted against the stream.

"Krukczy Straz," Bogdan murmured.

It surely was, Tamas thought. It was after all the road their grandmother had described to them, burned and dreadful as the mountains had become. They had come through the right pass, after all, and elsewhere the land was catching the sunlight still, like a promise of better things. "Quickly now," master Karoly said, silencing their chatter, and urged his horse faster down the road, that passed right alongside the tower crest.

Hisses then, sharp and quick, that no archer had to guess at; "Jerzy!" Filip cried. Tamas looked wildly about as horses bolted past and his own shied and reared. He saw Bogdan hit and falling as his own horse stepped backward on the road edge. He knew one heart-stopping moment of falling over the edge and onto the rubble, into a thunderous slippage of stones, battered and deafened in the rolling tide that carried him. He had time to despair of finding a stopping place. He had time to think of finding hold. The slide was a roaring in his ears and every handhold moved with him, slipping and tumbling as he went, down and down into choking dust.

3

CAME QUIET, AND COLD STONE BENEATH TAMAS' BACK. Water dripped and echoed in the dark around him. His body still felt the falling, but did not move, in a long, slow gathering of scattered wits, trying to reconcile sliding in a torrent of rubble, with this pervasive ache and this darkness and the regular echo of water drops.

The ceiling reflected a faint glimmering of light. None touched the walls. It was a broad cave, or a man-made vault— he could distinguish that much; but being here made no sense to him. He remembered going down, he felt the battering of the rocks—remembered he had outright fallen off his horse, no glorious end to his journey. Bogdan had been hit. Jerzy had. Dreadful images succeeded that one, arrows streaking black across a clouded heaven, horses and men screaming . . .

A second waking, how long after the first he had no idea. He was still lying on his back. Light from some source touched both shaped and living stone, a ceiling glistening with water and black mold, but nothing of the walls. It was the same place as before: he could hear the drip of water and smell the mustiness of wet iron and stone. But there was a thumping somewhere distant, like drums, he thought, or the beating of his own heart. He remembered the road, and he had to find his brother, he had to get back there, their father had told him take care of Bogdan—

But something held his hands fast above his head, and fighting that restraint sent a wave of pain through his back. He worked half-numb fingers, trying to feel what was holding him, and touched what might be rope about iron bars, but he could not be sure whether anything was warm or cold, nor tilt his aching neck further back to see.

A shriek reached his ears, far away—only a bird, he told himself, a crow, maybe a dog's injured yelp—not a human voice. His hazed wits could not shape it. He lay straining and dreading to hear it again, but the drip of water into some pool was all the measure of time and sanity.

Eventually, louder than the water dripping, came a slither like something dragging across the floor, with an audible breathing. It was a nightmare. He wanted to wake, now, please the god, he was very willing to wake up now, but there was no waking. One wanted to think of escape, but he could not so much as turn over. He asked himself who had tied him here, and why; and with his head lifted as far as he could, saw a large shaggy lump move out of the faint light and into the shadow beside him.

A troll. He was done. He knew he was. Only the bones left, he remembered Nikolai saying; and wondered if he was the only one imprisoned here. "Bogdan?" he called into the dark, with all the courage he could find.

"Ssss!" the troll hissed, trailed musty rags of wet fur across his face and clapped a massive hand over his mouth. Half-smothered, he struggled and, with his head beginning to spin, stopped, in token that he would be quiet, with no surety at all it would let him go. But it slowly drew its hand away and let him breathe.

Then it shuffled off as erratically as it had come. He listened after its departure over the beating of his heart, saw its retreating shadow against the light and, shivering, gazed into the dark for a long time after. He wondered where it went and why it had left and most of all what had become of Bogdan and Nikolai and the rest of them—not without reckoning master Karoly. A wizard might have defended them. Maybe Karoly had saved the rest of them, Bogdan and all of them, that was what he wanted to think—he might be the only one the trolls had gotten, lying unconscious as he must have. Bogdan and Karoly might be looking for him this very moment. They might save him if he could stay alive, if he was not going to be a troll's supper before they could get here.

And if he could somehow get his hands free, and get away on his own . . . that would save everyone the danger of rescuing him and himself the guilt of making them do it.

He refused to think of other possibilities. He worked at the ropes, not pulling at them: that would tighten the knots; but trying with every possible stretch of his fingers to find a knot within reach.

The troll had been cleverer than that; and while he was working, he heard the troll come shuffling back again, a humped shape against the illusory light, trailing cords of its shaggy coat to the floor as it walked.

He tried not to think what came next, as it crouched over him, as it slid a hand beneath his head, lifted it gently and put the cold hard rim of a cup to his lips.

He did not at all understand its reasons. But he saw nothing now to gain by fighting the creature, and the liquid against his lips tasted of herbs, nothing foul. It let him drain the cup, after which it let his head gently to the stone floor and crouched beside him, waiting, he had no idea for what. He only hoped it would go away and let him go on trying after the knots.

But he was in less pain than he had been. He felt his fingers and feet going numb, and then he began to be afraid, even while his wits were growing foggy.

He thought, I've been a fool. What does it want? What is it waiting for? Do they drug their victims? Poison—but would it poison what it was going to eat?

Hold Bogdan back, his father had said to him, and he had chased Bogdan down the road after that warning marker, instead of making a strong, reasonable objection to the decision that had put him here.

He was very sorry about that. He hoped Bogdan had gotten away. He hoped Bogdan would not come running in here to rescue him, even with Karoly's and Nikolai's help, because he much feared they were not going to be in time, considering the growing numbness he felt now in his limbs—he feared they would find nothing in this cave he ever wanted his father and mother to know about . . .

The road was deserted, so far as Nikolai could see, from his painful vantage on an otherwise glorious sunrise—he had crawled to this place on the mountainside, with a rock between him and the view of the road, but as for how he had gotten off the road and into the rocks in the first place . . . whether he had been left for dead and crawled up here or whether some one of his companions had carried him this far and left him to seek water or help . . . he had no recollection. He was, if he began to dwell on that thought, afraid, and confused; and the pain did not help him at all to sort out his thoughts.

He had gone down with the howling of goblins in his ears. He had waked with his sword in his hand, its hilt glued to his hand with blood, and he still carried it: his arm hurt too much to try to sheath it, and he had no assurance that what had brought him up here was not a goblin with a particularly selfish bent. He supposed he had had time to draw it and to use it, and that it was not his own blood on it, at least.

He had been shot—he had a sure reminder of that: the arrow had broken off, the black stump of it through his arm— through his side, too, except for the inside of his leather sleeve and the mail about his ribs. *Hell* of a pull that bow had had—he could admire the goblin archer that had drawn it; and damn him for the pain, in the next breath, when he moved his arm and the projecting head raked against his ribs.

Enough of trying for a view. He fell back and watched the dawn sky, trying to force any recollection out of his pain-fogged wits—where the boys were, what had become of Karoly, where anyone might be. He was halfway up the hill, hidden, as he hoped. He remembered—thought he remembered—the dirt of the road in front of his eyes—

So he had fallen. He remembered a confusion of rocks and brush. Maybe that was the climb up, a jumbled image of rock and sky. Karoly—damn his stubborn forging ahead into disaster—was not here to help. 'Listen to advice,' lord Stani had said. As well spit into the wind. Trust a witch or a wizard, listen to his advice, and this was where it brought you. The lady gran had had a cruel bent. He had known it. He should have suspected Karoly.

An eagle crossed the sky. It was the only feature in a sea of dawn, serene, without obligations to the world. But that was not his case. He shut his eyes, recalled the road last night, the tower hulking beside the stream, and thought, I have to go down there. I have to know. That arrow has to come out, doesn't it?

Damn Karoly for not being here.

An eagle cried like some lost soul across the mountainsides. On either side of the road, mere stumps and blackened trunks and stubs of trees. Nosing the ground, Gracja blew at the ash in despair, snorted, and lifted her head without resisting the reins. It was no place to stop, Yuri told himself, no matter how tired they all were. Even Gracja knew it, and kept moving on her own.

He had expected green grass, he had hoped to find his brothers not too far ahead once he reached the warmer elevations. His brothers would come off the mountain heights tired and in want of rest, and most probably they would camp and rest at the first opportunity—that was what he had told himself, before he met this desolation. He had found traces of their passage all along, seen tracks of their horses as late as this afternoon, on a wind-scoured crust of snow that he did not think was that old.

But no sight or scent of a campfire this day. Everything was charcoal. Zadny limped, sometimes on one foot, sometimes on the other, leaving blood on the snow this morning, but he was still going ahead, still tracking, nose to the trail— and that was assurance of a kind, but it was a scary place, this road, so void of every living thing.

The way began at least to be wider, steadily downward with another turn on the mountain, and there, lord Sun, was a deep stream-cut valley falling away steeply at his left. That encouraged him—because where streams cut, there were passes, Nikolai had said so.

The road became a steep descent, then, with the afternoon sun behind the mountains, a plunge deeper and deeper into the premature twilight of the valley. With every rest they took, once silence descended, the gloomier and the spookier the place felt. It was not like gran's stories. Not a leaf rustled here. There was only the wind, and once they were under way again, the solitary, lonely sound of Gracja's hooves made him think of walking through some vast, forbidden hall.

I don't like this, he kept thinking. Zadny seemed anxious—circling back closer to him, looking out into the shadowed valley and growling. Yuri thought, I don't like this open place. Anybody on the heights can see anybody on the road. I wonder if it is the right road, after all, or if we're even following the right horses.

But there was no going back now. He kept telling himself—if I just keep going, I'll surely find them. Some forest fire happened here, that's all.

The last of the grass had run out; the last of the rabbit was yesterday. Lord Stani's youngest had never missed a meal in his life, and he was so hungry he seemed apt to fold in half. As soon as the air had warmed enough to risk the wood, he had strung his bow, and carried an arrow ready in hope of rabbits; but now he kept the bow and the arrow resting against his knee because he was anxious and determined to get down to the streamside. The road was getting darker and darker, in a real twilight now.

Color touched the sky and cast a strangeness on the rocks and the surface of the road. He came to a milestone that looked the same as the milestones in Maggiar, old and worn and telling travelers nothing useful nowadays; but a dreadful painted face grinned at him from its whiteness, and the paint was not old. His heart jumped and for a moment everything seemed scarily sharp in detail, the white stone in the twilight, the grinning face, a boy on a fat, shaggy pony, a yellow hound, all brought together in this almost-night.

He rode further, slowly around the turning of the road and,

by the last light, into the valley beyond, where a great tower was set low beside the stream, its crest rising beside the road.

Men had made it. One hoped that they were men. But there was that stone back there. Gran had never told his brothers about such things. Or if she had, Tamas and Bogdan had never told him. And he had been too young to remember.

Would they go there? he asked himself. Should I?

Master Karoly was with them. Master Karoly undoubtedly knew what he was dealing with, and had planned everything, and knew exactly what he was doing, no matter how dangerous. So here came a boy, a pony, and a silly dog, into the middle of older people's plans that were life and death to everyone—not things he knew how to deal with, like cold and wind and getting food in the mountains—but places with strangers, in towers like that.

I don't belong here, Yuri said to himself. I should have stayed at home and never tried this at all. I can starve or I can go down there and knock on the door, or I can try to get past. What did master Karoly tell my brothers to do? Or why did they come this way, if not to find this place?

The more and less of haze seemed only part of slipping into unconsciousness, except Tamas found his joints stiff and his back numb and realized that he was on the other side of that dreaded sleep. More, something was still hovering near him with the same slithering movement and musty smell he associated with the troll. He saw its shadow loomed between him and the source of the faint light like a huge mass of shredded rags, all hunched down as it was. He did not want to be awake. He shut his eyes all but the least view through his lashes and tried not to betray that he was.

But it did not touch him. Eventually it got up and moved away, a shambling hump that, indeed, had a long tail. Tamas lifted his head and saw it dragging and snaking nervously in its wake, as the troll passed the dim lamp and its shadow crept up to the walls and the ceiling.

It was a nightmare. He heard that thumping sound again, or it was the beating of his own heart. Dizziness overwhelmed him as he let his head down. He was not dead. It had made him sleep long enough that his back was half numb and he could only wish his arms were numb, too. But why would a troll want to keep him here, and sit by him while he slept?

A bolt clanked and thumped somewhere above, a hallway echoed. The troll jumped, leaped, and a flare of its shaggy arm extinguished the lamp. It scrambled toward him, felt him over hastily and shoved his knees up perforce, smothering him with a raggy, massive hand over his mouth. Another clank. The creature settled its long, damp fur over him, and hissed, close to his ear, "Goblins. Husssh."

Goblins. Worse and worse—the troll crushed him into a bent-legged knot in the corner, against the bars, urging him to be quiet, and he lay absolutely still, breathing through the musty fronds as it tentatively let up its hand.

A door creaked. He saw a seam of light through the trailing fur of the troll's arm, past the shadow of its crouching body. Came the gleam of a torch, a silver sheen of weaponry and armor in that light, and he held his breath, ready to call out at any risk of his life, in a heart-clenched hope that it was one of his friends come looking for him.

Then the intruder turned his head, showing an animal's sharp ears in a mane of dark hair, a jutting jaw, a face human and beast at once. His heart froze as its gaze passed over them. It lifted the torch and scanned the vault in other directions, as if it dismissed them as some mound of rags.

Then the goblin slowly turned the other way, along the corridor and around the winding way the troll had always appeared and vanished. Tamas trembled beneath the troll's crushing weight, dreading the goblin coming back—and it did, a martial and dreadful figure in its silver-touched armor. It cast a slow second gaze in their direction, holding the torch aloft.

But it seemed blind to them: it went out by the same door it had come in, and shut it.

A bolt slammed home. The troll shifted its weight very slowly, drew back and left him as another door opened and shut, deeper inside the mass of stone.

Everything was dark and breathlessly still then, except the troll moving about in the utter night of the vault. Tamas slowly, painfully straightened his legs and settled himself, in a depth of despair he had never imagined. Goblins. *That* put more pieces together: Krukczy Tower, the clouds, the road, the outlook toward the valley, the long slant of loose stones . . .

He realized his horse had been hit, now that he put things together; he remembered its sudden jump before it hit the edge, and he pieced together an attack from the rocks above the road.

But it had not been trolls, in that attack: he had never heard that trolls were clever enough to use archery. Goblins were. And he remembered the stone marker, the dreadful living face he had just seen in torchlight, the doors and the echoes he had heard.

It was no troll's den, it was the cellar of Krukczy Tower itself; and goblins held it, loosed from what hell he did not know: but by all the late-at-night tales that had ever frightened a boy sleepless, he knew they were no solitary bandits, no witless bludgeoners, like trolls. Goblins came from deep and unfriendly places, they were clever and they came in armies, that was what he knew from gran's tales. Sorcerers and wicked powers used them to fight their wars.

What had happened this side of the mountains? Had not Karoly *known* they were in trouble, the moment he saw that stone—and still he led them toward this place? Had he not known in dreams before that? Had the mountain not told him, that morning on the heights, and he had said nothing to them?

Betrayal and Karoly had never seemed possible in the same thought. But whence this sister? Whence this mysterious sister Karoly had never mentioned to anyone? And whence this plague that Karoly could not stop—except from what was here in Krukczy Tower? Whence the smell of burning that had roused the whole household, but on this mountain? And whence the cries of lost children, if not here, in Krukczy Tower?

Ride quickly, Karoly had said, before the attack. Karoly had *known*, and he wished he could believe Karoly was free somewhere and plotting his rescue; but Karoly, if he was alive, well knew where he was—in this tower, and in the hands of creatures Karoly had already failed to deal with. He began to hope that everyone else was dead in the ambush—please lord Sun they were dead . . .

But if they were, he was not, and since he was not, he had no hope but the troll's slow wits and its intention to keep him to itself—which meant time to work on the knots, if not to rescue anyone, then to get away and onto the road and up the pass to home, to warn his father what was happening over-mountain, because he saw the next step in the taking of this tower: goblins raiding through the high pass next year, killing and doing in Maggiar whatever goblins did with their victims—which he did not want to think about. How he should escape, how he should survive the cold of the pass he could not imagine, but he could not imagine his father's son lying here and waiting to die, either. That was not what his father had taught his sons, and not what his father expected of the men he had sent over-mountain.

And once he heard the troll's slithering sound diminish down toward the end of the tunnel, he began to try again to feel out the knots, using what slight movement he had in his fingers, in the case that the troll might have redone its work and left him a knot in reach . . .

There was so little feeling left. He tried and he tried, and eventually decided he could just reach something curious that might be a knot. He stretched as far as he could and worked ever so patiently, tears of exhaustion running on his face, and his arms and back burning with the effort.

But while he worked, long before he had loosened the

knot, he heard the troll returning, in faintest light now, from some distant source. Unfair, he thought resentfully, if after all this time it wanted its supper, please the god it did not, and that it would not test the ropes. He knew now that it had the power of speech, and he asked it, "How many goblins?" —to gain what knowledge of his situation he could, perhaps to distract it, or, most improbably . . . even to befriend it and escape this place, if trolls could reason, if it conceived of itself in danger from the goblins.

But it hissed at him, then lifted his head as it had before, and put a cup to his lips as it had before, with no answer to his question.

He would not drink this time. He kept his mouth obstinately shut. But it shook him sharply, one snap that rattled his brain in his skull, and offered it again. He drank, flashes of color still hazing his eyes. It let his head down afterward, and sat close to him, waiting.

He tried again. "What happened to the others?"

"Ssss." It might be asking him to be quiet. Or it was an expression of its anger. He whispered faintly: "I can lead us out of here." But he was already feeling a numbness in his hands and his feet and a frightening confusion in his wits. His tongue was going numb. "I could help you." He was not sure it could even understand him.

It hissed at him, more intensely. He thought it might be answering him after all—if one had goblins upstairs, one certainly might want quiet in the cellar.

"I wouldn't bring them," he argued with it.

It said, "Not now."

There were drums, Yuri could hear them from here, the whole mountain echoed them crazily, and one had no choice but hear. He hunkered down on a flat stone in this concealing bend of the road, with Gracja's reins in his lap, holding her out of sight of the tower, waiting—because the more he considered knocking at that dreadful gate, the more he was afraid. It was not a tower where farmers came and went, it was a martial tower, where it was set and as simply as it was built, with no other possible use for it but border watching and bandit hunting. Whatever men might live here, if they were men at all—might be little better than bandits themselves, for all he knew. He was only waiting for moonset, hoping for clouds, and shadow—him with a yellow dog and a pony with a wide white blaze and a white foot. He had muddied up Gracja's blaze and her white stocking, with water from his canteen; but that was small good—he could not lay a hand on Zadny, who had gotten restless and run off on his own business, to bark at the tower, for all he knew, and rouse everyone in there.

Probably something had caught the dog. Or he was going to come back chased by a hundred bandits, and run right up to him. And the wind was getting colder or he was growing shivery with thinking about it and listening to the drums in the night.

He left Gracja tied to a cindery tree trunk for a moment to stretch his legs, and went far enough to steal a look down at the tower. It was lit up on top, torches all about.

No sign of Zadny.

"Stupid dog," he muttered to himself and to Gracja, and paced and shivered, and paced, and sat down and waited, and finally told himself that he had to go. The moon was setting and if he was going to try to pass the tower in the dark, he had as well do it while there was still noise and they were busy, not while they were sleeping—with the sound of a horse passing right under their walls. He started to get up, teeth chattering with the thought that he was really, truly about to try it.

Suddenly a pale shaggy shape came barrelling off the hill and into his lap, licking at his hands and his face and making his heart skip a dozen beats. He sat down hard on the stone, the hound a flurry of paws in his lap and on his arms. He shoved to protect himself, he flung anxious arms about what was warm and safe and alive in this dreadful place, and tried to hold on to him, for fear of what had sent Zadny running back to him.

"Where have you been?" he whispered. Zadny's pale shape, cavorting down the road, had been plain for any eyes to see. "What's down there, what do you know?"

But the hound jerked about of a sudden, braced and staring wildly up into the rocks, toward a dark shape and a gleam of metal.

A troll, Yuri thought, frozen as Zadny was frozen, expecting it to spring.

But it skidded down among the burned trees, human looking, and slid down against the rock right in front of him, saying, "You damned *fool!* What are you doing here?"

"Master Nikolai?" he said faintly, and, holding Zadny's collar fast, hugged him tight. "Master Nikolai?" He did not intend his teeth to chatter when he spoke: he tried to stop it. "Where are my brothers?"

Tamas waked with his arms free beside him, with a warm cloak over him, and blinked in a wild hope that he was miraculously rescued, that Nikolai or Karoly had found him, or that Bogdan had—

But it was the same dank, dreadful place. He hauled himself painfully onto his knees, felt about him in the dark, and up against the iron bars that he had lain next to. They made a wall, and a gate, and that gate—

—was chained shut.

He sank down with his shoulder against the bars, and leaned his head there until his heart had settled and the despair that welled up behind his teeth had found a bearable level again.

It was no worse than before. It might be some better. He bestirred himself to search the dark, and, feeling around him, discovered a slimed wet water-channel, carrying water that smelled and tasted clean. He washed his hands and face and drank and drank until he was chilled through, sure at least it was not drugged.

But when he had felt his way about the rest of the space of his prison, and found masonry walls on either side and the ceiling lowering at the end so he had no hope of squeezing further, he went back to the bars and sank down against them.

He could move; he had his cloak to wrap in against the chill; and when time passed and nothing threatened the silence or his solitude he crept back to the water-channel and washed at his leisure, although he was sore down to his fingertips and the cold and the effort hurt. Papa would not die in filth; mama would never tolerate perishing like this; Bogdan had not had to, he hoped that much for his brother, and for all the rest of them. And in the increasing cohesion of his aching and battered wits he told himself if once the troll opened the barred gate, if it once gave him the least chance, he was going to run for it, find his way out or find a weapon. If he did not make it, well—he had seen worse waiting for him, in this very cellar.

So he waited, nursing a headache and rubbing his chilled limbs to keep them from stiffening, and passed his time remembering good things, his home, his family, playing up and down the brook, sailing leaf boats.

Master Karoly's lessons—the tower room, the cluttered shelves with their dried leaves and books and curious objects; learning their letters, and their insects; and the name of the birds that built nests under the eaves. . . .

When Bogdan and he were boys together they had gotten bored with indoors and played pranks on the old man, turned the pages in his lesson book when he was out of the room, put live frogs in his tackle basket, rearranged every single book on his shelves, and never understood that they were doing wrong. Master Karoly had always seemed different from serious grown-ups, both wiser and more childlike. Master Karoly had kept his own counsel regarding the mischief they did; and derived his just amusement and his revenge (as they had duly expected) by posing them long, long cipherings or particularly arduous errands the next day. That always seemed fair, in the balance of things. And it had never once occurred to them that master Karoly should mind looking foolish, because dignity was not the province of young boys.

But as he thought back now, he decided the old man might have been annoyed at young fools who happened to be a lord's undisciplined sons—especially in the matter of the frogs, which had been his personal inspiration.

That was the forgiving master Karoly he wanted to believe in—not the short-tempered, close-mouthed old man on the trail. He was not sure now which man had really ever existed—but discovering what had lain next door to Maggiar unsuspected, and discovering that grown men fought and picked on each other like boys, and that sometimes good people died for no fair reason at all, everything else seemed in question, of things he thought he had understood. He was not likely to have the chance to use that knowledge . . . or to find out other lessons this place had to teach, only defeat, and his own limits of courage, and the fact of a lord's second son mattering very little to the creature that looked on him as its property or its supper.

In time he heard the troll returning. He waited, trembling with the effort to hold his limbs tensed to move. It came up to the bars, a shadow that cut off all the light on what it was doing. He heard the chain run back ever so softly, link by link, and suffered sudden doubt what he should do next, whether it might be wiser to await a better chance than to try to break past it—it was a clever troll, cleverer than any troll he had heard of. It seemed to have some obscure purpose in what it did; and it whispered, now:

"Follow me."

It was foolishness even to imagine it could mean something other than harm to him. It might have hidden him from the goblin, but it had hidden itself by doing that. He had provoked it, and it had cuffed him, using nothing of its prodigious strength—but none of that said anything at all of its reasons.

He got up slowly, thinking: What if it only wants me in reach? And again: What if goblins are about to search this place? He felt after the gate in the dark, ducked his head when his fingers met the low bar overhead. The troll moved away from him, affording him all the room to run he could wish. He saw its moving shadow in other shadows, heard the slithering passes of its tail along the stone floor, and followed it—like any silly sheep, he said to himself: Bogdan had always called him the slow wit of the family; and he could not make up his mind what to do or what to trust—but he had no idea whether that sometime source of light down the tunnel was open or barred or a route straight to the goblins.

A door creaked ahead, on the right hand, the same door the goblin had used, he was sure of it. He saw it open, heard the troll go through, heard it breathing, and thought—the troll did fear them. It hid from them. It wouldn't willingly walk into their hands . . .

He felt his way through the doorway, banged his shin and stumbled against steps. The slithering sound came from above him, as the troll climbed. "Where does this lead?" he whispered, as loudly as he dared; but it gave him no guidance but the sound of its tail trailing up the steps.

He felt the pitch of the stone stairs, climbed, aching from bruises, his head throbbing—there was no quickness or agility about it. A door creaked above, and when he had gotten there he felt his way through into another dark, smooth-paved passage, with an unfamiliar taint: goblins, he thought, dreading what he might stumble over in the dark, his worst fear that the troll might have made some understanding with them.

A door in front of him cracked on night and moonlight. The troll went out. He followed it onto the broad wooden roof, delirious with relief to have the sky and the stars over him.

But ringed about that sky, on pikes set in the ramparts, stood the skulls of humans and of horses. Heaps of bone were swept like offal against the ramparts, white bone with dark bits of flesh still clinging.

He spun about to escape the sight, to strike at the creature that betrayed him—

A slim, slight shadow stood there, wrapped in a dark cloak. A goblin, he thought at first blink—until the figure cast back the hood. A mere girl faced him, pale as the starlight and insubstantial as his grip on the world. She had a cleft in her chin. Would a sorcerer's illusion add that human detail? His wits were fogging, his legs were shaking—he felt the troll's shadow in the wind at his back.

"Who are you?" he asked.

"A witch," she said. "A powerful witch. I came here to find a wizard named Karoly. Do you know him?"

No, he thought distressedly, no, I'm not sure I ever knew him. He thought of the skulls at his back, and doubts and anger welled up, with a memory of his brother, and the road, and the warning stone. "Are you a friend of Karoly's?"

"My mistress is. Was he with you?"

"How should I say? I don't know your kind, I don't know if wizards die or not. He saw the stone, he didn't warn us, he didn't stop—" He was shaking in the knees, and it was not all the cold. "Look around you. Tell *me* if he's alive, and I'll ask him where my brother is!"

She looked distressed then. And the troll said, in a deep, deep voice:

"Ate them all. Only bones are left."

She glanced past him and above, and for his part, he wanted to sit down and let the troll and the witch argue out what to do or what more they wanted with him—escape was a far, confusing enterprise, and led probably to the hands of goblins, or witches, who knew?

"I have two horses," she said. "I've food enough. Krukczy, bring him."

He did not want to be brought. If there were horses, if there was a way off this rooftop, he was willing to go. The witch walked away to the edge of the parapet, and over the edge—onto downward stairs, as he saw; and he began shakily to follow, stepped over the brink and saw dark air and empty space as the wind rocked him.

But the troll caught his arm in a powerful grip and held him from falling—kept its grip on his arm and guided him all the way down the steps to the stones of the streamside, the witch moving constantly ahead of them, a cloaked black shape with now and again a pale wisp of hair or gown. He went without argument now, although the troll's grip hurt him. He thought: We came to find a witch; and I've found one, and she might even be what she says . . .

If she's not in league with the goblins herself.

4

"HOLD ON," YURI BEGGED. "DON'T FALL, DON'T LET
GO—"

Master Nikolai clung to Gracja's saddle as he walked, that
was how they descended from the road, Gracja stumbling on
rocks as they worked their way down near the slide. Of a
sudden, faced with a cluster of boulders, Yuri had to let go
the reins, because there was no more room for another body
as Gracja passed between—he had no idea whether there was
footing for her there, but the sheer slide on their right went
straight to the water.

"Look out!" Yuri pleaded, seeing Gracja stumble and
Nikolai's body hit and drag through a gap not wide enough
for him and Gracja at once: Nikolai had lost his footing, but
he was still holding on, his left hand wrapped in Gracja's
saddle-ties, when Gracja stopped unevenly in the shadows of
brush and rock right at the streamside. Zadny began jumping
up and pawing at Nikolai anxiously, the habit that made the
houndsmaster hate him. Master Nikolai, hanging limp from
a wrist wrapped in the saddle-tie, no more than lifted his
head and said, "Damn you," to the dog.

Yuri threw an arm about Nikolai, trying to help him stand,
but he was no better help than Zadny: the moment Nikolai
unwound his wrist from the leather, his weight was more
than Yuri could hold, and he collapsed with him, Nikolai
gone suddenly all limp and loose and maybe dead, for all he
could tell. Zadny licked his face and Nikolai's while Yuri had
not a hand to spare to hit the dog. His heart was pounding
from the climbs, one after the other, racing from the fright

just now of losing Gracja's reins and almost having Nikolai dragged to his death, and most of all from being very near the tower and the goblins.

But they were in cover now, finally, in the dark and the brush on the streamside where Nikolai had intended to go— or as close as he could manage. Gracja had just slid whichever way she could at the last, and chanced into this nook where only the starlight reached.

"Stop that!" he whispered, elbowing the dog's attentions away from him, "dammit, stop!"—language his father would by no means approve. Then to his vast relief he felt Nikolai move. "We're all right," he promised Nikolai breathlessly: he wanted ever so much to believe it himself. "We're all right, we've made it, we can rest here."

"Good boy," Nikolai said, "good boy," and might have been talking to the dog. The drums were still within the looming tower, long quiet, but it was a lonely silence, without even leaves to stir, only the soft rush of water in the stream.

Goblins, master Nikolai had said: they already had his brothers and master Karoly and everybody—even the horses. And master Nikolai had been going to see what he could do alone, when Zadny had found Nikolai and guided him—but Nikolai had run out of strength and bade them go down into the brush and get into cover. Without him, Nikolai had meant. But he had talked Nikolai into holding on; and he had gotten him down here, and once Nikolai had caught his breath he would tell him what he had to do next, please the god.

He began to shiver in the wind, knees and elbows tucked for warmth, saw Gracja pulling at the leaves of the bushes— she had found something alive, in the very shadow of the goblin tower, at least enough to keep her stomach from hurting, he hoped. Because his did. Master Nikolai had told him everything down to this point. But there had not been much of the rabbit yesterday; and he had a very sick man in his lap and he honestly did not know what to do with him here, where goblins could find them at any moment.

He knew at least where to get warmth. He unsaddled

Gracja, rubbed her down briskly with her blanket and took it, still heated from her body, back to Nikolai, and tucked it about him; then he took his water-flask from the saddle, held his head and gave him a drink.

"That's good," Nikolai breathed, in the waxing and waning of a pain he had never felt and did not want to imagine. Nikolai was stronger than he looked, he kept telling himself that, and kept believing they had only to do the right things, one after the other, and somehow the sun would come up in the morning and master Nikolai would be all right, and they would make a plan to rescue everyone alive from the goblin fortress.

But Zadny had lost Tamas' trail up there on the road. Zadny had cast about and then gone off after master Nikolai's scent, from all he could guess, as the only one who had walked out of the ambush, perhaps the strongest trail, the only one without goblin smell about it: he could think of no other reason Zadny would have followed Nikolai and left Tamas.

Nikolai breathed, "Damn you, why are you here?"

Following the dog seemed a miserably stupid thing to say. He said, with a lump in his throat, "Because I'm a fool, sir. What shall we do now?"

There was long silence. He thought Nikolai must have fainted again, and feared he might even have died, but Nikolai blinked, then, staring at the sky.

"A pair of fools," Nikolai said finally. "I'm not going to make it, boy. Can you get home from here?"

"No, sir." Short answers, Nikolai had always wanted from them, no excuses, when he was teaching them. He blinked tears and tried not to shed them. "I'm out of food."

"There's the horse," Nikolai said, and he did not for a moment understand that.

"No, sir," he said, "no, sir, I won't."

"Then eat the dog and ride the horse."

"No, sir!"

"Like your damn fool brother," Nikolai muttered, but which brother he meant, Yuri had no idea. Nikolai shut his eyes, and drew several slow breaths, then looked at him in the starlight. "The horse is goblin bait. So's the dog. So are all of us. You understand that, boy? Are you going to stay here and watch, and then be dessert? Your father's lost two sons in this place. You're the heir. Do you understand me?"

"So what were you doing? Were you going home without them?"

"I was going to see—" Nikolai stopped. Master Nikolai stared at him straight on, all shadow and starlight. "Don't you think about it. Don't you think about it, boy."

But it was exactly what he thought master Nikolai would do. Nikolai had been going down there, hurt as he was, to see if his brothers were alive, or if any of them were, or if there was anything he could do, and master Nikolai had not waited to get well, because there was no time to wait, if the goblins had his brothers in that tower. So he knew what he ought to do, then, first off.

And there was still night left.

"Boy," Nikolai said, when he got up to go to the tower. "Young lord." More respectfully, and struggling for his words. "Listen to me. . . ."

"I'll be careful," he said, and got his bow and his arrow case from Gracja's saddle.

"They can smell you," Nikolai whispered, evidently resigned to what he would do. "At least trolls can. Watch the wind."

Yuri came back and squatted down with the bow across his knees, out of Nikolai's reach, because Nikolai was devious, he knew that. "I'll find out where they are. Don't move around and make it bleed." Nikolai had lost enough blood. It was all down his side. Nikolai said he had pulled the arrow himself, and he flinched even thinking about it. "If I'm gone awhile I'm hiding, all right?"

"Don't take that damned dog," Nikolai told him. "Leave him with me."

That also seemed like a good idea.

The stream was cold water, stones slick with moss. Tamas wobbled along the edge, slid and slipped and saved himself from falling, but the effort left him hurting. Meanwhile the troll carried the witch-girl effortlessly in its arms and set her safe and dry-shod on firmer ground. Then it forged ahead of them, breaking a passage through the brush.

A whispering began to surround them, not alone the sound of water over stones—but the wind in living leaves. The branches he fended with his hands were pliant, and the boughs above their heads sighed with life. The fire that had blackened the mountains must not have reached downstream—and very far downstream, as it seemed to him, before the troll slowed to a stop, looking as satisfied as if it had gotten them somewhere besides the middle of a forest.

But he was glad enough to rest, and glad enough to find things alive, and sank down on the spot, covered in sweat and shaking. The troll for its part seemed to be leaving them—it walked back up the water's edge, passing him with no notice or apology; the witch girl called after it, "Thank you, master Krukczy."

It turned in the moonlight, looking like someone's abandoned mop, except the snaking tail. It bobbed a little and inclined as if it bowed, then turned its back and waded into the stream, a moving ripple, that was all.

Tamas muttered, "Good manners for a troll."

"He's not a troll," she said sharply. "His name is Krukczy like his tower. This is his Place, and he saved your life."

Troll was close enough, in his opinion. But he had not meant to offend her, or the mop, for that matter: he got up with the very last of his strength and put forth the effort of manners, starting to say, "I am grateful—" But she turned her back and began to walk away down the shore, evidently expecting him to follow.

Damned if he would stammer and protest after her. For a very little he would let her walk on alone to her business, and take his rest here, and go home.

But he needed a horse and she claimed she had one; he needed food and he had none—a bad position for any assertion of his independence, no matter that the arrogant witchling looked fragile as a flower and younger than he was. And she had claimed to know Karoly.

So he followed, on what breath he could find. He even recovered his manners, and panted, when he had almost overtaken her, "I apologize. He's not a troll. Whatever he is."

"The watcher here," she corrected him.

"Watcher."

"Of Krukczy Straz. And you can't bespell them, it only makes them angry."

None of that made sense to his ringing ears. He walked, stumbling on the stones and the roots, and asked finally, because nothing else of his situation made sense, "Why did you rescue me?"

She cast him a shadowed glance and never slowed a step. "I thought you might be glad to be out of there."

"I am." He had a stitch in his side that was only growing worse, never mind the bruises that hurt with every step. "I am grateful." They had started off badly, without names or courtesies; but, granting the complete justice of her displeasure, and the sting of her treating him as a servant, it still seemed foolish to volunteer too much to any stranger, who he was, who his father was, and hence that he might be valuable. He said only, when he had overtaken her again, "My name is Tamas."

"Ela," she said.

"Your name is Ela?" (Evidently it was. She said nothing else.) "I'm very glad to meet you." God, it was ridiculous, chasing the damned girl, trying to observe the courtesies when he could scarcely get a pain-free breath to talk at all. "What do you want me to do?"

"Walk," she said, and pushed a branch aside, that sprang back and caught him in the face.

Outrage only made him dizzier, and shorter of breath. He wiped the tears the grit from the branch had left, kept walking, and promised himself he could leave the surly girl whenever he liked, just let them somewhere find horses and a sense of direction—soon, please the god. The pain in his head had become blinding since the blow across his eyes, every bone end in his body was bruised from the slide down the hill, and he was weak-kneed from want of food.

But just when he thought he could go not a step farther, the space along the shore widened to a moonlit strand of grass, where grazed the promised horses, one dark, one light. Lwi, Nikolai's glass-eyed gray, and Jerzy's little bay mare: he recognized them the moment Lwi lifted his head, and he went and fell on Lwi's warm shoulder with his eyes stinging and a lump in his throat—an old friend in a bad place, Lwi was, his own horse's stablemate, who knew him despite the troll-smell and the dirt, and nosed him in sore ribs, in recollection, he was sure, of smuggled carrots.

"Nothing this time," he murmured shakily, patting Lwi's neck. "Good fellow. How are the legs? Better than mine, I hope. —Skory, good horse." Skory evaded his hand, skittish fool that she was; he remembered why he hated her; and he looked along her side to find the witch girl frowning.

"The saddles are over there," she said, pointing grandly to a brush heap, and he stared at it and at her, out of breath and out of strength, wondering if she even understood that he was doing well to keep his feet.

"I take you do know what to do with them," she said, as if she were far too exalted a lady to deal with horses . . . and he caught a breath and another and found himself moving— he had no idea whether it was anger at her that lent him strength or that he had suddenly found a last reserve somewhere at depth, but he went where she said and found the saddles and all the gear, including Nikolai's bow, lying under brush, on the ground, of course, in the dew and the damp—

Fool girl, he thought in growing contempt, and then realized what he had seen when he came up to the horses, that they had not even a tether—no tether, goblins all about, trolls running up and down the riverbank, and they were still waiting where she had left them? That was more evidence of witchcraft than he had seen out of master Karoly in his lifetime.

It gave him second and third thoughts about disrespect to

the girl, while he flung the brush aside and, staggering, re-
trieved the tack. If a witch's mere servant could do this much,
and expected such great respect for herself, then perhaps
master Karoly's sister was someone of immense consequence
in this land, the sort of help his father might soon need against
what was preparing, so he might do well to keep a civil
tongue, saddle the horses for the girl and meet this mistress
of hers face to face before he claimed anything about his
origins.

So he took Jerzy's mare, Skory, first, adjusted the blanket
on her back, took deep breaths until he could bend and snatch
the saddle up and fling it on—waited several more, leaning
against her side, before he could attempt the girth, that was
how scarcely he was managing. But through all of it, the
mare at least stood still, better than she had ever done for
Jerzy.

Lwi had better manners from the start. Lwi did not suck
in wind the way Skory did, Lwi took his bit without fussi-
ness: that was the kind of horse Lwi was, besides sure-footed
and level-headed; and the witch taking Skory's reins and of
course assuming the pretty mare was hers was entirely agreeable to him—he said not a word about Skory's character, only
gave the girl a hand up, gave her the reins and showed her
how to hold them. The elegant mare was beautiful and sly
and fractious—like Jerzy; but she did not go into her accustomed dance, she did not pitch the witchling off her back.
Somewhat to his disappointment she stood like a lady; and
he went and, with failing strength, got his foot into Lwi's
stirrup and flung himself into the saddle.

Through a haze of dark and moonlight, then, he saw Ela
ride the mare past him and felt Lwi turn of his own accord,
in a dreamlike slowness. Moonlight on the water beside them
showed only vague shapes of stones and turbulence. The
horses kept to a leisurely walk as if no goblins dared assail
them.

"Are we going to your mistress?" he asked.

"As quickly as we can," she answered him.

"To do what?" he asked, but got only silence. "To do

what?'' he repeated, more loudly, and had no more answer than before.

Damnable rudeness. If he could get to this sister of Karoly's, and prove who he was, and tell her what had become of Karoly, she might care what befell her neighbors—but now that he had leisure and breath to think about it, the witch's own land had not fared outstandingly well, if Krukczy Straz was any evidence of her authority. One could suppose matters might be better lower down, that the goblins might be a plague that had turned up on the heights, or the borders, and that Ela's mistress could deal with if she put her mind to it—but would she not, knowing that her brother was due over the mountains, as she must have if she sent this girl to find him—have done something to defend him? —Unless, of course, she had relied on Karoly's own abilities.

For some reason the goblins had quitted the tower—perhaps the girl's mere arrival had confounded them and driven them in retreat, but Ela had been anxious to leave the tower itself, and she had certainly been no help to Karoly, if that had been her mission.

A great many things did not make thorough sense. He began to take sober account that if he was wrong about following this girl, he could lose himself and leave no warning at all for his father—but if he left her without seeing her mistress, he lost all chance of the help Karoly had supposedly tried to find.

He could hear his brother saying, Brother slow-wits, can't you make up your mind about *anything*? —But, no, he could not be easy with what he decided, go on or go back. It was never his skill, to take a blind decision and wager others' welfare on it. *Doing* something required knowing where he was, or who he was dealing with—and his guide and her mistress and Karoly himself were ciphers. The girl might be a graceless shrew, but maybe she was the grand lady she claimed. Maybe she was unaccustomed to riding alone in the woods with strange young men who (he had to admit it) reeked like a troll den. Maybe she thought him some man-at-arms, accustomed to rude orders. Maybe—

In the starlight and the dizzy patterns which forest shadow made of his companion and Jerzy's mare and Lwi's pale neck, it was easy to become foggy-headed. He tried to reason clearly, he tried to maintain a recollection of the way they were going: descending straight along the river into the green land they had glimpsed in the sunlight, he thought, if it was the same stream as ran beside the tower.

He thought that if he should decide to go back, he could trace the water uphill at least to the road, but it seemed more and more deceptive: in the way of streams, that met and joined and carved narrow passages the horses could not follow, it wove back and forth and lost itself repeatedly beneath the trees. Leaves brushed his face and blinded him, then gave way to streamside again, the same one, a different, he had no more confidence he knew at all.

5

BARREN ROCK OFFERED FEW HIDING PLACES; BUT THE MOON was over the shoulder of the projecting mountain now and Yuri's heart was thumping like a rabbit's. The hulking shape of the tower rose up to blot out the sky. He had not known the place was so large and so high: that was his most daunting surprise thus far.

Try sneaking up on a watchdog, Nikolai had said, of the goblins. —Do that, and tell me you'll get away with your fingers. This isn't deaf Pavel you're sneaking under the nose of. They'll have guards posted, young fool, they're soldiers; maybe with noses keen as hounds', do you understand that?

Nikolai was angry; Nikolai called him young fool; but only because Nikolai had been sneaking down here with a hole in his arm and half his blood on the mountainside when they had run into each other, and Nikolai could not do it himself, that was what Nikolai was angriest about.

So Nikolai and he had agreed without agreeing; and Nikolai had stuffed his head so full of details and exceptions and instructions between then and moonset, he had to stop now and think it through and through again.

But the outpost that was Krukczy Straz sat directly on the streamside, and the plain fact, as Nikolai said, was that a castle of any use to anyone had to have water: where it got water it had either to sink a well straight down into the ground or build some fortified tunnel out so they could get to the stream, maybe both, the oldest castles tending to grow from small beginnings and be patched together with this and that owner's intention. And this one being set on mountain rock did not make wells a certainty. Nikolai said he had seen a lot of towers like this one in his travels; and Nikolai said he had traveled a lot, had been a boy up in the Rus, before he had come down to Maggiar.

That Nikolai had ever been a boy was a revelation. That he had seen castles more than one certainly was. But Nikolai sounded as if he knew exactly what he was saying, in every particular of the torrent of detail Nikolai had poured into him. Nikolai made him look at the lines of the tower and see how it was laid out, and where they would most likely have guards, and where their blind spots were. . . .

Where they don't have windows they'll post guards on the roof, Nikolai said. Where they don't have guards they think that face is too strong to worry about; where they don't expect attack they'll have fewer guards than where they do . . .

The strongest point of a tower is one direction to come up on, because they may not have guards there; and the water-channel or the drains are easier to get at than windows.

Nikolai added then: But they know that. And they may take precautions. Don't go inside. Just look it over. Remember every window, every hole, every nook that can give cover, to them or to us, and come back and tell me what you see. Then we can decide what to do next.

That last, he knew, was Nikolai trying to get him to be safe. And this back and forth bearing of careful reports made thorough sense, if one's brothers were not in there being eaten alive, or whatever terrible things goblins did with people they caught. Nikolai had said they had even hauled away the dead horses. And that did not sound good, in his ears, except they might take longer getting around to the men.

He moved very carefully, trying not to rattle the stones, and most of all to keep out of sight—Nikolai had grabbed his head without warning and jerked it down hard, pointing out to him that where he had sat the moonlight was on him, and below the rock shadow was where his head and his body and his arms and his legs all belonged, if he wanted to keep them when he was sneaking up on anybody. He could still feel the bruises of Nikolai's fingers on his neck. So he thought about that while he moved, crawling on his stomach and his elbows—likest, in his experience, to sneaking under orchard fences—and remembering always to take the long and patient way if that was the way with most shadow.

That way turned out to run right up against the wall, following the foundations down to the streamside, a shadow so black he went a great deal by feel. By comparison the water glistened brightly in the starlight, once he reached the water's edge; and by that same starlight he saw a barred iron gate in the stonework, facing the stream, stonework steps mostly awash.

He slipped up to the side, found the gate ever so slightly ajar, so that one would never notice if one did not happen to be pushing at it, hoping it was unlocked. The gate might creak if he pushed it wider. He might have to run if it did. He might have to throw himself in the water and hope it swept him to some handhold downstream, away from Nikolai, where he would not wish to lead pursuers in any account, and he did think he was being commendably thoughtful, to reason that out in advance. He knew exactly what he would do if he were surprised, he had a plan—so he gave the gate only the gentlest effort, ready to stop at the first hint of resistance that might make the hinges creak. It went wide enough for a skinny boy—which was good enough; and he thought, meanwhile, It's dark inside. I can at least see if it goes all the way in without a second gate in there—master Nikolai would need to know that, or we can be coming and going here all night, and every time we come and go is a chance for them to catch us, isn't it?

So he slipped inside, and had the foresight to pull the gate almost shut behind him, so it looked exactly as before.

The air inside was cool and dank the way one would expect next to water, and a little musty, as if someone used the place for storage or refuse. He felt to one side a fair distance before he found the wall; he walked carefully ahead and found no second gate—it felt like a tunnel of some kind, maybe even a natural cave, since he felt no mason-work. So far he smelled and heard nothing that indicated occupancy, only the odor of old, wet sacks. He debated whether to go back, decided to try just a little further, always keeping to the wall which could guide him back in the dark, and with one hand above him to watch his head, if it was like the cellars at home—because the starlight and water sheen that reflected into the entry rapidly ran out, and he needed to stop now and again and let his eyes grow accustomed to more dark.

This tunnel was certainly something Nikolai would want to know about—and more so if he could report a door or a gate through which the goblins in the tower might get down to the water and by which they might get up into the tower and rescue his brothers and the rest.

There *might* even be store rooms, as he thought about the probable use of this place: that was what the basement was at home, it did smell like it was used for that—and store rooms, he thought excitedly, were one place the goblins might lock up their prisoners, the way the servants said grandfather had locked up the bandits once upon a time, before he hanged them.

In that thought, he desperately wished he dared call out his brothers' names, and he stopped now and again, held his breath and listened for the faintest sound that might indicate a prisoner locked in this place.

Water dripping was all he heard—plunk, plunk . . . plunk. Louder and louder—until he heard another step, back toward the gate.

Lord Sun, he thought, heart in his throat, someone's in the tunnel behind me.

His first desperate thought was to press himself tight against the wall, and he did that, in the hope someone more used to this place might walk down the middle and miss him. But that was no good if they lit a lamp; and if they did not light a lamp it meant they were walking in the dark on purpose, which if they owned it, meant they knew a foolish boy might be in this tunnel. Noses keen as hounds', Nikolai had said, but he had never expected any guard would come in from the water side, from the same way he had, or move in the dark.

He hugged the wall, trying to think of some better choice, all the while trying to hear how many there were. The presence moved in two parts. Like a snake, he thought, swallowing hard. Or a single goblin dragging something, like a sack, or a body.

The gate to the outside might still be open. He might rush past the goblin by sheer surprise if he waited until it was almost on him and then burst for the exit. Or he might sneak as far as he could ahead, and hope the goblin turned off into some passage on the other side of the wall, at some branching yet unfound. The first offered a better chance: he knew the door was there, which he could not say about any other doorway; but it would alert the whole tower; the second was the quieter, and there had to be a door from upstairs, or how did they ordinarily come and go here, without getting their feet wet? If he could get past that, the goblin might go upstairs.

Except, god, they could *smell* him. And there was no surety the gate to the outside was not locked, now that whoever had gone out had come back.

Quiet was what he thought Nikolai would choose. Raising a general alarm was not a good idea—that could bring a search along the stream that might find Nikolai; that would be a disaster. So he edged along the wall, feeling his way past projections, along turns, utterly blind now, hurrying faster than he liked. He knocked into something, that, thank the god, he grabbed before it fell. A lamp, he thought, steadying it in its niche; and quickly he moved on.

Then he ran into bars, a shock that half stopped his heart. But he felt out an open gateway in them, ducked through it and went further; but then he was running out of ceiling—so he had to bend, and then to go on hands and knees, truly scared, now, that he had gotten himself into a trap, hoping desperately that beyond the bars might be a nook they might not search—hoping Nikolai was wrong about their sense of smell. He hunkered down, almost out of room altogether, trying not to breathe hard. He heard the movement behind him stop, and then a little gleam of red showed in the dark—he thought at first of demonic, glowing eyes.

But it was ordinary coals in a firepot, and a wick that caught yellow fire, and flared on its way to a lamp—showing him shaggy fur, a broad face, eyes dark and liquid with light, suddenly staring right at his refuge.

He hugged his knees tighter and tried not to shiver, hoping it did not see him in the shadow. But it said, "Another one," in a harsh, deep voice, and shuffled over toward him, with a long, ratlike tail snaking and coiling behind.

He looked back to see if there was anywhere at all else to go, but the ceiling was so low he could only crawl—

Which the creature could not. He scrambled for the low spot and heard the bars bang. He was crawling into it as flat and as fast as he could, trying to get beyond its reach, when something seized on his ankle and dragged him backward, burning his palms and his chin as he tried to hold to the rock.

It dragged him out to the lamplight kicking and struggling. He kicked it, but it held on, and looked at him, after he had run out of breath trying to escape it.

It was a troll, he was sure. He had gotten himself into a predicament master Nikolai had given him no instructions for, unless it slipped its grip. It had the lamp in one hand and his ankle in the other, and seemed perplexed by the situation.

But it set the lamp down on the floor, tore him loose from the bars where he had immediately anchored himself, and held him by both arms in front of its face—to bite his head off, he was sure, and he kicked it again, to get even.

"You smell familiar," it said—when he had never heard that trolls talked at all. "You smell of dog."

He did. Zadny had been all over him. And what did Zadny have to do with trolls?

"Where are my brothers?" he asked the troll, on what little breath he could get, suspended as he was. "What did you do with them?"

"Most dead," it said. "Only bones."

Most. He clung to that 'most.' And it had not bitten his head off. It talked about dogs. It looked him thoughtfully in the eyes, not looking particularly fierce, now that he had a longer look at it. It looked puzzled; and his arms were near to breaking, but it had not done more than hold him eye to eye with it. "Some not dead," he gasped, and kicked without intending to this time.

"Where?"

"Two rode away."

"Where?"

"Outside. Away. —You smell of boy, not goblin. Boys don't belong here now. Bad place, bad."

"I'm looking for my brothers." The pain was worse and breath was shorter. He thought his arms would break. "Where did they ride?"

"Looking for brothers," it rumbled. "Looking for brothers." It set his feet gently on the floor, eased its grip and patted him on the shoulder with a huge, shaggy hand. "Good. That's what to do."

"Do you know where they've gone? Do you even know it was my brothers?" It was magical. He had no idea of its capabilities. But sudden hope brought a wobble to his voice, and he hesitated to run. "My name is Yuri. I come from over-mountain. My brothers are Tamas and Bogdan. . . ."

"Don't know names. But look for brothers, yes, a good idea, very good idea."

For some reason a prickling went down his arms, like being with the priests, or hearing the winter wind, its voice was so deep. The troll did not look wicked or cruel to him, it looked sad, and wise, and it seemed to be saying more than it owned words to say. It said, "We'll go," turned him with a vast shaggy hand and urged him to walk.

He should run for his life, he thought. It was probably a trick. He was probably far faster than it was—it was very big and heavy; but it was already taking him where he wanted to go, beyond the light, back down the shadowy tunnel to the streamside and the starlight and the open.

"Go find them," the creature said, exactly what he wanted to do.

But he could not go with it anywhere looking for Tamas and Bogdan, not leaving Nikolai lying wounded and waiting for him and not knowing what had happened. Nikolai had killed trolls—it might not take kindly to that, if it knew—but maybe it would not know, and maybe Nikolai would give it no hints.

They walked as far as the gate and the river, with his stomach knotting tighter and tighter over the question.

But Nikolai had said himself, I'm not going to make it, boy. Nikolai believed that. Nikolai had believed it when he came down the mountain looking for his brothers, and Nikolai usually knew the score on things. So there was no hope for him—

Except if a boy could bring him help, and he hoped with all his heart it was the right thing to do.

It seemed forever, the waiting did. The damned dog at least had settled to rest. Nikolai had his belt around his wrist and its collar, and passed the moments scratching the soft hide under the hound's jaw, because it was warm, in the dark; because it was not really a stupid dog, just a clumsy, well-meaning dog, after all, that would track its master through hell.

And lead a boy into it. And wake every damned goblin in that fortress if it took a notion to bark, which he earnestly hoped Zadny would not, and tried to keep the hound comfortable and distracted—the right arm would not move, now, with any speed. He could not get a better grip on the dog, or hold it quiet. The pain came and went in waves that wiped sense out when the dog would get restless and pull at him in the least.

"Shush," he said, when it did. "He'll be back. He'll be back soon, hound. He's a clever boy. Lie still."

So he told it. So he wanted to think. The boy might be in serious trouble by now. He kept listening for any commotion in the distance, hoping against all reason for the boy to follow his instructions to the letter and only find out the lay of the place, then come back for more instructions—and more instructions, and more argument: it was the only delay he could think of to dissuade the boy. Maybe by morning he would be stronger—

And maybe pigs would soar, he thought. He needed to box the boy across the ears, get him on that pony and tell him get the hell home, was what he needed to do. He would keep the damned dog, who could atone for his sins in leading the boy here in the first place; he and the dog might get along, and he might somehow find fish in the stream—

More winged pigs, he thought. The stream had poured off the ice of the heights, and it offered only sterile water.

Water and a way . . . maybe a way to float downstream to safer territory. Damn. He had not thought of that. If he could just get the boy back . . .

If the boy would only come back . . .

Lord Stani's remaining son on his hands, the other two missing—but if they could go downstream, go back to the mountains once they were well away from here, then find another pass—

All this through a landscape barren as hell's doorstep and haunted by goblins, after which they faced a journey through the mountains with no food, nor forage, nor any hope of finding any on their way; with only the vague hope of finding a pass no one else had found, besides the fact that mountains tended to fold in unpredictable ways, and lead one into blind ends, and mazes . . . maybe floating downstream was a better . . .

Zadny lifted his ears, lifted his head and jumped to his feet. Nikolai tensed his arm against the lunge, got a grip on the belt and held to it, knowing the dog was going to bark, damn him—he jerked at the belt hard, to bring the hound to the reach of his fingers, and tried to bring the left hand to seize its muzzle.

There was a bark, a feeble, uncertain whine, then a boy's running steps—he hoped that was the case. "Hush!" he whispered to the hound, fearing the boy was running with goblins on his heels.

But the boy showed up and slid to his knees, babbling, "Master Nikolai! Master Nikolai, I found someone!"

There was no one to find but goblins. And Zadny's pulling at him all but took his senses away. He said, with greatest apprehensions: "Who?"

A huge shadow lumbered up behind the boy, a huge and shaggy shadow with a ratlike tail.

He snatched the sword that was by him, but his good hand had the damned leash tied to it, and the boy grabbed that elbow, and hung on it, objecting: "No, no, it's all right, master Nikolai, he's all right!"

The troll squatted down to have a closer look at him, rumbled, "Bad, bad hurt," and put a hand on his shoulder.

He had never imagined a troll could speak. He was quite out of his head. The creature had tricked the boy. It was contemplating supper, he was sure of it. But between the boy holding his arm and the leash on his wrist—

It said, "Krukczy is my name."

"Nikolai," he said, to humor it while he tried to think. The fool hound was trying to leap up and paw at the troll's lap like some long-lost friend, shooting pains through his wound while Yuri held its collar. The troll patted the dog, then reached and patted his shoulder.

"Nikolai," it said. "Yuri. Good. Good we find brothers."

"It says," Yuri panted, "it says two got away, it says it's going with us."

His heart could only beat so fast. He was not thoroughly aware of his fingers now, or his feet, and the rest of him was fading fast. He said to the boy, "Run, dammit." But the boy paid no attention, neither the boy nor the troll, which was working at the knot that held the dog to his wrist, hurting him and getting nowhere with it.

The boy took over. Fever had set in, Nikolai decided. He was dreaming now, how a troll gathered him up and carried him in its arms, and that Yuri rode along on his pony.

He dreamed that they went into the stream and under the walls of the fortress, and down a winding dark tunnel, pony and all. Lamplight cast shadows on the ceiling above his face. He heard the clip-clop of the pony's hooves.

"What about the goblins?" he asked, because even in a dream, one should not leave such details unseen-to.

The troll said, "Gone to their queen."

"What queen?" And more to the point: "Why?" Why always mattered most, of questions.

But it laid him on the floor without answering the important things. Dreams were like that. Yuri leaned over him to say they were safe, and that the troll was out looking for supper, which it had not been able to do while the goblins were in the tower.

"Fool," he murmured, "it's found it . . ."

Zadny licked him in the face. Yuri made him stop.

"Tell it eat the dog first," he muttered. "Boy, get away, get out of here."

But perhaps the dream had started way up on the mountain, when he had pulled the arrow. And the boy and the dog had never arrived, and there was no troll at all. Only goblins, who had gotten everyone but him.

The troll came lumbering back, shadowing him. There was a great deal of moving about then, in a haze of pain and light and shadow—he fell asleep until Yuri bumped his head up on his knee, and said he should drink.

Fish stew. It wanted salt. But it was hot. "Get away," the boy chided Zadny. "You have yours."

Amazingly detailed for a dream. So was waking again with a contemplative troll staring at him in the lamplight.

"Good, good," it said. "Better?"

He nodded, wanting the other part of the dream back, the one with the boy and the pony and the free sky still overhead. He glanced around him, lifting his head, and saw boy and dog curled up together with the pony's saddle for a pillow, saw the pony dozing on three feet within the tunnel.

The troll was still sitting there when he looked back. It looked very real. It smelled real. It made a shadow where it should. He did not at all like this persistence of imagery—or his situation, or watching the troll's flickering eyes watching his with too much awareness.

"What do you want?" he asked it finally, in his dream; and it said only:

"Sleep, hunter. Go to sleep."

6

"FISH," KRUKCZY ANNOUNCED, ALL DRIPPING, AND FISH there certainly was, a big fat one, flopping about on the floor. Zadny began to bark, threatening it. But Yuri got it and cut its head off, and cleaned it. So when master Nikolai finally opened his eyes on the morning there was breakfast cooking.

"We're still alive," master Nikolai murmured as if that surprised him.

"Goblins all gone," Krukczy said, very full of fish, as it seemed, and wanting to nap awhile, with Zadny, who had breakfasted on fish offal and roe.

"Damned good friends," Nikolai said under his breath. "Never ask where that hound came from. Friends with trolls, it is."

Yuri cast an anxious glance over his shoulder, but Krukczy only seemed to drowse, and Zadny had curled up and shut his eyes.

"Go home," Nikolai said in a low voice. "If there's fish in the stream, catch some, take the pony, leave me and the damned dog with the troll, and get *home*. Tell your father—"

"I'm not telling my father anything," Yuri said, with a lump in his throat, "because I'm not going home yet."

"You've no business in this—"

"You've no business either, you can't use your left arm. What are you going to do to rescue them?"

"I'm going to use my head and go home when I can walk, and get help over here, so there's no question of your going along—"

"Yes, there is. Because if you're going home you can ride Gracja and I'll take Zadny and I'll find them."

"You'll mind what you're told, young lord! I'm responsible for you—and don't think you've proved a thing, running off from home, trekking over-mountain with no damned sense what you were getting in to . . ."

"Did *you* know?"

Master Nikolai shut his mouth and clenched his jaw.

"And you wouldn't go home," Yuri said further. "Not except to make me go. Which you can't do. So there."

"Damn your disobedience."

He did not like being damned by master Nikolai. He was sorry to be disrespectful. But he said, to drive home the point: "You can have my pony, if you want. I got this far. I can walk." Master Nikolai was furious with him, but he was not going to do as he was told, not this time, he had made up his mind on that account, and he was more scared than he had ever been in the mountains. He changed the subject, since master Nikolai was not going to say anything helpful. "Breakfast is ready."

"We're not discussing breakfast."

"Krukczy can catch you more fish. They'll freeze in the pass and they'll be fine. You'll have food all the way home. And he brought greens for Gracja this morning. So she's all right."

Silence from master Nikolai. Nikolai was mad at him. Nikolai tried to sit up and hurt himself, which did not improve his temper.

"Go home!"

"I wouldn't go home without my brother's dog. Do you think I'd go home without *him*?"

"You've not a hope of finding the boys. We don't know where they went."

"Zadny will."

"Damn that dog, he'll get you killed, that's all he's good for. He's got no sense!"

"I'd rather have you with me," he said, with a glance from under his brows, and there was a lump in his throat, and in his stomach, too, where breakfast sat like a stone. "I followed everything you said, master Nikolai, all the way up the mountains, and I didn't have any trouble. I did everything you said last night. Didn't I? And things are all right. I can get along all right if you go home. —But I'd rather have you there. Gracja could carry you. And Krukczy says he's going with us."

"Damn," Nikolai said under his breath, and muttered to himself and winced, with his eyes shut, because it hurt him to sit up. "Damn and damn, boy! You belong at home!"

But Nikolai never for a moment intended to go home without him. Nikolai *wanted* to find his brothers and not to have to face his parents without them. There was never a time they were lost or strayed that Nikolai had not found them and brought them home, only this time was the worst, it was by far the worst.

"So will you go with me, master Nikolai?"

They were riding in the sun, and Bogdan asked him—asked him something, Tamas was sure—but, distressingly enough, he could no longer remember the exact sound of Bogdan's voice; or see Bogdan's face except in shadow. Sunlight streamed about them blindingly bright. Petals drifted down in clouds from the orchards, a blizzard of dying flowers.

If there were a means, he thought, to gather up all the flowers, if he could recover the recent springtime, if he could retrace their path on the mountain road and say, when they had hesitated at that dreadful stone, master Karoly, where are you leading us? Whose friend are you?—then everything might be different.

But he and the witch girl kept riding down the stream, and fever and sunlight blinded him. He might be home, in the orchards about the walls. But if he was where he remembered, a dreadful thing had happened, which in his confusion he could not recall, except the ominous curtain of petals, a sign of decay and change.

The stones in his dream echoed with drums. A goblin looked at him and was blind to him. A troll held him in its arms as skulls shone white under the moon, horse bones alternate with human, a goblin fancy of order. Their kind was not incapable of artistry.

Birds screamed from the thickets while the horses picked their steady way downhill. He saw huge lumps of rock, saw juniper and patient saxifrage, but nothing in this place of orchards, no tree so tame, only twisted shaggy bark, tough and resilient, and weathered gray stone. Gone, the soot-stained snows and lifeless rocks of recent nightmare. Roots here invaded rock and patiently wedged cracks wider, making mountains smaller. Master Karoly said so.

Came pine and linden, rowan and new-leafed, timid beech—he knew them by their names, master Karoly had taught him. Listen to their voices, Karoly had said: each sings a different song. So he knew with his eyes shut the sound and smell of each and every one. But what did that say of where he was or what did it say of the character of his companion, who refused all questions and rode in disdainful silence?

Wool-gathering again? he could hear Bogdan say. There are times to *do* things and times to think, brother. Figure it out, will you?

A dark-spiked shadow of pine ran along the streamside. The witchling led them down to the stream again—when had they ever left it?—and let the mare wade in and drink.

He stopped Lwi short of that: it dawned on him to look into the saddle kit, now that they were stopped in daylight. He was too stiff and sore to turn around to search the gear from horseback, so he slid down, thinking if anyone had food left in his saddlebags it might have been Nikolai; he had never thought to search this morning, and hunger had not much intruded through the pain.

That was a mistake, he thought, kneeling by the water's edge. Getting off was very surely a mistake.

Ela rode the mare between him and the sun, asked, disgustedly, "What are you doing?"

He had tried to get up. Instead he knelt with one knee on wet and soaking reeds, and wet his hands in the icy stream and carried them to his face, while Lwi wandered free in the shallow water. Ela dismounted, and he blinked wetly up into eyes green as glass, green as pond water. Her hair was palest gold. These details absorbed him, along with the frown that knit her brows.

"Fool. You'll catch your death. The stream is ice melt."

It might be. But it took the pain away, and he laved his face with it, ignoring warnings. He wished he could slip into it head-deep, and have it take all the ache, and the thinking, and the remembering. He said, conversationally, on the last of his self-possession, and the last shred of his strength, "I was looking for something to eat. Is there anything? I think I could go on, if there were."

As witches went, he vastly preferred master Karoly. Karoly would not have called him a fool. Karoly would have had some sympathy, long since, even if he had betrayed them. But she confessed there was something to eat, and said she would get it out of her packs if he would quit being a fool and not drown himself in the meanwhile.

She had not a kindly word to her name. She was the most unreasonable, ill-tempered, and arrogant creature he had ever met, including the troll. But she took packets from Skory's saddlebags, and thereafter Lwi and Skory browsed the shore while he and the witch shared the first meal he remembered in days—a little jerky and biscuit, and a sip of clean, cold water.

But after the work the dried meat was, he felt wearier than he was hungry, and set his shoulders against a gnarled pine so that the roots and the stones missed most of his bruises— only to rest, he protested, to her impatience, only a moment.

He was filthy, he was bruised down to the fingertips, there were cuts in his scalp, his bath in the cave had only moved the mud about, so far as he could tell, and she was right, he had soaked himself down the neck and now he was chilled and sorry for it. But he had a precious and clean bit of food in his hand, overall nothing much was hurting him, and his eyes drifted shut—as if, once the terror was past and food had hit his stomach, he could not keep his wits collected or his eyes open. He had found his land of once upon a time, but it was all dark, everything was grim and magical things lived here, oh, yes—trolls and witches. Of gran's stories—at least there were pine groves, and this brook which the goblins had not so far fouled. That was true. So he could still believe in her, for what little good those stories were.

Ela's mistress would prove wiser, and better natured than Ela *or* gran. And if not, if this ride was all for nothing, then he would ride away on his own, and trap and fish for his food and get home past the goblins somehow.

And his father would ask—

His father and his mother and Yuri would all ask, Where is Bogdan?

His only answer must be, I don't know. And his parents would ask why, and he could only say that he had not warned Bogdan, worse, he had fallen off his horse when Bogdan could have most used help, and he had no real answer for what had become of his brother. He never would have, unless he found someone who could tell him what had happened in this country and why goblins were loose and no one stopped them, and whether Bogdan had died with the others—he had not counted the skulls, he had had no such thought in his head last night, nothing but to escape the sight. . . .

A warm hand touched his brow. It confused him, or the tingling that followed it did. He opened his eyes in confusion, saw Ela with a frown of concentration between her brows. He felt warm and cold all over, felt . . .

She said to him, "Get up. Do you hear? Get up now."

He did not even think about doing it. He got to his feet with the bit of jerky still in hand, stumbled on the roots and went after Lwi, as the witch girl put her foot in the mare's stirrup—not a graceful mount, but the mare stood still: creatures did as Ela said. So was he doing, although it dawned on him while he was gathering up Lwi's reins that his pain was less, and while he was hauling himself into Lwi's saddle, that he was not so weary or short of breath as he had been.

Only tired. Unbearably tired, so that once he was in the saddle it was easier to let Lwi follow the mare.

"Wake up," Ela told him twice, before he caught a branch across the face, and, his forehead stinging, kept himself awake.

"I'm fine, I'm fine," master Nikolai panted, and Yuri bit his lip while Nikolai hauled himself painfully onto Gracja's back. Master Nikolai was not at all fine; but he wanted no help, he said, thank you.

"Are you on?" Yuri asked, holding his breath for fear that Nikolai might slide right on off the other side, onto the rocks. He held his hand ready to grab Nikolai's trouser-leg.

"Go now?" Krukczy rumbled, curling his rat tail around and around so it made ripples in the water; Zadny put himself under Gracja's feet as they started off, and scampered from a near miss. Gone to their queen, Krukczy said of the goblins; but Yuri had had no disposition to search the place to be absolutely sure. It was enough to be away, as quickly as they could.

The morning shadow of the mountain was still on them, the rocks dark and the water beside them murkily gray, but darkest was the out-thrust shadow of Krukczy Straz itself, where the going was so narrow Nikolai's leg brushed the tower wall, and he felt the shadow and the threat of the tower looming until they had made it away into the living brush.

"Green," Nikolai murmured, and it was. Grim as the mountains had been, they had come where there was forage. Gracja nipped leaves as she went, caught mouthfuls of grass, so that Yuri tore up handfuls to give her as he saw a chance, to keep her from jolting Nikolai. Zadny rolled in the grass and got up and ran circles until he panted. But the troll met them only now and again as they went, preferring the stream they could not at all times follow. Krukczy would emerge like a bear from the water, shoulders first, and then two large eyes, that might vanish again; or all of Krukczy might come out to walk with them awhile, dripping on the leaves, squishing like a sheep in a rainstorm, and trailing a watery snake curve with his long furless tail.

"Find brothers," Krukczy would say on occasion. And:

"Went this way, went this way." And, yet another time: "Going to see the witch."

"Karoly's sister," Nikolai said, with the nearest interest he had shown in Krukczy's wandering conversation. "Where does this witch live?"

It obtained an airy wave of a very large hand. "There, there, down."

"Fine directions," Nikolai said sourly. Nikolai was in pain, and sweating, and they needed to stop—No, Nikolai insisted, he was on the horse, he was staying on the horse, so they were still going.

Nikolai asked aloud, "Are there more goblins, master troll? Or what kind of place is this they went to?"

"Gone to their queen," was all Krukczy would say. "Gone to their queen. Queen sends them, queen says come back."

"Where?"

Krukczy gave what seemed to be a shrug as he walked, and his tail whipped about nervously. "Where the queen is." Krukczy seemed more and more agitated. "Goblins . . . goblins . . ."

"Where?"

"Gone."

"No sense," Nikolai muttered. "No damned sense, you can't talk to it . . ."

Krukczy was further and further ahead. Yuri tried to hurry, tugging on Gracja as branches separated them from Krukczy's shaggy shape—Krukczy was only a shadow now, a brown shadow quickly slipping away among the leaves.

"Give me the reins," Nikolai said. And when he started to protest, "Give me the reins!"

He passed them up, and Nikolai gave Gracja a fierce kick, sent her at a run on Krukczy's track—and, fearing Nikolai would fall, Yuri began to run, diving through brush Gracja and the troll had broken, Zadny racing ahead of him. He ran and ran, and heard Nikolai call out, "Damn you—"

But Nikolai had brought Gracja back to a walk by the time he had him in sight again. There was no sign at all of Krukczy. "Damned troll," Nikolai breathed as he caught up. But

Nikolai kept Gracja moving, so that he had nothing to do but to walk behind with Zadny and hold his side against the stitch he had caught running so hard.

Then he saw Gracja's reins fall slack, and Nikolai leaned perilously in the saddle. He flung himself forward to stop Nikolai from sliding off, heedless of the thornbush Gracja's forward progress took him through. He shoved at Nikolai, got the reins and made Gracja stop. Gracja was confused, and scared, and Zadny's jumping at her legs was no help.

"Easy, easy," he breathed, trying to steady Gracja with one hand and hold the other ready to keep Nikolai upright. Nikolai had caught himself against the saddlebow, but the whiteness of Nikolai's face and the set of Nikolai's jaw said he was in excruciating pain.

"Better lead," Nikolai said in the ghost of his own voice. "Do you know the way back, boy?"

"No, sir," he said faintly. The very sunlight through the trees seemed cold. "I don't think I do. We've been up and down so many hills . . ."

"I don't know either," Nikolai said. But he did not believe that. Nikolai never got lost.

He looked about him, and up at the sun, the way Nikolai himself had taught him. But lord Sun was hidden by the trees. He only believed he knew where west was. But west was a long ridge of mountains, and a maze of hills. Nothing— nothing was certain. He led Gracja a while, in the direction he thought was right. And when he looked back master Nikolai's eyes were shut and Nikolai was leaning again.

"Please don't fall off," he said. He was still shaking from running. His side hurt, and he could not get enough breath. "I think we need to find somebody, I think we need a place with people, very soon."

"Karoly's sister," Nikolai said. "The ones we're following—there were hoof-prints . . . some time back. Horse-hair—white—on the branches."

Yuri was embarrassed. He had been blind—leading Gracja, keeping his eyes on the troll, that was all. He had seen no such things. Nikolai, hurt as he was, lying much of the time against Gracja's neck, had kept his eyes open. But he had a dreadful thought then. "Do goblins ride horses?"

"Eat them, for all I know." Nikolai's eyes shut again, and half opened. "Shouldn't have run. Shouldn't have run. Damn, boy."

"Yes, sir," he said. "What should we do?"

Nikolai sat there a moment, above him, his eyes open—but Nikolai said nothing; only, for no reason, took his weight to the stirrup and began to get down—which, if he did—

Yuri shoved hard to stop him, put himself in the way so Nikolai had nowhere to step. "You can't get off," he told Nikolai. "Don't get down. . . ."

"Boy, I want you to take the horse."

"No!" he said. "No. If you get off, I'm staying here. We're both staying here. Do you want that?"

"It's left us," Nikolai said. "It's left us in the middle of the damn woods, boy, it's smelled goblins and it's run."

"Then don't make things worse! I can't get you back up on the horse if you fall, and I don't even know where home is."

"You can track us backwards. Back to the tower . . ."

"No, sir! I won't, I won't do it—you stay on, you hear me? If you get off, I'm staying with you until you can get on again. Do you hear me, I'll do it!"

Nikolai seemed to think about that. Or Nikolai was in too much pain to think at all. He leaned heavily on the saddlebow until all Yuri could do was steady him; and he knew it hurt Nikolai's wounded arm, but it was the only way he could manage. He started leading Gracja again, making as much speed as he could, looking back as he could to be sure Nikolai was still steady.

But a thread of blood was running down Nikolai's hand, staining Gracja's side.

He's dying, Yuri thought in panic. He's going to die if we don't get help, and there's nothing we can do any faster than we are.

Zadny went in front of them. "Find people," Yuri said to him—"Zadny, find people, do you hear me?"

There was no knowing whether Zadny understood a word,

but he kept to the front of them, sometimes losing himself in the brush, so he feared they would lose track of the hound, too, and be alone.

"Maybe we can find somebody besides Nikolai that got away," Yuri said to himself. "Everything's going to be all right, it's just trolls don't know what people need, it's just scared, probably Nikolai chasing it scared him, he'll come back. Nikolai shouldn't have run the horse, that's all—the blood will stop."

"Karoly's sister," Nikolai murmured, once, obscurely, and he stopped Gracja and went back to him to see whether Nikolai was all right. But Nikolai only said, "Are we still on the trail?" and he said, "Yes, sir, I think we are. . . ." realizing with a chill that Nikolai was off his head and lost.

He had made Nikolai come with him. He had been disrespectful, he had refused Nikolai's advice, and been smug about it; and offered Nikolai no choice but come with him— because he had known in his heart of hearts that Nikolai would never take Gracja and ride home without him. He had wanted Nikolai to get on Gracja's back and come with him this morning; and he had been so sure he was doing the right thing, so sure Nikolai was strong enough—although Nikolai had told him last night he would never make it.

He had not listened: he had not wanted to listen, that was the bitter truth. Nikolai had said go home and have his father send men who could do more than a stupid boy could do— Nikolai had never once asked him to get *him* to safety, Nikolai was too strong for that, Nikolai was supposed to be with him to advise him, that was the way he had intended things . . .

The woods blurred in front of him. He walked and followed Zadny, and looked for the hoof-prints master Nikolai had said he had seen, because there was no time to be wrong now—thanks to his cleverness and his disobedience, master Nikolai had no time.

The sun sank as they followed the watercourse downhill, sometimes among rocks, in the shadow now of tall beeches not fully leafed, and early willow, and brush as stripped as the brush the other side of the mountains. The plague of beasts had passed here, too, Tamas thought, in the numb lucidity that had come since he had had water and food. Leafless vines snagged the horses' feet and snapped, dry branches broke under their hooves. The horses, taller than deer, found browse along the way, a snatch of leaves, and in clear spaces, patches of stream-side cress that had grown since the depredations. Ela held the lead, no horsewoman, but Jerzy's mare went along as if it had home and stable in mind.

So did Lwi, without his urging; and when he protested the horses could not stand that pace forever, she declared they would be all right, that was her word, they would be all right.

"Are there goblins behind us?" he asked. And got no answer.

His bruised bones ached, after so much and so rough riding—but he was thinking clearly enough these last hours to realize that he had lost his grandfather's sword, and even the saddle knife, with his own horse. Nikolai's bow was all the weapon they had, that and its handful of arrows.

Well done, he thought bitterly, in Bogdan's tones. Well done, little brother. And only now wondering what you have for resources? You unfailingly amaze me. . . .

He tried at least to calculate how far they had come. In a clearer space he looked back and all about for the sight of mountains, but the trees still loomed taller: the forest was all their surroundings, the colorless and dimming sky with its high cloud making time itself uncertain. He was all too awake, in the dark that lived within the forest, where twilight was early and shadowed with leaves. The whole world tottered on the edge of reason, imagination led nowhere, and he had no sane choice now but the one he was following.

"We'll make it by twilight," Ela declared, the only words she had volunteered to him since noon. "We have to."

He repeated his question: "What do we fear in this woods?"

"All manner of things," she said, and added: "Everything."

Lwi tossed his head, sweating. Tamas patted his neck beneath the fall of mane, misliking vague answers, and disliking witches more by the passing hour. Maybe she could ease his aches, but the ease did not last. Maybe she could make creatures go where she wanted, but clearly that did not extend to goblins, and maybe not to bears; so what good was that?

Besides, who knew what women thought, or might do, or why? Here he rode in a shadowy, goblin-haunted woods asking himself not for the first time how Ela had escaped the goblins' ambush, or hidden the horses, or made bargains with trolls to rescue him.

Walls before nightfall had been his hope in mid-afternoon: the expectation that they would find some fortified and human hold, an unassailable place with a great lady who happened to be a witch, but who, please the god, would turn out to remind him a great deal of the Karoly he had loved, an old woman who would keep a study in equal clutter, who would answer his questions with equal sympathy, tell him the good and the bad that he had to deal with, and magic up a wise and potent answer he could bring back to Maggiar.

But by the beginning of sunset he still saw no fields such as a great hold would need, only this barely flourishing desolation of woods and stony hillsides. He was down to hoping for another tower, like Krukczy Straz. (And another troll, shuffling about the halls in service to Ela's mistress? He was over the boundaries of Maggiar and clearly things here were different.)

Madam, he would say to Karoly's sister—at least he imagined that was how to address a witch—I was with master Karoly, whom, I fear, the goblins . . .

. . . ate? Killed. Killed was far kinder, and he could get immediately to: Master Karoly came to ask your help, my father asks it—

Then the witch would say: What exactly do you want me

to do? and he would have not an idea in his head: he had no idea what a witch could do, or what she would ask of him—

Because witches asked payment, that was in grandmother's stories, along with trolls and magical waterfalls that made one young a thousand years, and undead creatures that haunted the site of their demise, different than ghosts, and bloodier. . . .

Madam, he would say, if you would help my father and my people—and my brother, if he's still alive . . .

What would he do in return for that? Anything, he said to himself. Anything. Bogdan had left him that duty. Master Karoly had. He was the last of their company and he had no choices, now that he had gone this far.

Madam, anything at all, if only you'd do something . . . if you *could* do something . . .

But the witchling pushed the horses both to the limit of their strength and spoke of being in after dark, and that was no recommendation of her mistress' power. "I don't like this," Ela said once, which instilled no confidence at all. He asked no further questions. But she said again, "She should hear me," and he thought she must mean her mistress.

"Where are we?" he asked. "How far yet?"

But for an answer, the witch-girl only put Jerzy's mare to a jogging, bone-jarring pace, slipping perilously from side to side of the saddle. They rode down a slope and along a winding hillside, and even in the clearings now, the light was dimmer. Sanity seemed diminished, feeble, overwhelmed.

"Be careful," he began to say, but it was far too narrow a trail to overtake her and Skory was already vanishing in the brush. Lwi had taken to running, too, through twists and doubling turns, under trees and headlong downhill. Alone, he would have reined Lwi back, but pride or fright said no fool witchling who could scarcely stay ahorse was going to lose him in a woods full of goblins—not now, with night coming.

Down to the trough of a hill and up again, up and up through a jolting series of climbs, then onto—thank the god— a well-worn footpath, that promised habitation hereabouts.

Earth and recrossed roots sped under Lwi's hooves, new-leafed branches whipped past. Then an archway let them through a stone wall so overgrown with vines it loomed right out of the woods, one with everything around it.

He saw Skory and her rider and the skull-topped poles ahead of him all at once, saw Ela sliding down from the saddle in the courtyard of this forest-wrapped tower and an outcry of protest stuck in his throat. With all the clatter they had just made, they could have roused the sleeping dead, but there was no need compounding the error: he kicked free of both stirrups and slid from Lwi's back while Lwi was stopping, chased a disappearing flash of blond hair and flying cloak into the shadowed doorway of the vine-veined tower. Goblin work was plain to see in the courtyard, the door dark and unbarred to all comers—and Ela ran inside and upstairs with the fleet surefootedness of someone at home on those steps.

He could not. He stumbled on them in the dark, hurrying as fast as he could to overtake a bereaved and frightened girl, intending to reason with her: after the rooftop of Krukczy Straz he had not the heart to blame her; but echoes were waking to her search with the dreadful sound of an empty house, and betraying where he was now seemed doubly foolish. They had two horses in the courtyard that might be their only way out of here, he had left the bow down there in his haste to overtake her, and if there was any mystery left of them, he hoped to preserve it, arm himself and reserve some surprise on their side if she came running . . .

A step rasped on stone below him and his heart skipped a beat. Down the dark of the winding stairs, the faintest of twilight from the hall below still showed at the edges of the steps and on the walls opposite the core. And the step repeated itself.

Ela, he thought. We're not alone. Do you know that?

He fervently hoped for witchcraft, recollecting that Ela had come and gone undetected among goblins, and got along with trolls; but that had been no trollish movement. That had been a shod foot, a scuff of leather on stone, and since the second footfall, silence: Ela's, his, and whoever shared the tower with them.

He leaned his back against the stone of the stairwell core, keeping still in the remote chance it would go away and not come up the stairs. *Ela* was silent now that she had roused trouble; Ela must have heard it wherever she was—in some hallway upstairs, while here he stood guarding her retreat, and he could only hope she had recovered her good sense.

Not a woman's step, below, he was sure. It had sounded to his ears very like a man's boot, edged with metal. And the silence persisted, as if the presence down there had realized its mistake, and waited for him to make the next move.

Which could just as well mean some guard of this place, some honest servant of Ela's mistress, who could end up in fatal misunderstanding of intentions on this dark stairs—fatal for him, counting he was empty handed. The intruder, if intruder it was, had come past two horses out there—and knew their number. He thought, I'm trapped. Maybe I should take the chance and call out—in the case it is a friend.

An outcry would warn Ela. But Ela was being wary now that it was too late, and he decided that he was in no hurry either. Let whoever-it-was move again. He wanted to be surer, before he made an irrevocable move, and meantime he wanted off this stairs if there was a hope of doing it in silence.

He heard a faint, faint movement below him—the tower was old. Its steps gritted underfoot, there was no helping it. So did his, he discovered, and the other was moving now. He pressed his back to the wall for steadiness and heard a whisper of cloth and metal, saw the illusory light at the lowest steps eclipsed by darker shadow. He set his foot to the next step and moved up and up, trying to mask his movements beneath the movements of the one stalking him, and meanwhile to widen his lead on it, hoping desperately for some doorway out of this place that would not compromise Ela.

But the next turning of the stairs showed a faint glow above him, a window at some higher turning, when he most prayed for deeper dark, and when he judged he was running out of stairs altogether.

That was no good. He had made his own mistakes, he could only hope in Ela's magic now, and he thought he had as well find out whether it was friend or foe stalking them, before someone died of what might, after all, prove a mistake. He called out, failing nonchalance:

"Are you a friend, down there?"

It glided onto the steps below him, a darkness on which metal glistened, a horrific and elegant armoring he had seen once before, in the cellars of Krukczy Straz—a jut-jawed countenance beneath a mop of dark hair and braids.

Fangs, oh, indeed it had. And eyes large and virtually whiteless. And an unsheathed sword.

"Well," the goblin said. "Well, shall we see?"

He backed up a step. He had not intended to, but the creature seemed to have more of the stairs than he had, as he took account of its reach and the sword in its hand.

"There's nothing up there," it said. It beckoned to him with an elegant, beringed hand. "Come down, come, you've nothing to fear."

"So goblins joke."

It laughed, showing fangs, and climbed another step closer. "Oh, often. It's a joke, you know, like that in the yard. Where's the witchling?"

"Out the door. Riding away. You can't find her, can you?"

"So men joke, too."

Man, it called him—not for his age or his facing it: it meant his difference from its kind, it meant no sympathy or mercy, and he backed another step, he could not help it. He was not ready to die. He contemplated a rush against it, perhaps to bear it over on the steps, or tear through its grip. Its nails were dark and long, on hands as beautiful as a woman's, as expressive, as graceful in ironic gesture. And somehow it had gained another step without his seeing it.

"Where is she?"

"I've no idea." His heart fluttered. It took another step

and he had no choice yet but to back up, feeling his way around the core. It was clearly in the light now. Its eyes were green as old water, its smile nothing reassuring.

"Afraid of me?" it asked.

"Oh, never. Why don't you go downstairs?"

"Why were you going up? Looking for something? A witch, maybe?"

"I'm a thief," he said. "Like you."

A second time it laughed, and flexed a hand about its sword hilt, beckoning with the other. "Then we should be friends. Come down. We'll have a drink together."

"Be damned to you."

The sword flashed, rested point down on the steps between them. "You've great confidence. Is it justified, I wonder?"

It meant to kill him outright, he had no doubt now. He backed up only for a feint, shoved off from the edge of the step and, bare-handed, struck the blade aside as he dived for the shallow of the turn.

The goblin warrior followed the blade about, full turn, that was how it had its arm in his way, and him pinned against the great pillar of the core, staring at it face to face. Its iron-hard arms were on either side, and the carelessly held sword leant against his neck as it shook its head slowly. "Not justified," it concluded, and grinned at him, a showing of fangs, a glitter of shadowed eyes behind a disordered fringe of mane—such details stood clear as his heart pounded away and he wondered could he duck down quickly enough, or dared he move—considering the cold blade beneath his chin.

"Lost its tongue?" it asked him. "Fellow thief?"

He had. And his breath. He brought a knee up. The goblin knocked his head against the wall, not grinning now. He made a second try—but the goblin was too tall, and breath was too short. It said, hissing into his face with that lisp the jutting fangs made,

"I want the witch, man."

"What witch?" he asked. "Which witch?" Light-headedness suggested rhymes. It could not be more annoyed, and he was out of strategies. He tried to pry its hand loose. As well dispute a stone statue. "I think you ate the last one—hereabouts . . ."

"Liar," it said, and tightened its grip. "Are you a liar?"

"Of course not," he had wind to say. It slacked its hold ever so little.

"A conundrum. How clever." Unexpectedly it let go entirely, and gave him room on the stairs. "Run, man. Run."

He did not believe it, not even when it dropped the sword point and gave him room. He drew a shaky breath, made a gesture downward, giddily, toward the stairs. "You first." If one was about to be beaten anyway, he had learned that from Bogdan—if one was about to be stabbed from behind, as seemed now, then play the game for pride, if that was all he had left. And to his own light-headed amazement he was not tongue-tied or wool-gathering. Bogdan would approve, if Bogdan were here, but this creature and his kind had—

He could not think about that rooftop. He refused to think about it now.

The goblin stepped higher on the stairs, trading places with him on the narrow steps, and tapped the side of his leg with the sword blade as they passed each other. "I'm letting you go, man. Go. Next time—find a sword."

It was going on upstairs. It was searching for Ela. It would come back for him, or others were below to deal with him. He contemplated attacking it as it turned its back on him in contempt and kept climbing—the troll had inured him to terrors, for days now, and he wanted to go for it bare-handed as he was. But that served nothing. In the hall below he might find a weapon, a fallen board, anything to throw a pennyworth weight onto his side of the balance and do it harm it might feel, if it followed him. Or get to the courtyard and his bow if it did not.

He sped down the steps, angry, desperate, blind in the winding dark below, expecting to run headlong into more of them at any turn. He saw the faint twilight from the doorway and bolted down the last turns into the entry, where his dark-accustomed eyes picked out cloth in the shadow, a cloaked figure that accosted him with:

"Shh!"

Ela's whisper—while his fist was knotted up to strike and his legs were shaking under him. "What were you *doing* up there?"

"There's a goblin," he stammered. The fury ran out of him, and he set his shoulder to the wall for support to his shaking knees. Hardly a hero, he: he had fled pell-mell down the stairs, and the goblin could come back down or call to its friends from the window at any moment.

"Then get out of here! There's a place I haven't looked—"

"Ela, give it up! Everyone's dead! The horses are out there. They know there's two of us! They'll find us. —Lord Sun—"

'I have to!'' she whispered, and tore away from him.

"Ela!'' he whispered furiously, but she was a wisp of cloak and shadows, headed for a door, another stairway, he had no idea. He took her advice and ran out the open door to the yard, where the horses were grazing on the grass that had sprung up in the half-buried cobbles.

"Aha!'' rang out from some window, from the roof, he had no idea, nor waited to see in his reach after Lwi's saddle. A knife thumped into the ground beside his boot, stuck upright in the weed patch beside the cobbles. He jumped—he could not help it, and Lwi shied as he grabbed the reins. The bow was not strung. He snatched up the knife as his only gesture of defiance and looked up at the tower.

"Ah. Do you take my gift?'' the goblin warrior called down. My gift, my gift, my gift, echoed off all the walls, loud as Lwi's hooves clattering on the pavings. Skory danced away, out of his reach, and he had visions of the goblin coming down the stairs and cutting off Ela's retreat. "And are you a thief, too?''

Thief, thief, thief, the echoes said.

"What harm have we ever done to you?'' he shouted up through the echoes. "What do you want?''

Want, want, want, the echoes gave back, as Ela came flying from out the door.

"Ho!'' the goblin shouted; "Witchling!'' But Ela never stopped. She caught Skory's trailing reins as the goblin disappeared from the window, downward bound without a doubt. He drew Lwi after him, held Skory's reins while Ela climbed up to the saddle, and without a second glance over his shoulder, flung himself for Lwi's saddle.

"Witchling, witchling, witchling," the echoes were still saying, as they rode past the grisly warning on the poles, through the gateway and into the tangle of the woods again, where the horses had to strike a slower pace.

Then he cast an anxious glance over his shoulder, and saw Ela's face as she looked back at the vine-shrouded gates. It was not grief, not a child's bewilderment, but a cold, white-lipped fury.

"What can we do?" he asked. "How can we fight them?" He was willing to hear anything but pointless defeat, nothing done, nothing even learned about their enemy, and their enemy in control of the place they had come to find and despising all they could do.

She laid a hand on her breast, and said only, "It's *mine*, it's *mine*, and he knows it."

"What, the tower?"

"This." The hand was pressed to something beneath her collar, and she looked at him with a set face and a defiance that challenged him along with the goblin as she rode past him.

So it was *not* for her mistress she had been searching the tower. Karoly's sister was dead, if those skulls could tell the story. And he—

"Where are you going?" he asked.

"To make them regret it," was all she would say.

7

THEIR GOING WAS A HASTY CONFUSION OF DARK AND branches by starlight. Leaves raked Tamas' shoulders as the horses struck out on a downhill and up again, on a ride in which any stir of brush might be goblin ambush, any twitch of the horses' ears might be the only alarm they would have. The witchling told him nothing—but, Tamas thought, nothing he had done back at the tower had deserved her confidence. The goblin had *let* him go: she might have bewitched the creature, or not, for all he knew—she might not know what had happened up there on the stairs and might ask herself how he had escaped, weaponless.

But it was not an hour to plead for trust. And counting her reticence and the fury he had felt in her glance, he began to ask himself whether she was in fact a white witch, whether in fact she needed help in which a fool would do very well—he had heard about *that* kind of sorcerer in gran's stories, too.

But how did one know the good witches from the bad? Ela moved by dark, in shadows, and by moonlight, and if that had not been a curse she had loosed against the goblin he never hoped to feel one. The horses' mad steadiness, jolting his exhausted, spinning senses, the goblin saying, "Run," as if it were a choice he had . . . its eyes looking into his, mad and malicious and amused with him and his plight . . .

Lwi stumbled, and the near fall and the slope beside him sent a chill through him. "The horses can't do any more!" he protested, with too much pride to add, Nor can I. He was crazed, trying to comprehend goblin games and witches, most of all for staying with her, and he began to think that his own staying might be more spell than reason.

"Not far now," she promised him.

But Not Far took them down a hill and along another and another, and maybe a third: he was drifting in nightmare corridors and remembering goblin footsteps somewhere along the second hill, in a forest darker than the night sky, Lwi panting as he moved.

Then he heard water out of the dark—their stream again, he thought; or he was dreaming still. He heard it nearer and nearer, until he saw Skory wading into it, Skory first and then Lwi dipping their heads to drink as they walked—he let out the reins and let Lwi drink as he could, never stopping, even yet—bewitched, as before.

"Have mercy," he pleaded. "This is foolish. What good to kill the horses? We've outrun the goblins. They aren't following us, Ela, for the god's sake—"

They were at the bank. She rode Skory further up before she stopped—but Lwi stayed on the bank to drink, no longer spellbound, as far as he could tell.

So they must have arrived, he thought, and slid down from Lwi's back, sore, and dizzy, and suddenly perceiving a stone wall and a gateway in the darkness of the nightbound trees. For one blink of an eye he feared they had ridden full circle back to the tower and into a trap, but at a second, he saw only an open gateway into, so far as he could tell, an overgrown ruin.

"Ela?" he said, but she was staring at the gate, simply staring. Lwi had had enough water, and he patted Lwi's sweat-drenched neck, and led him up gently to the grass that grew along the shore, while the mare wandered at will. This time he loosed the bow and the arrow case from the saddle; and looked around to learn in what precise place Ela decreed for their camp.

But she had vanished in that instant of inattention—through the gateway, into the ruin.

"Ela?" he asked the empty night, exhausted, lost, and suddenly outraged. He went as far as the dark doorway, and found no sight of her, listened, and heard no sound but the sighing of a cold night wind and the sudden jingle of harness as Skory shook her head.

So the girl wanted to slip away alone into the ruin after riding all day, finding her mistress murdered, and escaping goblins with something the goblins were looking for? Well and good. Maybe witches needed no sleep and no protectors and dined on moonbeams. He strung the bow in a fit of temper, set it and its arrow case against a man-sized lump of stone, and unsaddled and walked and rubbed the horses down—*there* were grateful creatures at least.

Afterward, in a calmer frame of mind, if no easier in conscience, he bent down at water's edge, cooled his face in water that chilled him to the bone—good water, clean water, that set him shivering as he washed and drank—but that was honest work that he had done, unlike some he could think of; honest work and honest sweat and trying to do the right thing.

He was chilled through. He took his bow and found a seat next to the wall, hugging his cloak about him against the night wind, and thinking that now that his stomach was quieter, he ought to try to eat—get into the packs and find something to eat for himself, since the girl would not deign to advise him where she was or what she was up to or when, if ever, she would come back.

But he had no real appetite left, and not to be pent anywhere or shoved anywhere, or bewitched off on another ride—that was all he wanted. It was enough to know there was food and water within reach, even if he was too exhausted to eat. He could sleep a moment, he decided. It was only his neck at risk, now. He need only shut his eyes and listen to the forest whispering in the wind.

"Men see so poorly at night," a goblin voice lisped, from the wall above his head. He flung himself to one knee, reaching for the knife.

The goblin leapt down with a light clash of metal as he reeled to his feet, drawing the knife—it was that near him. He heard the horses bolt and run.

"Well, well. Here we are again, and you threaten me with my own gift."

"It *is* you," he said, backing up a step, trying to clear the light-headedness that assailed him. *"Ela!"*

"Oh, hush, hush, man, she's not afraid of me. She should be, but she isn't. She's a great magician, like her mistress, don't you know? Undoubtedly greater. Ysabel wouldn't touch what she's taken up. Now Ysabel's dead, and her poor, slow-witted servant with her. I wonder how *she* will fare."

"E-la!"

"I tell you she won't hear you. She can't hear you."

It advanced. He stepped back again, giddy, keeping the knife between him and its owner—a wicked blade, with a backwards spine he could only guess how to use—but this creature most certainly knew, and it had the sword that matched it.

"Ungrateful wretch. Here." Jewels glittered in the star-light, in a black-nailed hand. Something thumped to the ground at his feet.

He was supposed to look down. He refused to take his eyes off the creature, who smiled at him, showing fangs, and leaned casually against the wall, long fingers, spiderlike, grazing the sword hilt at its side. "Oh, not at all trustful. Are we, thief? Lie to me, and all the time you were with the witchling. For shame, for shame."

"Where are the rest of you?"

"Of me? Why, altogether here, man, altogether where the witchling is and isn't. —But witches are like that, nor here, nor there, most of the time. While you—" Another smile, close-lipped, but the fangs still showed. "You are most definitively here, young gentleman, in possession of my knife, and, by my graciousness, its sheath, and your head. And here am I, seeking *your* gracious hospitality. What do you say to that?"

It was hard for a cobwebby wit to follow the twists and turns of its converse, but it seemed foolish to attack the creature, more foolish to die in contest with weapons it knew, when it seemed extraordinarily enamored of its own cleverness, and he had no idea the measure of it. He took a breath, adopted a careless stance. "What do I say? —That you're a common bandit!"

"Oh, uncommon. A lord among my kind, and grossly inconvenienced by this girl, this fledgling, this would-be sorceress. So here we are, thief and liar, and bandits both."

"I'm no bandit."

"But thief and liar you admit to?"

"No."

Again the sharp-edged grin. "Azdra'ik is my name. And yours, man?"

"Tamas." He gave no more clues to his family or his friends than he must. Exchanging names offered a familiarity he had no wish to share with this creature. He only hoped Ela had heard him call out, and was working some magic to deliver him: meanwhile he could no more than play for time, and he wondered how many other goblin warriors were slipping around them in the forest dark. Lwi and Skory had made no further sound, but he did not think goblins could overwhelm the horses without at least some commotion.

"So, Tamas, and are you a wizard, too?"

"The greatest."

It laughed. "Audacious man. Why don't you go find the witchling? I'll wait here for you."

"Of course you will."

"No, no, my solemn word. You're free to go."

It meant to follow him to Ela, he was certain of it. But he did not know what else he should do, that might give him a chance, or even delay this creature more than a single pass of its sword; and he no more knew where Ela was than it did. Perhaps he could lead it a chase and raise enough noise that Ela would know where he was. Or maybe they had already caught her, and it was only a cruel joke the creature played. But he had no better offers for his life.

He caught up the bow and case, dived through the gateway into the shadow of the ruined wall, and found himself in a maze of brush and broken walls. His footsteps sounded louder than he liked on patches of exposed paving stones. He tried to keep silence, and now and again glanced back, afraid the creature was laughing all the while and following him.

He dared not call out. He feared she might answer, unaware of the danger. It was not even his intention to find her, only to raise enough noise for her to take some magical precaution—and for him to locate targets at more than arm's length, if the creature had companions slipping through this woods. He had an arrow against the bow. He was ready for treachery.

Then he saw Ela's pale hair past a screen of head-high brush, and stopped and caught himself against a truncated wall, trying to think what to do or whether to go to her—

But she stood so still, so unnaturally still, paying no heed to his footsteps on the stones and his moving in the brush. She was gazing down at her cupped hands—working some magic, he told himself, but nothing evident to him, nothing to his observation that might have dispelled the threat outside.

He glanced back the way he had come, wondering whether to go back and try to lead off the creature rather than disturb her working—but that seemed supremely ill-advised. And if despite all he could do, he was followed, they had already found her.

He came to her and stopped at respectful distance, trying to say calmly, "Ela. Ela, there's a goblin—in our camp—"

She might not have heard him at all. He saw the flash of glass and starlight in her hands, held the bow and the arrow in his left hand, touched her arm ever so slightly, then shook at her, when she remained, statuelike, completely oblivious to his touch. "Ela. A goblin. It's after us."

A flutter of her eyelids then—a moment that she looked straight at him. "No," she said, shaking her head, as if what he said were patently foolish. "No. Not here."

Perhaps, then, the wall did keep something out. Perhaps there was some magical reason the goblin asked him to find her, and perhaps it had been a mistake to come in here and disturb her magic. Maybe that was exactly what the goblin wanted. But there was nothing to do now but make her understand him. "It's out there with the horses. It followed us from the tower." He tried to sound sane and reasonable. Breath failed him. "It *spoke* to me. It told me to find you. What should I do?"

She seemed to have understood, then. And the amulet in her hands began softly to glow and cast a light on her face— a mirror, it was, a simple mirror. He remembered the goblin saying that her mistress would not touch what she had taken up . . . and he thought: This small thing?

Then a feeling of malaise tingled through the air, through the earth, through the soles of his feet and the nape of his neck and the palms of his hands. He heard the trees sighing in the woods and the water of the brook running, and a distant shouting, as if it came out of some hollow hall. Ysabel wouldn't touch what she's taken up, echoed in his ears, like voices from the tower—taken up, taken up, taken up—

The dark around them receded. They stood beneath the ghostly lamps and hangings of a great hall, and all around them men and women fled in fear. The floors and walls began to crack as light blazed through, brilliant as the sun.

Everything whirled about them. Suddenly a veiled woman stood in this thundering chaos, her cloak and her robes cracking like banners in the winds that swept the hall. She looked full at them, at *him*, and pointed her finger, crying into the gale—" . . . one and the same . . . One is all! Remember that, above all! There is always a flaw—"

The image shattered, with a sound of breaking glass. Shocking quiet followed, isolation and dark, ordinary night around them, an ordinary moon above the ruined walls and the brush. He discovered himself breathing, and his heart beating and the sighing of the wind moving without his will.

"Wizard!" Ela cried, tearing her arm free, and hit him with her fist. "Liar! Damned *liar*, get away from me! You touched it, *you* changed it—"

"No!" Too many accusations of falsehood had come his way tonight, too many confusions. "Anything that happened, *you* did. That *thing* you have—did." Words were coming too rapidly, and he could not get breath enough, in the sudden stillness of the air. She began to walk away from him and he caught her arm and held her perforce. "I've nothing—*nothing* to do with magic, or goblins, or this thing of yours! I don't know what you were doing, but there's a goblin the other side of the wall where the horses are, it's looking for you, and it says you've inconvenienced it—that that *thing* you have, your mistress wouldn't touch! He called her name. Ysabel. And he told me to find you, don't ask me what for—I didn't know anything else to do!"

Light shone through Ela's fingers, reflected on Ela's pale face—the rest was dark, and sighing wind. "My mistress wouldn't touch it," she echoed. "Then why did she hide it from everyone but me, why did she tell me to use it, did he tell you that? —Let me go! Where do you get the right to shout at me?"

"You said you were a witch!"

"I am!" Light reddened the edges of her fingers and made the illusion of bones within. "I brought us away from the tower, didn't I? I brought us here!"

"Did you rescue me, or was it the troll's idea? This is the second time that creature's let me go!"

"He's not a—"

"I don't care what it is. Karoly is *dead*! Your mistress is *dead*! Krukczy Tower is full of goblins, and now your mistress' tower is! The one waiting out there—wants you." He struggled to keep his voice down. "It says its name is Azdra—Zdrajka—something. It says—"

"Azdra'ik!"

Beyond belief. "You *know* him?"

The glow had all but died within her hand, leaving only night above them, and a plain piece of mirror when she opened her fingers, that reflected nothing but dark and moonlight. "This is *mine*. I have it! It can show me anywhere in the land. It can open magic to me. It can defeat them!"

"Then begin with the one that's been following us! If it gets the horses, we're afoot here with its friends, with lord Sun knows what next! Send *him* off, for a start!"

She seemed to have run out of words. The bit of silvered glass flashed in the moonlight, inert as its delicate chain that sparkled in her fingers. "Let me go," she said. "Let me go! You've already changed something, I don't know what. What more damage can you do?"

He released her arm. She eyed him balefully, then began to walk, back toward the gateway and the horses. He walked with her, with a stitch in his side and with the disquieting understanding that she was going indeed to confront this Zdrajka-goblin with her piece of glass, and he nocked the arrow and had another ready as he walked.

"Let me go first," he said, "and tell him I found nothing." Perhaps after all, he thought, lying was his best talent. But it was not fair tactics he expected, from a goblin; and it was not fair tactics he meant to use, with the advantage all to the goblin.

Ela might have heard him or might not: she kept walking, and he saw her lips moving, shaping words that had no sound. That, he did not like: it might equally well be a magic to deal with him as with the goblin, so far as he knew, or blackest sorcery that might not care where it made its bargains.

But when they came to the gate, the horses were grazing peacefully in the moonlight, as if nothing had ever happened.

"Well?" she asked. "Where is he?"

"He *was* here," was all he could say—until, outside the gate, walking over the ground he and the goblin had occupied, he saw the glitter of jewels in the moonlight, and gathered up the sheath that belonged to the knife. "It *was* here," he said, showing it to Ela. "It was here and it left."

Why? was the next obvious question. But Ela only frowned and walked away in silence.

While the horses, that should have been off in the woods and the devil's own work to catch after their fright, might have had second thoughts about the grass growing in this spot, and hunger *might* have weighed more with them than goblin-smell—they certainly showed no signs of recent panic.

He could not answer that well for himself: he ached from running, he was ravenously hungry, which no one reasonably should be, who had just seen what he had seen. He was vastly relieved that the horses were all right; and beneath all that, he felt the complete fool. So far as he knew, Ela's magic *had* bespelled the creature, brought back the horses and secured their safety, and he had been unjust to lay hands on her and most of all to disturb what might have been a delicate and essential work of magic. He could no longer even swear that he had seen what he had seen either outside or inside the walls—it was slipping away from him, detail by detail, like a dream—but he did know that he found himself deeper and deeper entangled in what Ela would, and where Ela was going, and what Ela wanted.

He asked himself when and where he had passed the point of no return, because he no longer knew how to ride away—not alone because he no longer knew the way home through these wooded hills. He desperately wanted a hope to chase—anything but a blind flight this way and that from successive disasters, anything but a return without answers and without help.

But, damn it all, if magic was the help Karoly had placed all his hope in, a waking dream did not change what was going on in this place, or get them help, or get him home again with any answers.

He thrust the goblin knife into its sheath and that into his belt, and went and sank down on his heels where Ela sat. The mirror was in her hands. It seemed to occupy her attention, quiescent as it was, and he waited a long time to see whether she was doing anything or only brooding on his company.

"Ela," he began finally, most respectfully, most courteously, he thought, "Ela, I want to know where we're going, and why, and what's ahead of us. I want to know why that creature left and why he asked for you and told me to find you. I want to know why master Karoly believed it was so important to talk to your mistress, but he could never tell anyone why; and I want to know why he rode past a goblin warning and never warned us what it was.''

''Sometimes you can't,'' she said faintly.

''Can't what?''

''Can't break through a spell.''

''Is that what happened? He wanted to and couldn't?'' It opened a sudden hope for master Karoly's character. He wanted to understand Karoly's actions, even if it involved dark and damning things. But she looked away from him, evading his eyes the very way Karoly had done since his dreams began, and with gentle force he touched her knee and drew her attention back, with all the gentleness and patience he could muster. ''Is that the kind of thing that happens?''

''Sometimes. Sometimes—else.''

Oblique. Always oblique. She still evaded his eyes, even answering him.

''Like the goblin leaving? You made it leave?''

''I don't know.'' Her gaze roved distractedly about the wall of trees as if she were listening to something, to anything and everything in the world but his voice.

''What's out there, Ela?''

''I don't know.''

'I don't know,' began to take on a thoroughly ominous ring—recalling Karoly and the goblin stone, and considering their present situation.

''Ela. Are we in danger?''

''I don't know.'' A sudden pale glance, starlit. A frown. ''Yes. The moon. On the lake. There's danger. There's always danger.''

There was no lake. It was a stream in front of them. ''From where? What lake? What are you talking about?''

''The goblin queen.''

He rocked to both knees on the cold ground. ''Why should she be our enemy?''

Another wandering of Ela's eyes, about the sky, the streamside. The leaves whispered louder than her voice. ''Because. Because she is. Her kingdom—I don't know if it *appears*, or if it always is. But she can reach out of it, and this knows where she is.'' She held the mirror against her heart. "This always knows."

She looked so young—not the witchling now, but a frightened child, pale in the gibbous moon.

"And your mistress said to use this thing."

"My mistress said—if everything failed, if she wasn't there when I got back, that I should try to get help here."

My god, he thought. With no more than that instruction, the woman sent a girl off to Krukczy Straz? A great and powerful witch, Ela claimed to be—and maybe it had been her magic that lent him strength to ride, and not the first meal he had had in days. Maybe it had been her magic just now that had sent the goblin away, and maybe it was her magic that had waked him from the daze that had held him since Krukczy Tower—

But, lord Sun, was there not better hope for them than 'try'?

He asked, "Wasn't master Karoly supposed to come back with you?"

"Yes."

"So he was supposed to help you use this thing? He was supposed to know what to do? Is that what was supposed to happen?"

A glance aside from him, at the sky, at the wall, anywhere but his face.

God, he thought, murkier and murkier. He touched her arm gently and made her look at him.

"Ela. What would master Karoly have done with the thing, if he were here? Do you have any idea what that is?"

"Stop her."

"How would he do that?"

Her eyes slipped away from his.

"Ela?"

There was no answer. Their journey had been disastrous from home to the mountaintop—their canvas had ripped. They had had nothing but contention among themselves.

And Karoly—had gone silent when he most needed to speak.

"Ela. If you're a great witch, can you say what you want to say? Can you answer me?"

She did look at him, a pale, distracted glance. The mirror in her lap began to glow with light as she brushed its surface, and she looked at him, truly looked at him.

"I saw a castle," he said. "We were there. Weren't we? I saw a woman. . . ."

"It was a long time ago. The chief of the goblins came here. Right in that very gateway—"

He glanced toward that gate, he could not help it—and the goblin was sitting on the wall, long legs a-dangle. "God!" he gasped, snatched up his bow and scrambled for his feet.

The goblin leapt to the ground. It landed with grace and arrogance, and swept them a bow.

"Well, well," it said, "not paying full attention, are we, young lady? —You truly shouldn't distract her, Tamas. Keeping us away takes constant thought, especially once we've made up our minds about a thing."

It wanted Ela—that was what it had continually claimed. He felt of the arrow he had ready, and laid it to the string. But it made an airy gesture, refusing such unfavorable battle.

"Oh, no, man, there's no need of that. I've merely come to watch."

To watch what? was the natural question. But he disdained to ask it, and the goblin laughed softly and made a second flick of the wrist.

"Ah, ah, ah, pricklish pride. It does lead us by the nose, doesn't it? —I'd advise you *give* me the trinket, witchling. Or at least put it away and don't use it."

"You killed my mistress," Ela accused it, standing at his elbow. "You killed her!"

"I?" The goblin laid a hand where its heart should be. "I by no means killed your mistress. We were always on the best of terms."

"You just happened by today," Tamas scoffed.

"I just happened? Ah, no. I knew. No sooner than a foolish woman dismissed this girl to Krukczy Straz, the ravens knew and gossiped on the housetop. The whole woods knew. Did not you?"

He did not take his eyes from the goblin. But he saw a flare of cold light in the very tail of his eye, and saw the goblin's face go grim and hostile.

"Forbear," it said, holding up its hand. "Forbear, foolish girl, *put it away*!"

"Did you kill her?" Ela's voice cracked like a whip. "Don't lie to me, don't dare to lie, ng'Saeich!"

"No." A short answer. The goblin's nostrils flared and the scale armor on his chest flashed with his breathing.

"*I* am the witch in Tajny Wood. Am I *not*, Azdra'ik ng'Saeich?"

"You. Are."

A silence, then. Tamas dared not turn to look. He felt ants walking up and down his spine and on his arms and felt his heart beating fit to burst. The creature would spring. He raised the bow, gauged the gusting wind.

But the goblin shrugged a shoulder into a spin half about and a mocking flip of the hand. "Ah, well, a new witch in Tajny Wood and a bit of broken glass. And what do you propose to do with it, pray tell? To order me about? Does that amuse you?"

The feeling was dreadful then. Tamas drew the bow.

"Put it away!" Azdra'ik exclaimed, his voice trembling, and turned full about, holding up his arm. "Put it away, young fool, do you even know what you're dealing with?"

The mirror, the goblin meant. And the goblin took no step closer—took two away, in fact, and turned full about a second time, pointing with a dark-nailed hand.

"That—fragment—is not a toy for your amusement, girl! That is nothing for a human whelp to handle in ignorance! Give it to me! *Give* it to me before you destroy yourself!"

"Leave us alone!"

"Man. Tamas . . . this *thing* she holds—the witches of

Tajny Wood have feared to use, and this *underling* proposes to make herself a power with it."

"You seem not to like that."

"Listen to me, fool! A mirror stands in the queen's hall beneath the lake, a glass taller than the queen is tall; and in it she sees what is and what may be, and she shapes what she wishes and deludes those that will believe. *That* is that shard and the magic of it, a shard from its edge, against that and against the queen. *That* is the power your young mistress proposes to oppose. A gnat, man, a gnat proposes to assail the queen of hell—and for her right hand, lo! Tamas, with his bow and his dreadful knife! Tell me—what will you do first, young witch?"

It was laughing at them, this creature, as it sauntered away toward the wall, the dark, and the brush. It vanished.

"I'm not sure it's gone," he said.

"He's not," Ela said. He looked at her, seeing anger, and fear. Her hands shone like candlewax in the fire they covered. "But he won't do anything. He daren't. He *can't*."

He let the bow relax, caught the arrow in his finger along the grip. "It doesn't dare the gateway. I'd rather we moved there tonight."

She gave a furious shake of her head. "We daren't go back in there. Not tonight. No."

"Then why did we come here in the first place? What are we doing here?"

Her eyes slid away, toward dark, and nowhere.

"Is it because of the mirror? Is it something it can tell you—or something you don't want to meet?"

A frown touched her brow, as if he had said something curious.

"The mirror called me a wizard," he pursued the point, "and it was wrong about that. Did it show you the goblin?"

"No," she said, and walked away from him, a deliberate turning of her back. "But why should it?" floated back to him, supremely cold and disinterested in his challenge.

Maybe it was a spell that made her deaf to him. Maybe it was sheer arrogance. He inclined now to the latter estima-

tion, thought: Be damned to her—and went to see whether
the horses had come back unscathed.

Liar, she had called him. She and the goblin were evidently agreed on that point.

Well, then, admittedly he had not been scrupulous with
the truth, with witches or goblins. Or trolls. He saw no obligation to have his throat cut. Or to have his land invaded
and his kinfolk murdered by goblins. Or to die for nothing
because some self-righteous slip of a girl was too cocksure
stupid to take anyone's advice.

He found no harm with the horses, at least. He thought
again of taking Lwi in the morning and riding west, just
blindly westward, until he found the mountains to which
these hills were the foothills; and he thought how Karoly had
not been able to do what was right or sane either. Maybe his
own hesitation was a spell; or only his good sense at war
with his upbringing, that said girls were not safe wandering
the wilds alone: for her part, of course, she would very surely
hold him by magic or by any other rotten trick, because *she*
would not saddle the horses. *She* was too fine to soil her
hands, and *she* was too delicate to lift the tack about, but
forget any other use he was—*she* was too wise to need what
he knew.

He gave Skory's neck a pat and walked around her, with
suddenly a most unpleasant notion he saw something in the
tail of his eye. He walked behind her and around to Lwi's
side, to steal a glance toward the wall without betraying that
he had seen anything.

The goblin was back, sitting in the shadow, simply watching.

Damn, he thought, and turned his back on it, at wits'
end, exhausted, robbed of appetite and, as seemed likely
tonight, of sleep, by a goblin who made no more sense than
Ela did. At Krukczy Straz he had known where home was.
The troll had not even been that bad a fellow, give or take
the want of regular meals—

But the memory of that roof-top brought a haze between
him and the world and he was too tired to dwell on horrors.

They twisted and became ordinary in his mind, an unavoidable condition of this land; and he found himself a place at the foot of a tree with his bow across his knees and his eyes shut, refusing to care what the witchling thought. She was awake. Let her watch. Let *her* worry.

But he had not succeeded in sleeping when Ela came back and made a stir near him, getting into the packs. He tried to ignore her, but what she unwrapped smelled of spice and sausage, and it was impossible to rest with that wafting past his nose: he gathered up his bow and, with a glance at the goblin still sitting in the shadows, he served himself a stale biscuit and a bit of sausage and sat down.

"Was Karoly your father?" she asked straightway.

"No." Appalling question. With *his* mother? The girl could have no idea. So much for witchcraft and farseeing.

"Someone in your house was a wizard."

"Karoly—just Karoly. And he's no kin."

"Or a witch," Ela said.

"No."

But gran leapt into his mind, gran, whose grave—

"There had to be someone," Ela persisted. "A cousin? An uncle?"

"There wasn't," he lied: god, he was growing inured to lies. He was surrounded with them. He had the most disquieting feeling if he looked toward the wall this moment, he would find the goblin staring back at him—

—mirror image, down to the arm on the knee. He shifted his posture, suspecting mockery in its attitude, and fearing suddenly that its sharp ears might gather every word they spoke.

"I'm no wizard," he muttered, lowering his voice to the limit of hearing. "Master Karoly taught me, just simple things. Maybe he taught me a deal too much, maybe that was what you saw. . . ."

But gran was from over-mountain, from these very hills.

Gran had shown them little tricks, move the shell, find the coin—two young boys had been oh, so gullible, once, and gran had laughed in her solemn way, and said there was always a deceit, gran had called it. —Always look for the deceit, even in real magic.

Please the god, there was a deceit.

But the only deceit he could see was over there, by the wall, staring back at him.

"You were Karoly's student?" Now, *now* the girl wanted to talk, suddenly she was brimming with questions, worse, she had made up her mind to what she thought and there was no shaking it.

"He taught me letters. And how to name birds and trees. That was all. —It's listening to us, you know that."

"It doesn't matter. What you are, his kind can tell without your saying."

He muttered: "I'm the lord in Maggiar's second son. And my brother is his heir, if he's still alive. I'm *not* a wizard, none of our family have ever been."

"I *felt* what the mirror was doing. It answers you. It won't do that except for wizards."

"Well, it makes mistakes, doesn't it? It didn't see him— and is he there, or isn't he?"

She was not as sure of herself on the matter. Such as he could see her expression in the dark, she was not utterly sure, and he was relieved at that.

Gran was not a witch. Gran was gran, that was all.

(But the country folk to this day hung talismans about her grave, straw men and straw horses, sheaves of wheat— childless couples brought straw children to gran's graveside, and . . .

. . . burned them. He never had understood that part.)

"All the same . . ." she said, frowning. And took her blanket, flung it about herself and settled down with Skory's saddlebags for a lumpy pillow, having had the last word, and giving him no indication at all what he should do about the goblin.

There were worries enough to keep his eyes open, if they had come singly, if the whole whirling chaos of them had not exhausted him. The suspicion of gran was the final straw, the absolutely overwhelming weight on his mind, and, back at his chosen resting place, while the girl slept, he began against his will to rehearse memories, gran's friendship with Karoly, gran's possets and potions—gran's staying up all night. One could see the light in her window, late, later than a boy could keep his eyes open—but was that incontrovertible evidence of witchcraft?

He remembered the day she died—and the storm and the lightning, and the people and the horses all drenched, lit in the flashes, while they rode back from the burial—the rain and the bitter cold. He and Bogdan had taken chill, and their mother had had a fierce argument with their father, giving them hot tea and vodka, wrapping them in blankets—their mother saying . . .

. . . "This is *her* weather. God, when's morning? When will it be morning?" And their father: "Be still!" But the vodka had woven through his wits, and hazed everything. Their mother had said something else, that their father had shushed, and their father had said, "I never knew her. The god knows she was no mother to me. But she loved the boys."

And he had thought, half-asleep then and sleep-haunted now, Gran was gran, that's all, gran loved what agreed with her, gran would ride out with anyone who'd ride with her—she loved the open sky, she said—she and Karoly used to—

He did not want to think about that. He twitched and shifted position, but he kept seeing gran and Karoly grinding herbs, gran and Karoly riding in the gates one early dawn . . . gran being so long a widow, people talked, but people somehow looked past the indiscretions. . . .

While grandfather Ladislaw had been alive, there had surely been no such suspicions, god, it was not *true*, his father could not be Karoly's bastard, wizardry would have out, would it not, if gran were a witch—Karoly most certainly being a wizard? That was the way he had always reasoned, when the unwholesome thought had nudged him— but *no* one thought twice about it, no one ever thought, the thoughts just—

—slid right past it, like water around a rock. Like questions around a wizard.

He felt cold inside, false and hollow, as if he might not be who he had always believed he was, as if the lineage of Maggiar might not be his at all, and his uncles and his cousins— Who knew in what degree they were really related, any of them? If Karoly was in fact his grandfather, and Ladislaw no kin at all, then his father had no right to the lands or his house. If Karoly was in fact his grandfather . . . had his father known, and faced Karoly every day of his life?

But it was ridiculous, patently ridiculous. No one in his house had taken it seriously or put themselves out about the gossip—

—As if, lord Sun, gran being widowed and Karoly and gran being mostly discreet about their nighttime rides, no one wanted to say anything, no one had ever *dared* say anything. Mother would never put up with unseemly talk in the house, Mother would never tolerate a breath of impropriety, everyone knew that, certainly never any scandal touching the household—and Father having not a shred of magic about him . . .

Everyone had known so many things without knowing them, without anyone taking rumors to heart, without anyone ever blinking at an association that, however flagrant, never—somehow—seemed to be anyone's business.

God, he did not want to think about it now. He saw the horses eventually asleep, forgetful of the goblin presence near the wall, and if an old campaigner like Lwi had smelled out the situation and decided to rest, a tired young fool might be excused the fault. He tried to chase away the worries, angrier and angrier that Ela had first upset his stomach and then assumed *he* would watch while she slept. Probably she made it all up on purpose, so he *would* stay awake.

He saw the goblin's head fallen forward, now, as if even the goblin found it too much. Now, surely, he thought, he could watch the creature a while, and if it was no trick, then maybe he dared catch a wink himself.

But before that happened he heard a bird begin to sing; and another; and he sat there while the goblin slept on, dark head bowed, braids hiding his face.

So in this country such things were not nightmare, they lasted unabashed into sunrise.

And this one feared no harm from them—that seemed evident, whatever its reason.

8

GRACJA HAD TO REST AND NIKOLAI STAYED ON HER BACK, sleeping, Yuri hoped, but Nikolai had been very quiet, scarily quiet, this last while, and he hesitated between touching him to be sure he was all right or letting him sleep if it meant he was out of pain.

He decided the latter, weary as he was himself—his feet ached, his legs ached . . . he stopped counting there, except the stinging scratches he had gotten from brush. He was not cold. His rests were too short and the going too hard to let him chill, and he had given Nikolai his cloak, because Nikolai's wounded hand was growing colder and colder, even while Nikolai's face was warm to the touch.

"I'm fevered," was the last thing Nikolai had said, the last thing that made sense, at least. Something about goblins and trolls, and the folly of trusting one.

There had not been another sign of Krukczy, but thank the god and the lady, Yuri thought, there had been none of goblins so far, either; and the sun was coming up now, as he tugged at Gracja's reins and coaxed her to move. Zadny was already off down the trail, too fast, always too fast—he had given up worrying that he would lose the dog, Zadny came back when he had gone too far, and he just slogged along at the best pace he could until Gracja had to rest again.

His side hurt. He tugged Gracja up one hill and down the other, with never a sound out of Nikolai.

But Zadny had been out of sight a very long time now, and he was beginning to wonder and to fret, and finally, though he hated to make a sound in the woods, he called out, "Zadny!"

Echoes came back. "Zadny—Zadny—Zadny . . ." And Nikolai moaned and lifted his head.

"He's just been gone a long while," Yuri said, and went back to Nikolai's side and touched his face. Nikolai was burning hot. "Do you want a drink, sir?"

"Find the damn dog," Nikolai said fuzzily. "Something's the matter."

He did not know whether that advice was fever-inspired or not, but it was his own sense of priorities. He got back to the fore and led Gracja along the base of a wooded hill, along a leafy track, and a muddy spot.

A horse had trod there. So they were still on the right track. He pulled at Gracja, wanting her to hurry, thinking— if only they had made enough time during the night, if the ones they were following had made camp and slept, then they might overtake them, and they might find help in time for Nikolai—

Zadny came panting back, just close enough to catch sight of a shaggy flash of his tail through the brush. Then he yipped and was off again. Maybe, Yuri told himself, struggling to pull Gracja along faster, faster. Zadny was excited, Zadny might have found something—please the god it was not just a rabbit hole.

He was watching his feet, trying not to trip, his arm feeling near pulled out of its socket by Gracja's resistance, but he glanced up to see where the slope upward was leading, saw stones and vines through the trees, saw . . .

"We've found somewhere," he breathed, holding the ache in his side. "Master Nikolai, there's a gate—"

He could see it clearly in the dawn. He saw Zadny dart into it and out and back again into some courtyard. It looked dreadfully deserted. If *he* owned a tower in the middle of a forest full of goblins, *he* would not leave its gates standing open or let its walls grow over with climbable vines like that.

"Master Nikolai," he said quietly. "I think you'd better stay here and let me see what's inside."

"Doesn't look too good," Nikolai murmured. So he was aware of what was going on around him. Yuri patted his shoulder, eased his bow and his arrow case free of Gracja's saddle and said,

"I'll be right back."

But he strung the bow and he took out an arrow before he slipped up to the gateway and had a look.

God.

He shut his eyes and looked away, and had to look back, at the poles, and the dreadful skulls. He felt cold all over, and his heart was thumping from the shock.

Goblins, he thought.

And then he realized there were two skulls, besides the animals, and he remembered they were following two people, and his knees began to shiver under him, and his heart to thump harder. He did not want to worry Nikolai until he knew something—he could not think that those grisly bones were his brothers, he refused to believe that could be them. His teeth chattered, he was so scared, so he clenched his jaw, and, shoulders to the wall, eased inside, behind the cover of a bush that should never have been allowed to grow right next to the gate. His father would have such a sorry castelan horsewhipped, his father would say, his father would never let a place get into this condition . . .

Nothing stirred. Zadny was gone, somewhere, and nothing had eaten *him*, yet, or if it had, it had been quiet about it. He spotted another place to hide and slipped toward it, did not feel comfortable in that one, and went for a second nook, closer still. There he waited for Zadny to come back, waited what felt like a very long time, long enough almost to start thinking again about those awful bones and wanting and not wanting to look at them to see if there was anything familiar in them.

So he moved again, because if Zadny would only come back, so that he could get his hands on him and be sure Zadny was not going to do something stupid, like start barking, he urgently needed to get back to Nikolai, who was waiting alone out there.

More bad yard keeping. Maybe goblins had raided the place, but if they had not broken the house door down, they had probably climbed right up the huge vines that led to that open window . . .

He had a sudden spooky feeling that something might be watching him. He held his breath and wanted out of sight of that window, looked for a place to go, and ran for the side of the tower itself.

Then he heard something like claws on stone, that might be Zadny or might not be. He was furious at the dog. Come out here, he wished Zadny; the faintest whistle might bring him, if he was in the hall—or it might bring something else.

If the place *was* deserted, he thought, and the goblins were gone, the same as they had left the other tower, then he and Nikolai might be safe here tonight. They might find a bed for Nikolai and doors to shut, maybe not the outer one, that would betray their presence here; but some inner one, maybe the lowest rooms where they would never think to search, and Nikolai could rest—

His brothers might have thought that. He had followed two horses this far, and if they had seen the same thing in the courtyard that he had seen, they might have ridden out of here on the instant, the way they would if they could—or they could even have done what he proposed to do, and bolted themselves inside.

A dog yipped, and yelped into silence. His heart bounced into his throat and sank again. He thought, I should get out of here. Now.

But if it were not his brothers—if it were *not* his brothers— why had Zadny led them in here, what would keep Zadny occupied here, when Zadny would hardly quit the trail to eat or sleep?

The goblins were surely gone. The goblins in the tower in the mountains had made no secret of their being there.

He eased forward, then stopped, at the clatter of a horse in the courtyard behind him, saw Gracja, with Nikolai upright in the saddle and holding his sword in his left hand, the god only knew how he had drawn it. Gracja woke echoes in the place, a slow clatter of hooves as he rode in, and Yuri held his place, shivering, thinking, If there's anything here, they'll see him and he can't see me. Father Sun, what's he doing? Is he thinking about that? Nikolai's too clever to ride in here making all that noise . . .

Then he understood what Nikolai was doing. Nikolai had a fool boy overlong inside this place, and Nikolai was making a racket and putting himself right in the middle of the court-yard, to turn up whatever was hiding here, maybe to create havoc enough to let a stupid boy get out of here if he had run into trouble.

There was the scuff of a footstep, inside. Yuri glanced at the door, looked frantically back at Nikolai, stepped out as far as he dared, trying to signal him—but there was a bend of the wall in the way—and whoever was inside was coming out.

Someone was going to get an arrow in his back the moment he went for Nikolai. Yuri lifted the bow and drew in the same motion, taking calm breaths, the way one had to, who expected his hand and eye to be steady, and he did not think about killing—never think about that, Nikolai had said, just aim.

He drew his arm back, full, as a gray-cloaked figure came out the door, only at the last moment remembering goblins were not deer, goblins might wear armor and the back was a hard place to find a target . . .

But Nikolai was looking at the creature, and Nikolai was not even lifting the sword—Nikolai said, "You bastard," and slid down off Gracja's back.

Then the creature said, "Where are the boys?" in master Karoly's voice. . . .

Yuri held the arrow steady. Magical creatures were full of tricks, and they might look like what they were not, so he had heard. But he did not fire, even when master Nikolai fell, the sword clanging to the dirt-covered cobbles.

The might-be master Karoly hurried to him. Yuri saw white hair beneath the hood, and master Karoly's aged hands, even Karoly's frowning face. But he did not believe it until he saw the old man trying to help Nikolai, and then he knew it was Karoly. Then he let the bow down and came to help.

Master Karoly looked around, startled. "Damn you! What in hell are you doing here?"

"A goblin shot him. I think it could have been poisoned."

"It didn't need to be," master Karoly said, and turned his attention back to Nikolai, swearing as he felt over Nikolai's neck and shoulder. Yuri kept quiet, standing there with his bow in his hands while master Karoly unfastened Nikolai's collar and felt of his heart and his head. "The goblins left us damned well nothing," master Karoly said, to him, Yuri supposed, and he waited anxiously for orders. "I don't suppose you've got blankets. Or a pot."

"Yes, sir." He went and got them from Gracja. And the rest of the herbs Krukczy had found. "The troll gave us these. He made tea with them."

"Troll, is it?" Master Karoly's face was drawn and strange as he snatched the things he had brought. "Troll be damned. Lucky if he lives the day."

"Don't say that!"

"Lucky he's alive this long." Master Karoly started pulling at Nikolai's buckles, trying to get the armor off, and he was being too rough about it.

"Let me," Yuri said, and got the ties that held the sleeve on, while Karoly took his knife and cut off the bandage Nikolai had tied around the outside.

"Damn, it's stuck to it. Get that pot, get some water."

"I've salve—"

"Not for this you don't," Karoly said. "Move, young fool! We need a fire, and the god knows what it'll bring, but there's no damned choice—don't stand there with your mouth open waiting for flies! Move!"

"Yes, sir," he breathed, and grabbed the pot. Zadny was barking again, waking echoes inside. "Where's the water, sir?"

"In the back of the yard!" Karoly snapped at him. "Where would you expect a well? —And, boy . . ."

He stopped and turned on one foot. "Sir?"

"—Shut that damned dog *up*, will you?"

The goblin watched them make a fire, the goblin watched them make breakfast, the goblin watched them eat it, and Tamas glowered at it. His head was throbbing, his eyes felt full of sand, and only motion kept his mind from straying down the same unpleasant and useless paths it had followed all night.

"What do we *do* about it?" he asked.

Ela merely shrugged. "Let be."

"Are we staying here?"

Ela shook her head.

He kept his temper and asked the next question. "Are we leaving now?"

Well, then, Ela would not talk. *He* would not talk. He got up on legs that felt wooden, limped over to the horses in a temper and began to saddle them to leave this place, Ela nothing gainsaying.

The goblin turned up next to him, at the edge of the woods, making the horses nervous, watching him as if *he* were the object of its intention.

"You wanted to see her," he said to it, hauling on Lwi's girth. "All right, you've seen her. She doesn't want to talk to you. Why don't you leave?"

"She's not reasonable," it said. "Or wise."

He leaned on the saddle, looking across it as the goblin stood, arms folded, foot tucked, leaning against a tree. "Not wise—because she won't listen to you?" Humor failed him. "What do you want? Why do you destroy things? Is it just your nature?"

"You mistake us."

"Mistake you! Did I mistake what I saw in the courtyard? Or on the roof of Krukczy Straz?"

"I'm i'bu okhthi. That's itra'hi work."

Goblin babble, to his ears. He glared across Lwi's rump and rested his arm on it. But only a fool turned down knowledge. Master Karoly used to say so. So he overcame his headache and his temper and advanced a surly, "So?"

"Itra'hi aren't my kind, man."

"I'm sure it made a difference to my brother. I'm sure it made a difference to her mistress. They didn't introduce themselves. They didn't exchange formalities."

"They're not the brightest."

"And you are."

"Are you a horse? I think not. One has four feet. It's easy to tell the difference in your kindreds. Easy in ours, if you have half a wit."

"Are you saying you're something different than these— whatever you call them?"

"Flat-tongued human. Indeed, different as you from your beasts. One sends and they do. One doesn't talk to them. One doesn't deal with them. They're dogs. The i'bu okhthi are clearly *civilized*."

"God." He turned his back on the creature, turned to Ela, sitting on the margin of the stream, and said, "We're ready."

But when he looked back to the goblin—only trees were there, and not a leaf stirring to mark where it had been.

"Butchers," he said after it, hoping it did hear. "Murderers. You loose your hounds to do your work, what's the difference? What's the damned difference, tell me that!"

"Don't," Ela said, behind him when he had not heard her move. His heart jumped.

"Don't what?" He was still angry—with her, now that Azdra'ik was out of sight. "Don't ask what happened to my brother? Don't ask where we're going?"

"There." She nodded at the gateway she had not been willing to pass a second time last night. She was bringing the packs. Ela—was bringing the packs they had been using, practical girl: he was astounded.

"Thank you," he said, not with his best grace, and tried it again, with a sketch of a bow, after he had taken them: "Thank you."

"It's not a safe place," she said. "There's a woods past the second gateway. People go in and don't come back. My mistress said she wasn't sure it has another side, or not always the same side, if you can't see the path.''

Three thoughts in a row. Twice amazing.

"Can you?"

She lifted her chin slightly, frowning, and said, "Of course. Can't you?"

He did not understand for a moment, or care to: he was exceedingly weary of her moods and her offenses. Then he realized it was the wizard business again, *and* an accusation of lying.

"No," he said, and then (he could not help it) had a look toward that gateway to see if he *could* see anything. "There's nothing."

She went on frowning, while he tied the packs to Skory's saddle and gave her a hand up.

He cast a second glance toward the woods as he rose into Lwi's saddle. And there was still nothing that he could see from that vantage.

She started Skory off, and he followed her, thinking that here was one more choice made, that, dangerous as it might be to try to go back from here, it was going to be worse hereafter.

"Where are we going?" he asked. "Are just the two of us going to go up and knock on the queen's gate and say Shame on you, or what are we going to do, for the god's sake?"

"Banish her," Ela said. "Unweave her spells."

We're both mad, he thought. He thought: What if I *were* Karoly's grandson, and not Ladislaw's? What if, after all, Karoly's gone and her mistress is and we're all that's left for everyone else to rely on?

What if we were? We wouldn't know. We wouldn't know unless we turned around and came back, and then it would be too late, wouldn't it?

They passed beneath the arch. They rode a weaving course through brush, around piles of rubble, past the walls that had been rooms and vaults and hallways. There was still no path, only half-buried paving-stones, through which weeds and brush grew up. There was no magic. He waited to see something happen.

"My mistress' grandmother lived here once," she said, in answer to nothing. Or maybe it was part of her last answer. "She was born here."

"What was this place?"

"Hasel."

"Hasel!" But it was a strong place, a place full of people. His dream of last night came back, when he was wide awake, people and disaster, and stones riven with light.

"Do they know about Hasel, over the mountains?"

"My—" —My grandmother told me about it, he had begun to say. Gran had relatives here. God. What if it *were* true? And all those people last night . . . they're dead, dead as gran. The stories were yesterday in his mind, forests and fields and villages where people lived and went about their lives.

"Your—?" she prompted him, but he was not ready to talk to her about gran, or to trust her that much.

"What happened to it?" he asked.

"What happened to it? The mistress here died. The people here died. Ages ago. Hundreds of years ago. If they know about Hasel, don't they know that?"

He heard her, and it sank right to the pit of his stomach, refusing reason. Nothing gran knew could be that long ago. It was some other Hasel. Or the things gran had said she had seen were only stories gran told—only lies.

He might be Karoly's grandson. And now for all he knew gran had lied to him about this place. Too many things were shifting, that he had never doubted in his life—while beyond the farther arch he saw a forest that the witchling called dangerous, a gateway that showed only green shadow and the trunks of aged trees.

"What happened here? Was it a war?"

"With the goblins. When the mirror broke."

"That mirror."

"This mirror. Mistress had it in Tajny Tower; and the

goblins killed her and killed Pavel but they couldn't find it and they couldn't find me.''

"Who was Pavel?"

"Just Pavel. He came from Hasel when it fell. And he was never right after, mistress said. But he would have fought them when they came. He would have.'' There came just the least wobble to Ela's voice, true distress. But he was thinking more about what she had said, and about finding her in a lie, as they rode through the archway, as the horses' hooves rang on the threshold of the forest, and went thereafter with the soft scuff of fallen leaves. Wind sighed above them, and morning sun dappled the ground. It did not look so terrible a place, not to left nor right nor straight ahead. The horses certainly took no alarm—Skory most irreverently snatched a mouthful from a bush as they passed, and ate as they walked.

He considered whether to challenge Ela. And decided. "You said Hasel fell a hundred years ago."

"Hundreds.''

"So how could this servant of your mistress' be from Hasel? That can't be true.''

She frowned and seemed to think about that a moment. "I don't know, that's what she said.''

"Hundreds of years ago?"

"Witches—can be that old. I think she was.''

"How old are you?"

"I'm not sure . . . I think, I think maybe fifteen.''

God, she was hardly older than Yuri. Than *Yuri*, for the god's sake. And had this laid on her?

"Where did you come from?"

"From Albaz. I think from Albaz. Mistress got me when I was very small. I thought she was my mother when I was a baby. But she wasn't.''

After silence it was a torrent, in a silence so profound the whispering of the leaves and the horses' movements were the only sound. He thought it sad she had mistaken something as vital as that, and not been sure even where she had been born. At least, with all the confusion she had set in him . . . he knew who his parents were, and what his home was.

"Or maybe I *was* hers," Ela said, after a moment more of riding, in the whisper of leaves under the horses' feet. "It wouldn't matter. —Who was your mother, if she wasn't a witch? —And how old are you?"

"Seventeen. And my mother isn't a witch. She wouldn't approve of witches."

"Why?"

"She just wouldn't. She's very much on things being—solid. She wouldn't want to think about goblins. She—"

—never liked gran's stories, he thought to himself. She was afraid of gran.

Gran *wasn't* like everybody else, was she? Nobody did say no to her.

God, maybe nobody could.

Maybe, he thought, maybe I could have learned magic from master Karoly, if he had wanted to teach me—but if he could have taught me . . . why didn't he?

"Ela. *Why* didn't Karoly stop the goblins from attacking us?"

She looked at him, across the distance between their horses. "What?"

"The goblins that attacked us. Why didn't master Karoly stop them? He was with us, he saw the warnings. Why didn't he stop us?"

Ela cast a look ahead, as if she were looking at something a thousand miles away.

"Ela. Why. Didn't. He?"

"Pardon?"

"Why didn't master Karoly stop us from that road? Why didn't he work magic and protect us?"

"Why didn't *you*?"

"Because I'm not—because I couldn't. Whatever I am, I never learned, because *he* never taught me. Why can't you answer a plain question? You were there, weren't you? Why didn't *you* warn us?"

She shook her head. The air around them seemed unnaturally still and heavy. He had thought the frowns were arrogance. Or anger. But *he* felt uneasy now. It seemed the sunlight was less ahead. And if there was a path here he could not discern it.

"Ela?" he asked, because the spookiness of the place made him think about that road. Or maybe thinking about the road made him remember ambush too vividly. "How did Karoly do nothing to warn us?"

"Because—because the magic wanted it."

"Whose magic? Goblin magic?"

A shake of her head. "No one can know. No one can know, when magic fights magic. It could have been anyone, it could have been my mistress. It always could be anyone. Contrary magic can go anywhere. You can't tell what will happen."

'It always could be anyone.' It sounded like Karoly.

"Sometimes," Ela said, "sometimes you can't avoid things because you don't even know if you did them. Sometimes you're afraid not to do something. My mistress said— said Karoly might make things worse, she wasn't sure he should come at all, but she couldn't wait any longer. You don't know whose idea it was—her magic or the queen's. She called him, all the same. And it turned out—it turned out the way it did."

"And our going now? We don't know where, or why, but we're just going?"

"To find the center of the woods," she said, "but I don't know whose magic is leading us. I don't know who's stronger."

That was not at all a comforting thing to hear. "We're going against the queen of all the goblins and you wonder whose magic is stronger? Ela, you're not—" —Not as damned good as you think, he thought, in Nikolai's way of saying.

But was not he going where she led? And had he not reasoned half a score of times that if he had any good sense he would have gone home? And where was he now?

Looking about him at the trees, at a woods pathless to his eyes—where, indeed, was he?

"Not just me," she said faintly, "it's all the witches of

the Wood. I may be the only chance they have. And I think we should go and try—because I think that, that's all. Everything they've done and everything she's done, I'm what it comes down to—so I *am* the greatest witch in Tajny Wood, do you understand? And I don't know whose magic brought you, but neither can the queen. Neither of us can know whose magic is working.''

''Then what good is it, if no one can tell what will happen?''

''But things change. And if you do something small, it could be because of something large—and if you do something very large, you'd better know what you're doing, that's what my mistress said.''

How do you *do* something very large? was the question that leapt to mind. If he were Karoly's working, if what she said was at all true or sane, then he wanted to challenge the situation and *do* something magical—please the god, that could fail outright; or prove whether he had any magic at all in him. If he was at all a wizard he could magic up an incontrovertible proof, could he not?

But then—if magic worked the way she said—one could never know. Was that not what she had just said—in all her reasoning: there's never a way to know?

Where had the damned goblin gone, and what was it up to? Bearing messages to its queen?

And why had Karoly never told him, if he was a wizard? And why had Ela said what she had said, when all this time . . . she would or could say nothing?

Has something happened? he wondered. Has something somewhere changed? And is it our magic or theirs that's brought us into this place?

Hell of a wakening. Dark and fire and something clanking in his ear. Shadows on stone ceiling. Dull pain. And that damned dog. Nikolai put up the hand that worked and shoved it away. Karoly leaned over him. For a moment he had trouble sorting it out. But the images lingered in his vision.

"Well, well," Karoly said. "Good afternoon, master huntsman."

"Damn you," he murmured. *"Where were you?"*

"Afoot, as happens. While you had a horse to ride on. At least a pony. Followed the dog, young Yuri says. And doesn't know where his brothers are, except he hopes they got away, he was following them in company with a troll, and he hopes they aren't the skulls in the courtyard." Karoly slipped a hand under his head and stuffed a wad of blanket behind him, then went to the fireside and poured something, which he brought back. "Drink this."

"It smells like stable sweepings."

"It's been a little through the damp, just drink it and stop complaining. You're alive. That's more than some of us can say, isn't it?"

He drank it, sip by nauseating sip. The dog had gone somewhere—where the boy was, he hoped. "Where's Yuri?"

"Asleep," Karoly was putting jars in a sack, scores of little jars, all over the table. And scattered powders and leaves and herbs. Nikolai finished the cup and set it on his chest, looking at the ceiling of what he supposed was the hall in the tower he had fainted in front of, and a fire that was not a good idea, if there were goblins about.

"Is this your sister's place?" he asked when Karoly took the cup.

"It was."

He recalled the skulls in the courtyard, and gave the old man latitude for rudeness. He tried to think ahead of things, tried the fingers of his wounded arm to see if they worked, and they did, enough to serve. But whatever tea Karoly had just served up was the same sort as the troll's, so far as his head could witness: he could count the beats of his heart, thump, thump, thump, louder than the crackling of the fire, louder than the old man sitting with his hands between his knees and his fingers weaving cat's-cradles with a bit of yarn.

He thought of slender fingers, the same game, the same tuneless humming . . . thought of the lady gran, by the fireside, the lady gran looking up at him with dark, dark eyes, and saying, "Aren't we the curious one? Spying, are we? Do you know what happens to boys who spy?"

"I was looking for Stani," he had said—to go hunting, as he recalled. Stani and he had used to do that in those days, when Stani was a gawky young man and he had been—

He had been—

"You're often about with my son," the lady gran had said. "What do you do in the woods, you? Watch the birds?"

"Yes," he had said. And:

"Look at me." The lady caught his eyes and he could not look away. A long while later she ceased to frown, and he could breathe again. "You have no lies. That's remarkable. I don't think I've ever met a boy who wouldn't lie. Are you loyal to Stani?"

"Yes, lady," he said.

She said, "You're a clever boy. Too clever to catch at lies. Don't spy on me again. Do you hear?"

"Yes, lady," he had said. And all the while watched the patterns that she wove. . . .

Karoly had said, "Let the boy go, Urzula." Urzula had been her name. But no one ever called her that. She was the Lady from the day the Old Lord had his fall until the day she died: only then had Stani become the lord and his wife Agnieszka became lady over Maggiar, and Stani had been a man with three sons by then.

The same weaving as the lady gran. He had not seen Karoly do that in years.

"What is that?" he asked muzzily, the question he ached to ask the lady—but she was dead. She had died in the storm, and it had rained continually until she was in her grave—a cold and comfortless rain, with lightnings and thunder . . .

"What do you imagine it is?" Karoly asked. The firelight caught Karoly at disadvantage, cast his face grim and his hair fire-colored. The fingers caught another loop. A cage, Nikolai thought, for no reason. A trap.

"I don't know." The years had taught him to lie, at need. "Where's the boy?"

"Asleep. He's exhausted."

"What about Bogdan and Tamas?"

"I don't know."

"Well, where were you? Where have you been the last two days?"

"Three. It's afternoon of the third."

"Where the hell were you?"

"My horse bolted," Karoly snapped. "I fell off. I went for help. As of yesterday—there wasn't any here. Is that enough?—" Zadny broke out barking again, and barrelled through the room, oversetting a bottle from the table. "Dammit!"

Zadny was scratching at the door, furiously. Nikolai bethought him of his sword, and felt for it, as Karoly abandoned his cat's-cradle and stood up.

Nikolai asked: "Where does that lead?"

"The cellars."

"Master Karoly?" Yuri stumbled from around the corner, wiping his eyes, his hair tousled. "Master Nikolai?"

"Hush," Karoly said, went and gathered up a staff standing against the door. Nikolai tried to get up, feeling around him for his sword. Yuri had his bow in hand, and strung it.

"Hush!" Karoly said again, and Zadny whimpered into silence. One could hear something being dragged, slowly, slowly, step at a time.

"It's the troll," Yuri whispered. "It's Krukczy!"

"Krukczy, is it?"

"Where's my sword?" Nikolai hissed, but Karoly shot the bolt back and shoved the door open.

It was a troll, that was sure. It looked as if someone had deposited a brush heap on the steps: it stood there covered with twigs, with two great eyes in the shag of its mane. And Zadny, loyal hound that he was, leapt into its arms, licking it and wagging his tail.

"That's Krukczy, for sure," Yuri said.

"Oh, hell," Nikolai breathed, sank back against the support of the corner and watched the troll and the hound come inside.

* * *

The sun was a green brightness in the canopy. "I never saw trees so tall," Tamas said, and added, "I never heard a forest so quiet," because there was not the least sound now but their movement, not the sound of birds or insects, not the scamper of a rabbit across the leaves. "Do you still see a path? I don't."

"I can see it," Ela said, following whatever she had been following, and for all her claims that he had wizardry of his own it only seemed to him a spookier and spookier place, a place that gave him a feeling—he could not quite surround the idea with a thought—that the woods had no definite edges from here. That was a peculiar kind of impression to have, as if it could be different from inside than out. But that was the way he saw it. And it looked darker ahead than anywhere left or right, while Ela steadfastly maintained she knew her way, and that when they got to the right place, she would know it, and use the mirror, and have all the magic of the woods at her command. The horses trod a brown mottled carpet, the leaves of many summers, and the trunks of the trees were huge beyond anything he had ever seen—as if they and the horses had shrunk or the scale of the world had changed. Only the dead leaves were of ordinary size, and very thick, as if winds seldom reached here. The horses trod carefully in places where the packed leaves concealed uneven slopes or hid the roots of trees—the ground was full of deceptions and traps. And from green above them, there gradually seemed more brush and tangles, in a premature twilight that persuaded the eye that the sun was setting.

But it could not be. It had only just been noon, and they rode now in such shadow that it seemed the sun itself had failed, or the hours had slipped away toward dark and night in furtive haste. The eye believed it. The body did. Tamas found himself fighting a yawn, and arguing that it was not that late, that he was sleepy from too long last night goblin-watching. With Lwi walking sedately at Skory's tail in this tangled undergrowth, with Ela sunk in thought or magic the while, he found it harder and harder to keep his eyes open.

His body swayed to Lwi's gentle motion. Why resist? the leaves seemed to whisper.

"How long do you suppose to sundown?" he asked, if only for the sound of his own voice above the sleepy sigh of leaves. "I can't think it's that late."

"I don't know," Ela murmured. He had only her back for a view, but a downhill slope encouraged Lwi to overtake Skory, step by slow step, so that for a while they rode side by side. Ela herself repressed a yawn, the back of her hand to her mouth, and he shook his head, because it made him have to.

"I can't keep awake," he said. "It's this place. It's this woods. Damn!" A third yawn. It was beyond foolish. He shook his head.

"It's very old," Ela said. "That's all. It's an old place. Mistress said—"

She stifled a yawn of her own and he could not resist. It was ridiculous and frightening at once. The shadow was like a blanket coming down on them, and the air beneath the aged trees should have been cold with that shadow, but it had no feeling at all. He could not remember now what their immediate aim was, but he recalled it was important and they dared not stop—there had been too many deer and too many wolves, and he had given his bow to his brother, back in the yard. A girl had given him a cake and they had had it that night at the fire—Lwi caught-step of a sudden, over a fallen branch or his own feet, and shook him off his balance.

"Damn!" His wits were wandering. The horses' steps were heavy and slower and slower, and that was not right. He leaned over and hit Skory. Skory jumped and Lwi did, startled awake. But by the time they had come to the bottom of the hill, the horses were only ambling again, and resisted a second such trick, only did a faster step for a moment, and slacked off again.

"This isn't right," he said, "this isn't right at all . . ."

Ela lifted the amulet to her lips and held it aloft, her eyes shut and a dreadful concentration on her brow.

"What are you doing?" he began to ask, but just then

came a spark of light, as if the mirror had caught the sun, then another, and another, and another. Her eyes opened and she let slip the mirror to dangle from its chain, as sparkles of light began to dance about them, on the ground, on themselves.

"Keep on!" he said, and in a numb, distant daze saw sunlight from the mirror glitter on the trees and sweep the ground. He had no idea now whether it was the right way they were going. He could only ride with the sparkles of light, that seemed to dance and beckon further and further amid the gloom.

A long time it seemed they went that way, the horses walking more alertly, their way lit with dazzle from an absent sun, a giddy, spinning dance of light in which Tamas began to hope there was safety . . .

Until they came to a steep descent, and that light glanced off metal.

"Ela!" he whispered, reining back. He saw goblins, hundreds and hundreds of them, arrayed in ambush among the leaves.

But his own voice seemed to come from far away, and Lwi stumbled when he began to turn on the slope. He saw Ela riding on, and he tried to bring Lwi about again on the leaf-buried slope, to reach her and turn her aside—but before he could persuade Lwi to overtake her it was too late: she rode within the goblin ranks, and those ranks tumbled, one and the next and the next, into piles of metal, moldered leather, and bleached bone.

He stared, overwhelmed by the strangeness of the sight, so that he questioned whether he was awake or seeing what he thought he was seeing. Lwi had stopped with him, and he tried to urge him to overtake the witchling, but Ela was further and further away, from the moment he had reined back. Now the sparkle of the mirror swept the ground ahead and danced among the trees, but not where he was. The whole woods seemed darkened, and Ela and the light seemed far, far away.

"Ela," he called after her. "Ela!" The woods seemed to

swallow up the sound. He struck Lwi hard, for both their sakes, but Lwi would not go faster, not even take alarm at the heaps of bone that tumbled and rattled where they rode. He saw Ela look back as if at great distance. She was almost to the top of the next hill, and then at the crest of it.

"Tamas?" he thought he heard her answer him. But the sparkle went out then, and left no traces in the woods where he was. Lwi stopped listlessly, and he slid down in desperation and took the reins and began to lead him, insisting he keep moving, up and up the hill.

But perhaps he had turned aside on the hill and mistaken his direction—hills had so many faces, and deceived the senses so easily. He trudged the whole wide hillside, and found, everywhere, the ghastly dead, as if he had wandered onto some forgotten battleground, of some unchronicled war. There was no sign of Ela, not the least glimmering of the light he sought, only the rattle of bones falling, of armor clattering, and the sight of unhuman skulls—Azdra'ik's kind, and in like armor. He gathered up a sword from one of the dead, a frightening thing with backward spines for one of its quillons, the use of which might be to disarm . . . the god knew, else.

With that, he kept going about the crown of the hill. Ela could not have had that much time to disappear. Skory might have had her way and gone off without direction, or even, the god forbid, thrown her and left her hidden in the brush. If that were the case, he might see her from the height.

But when he had trekked all about the hill, he found only more white and eyeless dead, and endless tracts of forest. He set out in the direction he thought they had been going, the sword thrust through his belt and Lwi's reins in hand, dragging at him so his arm ached. He called Ela's name from time to time, but, dreamlike, the forest smothered his voice. He said to Lwi, in the numbing whispering of leaves, "We'll find her. We won't lie down here. The silly girl says I can work magic. So let's try, shall we? Let's say we should find her, let's think about that, that's a good horse. . . ."

Easy to sleep. Far too easy to shut his eyes, even walking;

while he still came on scattered stragglers of that ghastly army—as if some of that number had attempted escape from whatever had left them waiting for all time—only to let their eyes drift shut, losing their war to a gentle enemy. If he had magic, he called on it to save him and Ela from this place. If he had favor with the gods, he pleaded with them, but he was not sure they could reach within this realm, and he was not sure he had been as devout as the priests would wish.

"This way," the leaves seemed to whisper. "This way, Tamas."

Fish roasted on the fire, and there were greens such as Krukczy had found unspoiled in the garden and a few kitchen stores, but goblins had gotten the rest. It was a strange night, with Krukczy's musty fur drying in the heat of a fire, and Zadny with his head on his knee, and the dreadful warning still standing in the yard. Yuri did not like to think about it, and master Nikolai himself had asked if Karoly did not want them to try to bury the remains, such as there were, but Karoly had said no, said it with such harshness as invited no second question on the matter.

So here they sat, roasting fish in a ruined hall, amid the clutter the goblins had left of the place. Nikolai was able to sit up and have his supper, one-handed, and they had found master Karoly, and they had a roof over their heads and a wall around them tonight, but over all, Yuri found no appetite—thinking about Karoly's sister, and the servant, Karoly guessed it was, out there in the yard; and most of all thinking how it must have been Karoly's trail Zadny had followed, not his brothers', after all. This might be the end of it, beyond which—beyond which was nothing but going home, with Nikolai and with Karoly, at least, but—

He felt Zadny's head on his knee, absently scratched the soft, shaggy ears. Zadny had had his fish and probably wanted his, that was growing cold on a broken dish, so he began to break off bits, and pick out the bones, and give it to him.

But he heard master Karoly say something to Nikolai about tomorrow. Then followed an exchange he could not hear, the

two of them talking in low voices; so he listened harder, and
heard, "—going on from here."

"Alone?" Nikolai asked, then Karoly said something, but
Krukczy switched his tail just then, and a coal snapped in
the fireplace, making Zadny jump.

He listened harder. And suddenly saw two grim faces look
his way in unison.

He set his jaw and said, "Master Karoly. Are you talking
about finding my brothers? Because if you are I'm not going
home."

"Damned right you're going home," Nikolai said.
"You're going to do as you're told for once, young my lord,
and if you've any regard for your brothers' lives you won't
take *me* from Karoly to make sure you get there."

"They're alive."

"I've the notion one is," master Karoly said, at which
Yuri's heart beat faster and faster. "I'm fairly certain Tamas
was here, and not so long ago."

"Then where is he?" His voice startled Zadny, who
jumped up, darting from him to Krukczy, who crouched by
the fire, and back, and back again.

"He knows," Krukczy rumbled, and rubbed Zadny's
head. "Hound, he knows—brother. Hound, he knows."

"It *talks* to him?" Nikolai asked, but master Karoly held
up his hand and said,

"Say on, master Krukczy. What else do you know?"

The troll's tail spun a nervous, curling trail, and ended in
its broad hands, for safekeeping, as seemed. "Witch."

"What about a witch?"

"Young witch. Belongs here."

"Her apprentice," Karoly said, and got up and paced as
far as the door to the outside. "Damn! her apprentice . . .
that's who. *That's* who! I couldn't see her!"

Who what? Yuri wondered, but it was Nikolai who dared
ask it.

"Who are you talking about?"

Master Karoly turned about, and it was a frighteningly
different old man, it was not the amiable master Karoly who

had shown him the weather-glass, it was an angry man whose sister was dead outside, who had seen friends struck from ambush, and who had walked for days to get here.

"A young and desperate fool," he said, and cast himself down again by the fire. "God, god—she might have taken it. I'd forgotten all about her."

"Taken what?" Nikolai asked.

"What she has no business on earth to have in her hands. But if I weren't here, if she did survive . . ."

"What?" Nikolai asked, but Karoly shushed him and stared into the fire and thought and thought.

Yuri ate a cold bit of fish. And another. The troll said that one of his brothers was alive. And the way Zadny was after the trail, it might be Tamas—he hoped it was Tamas. He did not know if that was wicked or not, but he liked Tamas better.

But if it was Bogdan, he was still not going back without him. He watched Karoly, and waited, and so did Nikolai, uncommonly patient with master Karoly.

Yuri sucked his fingers clean of fish, and held the bones in a napkin on his lap, waiting; but finally he saw master Nikolai lean his back against the wall, seeming in pain; and he said, very so quietly, "You should go to bed, sir, I'll wait up. I need to talk to master Karoly anyway. I'm *not* going back."

Nikolai frowned darkly at him, cradling his wounded arm.

"It's *my* brother, sir."

"My *god*, your father should take a stick to your backside!"

"The boy belongs here," Karoly said.

"What do you mean he belongs here?" Nikolai cried, and winced. "Lord Sun, Karoly, your wits are addled."

"My wits are in excellent form, master huntsman." Master Karoly had pulled a twig from the bit of wood he added to the fire, and he stripped bark from it with his thumbnail. "If the boy went back now, he would be in worse danger. There are things abroad that would smell him out in a moment."

"We're not safe company," Nikolai said.

"No. Nor is he. Nor is my sister's apprentice." Master Karoly's mouth made a tight line as he tied the bit of cedar in a cross, and split it further. It made, Yuri realized of a sudden, the shape of a man.

Karoly cast it into the fire.

"Why did you do that?" Yuri asked.

"One pays," Karoly said. "One at least acknowledges the obligation to pay. Be polite with the gods. These are dangerous places."

"No riddles," Nikolai said. "I'm full to the teeth with riddles, master trickster. No more flummery. Where is Tamas, what did the apprentice take, and where are they going?"

"In over his head, a bit of mirror, and the heart of hell. Now do you know what I'm talking about?"

Two grown men were about to argue and nothing was going to get done. "Please," Yuri said. "What about mirrors, master Karoly?"

Karoly looked him in the eyes so long he felt the silence grow, but Krukczy the troll rumbled,

"Mirror of the goblin queen."

"A fragment of it," Karoly said. He had pulled another twig and peeled it, turning it in his fingers. "A fragment of the goblin queen's mirror. It has the power of delusion, the power of bewitchment . . . the power of misleading and confusion and seeming."

"Where is it?"

"It used to be here. Since it isn't, I can only hope the apprentice has it. I can only hope my sister warned the girl what it is, and most of all what it isn't."

"For the god's sake," Nikolai said, "in words without their tails in their mouths—what does the thing do? Or what doesn't it?"

"It doesn't make clever out of foolish, it doesn't rescue lambs from the slaughter, and it doesn't help a mouse catch a cat."

"What can it do?"

"Too damned much to have it wandering the countryside. When the mirror cracked, a goblin carried one shard to the upper world, so I had the story. That was a long, long time ago."

"Young mistress got it," Krukczy said.

"*Did* she, now?" Master Karoly lifted his brows and stared at the troll.

"Young mistress took it from the goblin. A present. A long, long time ago."

"What does he mean?" Nikolai asked.

"It means I know now how it came to my sister. Urzula never said. Damn."

"Urzula never said?" Nikolai asked.

Gran? Yuri wondered. *Our* gran? Meanwhile Karoly nodded to Nikolai's question and chewed on the twig, staring into the fire. "I wish the girl had waited. I do wish she had waited."

"Young witch came to my tower," Krukczy said, "to find brothers. One fell to the river, down with rocks. I give him to her."

"It *is* Tamas," Nikolai said. "He and his horse went down the slide."

Yuri drew in a breath. He remembered the road and those sharp rocks from the bottom side, as it slanted down and down toward the stream that flowed past Krukczy Straz. But Tamas was alive, even Nikolai believed it, now! He rested his arm on his knee and his fist against his mouth, trying not to ask silly questions while his elders were thinking, which they clearly were.

"I don't like this," Karoly said. "It doesn't have a good feeling at all. That fragment is moving."

"Moving where?" Nikolai asked.

"Toward its owner. It's been in a safe place all these years. The goblins were no present threat. Now the girl's missed me and gotten Tamas, and they've taken the piece and gone east, no question but what it's east. . . ."

"Goblin follows them," Krukczy said. "I smell him in this room."

"Ng'Saeich," Karoly murmured, or something like that, and Karoly's jaw stayed open, twig and all. "God. That scoundrel! Of course he is!"

"Who?" Yuri asked, he could not help it.

"The thief, of course, the thief, damn him! The fools murdered her and they probably didn't even know who she was. They didn't care. But *he* knew. He knew, damn him, he felt it the same as I, and he beat me here!"

"I need to speak with you," Nikolai said to Karoly, in that way grown-ups had when they wanted boys out of ear-shot.

Karoly said, "The boy is going with us. There's no choice now."

"How far is he going to make it? To a den of goblins? To what the rest of us made it to? What they did to your sister and her servant . . . god, they probably *ate* them, man, this is not an enemy who'll fight fair."

"Neither do I," Karoly said, and spat a bit of the twig, that hissed in the fire. "Neither would my sister. That's why I won't bury her. Go to bed. Both of you. You'll not dream tonight."

"I thought we were going after my brother!" Yuri protested. He did not understand what Nikolai and Karoly were arguing about. He did understand Tamas and a witch's apprentice being somewhere in the forest and someone named ng'Saeich looking for the piece of mirror they were carrying. Most of all he understood what he had seen in the yard, and that goblins had done it. "What about Bogdan? What about Jerzy and Zev and Filip? What about . . . ?"

"In the morning," Karoly said. "In the morning we'll go, and go quickly. Don't wake for any sound you hear. —Master Krukczy. Watch the deep ways. And take the dog. He'd be better with you tonight."

"Master Karoly," Yuri protested, upset and angry. But Karoly got up, making a shadow above him, and caught his face painfully in his hand, after which Yuri found his eyes closing.

"There's too much, too much to explain. Go to bed, boy."

Yuri found himself doing that without knowing why or remembering quite what they had been saying. He only remembered Zadny after he had gotten to the pallet master Karoly had made him in the wreckage of the hall.

And once that night he opened his eyes to think that a stranger stood near him. He thought it was a woman. He could not say why. He only knew whoever it was, was angry, and looking for someone who was not him.

Whoever it was brushed his hair with its hand and went away. He shivered after that. He had no idea why it had scared him, since none of the anger was aimed at him. But he was afraid, all the same.

The boy was quiet—exhausted, Nikolai could think, except he had the evidence of magic in himself with every breath he took. He kept expecting the pain to come back. The memory of it was so vivid he expected it to return if he so much as shifted his back against the wedge of blankets between him and the corner. And he had never given that much credence to the old man's abilities, true, but he had never forgotten the lady. He had tried to tell himself all his life it had only been a boy's imagination that had tingled through his bones that night and spooked him down the stairs—and that the pain in his arm was fading steadily was all very fine, he supposed, but no one had consulted him in it. It had been his pain and it was still his arm, and he sat there in a witch's ruined hall with the acute feeling he had had something thoroughly unpleasant done to him, but he could not swear to what; and the equally acute feeling that he both knew and had never known the old man across the room.

He watched Karoly throw a log on the fire, watched Karoly press his ear to the stone of the fireplace and shake his head as if he did not like what he had heard. Karoly patted the stone as if it were alive, then pottered about some more, putting their pans away into the packs. Finally he came and sat down on the bench next to the bed. The fire cast a halo around the old man and the shadow fell on Nikolai's face, making him feel, for some reason, cornered.

"How's the arm?" Karoly asked.

"All right," he said. "Twinges." Which was the truth. The old man's magic was not perfect. "—So what do we do about the boy?"

"Nothing we can do." Karoly was still chewing that bit of twig, and made it turn in his mouth. "When magic works it pulls things. If something's going the way its various parts are, it's safer for that particular something, you understand?"

"You mean the boy going with us."

"I mean *you* going with us. Leave us and you'll be goblin bait by morning. The boy has to go where everything else goes—getting him away from the magic at work in this land would be impossible."

"Impossible! Tell me 'impossible!' " He remembered the boy asleep and dropped his voice. "I can get him home. Trust me!"

"Not a chance. He'd come back, probably because you were dead. You're alive now because of him, and don't ask me why. I don't know everything."

"But you know *that*, do you? You're so damned sure of that? One of Stani's boys is wandering around the woods—"

"One of Stani's boys is in serious trouble. Shut up and listen, master huntsman. Tomorrow morning, at the crack of dawn or just before, I want you to take the boy and the horse and the dog and get outside the gates. I may join you. If I don't, and you don't like the look of things, head east, bearing along the wall. Krukczy will go with you."

Something about not fighting fair. The skulls in the yard. And not burying his sister.

"What are you up to? What's this—'take the boy'? Where will you be?"

"Tomorrow will tell, won't it? Behind you, in one sense or the other."

He did not like that in the least, either. "Take the boy and do what?"

"Find Tamas. I'll find you, if I can. I *think* my sister forgave me. We'll find out tomorrow."

"What do you mean—find out? Isn't she dead?"

"Oh, she's dead. Dead without a stroke struck or a goblin suffering for it, and that's not her style, not Ysabel." Karoly took the twig from his mouth and spat a piece at the floor. "Raising a ghost—you never know what you'll get; that's the trouble."

"Is she around here?" The room seemed too full of shadows. "Is she listening to us?" It was deeper into magic and wizards' business than he ever wanted to delve, but Karoly said, so quietly the snap of embers seemed to echo in the hall:

"I don't get that feeling. That's why I don't know how much of her I can get back. Sometimes it's just a piece or two. That's the danger."

"What's the danger?"

"Of only the anger coming back."

An ember popped. Nikolai jumped, and the shoulder sent a warning ache. Karoly looked about him with an absent stare, and spat another bit of twig.

"Was that her?"

"That's the other problem with ghosts. Ysabel, Ytresse . . . I wouldn't put it past any of them."

"Who? Put what past them?"

"The witches. Doing anything. I went to live over-mountain. My sister refused to deal with me after that. But she spent everything to call me home. She deserved her revenge. No one should die like that."

"And you brought the boys into this? You led us down that damned road and you knew all along what was going on here?"

"Keep your voice down. No, I didn't know what was going on here, I dreamed it, and there's a difference."

"What difference? You *saw* that marker!"

"And what could we do, then? Get back across the pass, with no supplies? Wait for the goblins to invade Maggiar? We were as close to their source as we might ever get—as close to the *only* place anyone can stop them, and close to the one who might have done it, with my help. But I wasn't in time."

"In time for your sister? What could you have done?"

"That's to be seen. That's still to be seen. —Let me tell you a story, master huntsman, if you care to hear it. Someone but me should know the truth."

He frowned and waited. Anything that made sense of the business, he was willing to hear—but he had limited faith the old man would make any.

"Some hundreds of years ago," Karoly said, "many hundreds of years ago, in fact, before there even was a Maggiar, there was a queen in over-mountain, and a tower at Hasel. The queen in Hasel had a daughter named Ylena. And nothing was good enough for Ylena. In her household, she had golden tables, and silver plates. Even her bed was silver and her washbasin was gold set with jewels. . . ."

"This sounds like one of those tales," Nikolai muttered.

"Of course, but that's Ylena the tales talk about. They don't know it's Ylena, but I assure you it is. Nothing but the best. And being a princess, as well as a witch—"

"Were all of them witches?" It seemed to him that essential things were being left out. A bard, Karoly was not. "Or was it just Ylena?"

"Oh, mostly they were. The queens of over-mountain all knew the arts to one degree or another. Anyhow, the queen discovered one day what a truly vain and ungrateful princess Ylena was, and she worried and worried about this."

"Too late," Nikolai interjected. "She should have taken a switch to the brat."

"Far too late for that. Ylena would ruin the land when she became queen, and queen Mirela, knowing that . . . looked for some magical solution: a failing in lazy witches. So she went to the goblins."

"Just like that? Walked up to the front door and knocked?"

"Oh, being a witch, Mirela rattled a few dark doors at night, some few that wiser witches wouldn't touch. Remember, she wasn't a particularly wise witch. She'd brought up Ylena. But she was a desperate witch, and good-hearted. And the goblin queen, in exchange for a promise of access to the world of men for one night a year, gave queen Mirela a potion that would assure her youth and beauty. The usual bargain. So queen Mirela came back young and beautiful and healthy enough to reign forty years more at least. Ylena was *furious*."

"Naturally Ylena worked a spell against her."

"No, not immediately. It was a very powerful magic that surrounded her mother, and if you go against something that strong without knowing exactly the terms of it, you can do yourself harm. So Ylena waited a whole year until that night the goblins could come into the land, and approached their queen to ask her how to get the throne. So what was a little treachery against one's mother? And what was murder? Because Mirela had asked for youth and beauty, not a charmed life. So Ylena promised the goblin queen a whole year of access to human lands, when she should rule, in return for that advice. And that let the goblins into human lands again."

"Again?"

"Oh, they'd begun here. That's how queen Mirela first found the key to calling them. They'd left their signs on old stones, they left their spells—in magic, one wanders through them like old landmarks. Of course the goblins had their own reasons for leaving such clues in the world when they were banished—but that's another story. At any rate, Mirela perished under most suspicious circumstances, Ylena became queen, and the goblins arrived in the world with banners and circumstance. They were on best behavior. They did no mischief. They were courtly, they were flattering to the queen, and they oh'ed and ah'ed over the new princess—"

"Ylena got a husband."

"At least a daughter. She was named Ytresse. She was very beautiful even as a baby. But Ylena had never planned to have an heir, and she hadn't succeeded in preventing her birth, if you take my meaning. Nothing worked. She suspected goblin treachery, and she fell out with the goblin queen until the day the year was up and the goblins were preparing to leave. They professed their regret to give up so much grace and comfort, and the goblin queen remarked to Ylena that she wished they might make a further bargain."

"The fool."

"Ylena? Of course. Ylena sensed magic in that baby. Powerful magic. She sensed goblin work. And the baby, Ytresse, had survived some very determined efforts. So Ylena wanted a spell stronger than the baby's determination to live. And the goblin queen said there was a lake—a particularly beautiful lake they had come to revere—"

"Goblins revere something?"

"There are goblins and goblins. Certain ones, yes, apparently do. This lake had a perfect reflection. It's quite shallow, very still, and it was a place of power in this world that the goblins wanted. So the goblin queen swore that Ylena might live so long as they had possession of that small lake. It was just tricky enough that Ylena believed in it. So she agreed on the spot."

"Clever woman."

"Ah, but when you deal with devils, beware the loopholes."

"The youth and beauty part?"

"Exactly. But—the goblins were of course willing to give Ylena spells to stave off age—by their magic, of course. So Ylena was trapped in her own bargain. But—*but*—" Karoly spat another bit of twig. "Ylena wanted to deal no more with the goblins, and began to sustain herself by . . . well, say her subjects grew fewer and fewer. She knew of course she'd been betrayed. Then a certain goblin came to her and offered her a secret—a secret, he said, in return for which he asked three wishes."

"You're joking."

"Three is a potent number. And he used his first two, but the third—not yet, for all I know. But for whatever reason, he told her how the goblin queen's power lay in a mirror, a working of magical smoothness and exactitude, and that if Ylena wanted power to equal the goblin queen's spells, that was what she had to defeat. So Ylena had a mirror made of silvered glass as smooth and perfect as she could obtain, and put into its making every spell she knew. —None of which, of course, went unreported in the territory around the lake.

So on a snowy midwinter's eve, when everyone should be asleep, and, as it just happened, the night before Ylena was quite ready to take her on, the goblin queen sent out her army and turned her spells against Ylena's mirror. When all was done there was little left of Ylena but a wraith, nothing left of Hasel but the shell, and nothing of Ylena's mirror but silver powder—so they say."

"And the goblin queen's?"

"Cracked right in two, with a small fragment fallen, that was the price she paid for defeating Ylena. But the same goblin, so he claimed, the very one who had dealt with Ylena, stole the piece and took it straightway—you guessed it—to Ylena's successor, Ytresse, who had grown up into a wicked, wicked woman. But Ytresse no more trusted the goblin queen than her mother had. She made sure of her own heir— nothing of the goblin queen's doing, a witch named Ylysse. And Ylysse, after a long, long lifetime, passed the power to Ysabel—"

"Your sister."

"My sister."

"But it's a goblin trap, that fragment. It was from the beginning. —Isn't it?"

"Consider its history. Is the goblin thief lying or not? And why that knowledge he gave to Ylena in the first place, and why the three wishes, and the unfortunate issue to Ylena? It certainly *is* to ask. . . ."

"Then—" Certain prying questions occurred to him, that did not seem entirely unwise, also considering the history.

"Then—?" Karoly asked.

"Where do you come into the story?"

"I? Nowhere. Or only at the last. Ysabel and I weren't descended from Ytresse. Not even from her apprentices. *Urzula* was."

His heart gave a thump. "The lady gran?"

"Exactly."

Nikolai let go his breath and drew in another one, thinking. My god. What else isn't what we trusted?

"You and your sister? —Where did *you* come into this?"

"Urzula's apprentices."

Apprentices, for the god's sake. "And what brought the lady to Maggiar? And don't tell me 'adoration for Ladislaw.' I was at the funeral."

Karoly laughed grimly. "Not overmuch of adoration. But a fair bargain on both sides. Ladislaw got his heir. And dare I say—if one hopes to undo a spell, one has to reach outside its arena of influence, one has to do the unexpected, work where one won't be spied upon—conditions which don't pertain to *this* side of the mountain."

"But she never *warned* anyone, not m'lord Stani, not—"

"I knew."

"Damned lot of good it did anyone. You knew, you knew when you saw the trouble start, let alone that business on the trail."

"It might have been trolls."

"Might have been trolls! The *troll's* not guilty, master wizard, the *troll* was hiding in the basement at Krukczy Tower, in fear of his life, don't tell me you hadn't clearer messages out of your dreams than that, once every wild creature in the over-mountain began pouring into Maggiar. . . ."

"There could be other causes. I hoped for other causes. That's the nature of magic, master huntsman. When will it rain, do the birds tell you that without fail? Better yet, do they tell you where? Or are there ever false signs? The goblins have been in this world for hundreds of years now—and will be, so long as the agreement with Ylena stands."

"It doesn't."

"Oh, but to this day, Ylena has never given up her power— power to frighten, power to kill. She's still in this world."

"You mean she's not dead."

"That describes it. Not dead. Not alive either. So the goblins hold their land—and the mirror is mended, with its one piece missing. As for mistress Urzula—what she did, and how much of this is the queen's doing, the Lady knows, but I don't—nor can, I've realized that, long since. Let me tell you another secret. Urzula's real name was Ysabel."

"Your sister?" More and more crazed, it was.

"Both were named Ysabel. Our mother was a servant in this tower, a very minor witch, a distant cousin. Ylysse gave Ysabel to our mother to bring up and gave out that we were *her* children. Which put us in danger, certainly. But Urzula—"

"Your sister?"

Karoly shook his head. "Use the names they lived by. It's less confusing. And listen. Urzula wanted me with her because I wasn't gifted enough to leave here in danger—that and other reasons. . . ."

"Were there other reasons?"

"Were we lovers?" Another spit of twig, and a dark, silent laughter. "Yes. Ysabel—my sister Ysabel—and I had a falling out on that point. We were twins. Ysabel expected loyalty, since she was getting the short end of things, and standing in the most danger. Ysabel wanted the teaching more than she wanted life and breath and I wanted—Urzula, that was the sad truth. I wasn't so gifted nor so dedicated as Ysabel. Magic for me didn't take fire, the way it did for her. I never trusted it. Still don't. Ysabel drank it, breathed it— and she never could have the magic she really wanted, could never *be* the witch she claimed to be. And Urzula—Urzula . . . the way she felt about it—you know, I never understood whether she was, inside, like Ysabel, in love with magic, or more like me. Urzula held everything inside and you never knew. But with her birthright, the god only knows what she *could* do if she used it as freely as Ysabel—if she let it use her, like Ysabel. I always thought—leaving Ysabel on watch here was like leaving the fox in charge of the henhouse. Fond of designs, she was. Fond of workings and intrigues."

He found himself uncomfortable, in wizardly confidences. Embers popped, again, and Karoly's brow wrinkled with an upward glance.

"Are you there?" Karoly asked the shadowed air and the firelight, and Nikolai held his breath waiting for an answer, but Karoly gave another humorless laugh and looked down at his hands. "I chide the boys for moongazing. But boys are silly longer than girls, aren't they—and that I wasn't her ally, that was something Ysabel never could understand. That Urzula wanted me with her was something she thought she did understand—god, Ysabel was furious. And Urzula was on her way to get a husband and a successor the goblins wouldn't know about. That was—a painful realization.''

A successor. Nikolai found his heart thumping so loudly of a sudden he could not believe Karoly did not hear. He asked, quietly, carefully, the gossip of every servant in the house: "Whose is Stani?"

"Urzula's, of course."

Damn the old man, up to the edge of truth and no further. But Karoly added, then:

"That's enough, if you want the truth. As witches reckon lineage it's enough. Ysabel and I lived this lie all our lives. And Urzula—'' A private and lengthy silence. "She was really a reprehensible woman, Urzula was . . . short-tempered; cruel, at times . . . most times. Dreadful things amused her. But she worked for the right. —And defend her own people—god, she would do that." Karoly drew a long breath. "You know what disturbs me most?"

I couldn't possibly imagine, Nikolai thought distressedly, and simply answered, "No."

"That so much of the business with Ylysse began with Ylena."

"What do you mean—began with Ylena?"

"In sorcery—and far-working is necessarily sorcery—one wants to affect events at a great distance and over time, and one can't predict whether the outcome is good or bad for one or another person, only *numbers* of people. Urzula could dismiss consequences like that: Urzula didn't see one person, or a son, or a mother. Urzula saw—I can't tell you what Urzula saw, or, for that matter, what Ysabel saw. I only loved certain people. And I couldn't *change* what Urzula worked, I couldn't even change myself, or Ysabel. . . .'' Karoly cleared his throat. It had gotten very still in the room, and uncomfortably close. "Anyway, I chose the small magic, I'm a wizard, not a sorcerer, not even a good wizard until

I've something I want with a clear conscience. I follow along after a sorcerer like Urzula, you understand, just picking up and patching what I can. Work *against* sorcery? That takes sorcery. That was Ysabel's domain." He took the twig from his mouth and shredded it in threads with his nail, as if the need to do that utterly occupied his attention.

"You mean you can't change anything? You can't do things differently than they've done?"

A moment's silence. "That's sorcery, too. Change the things they've done, means you change the far things. One thing touches everything. It's only the broken bits, the used bits, the bits passed over . . . that I can patch. The pieces in use—I can't help."

"Like Tamas? Is that what you're saying?"

"Like any of us. —Ysabel was as dangerous and as much in danger as anyone. It was a long and lonely time here, weak as she was, pretending so much more strength. Thank the god for Pavel."

"Pavel."

"The chap in the yard." A motion of Karoly's eyes. Up. Meaning the second pole and the second skull, Nikolai realized with a motion of his stomach. "He came from a long time ago. From Hasel. Half-mad, but he was devoted to Ysabel. Supposedly he kept the grounds—now and again. Mostly he kept Ysabel. —But beware the apprentice. Beware anyone who learned from Ysabel. The girl will have no conscience, Tamas, she won't know right from wrong . . . not if she learned at my sister's knee. Only the faraway things matter. Only the outcome, to anyone Ysabel would have taught . . ."

The old man was staring off at nothing, spinning the chewed twig in his fingers, talking to Tamas as if he were there, and the hair rose on Nikolai's nape. It took more than ordinary craziness to spook him, or ghastly sights to scare him—he had seen so many on his trek south, through the wars of wizards and petty tsars.

"Urzula saw the boys born," Karoly said, for no reason that Nikolai could understand, but the god only knew who he was talking to now. "She was satisfied then. She'd lived a long time. And she said they weren't her responsibility any longer. And I wasn't. So she died."

"Suicide?"

"No. Sorcery's like that."

"Better to wish your *enemies* dead. Damn. —And why didn't your sister know the goblins were coming? Why didn't she blast them with lightning or turn them to pigs or something? If she could call you from over-mountain, she wasn't helpless."

His caution had deserted him: he had asked too bluntly, perhaps, and he thought he might have angered the old man. But it was not a challenge. He honestly wanted to know why reasonable things had not happened, in a war of sorcerers.

Karoly frowned and finally said, very slowly, as if he were explaining to a child: "Because, master huntsman, do you forget? We aren't the only side in this war. The other side casts spells, too."

"So she couldn't just—send earlier?"

"So she couldn't *think* of it—at least not well enough to do a number of things all at once. It's often the little things that slip your notice—and sorcery doesn't leave tracks *on* objects that cause you problems, the way magic does. Mostly it's a gate unlatched, a moment of forgetfulness. Forgetfulness and looking past a thing are both deadly mistakes. The object on the shelf for thirty years, that you never think of being there, the thing you do every day, so you never remember whether you've done it or not, on one specific day. That sort of thing."

"Like this mirror that's so damned important? What does this mirror do? Why didn't the gran take it with her to Maggiar? Why did she leave it with your sister, where they could get at it?"

Karoly blinked and stared off across the room—looked back at him then as if he had only then accounted of his presence. "What did you say?"

"I said—why did the lady gran leave the mirror with your sister, if this tower wasn't safe from sorcery?"

Karoly blinked, shook his head, bit his lips a moment, frowning as if he were listening to something. Then he rose up, a shadow against the fire.

"Old man?"

"Find Tamas, do you hear? Find Tamas. Nothing's more urgent than that."

"And do what with him?" All his senses seemed foggy of a sudden, and the wound on the edge of hurting. "Shall we say, Excuse us, your goblin majesty, but we're not really interested in your war, and may we please go home? —I've been in bad situations, master wizard, I've been on battle-fields and I've seen a city burn, but I didn't have a boy and a pony and a damned dog for an escort. And what do we do with the mirror if we find it?"

Karoly pressed his fingers against his eyes as if he were fighting headache. "It's hard to think about. Ask it again, master huntsman."

"Why . . . ?" He must be falling asleep. He could not recall himself what must have caught Karoly's attention, god, he'd said it three times—did the man want it again? "What do I do? Where do I take the boys? If we get the mirror, what do we do with it? What can it do?" He remembered another piece of his question. "Why didn't the lady gran bring it with her?"

"Again."

"The damned mirror, master Karoly. What about it? Why didn't she take it to Maggiar? *What's going on?*"

Karoly looked . . . frightened, of a sudden, his eyes darting about the room. He's gone mad, Nikolai thought in distress. The old man's not sane . . .

Because he had never seen anyone do that in the middle of talking with someone, had never seen anyone take to watching something immaterial that flitted and darted and circled the room.

"Karoly?" Nikolai insisted.

Karoly stood up, and turned, a shadow between him and the fire as Karoly stared down at him. "Go to sleep," Karoly said, and suddenly Nikolai found his eyes so tired and the crackling of the fire so intense and so absorbing that he could not keep his wits collected. "Dammit, stop it," he protested—but his thoughts and his anger ran off in various directions, into memories of the road, the mountains, the woods and the pony. . . .

"The boy's in trouble," he dreamed that Karoly said. And Karoly said something more, concerning a place called Hasel, or where Hasel used to stand, but he could not hold onto the thought, not even enough to tell the old man what he thought of him. . . .

And Karoly for so many reasons deserved cursing.

9

LWI AMBLED TO A STOP IN THE TWILIGHT OF THE EVERLAST-
ing woods, and it would have been oh, so much easier to
give up and let the struggle go, Lwi refusing all reasonable
urgings to go on. The morning had to come, and Tamas was
so confused and so weary—but the easy way was the dangerous way, the easy way must always be suspect, master
Karoly had always said—think twice and three times before
you take the easy way.

Enough bones in this woods to make anybody think twice,
he thought muzzily, and tugged at the reins and led Lwi's
irregular steps on the straightest line he could walk among
the trees, one step after the other, no wit left to reason what
way he was going, except that everything ended, and that
this night, like this woods, surely had an other side if he only
persisted long enough in one direction, in one choice and
not the dozen his mind wanted to skitter off into . . .

It seemed to him at last that the woods was growing lighter
ahead—like the moon at forest edge. He hoped then, that he
had found the way out he was looking for, and the trees
began to appear like shadowy pillars in some great hall, but
he saw more trees beyond, and that light nearer and among
them, as if the moon itself had come to rest in the very heart
of the trees.

"Come here," a voice said softly, from everywhere at
once. Ela, he thought at first, Ela's magic was talking to him,
she had found the magical place she was looking for and she
was calling him to her—and then he thought that the speaker
seemed older than Ela: so readily a mind beset by spells

164

began to apply ordinary judgments, as if such manifestations happened by mundane rules.

"Who are you?" he asked it.

"Why, the mistress of this woods, boy. What and who are you? Do you have a name? It seems I should know you."

The voice that had seemed to come from all about him came from his left this time; and he looked in that direction, seeing only massive trunks of trees.

"Tamas," he panted.

"What are you doing here?" The voice came from behind him now, the self-same voice, as if it were stalking him, but it was nowhere, when he turned unsteadily and looked. "What do you seek here, Tamas?"

"Are you a witch?" he asked, he hoped without a tremor in his voice.

"Of course," it said. It was behind him again. He turned back the way he had been facing and saw a shadow between the trees, a woman, he thought, with a cloak drawn tight about her. "Where are you going, Tamas?"

"Out of this woods," he said, and decided that if it was her woods, disrespect to her domain would never help his case. "I'm only going through, good lady. If you know the way out I'd be grateful."

"Why so anxious? Are you afraid?"

"I've no reason to be. I haven't taken anything, or touched anything." Those were the magical rules as gran's stories had them. He pulled Lwi to the side and took another direction. Or perhaps he dreamed he did. She appeared in front of him again, saying:

"But what's that at your side, Tamas? Is that yours?"

A chill went through him. He reached blindly toward the goblin sword, and pricked his finger on its spines. "I didn't think it was stealing."

"But this is my woods, Tamas. Everything in it is mine."

"I beg your pardon," he said. Breath came short, shameful panic. "I didn't think there was anyone to—" He drew Lwi in the other direction, and caught his foot painfully on a tree root. He recovered his balance and she was still in front of him.

"—anyone to care?" she mocked him.

"Are you a goblin?"

"Do I look like one?"

"I've only seen one, face to face. You don't look like him. But how should I know?"

She laughed softly, and beckoned him toward her. "Come inside. I'm not so stingy as that. And you don't look like a goblin, either. You look like a young man who's far from home."

For the first time he saw the dim outlines of a doorway behind her. Perhaps he had been looking so hard at her he had seen nothing else. But gran's stories had never encouraged him to accept such offers and he shook his head no. "Thank you, no, madam, I'm looking for someone."

"Have you lost someone? I can help you. There's little goes on in this woods that I don't know. —Oh, come in, come in, no sense to stand outside. The horse will be safe. Nothing harmful comes here."

It was dark, beyond that doorway. Everything about it seemed untrustworthy. "You can just tell me the shortest way out," he said, but she stooped and ducked inside—perhaps, he reasoned with himself, only to light a lamp or poke up a slumbering fire, and he might be foolish to object—but Ela had told him nothing of houses or cottages in this woods, especially not ones lit by a moon that, by his reckoning, ought not to have reached mid sky yet, a waning crescent by now, and not so bright as the light that filled this grove.

He did not want to go into that place—but what else might he do but wander on in the dark? he asked himself. Her invitation was the only choice he saw.

Much against his better judgment, he lapped Lwi's reins about a low live branch and went as far as the entrance, with no intention whatsoever of going inside until there was a lamp lit or a fire to show him what he was walking into. The air that wafted out to him had the chill and damp of a cave, but it looked on the outside like a peasant's cottage. He touched the rough stonework and it felt real enough, down to the grit of old mortar.

"Will you help me?" she asked from out of the dark.

"Madam, I would, but I'm sure you know your shelves better than I do. I'd only be in the way."

"Cautious boy." He heard further small movements within. "Afraid of me, are you?"

Less and less trustworthy. "Madam," he said uneasily, "I've seen nothing in this whole land but trouble." He heard Lwi tearing at the leaves behind him, and thought that if he had the sense his father hoped for in his sons he would walk away now, take Lwi in hand and keep going in his own slow and uncertain way, in hope of sunrise, eventually.

But of things he had met in this land, witches seemed thus far a power opposing the goblins—and light *did* spring up inside, a golden and comforting light, that cast a warm glow over an interior of curtains and shelves and domestic clutter—just the sort of things a woodland wise-woman might collect, birds' wings and branches and jars and jars of herbs and such. It reminded him acutely and painfully of master Karoly's study.

"Well?" she asked, from inside, and beckoned to him. "Oh, come, come, boy, I don't bite."

He could see all the inside from the door. He entered cautiously. She was standing at her table, pouring from a pitcher into two wooden cups.

"I don't really think I need anything," he protested, because he had no desire whatsoever to eat anything or acquire any obligations of hospitality with a witch. But she set one cup into his hand and waved him toward a cushioned ledge, settling herself at the far end of that small nook, a very proper witch, very—beautiful, he decided, which bore not at all on whether he should trust her, of course, but she did not look wicked. She had put off the dark cloak, that was not black, but deep, deep red. Her gown was embroidered and fringed and corded and tasseled with intricate work of black and colors, of a fashion both foreign and strange—in fascination with which, he took a larger sip than he had planned, and felt the liquid go down like fire.

"*Are* you honestly a witch, lady?"

"Honest people have certainly called me that. And for your question, my question: What are you doing in my woods? Was it a way out you wanted—or were you looking for someone? Have you decided which?"

Perhaps she had the power to help them. Perhaps he had grown confused in his wandering. "Looking for someone. Who probably found the way out." Perhaps witches all knew one another. The tower was not that far away. He took the chance. "Do you know a girl named Ela? She came from Tajny Straz."

"From Tajny Straz. And don't you know these hills are a dangerous place?"

"Madam—" Words failed him. Everything he had seen came tumbling about him, with too much vividness and too little reason. "Are you at all acquainted with Ela's mistress? You are neighbors. And I know it's a dangerous place. The goblins killed her."

"A sad business. Yes, I'm aware. But that still doesn't answer why a young man is wandering these hills looking for a young lady from the perilous tower. I could wonder why I should answer his questions or tell him what I know—which might be something useful to him or not. How could I tell, if he won't tell me what he has to do with Tajny Straz and if he won't tell me the truth of what he's seeking?"

"We came to stop the goblins. They drove the deer and they burned the woods and when we came to see why, they ambushed us . . ."

"Did they? Why would they do that?"

"I've no idea." He held the cup locked between his fingers and wanted no more of what it held. His head was spinning and his thoughts fell over one another. "A girl is lost somewhere in this woods. I have to find her . . ."

"Poor boy." She got up with a whispering rustle of cloth and taking the cup from his fingers, set both cups on the table nearby. "Poor boy, you've hurt your hand—you've bled all over the cup."

"I'm dreadfully sorry. . . ."

"Oh, let me see." She began searching among the jars on the shelves, when he was only thinking how he could gracefully retreat. She found something, brought it back and reached for his hand. "Come, come," she said, and he felt like a fool, hesitating like a child with a cut finger—he truly did not want her to touch his hand, but she insisted.

"The sword did this. A wicked thing, and maybe poisoned." She carried his finger to her mouth while he was too confused to pull back or to protest her licking the blood off— quite, quite muddle-headed, then, and a little dizzy, as the pain stopped, and nothing seemed so comforting as her lips against his hand. "There," she said, edging closer, pressing his hand in hers, "isn't that better? Perhaps I can help you find your young lady. I do have my ways. And I can show you so many things, if you only pay some little token—the magic needs that, it always needs that, if someone asks a question."

He had not remembered about witches and payments. He regretted coming inside in the first place, or drinking anything, or letting her lips touch his hand. "I think—I think you never answered me—who you are, whether you know where Ela went."

"I don't. I can learn, ever so easily. Only I have to have something from you to make it happen. And you don't look to have any gold about you. What if my price were a kiss? Would that be too much to ask?"

He had never—never kissed any woman but his mother and his cousins: the truth was, he had never had the remotest chance, and her offer flung him into confusion. He was not courting some maid in Maggiar, he was sitting on a ledge in a strange little shelter with a witch who, he suddenly feared, was edging her way to more than a kiss. She might ask things he by no means wanted to do with a witch and a stranger. But he might be wrong about her intentions, and others were relying on him for their lives. So he leaned forward—it was not far—and paid her what she asked.

Her arms slipped about him. She held him that way and looked him closely in the eyes, laughing gently. "Oh, come, come now, was that a kiss?"

He had to allow it was not the way Bogdan would have done it. Certainly not Jerzy, or Nikolai. So he made a more honest try, but that did not satisfy her either: she made that kiss linger into two, and three, wandering from his lips to his neck, at which point he grew confused, what he should do, what he should agree to, what was right or wise to agree to or whether help that might be bought with dishonor could be relied on at all.

But what honor was it, if it let Ela go lost or goblins come at his land or his brother die without any justice for it?

She undid a buckle at his collar. He tried to think what to do, but when he shut his eyes to think he saw a dark tower, surrounded by goblin armies, saw war, men and goblins, a queen against a queen, not knowing how he knew that. He saw the great mirror cracked, and all the world rippled and changed like a reflection in water. Images flitted by, true or false, or what had been or what would be, he had no comprehension. What was happening in this world and the other tumbled event over event in confusion: he saw Lady Moon, in thinnest crescent, shimmering on a mountain lake. A goblin warrior stood on its dark and reedy shore, a knight whose countenance changed from fair to foul with the waxing and waning of the moon's reflection, with never a sun between.

That goblin figure turned and stared at him, the image of the goblin in the cellar, a hoped-for rescue turned to threat. Fair turned foul and fair again, not a human beauty, but beauty all the same, constantly changing with the reelings of the moon across the night.

But the shadow came across that goblin face and that armored body like the passing of a cloud across the moon, and when that shadow was full the body seemed broader, more familiar to him. The whole attitude was an echo of someone he knew—god, he *knew* with a pang at his heart, even before the cloud drifted on and the moon showed him Bogdan's pale face, remote, as a stranger to him. Slowly Bogdan began to turn his head, the very image of that creature in the cellar. He sought to escape that moment that their eyes should meet—but he could not turn away, not though his brother's eyes were dead and dark; and after that single glance Bogdan began to walk away, along the shore, into the dark.

"Wait!" he cried, and his voice echoed in vast halls that were suddenly about him, a structure of palest green stone and deepest black—he saw goblins standing about him, tall and grim, in the vaulted hall where the goblin queen issued her decrees. He saw her dusky face, dreadful and beautiful at once, with eyes of murky gold. Her braids were bound with silver, her necklaces were silver and gold, her long-nailed fingers were ringed and jeweled, and her arms were braceleted from wrist to elbow. "Well," she said, with that lisp that fangs made in a voice, and stared right into his soul. "Well, well, a venture against me. How nice."

"No," he cried, as she lifted a long-nailed hand and beckoned him closer, closer, with the force of magic. His body longed to go. He saw that Bogdan already stood there, among the dead-eyed courtiers. "It's all right," Bogdan said. "You've nothing to fear."

For a moment he looked at Bogdan, wanting desperately to believe in his safety—but it was shameful, it was horrid, Bogdan believed in no one's promises, and Bogdan was saying trust and believe that the queen had no wicked purposes.

"This is only the beginning," the witch in the wood said, standing beside him. "Is this someone you love? She'll find them, every one. She'll take them all from you, if you stand in her way. Believe what I say, believe what *I* say, and lend me your strength, boy, and there's nothing we can't do."

But nothing else had proven what it ought. And he felt cold in her touch, he saw shadow about him, and edged away.

"Not wise," she said.

He turned away and flung himself desperately at hall doors that shut in front of him—turned to run and found himself in the witch's forest cottage again, caught in an embrace that clung with frightening strength, arms with nothing of soft-ness or flesh about them. Everything was lies—he had not seen his brother in that place, it could not have been Bogdan, no more than he had stood just now in the goblin hall. He began to push away with all his might, tore from the witch's embrace and caught himself against the table, the wall, the draperies. The door was shut. The bolt was shot. When had that happened?

"Tamas," the witch reproved him, as his cold fingers struggled with the bolt. He heard the rustle of her garments behind him and he could only move in nightmare slowness.

"Are you afraid, Tamas? Look at me. *Look at me*, Tamas. I showed you a symbol of things as they are. But will you run away now, and be blind to what will be? Do you want the truth, Tamas? Have you no courage for the truth?"

He shot the bolt back. The door resisted like heavy iron. He scraped through the slight opening he forced and caught a breath of cold clean air as he fled, stumbling over the un-even ground on legs numb as winter chill. He met a shad-owed trunk, clung to it and struck out for a further one as his knees went to water. Lwi was standing where he had left him, and he flung himself in that direction, but the empty space was too wide. His knees gave way beneath him and sent him sprawling in the damp leaves.

"Well, well," a deep voice said, a voice that made his heart jump—but he could not recall if that voice belonged here, with a witch in this woods. He lifted his face from the leaves and rubbed the grit from his eyes . . . saw Azdra'ik standing among the trees.

They're in league, he thought. The witch and the goblins, all of them—

With a dry rattling and a whisper of cloth and leaves, the witch arrived beside him, her skirts in tatters, her feet—her feet beneath that hem were a pale assemblage of bone, which moved as if flesh contained it.

Azdra'ik sauntered closer. "Three wishes, mistress, wasn't that the term? I think I do remember your swearing it once upon a time, in exchange for my services." Three long-nailed fingers ticked off the items. "My first wish, I recall, was that you have no further power over me. My second . . . that you never oppose my purpose. And the third . . . the third, I fear, must be this wretched, foolish boy."

"Damn you," the witch whispered.

"Oh, I've served you more faithfully than you know—certainly more faithfully than you deserve. Now he's mine. By the terms you yourself proposed, he's mine. So begone, Ylena!"

A sound of breath, or angry wind. A soft and bitter laugh. "Cheaply bought, that third wish of yours. I feared so many worse things. But they're done. You can't banish me hereafter, ng'Saeich. I never need fear you again!"

"Begone, I say!" The goblin stood up tall and flung up his arm, and for a moment there was a dreadful feeling in the air. Lwi whinnied as a gust of wind blew decayed leaves and grit into Tamas' face, chilling him to the bone. He ducked his face within the protection of his arm, and hoped only for a cessation of the wind that turned his flesh to ice.

But in the ebbing of that gale an armored boot disturbed the ground near his head. A strong hand dragged him to his knees, up and up toward Azdra'ik's very face. He tried to get his feet under him, and Azdra'ik struck him across the mouth, bringing the taste of blood.

"You are an *expensive* bit of baggage, man. Shall I begin by breaking your littlest finger, and work up to your neck? I would do that ever so gladly." A second blow, harder than the last. "Stand *up*, damn you!"

He tried. Azdra'ik seized him by the hair and by that and a grip on his belt, half-dragged, half-carried him as far as Lwi. He staggered against Lwi's yielding body and groped after the saddle with the desperate notion of breaking for freedom, if he could only get a foot in the stirrup, if he could only find the reins, if Lwi could do more than stagger away from this cursed place.

Azdra'ik grabbed his shoulder and faced him toward him, his back against Lwi's shoulder. "You," Azdra'ik said, "you can walk, man. You richly deserve to walk."

"Where's Ela?"

"Oh, where is Ela? *Where is Ela?* Now we're concerned, are we?" The goblin flung him away and took Lwi's reins in hand as he staggered for balance.

"Fool," Azdra'ik called after him, and somehow he found the strength to walk, shaky as his ankles were. Azdra'ik had neglected even to disarm him. So had the witch, that was how much threat he was to them. He might draw the sword now and offer argument—he might die on the spot instead of later, less quickly. He was no match for Azdra'ik as he was: he suspected that not on his best day was he a match for a goblin lord—foolish Tamas, Tamas who had no natural talent with the sword, Tamas who was scarcely able to keep his feet under him at the moment, who needed all his effort to set one ahead of the other—he was cold, cold as if no sun would ever warm him. When he faltered, whenever Azdra'ik overtook him, Azdra'ik struck him and made him walk, but that he felt anything at all began to be welcome—anything to keep him awake and moving and on his feet.

"You cost too much," the goblin said again, hauling him up by the scruff when he had fallen. Azdra'ik struck him hard across the face and cried, in this space distant from the witch, "Do you know what you've done, man? Do you remotely comprehend what I paid for you?"

"A wish," he murmured through bloody lips, the only answer he understood; and Azdra'ik shook him.

"A wish. A wish. —She ruled this land when these trees were acorns, and she's not all dead, do you understand me? Wizards can be trouble that way, and among witches in this wood it's a plague! Didn't you see the warning in the forest? Didn't you apprehend there's something wrong in this place, before you went guesting in strange houses?"

Curiosity stirred, not for Azdra'ik's question, but for his own: incongruous curiosity, held eye to eye with an angry goblin, but pain seemed quite ordinary by now. "Why?" he asked Azdra'ik. "Why pay so much? What am I worth to you?"

A long-nailed finger jabbed his chest. "Because, thou innocent boy, if she had had the rest of you she would have gained *you*, and gaining you—gained substance in this world, among other things neither you nor I would care to see. But thou'rt mine, thou art *mine*, man—she can't touch the horse while I hold him nor touch me or thee by the terms we agreed to. So walk! You're bound to the witchling by magic nor she nor we can mend, and, by the Moon, you're going to find her!''

He did not understand. Bound? By magic? He stared stupidly at Azdra'ik, until Azdra'ik flung him loose, with:

''*Walk*, man, or *fall* down that hill, I care nothing which, but find her you will, so long as you have breath in you—don't look back, *don't* look back now!''

It was his worst failing, curiosity: the moment Azdra'ik said that, he could not but look back—and he saw the witch as if she were very far away, in the dark between the trees. Faster and faster she came as he watched—

''Fool!'' Azdra'ik shook him and spun him about to face him. ''Don't go back, you've no right to go back now, don't think of her!''

''I don't want to,'' he stammered, shaking with cold. It seemed when he shut his eyes she *was* there and he was *not* free . . .

''She can't claim you again unless you will it, man, don't think of her!''

''I'm not,'' he said, and it was the truth—he had rather Azdra'ik's company than the ghost's, for ghost she must be: Azdra'ik at least was living, and solid, and where he had been and what he had let touch him he wanted not even to think about now that he was clear of it.

''Then keep walking!'' Azdra'ik shoved him and he walked. But constantly he had a compulsion to look back, or to shut his eyes to see whether or not she was there—but it was not her, it was the goblin lord behind him, he convinced himself of that without looking back; he heard the constant meeting of metal and Lwi's four-footed stride in the leaves. He did not need to look over his shoulder, or even to blink so long as he could resist it—because at every blink of his eyes that place was waiting and at every weakening of his will that ghostly touch was brushing at his shoulder.

A light glowed through the trees, with a source beyond the next hill. The witch again, Tamas thought, reeling blindly through the dark—it seemed to him in his despair that they must only have gone in circles or that the witch had won and Azdra'ik was defeated, finally, fatally for both of them.

But the forest seemed to grow thinner as he went. Thorns and brambles grew more frequent. It was the east, he began to hope at last, the east, and the edge of the forest, and the faintest of rising suns.

He lost his footing in his anxiousness to reach it, skidded and fell—the second time, the third, he was not sure, a slide over dry and rotting leaves. He made it to his knees, hearing Azdra'ik behind him as sound and sense spun and whirled through his wits. He reached his feet, and Azdra'ik had not struck him. His next reeling steps carried him to a massive rock, from which he could see a dim gray dawn, a last fringe of trees, a vast and open valley: he launched himself down slope for that light and glorious sky with a first real belief he might escape.

An iron grip spun him about and slammed him back against the stone. Azdra'ik's hand smothered his outcry, Azdra'ik's whole armored weight crushed him against the stone, and for a desperate, bewildered moment he fought to get free, expecting the god knew what betrayal.

Then he caught from the tail of his eye a chain of dark figures crossing the open hillside below them.

Azdra'ik's enemies might well be his allies; that was his first thought. If he might free himself if only for a moment and attract their attention—but the least small doubt held him hushed and still. He felt a short, sharp movement as Azdra'ik jerked Lwi's reins, warning the horse to be still—and in only that small interval he saw more and more amiss in those figures down the hill, a foreignness in gait and armor.

Not men, he began to be sure now: they were goblin-kind, broader and smaller than Azdra'ik, like bears walking on two legs, armored and bristling with weapons.

"Those," Azdra'ik whispered, the merest breath stirring against his ear, "those are itra'hi, man, do you see the difference now?"

He tried to speak. Azdra'ik lifted his hand a little.

"No noise," he managed to whisper.

"Wise of you."

"Where are they going?"

"To mischief, always. Be still."

He was still. He watched until the goblins passed out of sight around the rock, and for a time after. Then Azdra'ik seized his arm and led him, Lwi's reins in his other hand, down a stony flat somewhat back of the track the goblins had crossed, and for the first time under the open sky.

Wooded hills rose on every side of them: huge boulders tended down to a straggle of grass and a dizzying prospect over a dawn-shadowed valley. It seemed to him that smoke stained the sky. Fires glowed within that smoke, hundreds of them, in a distance so far the eye refused the reckoning.

"Burdigen," Azdra'ik said. "Albaz."

"There's fire," he said faintly. "Why?"

"Have you never seen war, man? This is war."

"Against whom? Why?"

"Need there be a reason? That men exist. That the queen wants the land. *That* was the betrayal the witches of the Wood made inevitable."

"Why?"

"You do love that question. How can I know a human's thinking? Greed, perhaps. Or merely whim. A foolish witch wanted all that the queen had, and she tried to take it. While I—"

There was long silence. "What would you?" Tamas asked.

"I wanted what was ours," Azdra'ik said bitterly. "I wanted what was ours from time past. I thought there was a hope in humankind."

"Of what?"

"Of common sense." Azdra'ik seized his arm and shoved him along, and he saw no choice but walk—in a place made for ambushes, and not for silent passage with a shod horse.

The rising sun picked out the faintest of colors, warning them they were vulnerable; but if he were free this moment he could not face that woods now, or bear its shadow. The witch began to seem to him a recent dream, a nightmare in which he had not acquitted himself with any dignity or sense . . . but the consequence of it was with him, in the cut finger, the chill in his bones, the vision of the dark and that cottage at any moment he shut his eyes.

"I'll walk," he protested faintly, trying to free his arm. But he stumbled in the next step and Azdra'ik jerked him hard upright and marched him a hard course downslope and among the rocks.

"It's where they went," Tamas objected, and jerked at Azdra'ik's hold a second time. "Where are we going?"

"To our little would-be witch. The fool's using the mirror."

"How do you know that?"

"Does the sun shine? How do you *not* know? Are you numb as well as stupid?"

He did not know. He did not know how the goblin knew, except by smelling it or hearing it in some way human folk could not. "Why?" he began to ask, hauled breathless along the slope in the wake of what he had no wish to overtake, and with the vision of smoke and distant fires hazy beneath them. "Inside or outside the woods? What do you—?"

Another jerk at his arm, that all but lifted him off his feet. "Quiet!" Azdra'ik whispered, and led him down and down the hillside, all the time holding Lwi's reins in his other hand. On a steep, gravelly stretch Lwi slid past them and all but broke free. But Azdra'ik held on, the reins wrapped about his fist, and meanwhile gripped his arm so hard the feeling left his hand—stronger than a man, Azdra'ik was; but what Azdra'ik proposed to do on the track of a dozen of his enemies Tamas had no idea: no idea what Azdra'ik intended and no idea whether he was not better off drawing the weapons he still carried and trying the small chance they offered—

Were they going down there? he wondered. Were they going into war and siege? Nikolai's tales had seemed adventurous, distant, long-ago—but facing the fires in the haze across the plain, he found such destruction not romantic at all, rather a promise of terrors, in a land where goblins were the rule and humans were the prey. The fate of this valley might next spring be Maggiar's and the people suffering next year might be his own—while a goblin hauled him willy-nilly along the hill with what purpose he could not decide.

"I'll *walk*," he protested again, hoarsely, and jerked his arm to make the point. Azdra'ik did not let him go, but he kept his feet under him for the next dozen steps without wincing and Azdra'ik eased his hold.

Then without his asking or expecting it, the creature let him free.

He had thought he understood goblins, since Krukczy Straz—until this one, damn the creature, twice spared his life, and rescued him, and kept him on his feet last night, when sleep would have left him prey to . . . whatever he had dealt with in the deep woods. Did one stab in the back a creature who had thus far led him nowhere he would not go?

Not when he was doing very well to keep his feet under him, and skirting hill after hill in the very footprints of a goblin patrol, above a smoke-hazed overlook of cities under siege.

It was scarcely light outside when master Nikolai roused them out of sleep, gathered up all the things they could use and ordered Yuri to take Gracja's tack and get out of the hall—Karoly, poking up the fire in the fireplace, with no evidence whatsoever of breakfast in preparation, said he would follow, go on, get out, go with Nikolai and Krukczy as far as the gate: he had something yet to do and, no, he did not need help and he did not need boys' stupid questions this morning.

"What's the matter?" Yuri asked Nikolai while they were saddling Gracja. "Are goblins coming? Does he know where Tamas is?"

Master Nikolai said, "Does any wizard make sense, ever?" and ordered him to stop asking questions and go.

So they led Gracja out as far as the gate in the shivery half-light of morning, with Krukczy stumping along like a moving rag-heap, Zadny loping from one to the other of them and around and around Gracja's legs. Yuri found his teeth chattering, and told himself it was not fear that did that, he always did that when he slipped out in the morning cold without breakfast.

But what master Karoly was doing in there must be serious, the way he had snapped at them and wanted them out the doors before he started.

Maybe he was burning the tower down, so the goblins could not use it. He had heard that a general should do that, if a tower was likely to give an enemy a place to hold. But there was all of the forest around the tower, that could catch fire if that was the case, and burn all of them with it.

Surely he's thought of that, Yuri thought to himself, but one never knew about Karoly—sometimes he was fearfully absent-minded.

Maybe instead the old master was laying a curse of demons on the doors and locking the goblins out. Karoly was certainly a stronger wizard than they had ever believed in Maggiar: Yuri was in retrospect chagrined and on best behavior, thinking he and his friends at home had been lucky Karoly liked them.

"He's taking a long time, isn't he?" Yuri asked. But Nikolai gave him no answer and neither did Krukczy, who was sitting like a brown lump among the vines. Zadny whined and pressed close against his legs, nosing his restraining hands. Zadny was shivering, too, feeling the uneasiness, Yuri thought, the way he felt Nikolai's anxiety.

"Master Nikolai, what's he *doing* in there?"

"Wizard-work," Nikolai said, his jaw clamped so tight the muscles stood out.

Zadny whined. A wind began to rise. Brush crackled near them—that was Krukczy, heading away from them in a great hurry.

"Troll!" Nikolai said, and made a grab for him. "Krukczy! Troll! Come back here!"

But Krukczy was through the vines and out of their reach.

Came a sudden blast of wind and leaves began to fly and vines to whip about the wall like snakes, blowing loose around the open gateway. Came a dreadful wailing inside the yard, loose boards or something—Tamas had always said that was what made sounds like that in the night. It was loose boards.

Or owls. It might be owls.

Gracja tried suddenly to bolt. Nikolai hung on to her reins as she rolled her eyes and tried to stand on her hind legs. Then light burst inside the gates, light bright as noonday flooding out over the paving stones, casting the skulls and the poles into eerie shadow, as if the sun had invaded the tower. Wind shrieked. Dust flew into their faces and stung their eyes. It wasn't owls. It wasn't boards creaking. It was the shriek of iron bending, it was a roaring like flood coming down, it was cold, and the thump of loose shutters and banging pails and the gate hitting the wall.

"Come *on*," Nikolai shouted, starting to lead Gracja away. Gracja was more than willing to go, to run over him if she had her way—but, Yuri thought in dismay, they were deserting master Karoly, leaving him in that place with that banging and shrieking going on: and Nikolai would not do that. "Wait!" Yuri cried, "wait! He said—"

Nikolai only grabbed him by the arm, holding Gracja with his other hand, and yelled, above the wind, "Get on the horse!"

"We can't leave him!" he cried, but Nikolai yelled louder: "Get on the damn horse, boy, it's Karoly's business in there—he told *me* he'll follow us!"

He was used to moving when Nikolai yelled at him in that tone—his feet began to move, without his even thinking; and then he drew another breath to argue right and wrong. But whatever-it-was shrieked around the walls, scattering gravel from the crest, and Gracja was struggling to break away from them.

"It's wizard's business!" Nikolai yelled into his ear. "Get up on the horse and stay out of it!"

He found the stirrup and got on, while Nikolai held her—

Nikolai did not give him the reins; he began to lead her instead, while she was trying to get free and run. Bits of twigs and leaves were flying around them, Nikolai was hurting himself trying to run and hold on against Gracja's wild-eyed fright, and he could only duck down and try not to let a branch rake him off.

He hoped master Karoly was all right, he hoped Nikolai knew where he was going, he hoped—

He hoped they would only get to somewhere quiet and warm, because the wind was more than cold, it had the chill of earth and stone and it cut to the bone.

"He's in trouble in there!" he objected to Nikolai: if Nikolai had more confidence than that in master Karoly, he did not. But Nikolai kept them moving until they had left the stone wall behind. Then he gave up running, only limped along at Gracja's head in a wind-tossed dawn.

Zadny was still with them, Gracja had run her fright out, but anything could scare her into another panic; and Yuri had a cold lump of guilt lying at the pit of his stomach because he had been a boy and a burden. Nikolai had had to protect him, instead of helping master Karoly, Krukczy had run off from them, and Nikolai was doing the best he knew to get them somewhere—he began to understand that master Karoly had given Nikolai orders: Get the fool boy to safety, was probably what Karoly had said.

He slid off Gracja's back as she was still moving, hit the ground at Nikolai's heels. "Master Nikolai. You ride. You shouldn't have been running. . . ."

Nikolai gave him a look in the cold daylight, a drawn and dreadful glare—'run' was a sore word with Nikolai right now, he realized that the instant it was too late to swallow it.

He amended it, with a knot in his throat, "I know you'd have stayed if I wasn't there."

Nikolai kept walking, all the while casting him foul looks. "Maybe I wouldn't," Nikolai said. "Damned wizards shove you here and there and don't ask your leave. . . . Who's got a choice? Who's got a bloody choice, lately?"

"He magicked us to go?"

"He did or common sense did," Nikolai said. "Get back on that horse, boy. *Get on!*"

Nikolai made Gracja stop. Nikolai's pride was sorer right now than his arm was and it was not a good time to argue the point: Yuri scrambled back into the saddle and shut up, but it grew clear in his head that Nikolai had all along been put to bad choices. Nikolai would have gone after Tamas to the ends of the earth, if he could have, but he could never have made it alone.

And if wizards and witches were at work, it was a good job that Zadny had broken that rope, because otherwise Nikolai would be dead on the hill at Krukczy Tower, and Tamas would not have any help at all, that was the way he added it up—so he was *not* all to blame for things.

And, more to the point, Zadny had found a trail, running along with his nose to the ground, blundering into this thicket and that bramble, as if the wind, gentler once they were past the walls, were playing him tricks, but he was clearly onto something.

"He's following them," he said to Nikolai. "Tamas went this way—Zadny wouldn't follow, else."

"Good," Nikolai panted, not in good humor.

And finally: "Maybe we should slow down for Karoly," Yuri said, when Nikolai was well out of breath. "You said he was going to follow us. . . ."

"I don't know what the hell's following us! —No. We don't slow down. Damn that troll. 'It'll help you,' Karoly says; 'It'll go with you,' Karoly says . . . 'I'll follow you one way or another,' he says. Probably as right about the one as the other."

"There's tracks."

"I'm not blind. —Dammit!" Nikolai was in a great deal of pain, and Zadny crossed his path and bothered Gracja; but Nikolai would not agree to take his turn riding, not even after they stopped for rest and water.

So there was nothing to say—Zadny came back from an inspection of the area and tried to climb into Yuri's lap, whining and clawing at him, wanting to go on, and Yuri wrapped his arms around him to keep him out of mischief while they sat and rested. Nikolai's face was white and he was sweating, but he was clearly not going to listen to advice, or reason. In a moment more Nikolai got up, took Gracja's reins and told him to get on, and they waded the stream, where the horse tracks were clear—two sets of tracks, Nikolai had spared breath to tell him, which confirmed what he thought he saw; and on the other side they found horsehair snagged on thorn-bushes, where horses had climbed the bank.

"One white," Nikolai said, and added, short of breath, "It's the same ones we've been following."

But why was Tamas even going this way, instead of home, Yuri wondered, once they had found Karoly's sister dead?

And what had master Karoly said last night about a piece of mirror and the heart of hell? Everything he had overheard jumbled in his head. He had not understood all of it at the time, and now it slipped away from him in bits and pieces—

But Zadny was smelling something else as they went, shying back with his nose wrinkled and his hackles raised, and Nikolai squatted over the prints a second time. "What is it?" Yuri asked, about to get down to see for himself, but Nikolai shoved Zadny out of his way and got up.

"Someone wearing boots, moving at a fair pace. Someone a little taller than I am."

His heart sank. "That's not Tamas."

"No," Nikolai said, and led Gracja further down the bank, to thoroughly trampled ground. Horses had been back and forth here, had drunk, perhaps, had torn up the earth in deep, water-standing prints.

"That goblin Krukczy smelled?"

"Very probably. It's a narrow foot. And long."

He did not want to think about that, he did not want to wonder and to worry when he could not help—but there were other prints, and Zadny stayed bristled up and uneasy as they went.

But toward afternoon, and still following those tracks, they came to an old foundation, a well, overgrown with vines. People of some sort had lived near here, unless goblins had, and if Tamas and the witch were going anywhere looking for somewhere, this certainly began to look like more of a somewhere than the forest was. He began to imagine riding just around the bend of the water, finding another ancient tower, and a white and a black-tailed horse waiting safely in the yard.

What are you doing here? Tamas would say, all upset with him; and he would answer shortly that it was a very good thing he was, and they should go back and get Karoly: a witch and Karoly together ought to be able to deal with the goblins and they could all go home.

But he could not help thinking of Tajny Straz, and the skulls and the poles; and about that light and the wind that had broken out around the tower. When he thought about that, the whole forest seemed cold and menacing, and he began to hear every rustling of the leaves.

Something suddenly bubbled in the stream beside them, rose up with a rush of water and scared an oath out of Nikolai. It looked like a mass of water-weed, or a huge mop upside down.

Krukczy.

"Damn you, get up here!" Nikolai said. "What's happened to Karoly? What happened back there?"

Krukczy ducked under again and resurfaced somewhat downstream in a reedy area, just his eyes above water, his snaky tail making nervous ripples along the surface.

"I don't trust that thing," Nikolai muttered. "I don't trust it."

And just beyond where Krukczy was—

"There's *two* of them," Yuri exclaimed, and pointed, seeing a second lump in the water, another snaky ripple just beyond.

It vanished just as Krukczy did.

"Dammit!" Nikolai cried.

But Krukczy was not running away from them. He came squishing and dripping out on the shore further along beside a ruined wall, and a gateless gate. Before they reached him, Krukczy had shaken himself off and sat down to rest on one of the old stones; and Zadny had raced ahead of them and leapt all over Krukczy, getting wet as Krukczy patted him with huge hairy hands and tucked him into his lap, in curtains of dripping fur.

Then the second troll came out of the stream, shook itself, and came and sat down by the one they had now to guess was Krukczy.

"Well," Nikolai panted, leaning on Gracja's shoulder, next to his leg. "Well, now, we've got *two* trolls—they've sat down, and I suppose we wait here and hope Karoly makes it. Or we think of something. Or the goblins find us—in which case—" Nikolai caught a breath and looked about them, at their grassy space between the woods, the stream, and the ruined wall. "In which case I want us solid cover and a place to hide the horse. —Is that bow of yours any good, boy?"

"Yes, sir." He took it for leave to slide down, with the bow in hand. "It's Tamas' old one." He did not like this planning for goblins, as if they were a certainty. There was no tower beyond that wall that he could see, no door that they could bar, just the sky and the woods and the old stones around them. And he was tired, and scared, and cold, and there was no sign of Tamas but the tracks and a bit of horse-hair on a thornbush.

"Goblin was here," Krukczy said, holding Zadny in his arms. "I can smell him. Smell him lots."

"The same one?" Nikolai asked him.

"Followed them," Krukczy said, and the other troll bobbed its head in agreement.

10

"Hssst!" Azdra'ik said, catching Tamas' shoulder, and hauled him back to cover among the rocks, next to Lwi. There was not a sound but the horse and a bird singing somewhere near, in the late afternoon of this bad dream, on a long and rocky ridge. Then Tamas heard the faint jingle of metal, more and more of it.

"Another patrol." Azdra'ik extended his arm and pointed off along the slope. "I want you to go down and along that hillside, do you see?"

"Me."

"I'll keep the horse here."

"It's *my* horse. . . ."

"It's a large horse, fool. Go down there now and don't argue. Do you want him seen?"

"You're not going to eat him!"

"I much prefer young fools. —Get down there! Now!"

Tamas made a violent shrug, threw off Azdra'ik's hand and scowled into his face. "What is it you want? —Bait?"

Azdra'ik frowned at him, dreadful sight from his close vantage. "At least you stand a chance that way. —Take that damned thing away from her!"

"The mirror?"

"The mirror. The mirror. *Yes*, the mirror. Lady Moon, stand in a field and shout, why doesn't she? —Get down there, fool, before the rest of the world hears her business."

"How do *you* hear—"

Azdra'ik's hard fingers bit into his shoulder. "Because *you're* with me, because you resound of it, man, like a hammered bell; it bounces off every magic in the world, particularly if she wants to find something. That's why that patrol is hiking about the hills chasing its own tail. And that's why they haven't found her yet. But *you're* here with me, do you comprehend me yet? No? —Twice a fool. Go!''

He did not grasp Azdra'ik's purposes, but that patrol they had both seen he understood. That something had gone amiss with Ela's plans, he was sure; that Ela was making a magical commotion of some kind, he had Azdra'ik's word for it— and there was no question of her danger if the patrols found her. He scrambled away among the rocks, ignominiously dismissed, vowing he was going to live to rescue Ela, then take Lwi back and avenge himself on Azdra'ik ng'Saeich, sorcery and all—

But if Azdra'ik had told two words of truth, Azdra'ik wanted him for a way to obtain what a goblin dared not touch: he did not in the least believe that Azdra'ik meant to wait up here with his hands folded while he located Ela. It might be that Azdra'ik could not find Ela past the confusion he claimed existed. It might be that Ela's magic overwhelmed some sense goblins possessed and ordinary folk did not, and it might be that all that Azdra'ik *could* do now was to loose him like a shot in the dark—something about geese in the autumn, silly pigeons to their roost, he thought as he worked his way along the hill, exhausted and at wits' end. He had no more idea than Azdra'ik where he was going, he only hoped if there existed any shred of magic in him he would find Ela before the goblins did.

He passed along the long hillside, wary of ambushes. But perhaps Ela's magic did possess an attraction of its own, because something told him bear left and uphill, and, once he had gone far enough to have himself irrevocably confused, after the last split in the ridge, and once he had climbed down and up again, whether he was still on the same hill or not, he saw Skory's brown shape among huge pale rocks. The mare was still under saddle, grazing the coarse grass on the hillside.

He slid down the dusty slope toward the horse, losing skin

on his hands. Skory interrupted her grazing to look at him, then went back to cropping the grass, loyal horse, while there was no sign of her mistress.

He dared not call out. He only followed the impulse that had led him this far, walked along the hillside among the head-high boulders—and seeing shadow where no shadow should be, looked up, expecting a cloud overhead but there was none, just a darkening of the air and ground ahead of him.

I don't like this, he thought, and imagined some sorcerous goblin trap, but he could not think of going back. It was this way—he was sure enough to keep walking; and nothing visible threatened him, not the towering rocks, not the deadness of the grass or the leafless bushes. Perhaps by the sky above there ought not to be shadow on this ground, but it was no illusion: the air seemed colder as he walked, a wind began to blow, and when he looked back in unease, he saw nothing of the rocks he had just passed.

Worse and worse.

"Ela?" He dared not call aloud. He felt the cold more bitter than he had expected—whether it was the lack of sleep, or the dank chill in the air and the way things of magic tricked the memory. He had the feeling of walking toward some kind of edge, some place where everything he knew ceased.

Then there was that jingling of metal he had heard before, soft and growing louder: the patrol, he thought, and sought some place to hide. Dust whirled up on the wind, and through the veil of the wind came riders all in goblin panoply, banners flying indiscernible in the thickened air. He hid himself among the rocks as they streamed by him unseeing, riders on creatures shadowy and dreadful, with eyes of lucent brass and the sheen of steel about them—they passed, and the sound diminished to a thumping in the earth and in the stones, that itself faded.

The rocks remained. The dust did. He was uncertain of everything else: it fled his mind like a dream—they had been goblins, they had been men—he held to the solid stone and felt the world unpinned and reeling around him—felt the rock shift in his grip, thump! once and sharply, as if the earth had fractured, and might do so again.

He made himself let go of that refuge, while his heart said danger—he let go the stone and walked, then ran across the trembling earth, through the dust and the howling wind. The jolts in the earth staggered him. The ground was darker and darker ahead—the quaking rocks hove up like ruined pillars.

Beyond them the air was ice—and sound ceased. He came on Ela in a frozen swirl of shadow and dust, the wind stopped with her garments still in motion—the mirror blazing in her hands like a misplaced piece of the moon.

He reached for her—reached and reached above a widening gulf, as wind began to roar and move about them, storm that whipped Ela's cloak about him and his about her.

Ela struggled at the envelopment, struck at him and tried to escape; but he would not let her go—not her and not the mirror: it burned his hand with fire and with ice, and he would not believe in the dark or the wind any longer. He believed in the hillside, and Skory waiting, and the rocks and the morning sunlight, no matter the shapes that came to his eyes. Fool, his brother called him, fool who would not make up his mind, but he knew what safety was, he remembered the stones and the brush and the mare and the sun on the stones and he meant to reach that place.

Then it was quiet, and they were there, almost within reach of Skory. Ela tore at his hand to free herself and take the mirror back.

"Stop it!" he protested. "They're after us, for the god's sake, get on the horse, they can hear the magic—they're looking for you!"

"Don't ever," Ela gasped in fury, "don't ever, do you understand me?"

"Girl, they hear it, everyone hereabouts hears it—" He had not yet let go her hand or the mirror, and she had not stopped kicking and struggling to have it away from him. "Stop it! Listen to me!"

"Where were you? I *told* you stay with me, and you go

wandering into the woods—you're the cause of all this! I don't need your help! Let me go!''

All right, he thought, all right, others had told him so in his life—Bogdan said it: everything was his damned fault. But her shouting was going to bring trouble on them, and he could not hold on to a furiously fighting girl and catch the horse at the same time. He abandoned his argument and his hold on her and the mirror in favor of catching Skory before she bolted along the ridge.

But when he had caught the mare's reins, he looked around to find Ela disappearing straight up the slope.

He dared not shout after her. He muttered words only Nikolai used and hurled himself to Skory's back, out of patience with the mare's opinion what direction they should go, out of patience with contrary females altogether, and rode breakneck after the wretch, steeply and more steeply uphill, until he had to dismount and climb.

He had left Skory in a stand of scrub pine. Ela was not hidden. She was sitting down when he came up behind her, crying her eyes out, he could hear it—and he refused to be moved.

"Get up," he said. "Take the damned horse and the mirror and go where you like, I didn't come to rob you."

"I can't do it," she sobbed, "I can't do it, I wasn't strong enough . . . I lost the woods, I wasn't *there*—"

That was the first admission of truth he had had out of her—and, god, at this moment she looked no older than Yuri was.

He sat down beside her, weak in the knees, now that he had stopped running. She buried her face in her hands and sobbed for whatever reason stupid girls cried for—while he had a lump in his own throat, of self-pity, it might be, counting *he* had no prospects but the goblins hunting them.

"Look," he began, "crying's no good."

She made an effort to get her breath. "I was trying," she sobbed, "I was trying to find my way in the Wood, but it wasn't doing what it ought—nothing's done the way it ought ever since you came—"

"All right. All right, maybe that's so—but maybe mistress didn't know everything."

"You don't know!"

"That's not the point, Ela!" God, he could hear Nikolai shouting it at him and Bogdan on the practice field. "The point is, you're not winning, are you? You're not winning. *Maybe* it's my fault. *Maybe* I'm not going to do anything I ought to do. That's not the point either. What are you going to do to win?"

She swallowed a breath and another one—while her lips began to tremble and angry tears welled up.

"Don't dare," he said. "Don't you dare. You were left with a weapon, girl, a damned important one, by the commotion everyone's making over it. Azdra'ik wants it. Do you want him to have it? Or what are you going to do with it, now the first try's gone bad?"

"If mistress' brother hadn't gotten killed—if you were any help, but, no, you were off in the woods—if anything mistress told me had worked the way it was supposed to—"

"That's not the point either. What are you going to do to *win*?"

"You've no right to talk to me that way!"

She was the most maddening creature he had ever met, but the goblin lord himself. He was at the end of reason, and sanity. "Then take the horse," he said, not even angry now, only reckoning what he would be worth, and how long he would last as an obstacle once Azdra'ik caught up, or the patrol did. Longer, he thought, if he could get clear of Ela, by going afoot, and maintain whatever magical echoes Azdra'ik said confused goblin pursuers. "Just take the horse, get out of here, and good luck to you. I'm tired, I'm just very tired, Ela. If you're going to be a fool, go do it by yourself."

"I'm not a fool," she said, her chin trembling. "She didn't tell me how it was going to be, she just said it would work, go and do this and this and this, and if that didn't work—if that didn't work, I had to find a place where magic was . . . and we can't get into the Wood in the right place, I can't find the center of it—I don't know what to do!"

Her mistress was a liar, her witchcraft was a muddle of truth, misinstruction and guesswork, and nothing in her life had prepared Ela to guess for herself. Entirely reasonable that she offered no answers and no reasons, he thought: she had none for herself. And such chances as he had to take, he could not do with a fifteen-year-old girl hanging around his neck.

But another sort of coming-to-senses occurred to him, seeing she wanted to act the child: he pulled her up by the wrist, took her face between his hands and kissed the second pair of lips he had ever kissed, neither kindly nor gently, intending to finish it with a cold Goodbye, I'm leaving—after which, in his fondest and most foolish imagination, she would come running to his heels and ask his help; or at least grow up a week or two.

But came a curious giddy feeling—it might be the mirror or it might be something as mundane as his lack of sleep. He grew short of breath; Ela's arm had arrived somehow about his neck and he found himself doing exactly what the ghost had done—passing on what had happened to him. He began to draw back in dismay, but the look in her eyes was as astonished, as bewildered and as frightened as he had been, and her fingers were knotted into his collar and the fist with the mirror was clenched into his sleeve.

"I'm sorry," he found breath to say—from which beginning he did not know how to get to Goodbye. He blurted out, "I'll get you to your horse," and bundled her downslope where he had left Skory tied.

"I don't know where we're going," she said, putting the chain over her head.

"Where *you're* going," he said, and untied the reins.

"I am not!"

"Just get on the horse," he said, and faced her toward Skory's saddle. "Don't argue. And be careful. Azdra'ik's out there looking for you."

She had her foot in the stirrup. He shoved at a clinging mass of skirt and cloak, and she landed astride, with a frightened grasp of his hand.

"What have you to do with him?" she demanded. "What happened to you? —*Where were you?*"

"I met a ghost," he said, and intended to give Skory's rump a whack. But she still held his hand.

"Whose ghost?"

"Ylena. That was what Azdra'ik said. He said she owed him a wish. It was me he asked for, or I don't know what would have happened." Skory's restlessness was pulling at them, scattering shale from underfoot, and he had to move a pace to keep up with her. "Get out of here."

"No. —No, I'm not going without you, I *need* you!"

"That isn't what you said."

"I never said, I never said that. I tried to bring you back— I *did* bring you back, and you can't leave!"

"You worked magic on me? You put a spell on me?"

"I brought you back! I brought you out of the woods, I rescued you! You can't leave, I won't let you!"

Wait and see, was on his lips to say. That she had bespelled *him* was treachery. But the touch of her mouth was on his lips, and maybe it was a spell: he was still moving beside Skory's drift, with her stupidly holding his hand.

"*That's* why I couldn't stay," Ela protested, "*that's* why I couldn't find you, I couldn't work in that age of the Wood . . . Ylena's the worst ghost we could meet! She's the witch who started the curse! She wants the magic! —Tamas, you can't stay here, you can't stay near this place, neither of us can! She's too powerful in the Wood, mistress didn't know that. She wants the mirror, that's what's gone wrong— She's planned this forever—"

He all but tripped over a bush trying to keep up with the mare, and fell behind, but no longer with the notion of going back and disputing passage with a goblin. He began to follow at Skory's tail, with the deep woods of yesternight too close in memory, and a shadow whispering in the dark, saying that there was no freedom from the magic the witches of the Wood had already made.

"So where else can we go? Do you know?" They were

not headed back into the woods, but further along the hillside. "Ela?"

(A place of power, Tamas. My place is strongest, and safest. They dare not kill me, by the spell that binds them here, they dare not—I *am* your ally, if you would only listen. . . .)

He stumbled, so clear the voice was to him, like a memory of something he had never heard, something that had to do with that place behind his eyelids. He was cold through and through, he was lost in dark—

Azdra'ik! he called in that dark territory, and for a heartbeat believed Azdra'ik his hope and his safety—but that was a fool's thought, a dangerous thought—god, if Azdra'ik should have heard him . . . if the witch had . . .

God, no, he had escaped that embrace once—he had no desire to court it again, no desire even to think about it. He overtook Skory and limped at Ela's side. The sky had gone to milk and brass. His chest burned, and from brass the sky went to palest violet against the ragged shadow of the pines. Ela drew Skory to a walk in the slight cover of the trees, and he found a saddle-tie to hold to, half-blind with exhaustion, stumbling on the crumbling shale—while something within him said, dark and cold as night—Tamas. You can trust me. It's my own interest, Tamas, as well as yours, your defeating her is in my interest, and I've no quarrel with the girl—

Listen to me, Tamas. . . .

Curse all witches who made this folly, he thought in distraction. Curse the ignorant witch who had taught Ela by guess and by supposition: he had that clear now, too: Ela had had reason to be distraught, realizing of a sudden that all her resources were unreliable—so she looked to him?

Gran, he thought, and could all but see that charm-hung tomb in the rocks of Maggiar: Oh, gran, if spells are at work here—if her mistress has lied—if one ghost can harm us—I know you wouldn't. Can you hear me, gran, where you are? I need you, if you can hear me.

Foolish way of thinking—expecting magic, thinking that

gran could possibly hear him . . . he was down to such boyish imaginings.

But would not magic work that way? Was that not what a
wizard was for—to demand the impossible of the world?

The peasants did—the country-folk came with their barley-
straw men and their offerings of food and their requests for
children. . . .

What had gran to do with that? What had gran to do with
them?

If gran's ghost *could* come back, she would stand between
him and that apparition of bone and shadow—gran would
never abide threats against what she called her own.

But where did he begin thinking such foolish things? As a
shield against the dark? As a wizard-wish? Or a boy's longing
for gran's stories not to have been lies—when everything
around him spoke of desolation and death. Gran's sunlit
woods, gran's bright towers and gran's fields and villages
and gran's faery. When was it so? Why fill her grandsons'
heads with such hopeless, bare-faced fables? Was it an obligation of witches to deceive? Was that all that magic was?
He had never felt that in Karoly.

Gran had crossed the mountains and gotten children with
the lord of Maggiar—or—whoever his grandfather was. . . .

Why? To escape the folly the witches here had done? But
why *lie* about what was here?

Because below them now was devastation. And Ela went—
lord Sun knew why or where: he doubted she knew, except
it bore them away from the hunters, and away from the
haunted woods.

There was a hot supper, even a decent one. Nikolai insisted
on making a small fire at sunset, saying if goblins smelled
the smoke, they were apt to smell horses and human beings,
just as likely, and tea and flat-cakes would put spirit in a
body—but supper lay like a lump in Yuri's stomach. The
trolls had gone off somewhere—into the stream, most likely.
Zadny had had a flat-cake and part of his, and was off inves-

tigating a frog or something at the water's edge, among the reeds.

The time was, not so many days ago, when he would have been over there himself, as lively and as curious as Zadny, inclined to poke about with sticks in the water and turn over rocks, but right now he thought that he had seen enough strange things to satisfy him for months and months to come. He wished the trolls would come back, he wished the wind did not sound so lonely in the treetops; and he understood why Nikolai was sharpening his sword, scrape, scrape, scrape, but that was not a cheerful sound, with the wind and the sighing of the tall trees and the flicker of what was, after all, a very small fire against the night in a probably haunted place.

Most of all he wished he had some idea where Tamas was tonight, and whether Tamas had had a good supper.

And what had become of Bogdan, to be evenhanded about it. He knew he should feel dreadfully guilty for being glad it was Tamas they had a chance to find. Unquestionably he would still be here if it was only Bogdan they were tracking . . . he had gone out from home and over the mountains when it had been just Zadny, for the god's sake, so he had no question about his courage or his resolution on his brothers' behalf, but he had never considered before now that he really would not miss Bogdan that much if he could only find Tamas alive, and he did not think that made him out a very honest boy, when it came down to it.

He had found out a lot of things about himself since he had set out across the mountains—he had always thought of himself one way, that he did not have to be serious, *he* was not the heir to Maggiar. He would always be the youngest and he could do fairly much as he pleased in his life.

But Maggiar seemed very far away tonight, even if it was the same sky and the same stars over them. All the things he had used to do and all the friends he had used to have and all the things he had used to be interested in were on the other side of mountains—on the far side of sights none of the other boys had seen and experiences the other boys would never have, that was the truth of it. Tamas had given him his bow and he liked holding it now. He felt better for touching it, as if, as long as the wood was warm against his hands, things were not so bad.

It would grow cold if Tamas should die, that was the stupid kind of thing the ballad-makers said; but he had seen so much of magic in this place he was not so sure it was all stupid. He felt better if he had something of Tamas with him tonight, so maybe anything would do. Maybe the stories had something true about them, and it mattered less what it was one held to than how hard one thought about the person. Maybe if he could hold it tight in his arms and think of Tamas very, very hard, he could make him hear him:

We're here, we're looking for you, don't give up and don't do anything stupid. . . .

The wind whipped up of a sudden, a dreadful, sudden blast that chilled the air, that blew even the blankets into a rolling tumble and the fire into a trail of sparks and embers. Gracja whinnied in alarm and Nikolai leapt to his feet.

"It's the wind!" Yuri cried, cold through and through, and trying to stop the blankets and the pan from flying away, while Nikolai was grabbing after Gracja. "It's the same wind—"

Things that had started flying toward the gate started blowing back again, as if by magic—a gale was blowing from out of the gate, too, with equal force, and Yuri felt it hit from both sides at once, blowing his hair and his cloak straight up and around and around, and when he had fought himself clear of the cloak and prisoned it in his arms he saw the cooking plate fly up into the air, high as the trees, and come back down with a clang.

He stared at it, in a sudden silence, in the starlight. And looked up at a disheveled figure standing on the shore, at an old man in a pale cloak, with his hair all unkept, a man—

Lord Sun—it was master Karoly, walking as if he were very, very frail . . . or hurt.

Zadny ran up to him—shied back again, circling about in bewilderment, at master Karoly's feet.

"Karoly?" Nikolai asked cautiously, and Karoly kept walking slowly, until he had gotten to the flat rock where they had made their fire. The wind had died. So had the fire, once, but it immediately sprang up again at Karoly's feet, with no cause that Yuri could see.

"Master Karoly?" he said, advancing cautiously, Zadny close about his knees. "Master Karoly?"

"I would very much like some tea," Karoly said in a faint, hoarse voice.

Tea, Yuri thought, and remembered the pan falling, and ran to get it, while Nikolai came near, stuck his hands in his belt and remarked, "Hell of a woman, your sister."

"God," Karoly said, with a shudder Yuri could see from there. He swept up the pan and filled it with water from the brook and came and balanced it on the fire at Karoly's feet.

But Karoly was talking to master Nikolai, saying something about his sister, and when Nikolai asked how things had gone, master Karoly said only: "Not totally—as I'd hoped. It's Ysabel. I've kept her company . . . all the way from Tajny Straz. But I think it's Pavel, too—he wasn't altogether sane. I'd hoped . . ."

Master Karoly was shaking. Yuri grabbed up a blanket from its grassy tangle, shook it out, and master Nikolai put it around Karoly's shoulders.

"She got ahead of me," Karoly went on, and his voice was so faint and strained it was scarcely louder than the creaking of frogs in the brook. "I'm afraid she's reached something else, something *here*, that shouldn't be. Her and Pavel. This was his home. —I would really like supper, Nikolai. I don't think I can do any more."

The sky lately ablaze with colors had gone to dark as they picked their way along the barren heights, seeking the cover of scrub and rocks as much as possible. A faint smell of smoke was on the wind. In the valley below, the sullen glow of goblin siege-fires made constellations and clusters of hellish stars, and the number of those fires, Tamas did not know how to reckon. He only knew that Maggiar could never withstand that tide once it lapped up against its eastern borders. Those lights went on and on to the horizon, where the hills narrowed in, and beyond, for all he could tell: campfires, the burning of human homes and livelihoods, the god knew.

(Many, the voice within him said. They have no mercy.)

He tried not to listen, resisted even blinking as much as he could, the dark around him matching so well the dark behind his eyes. Hard enough to keep walking, hard enough to keep his ankles from turning or his knees from failing. In the easier places, he clung to Skory's saddle-strings and guided himself by that, because his wits were so muddled and weary he tended to nod even while he walked. He suffered dark moments in which he was aware of nothing, no ghostly voices, no visions, just dark, and rest, and that, he thought in his muddled way, might be the witch trying to lull him into trusting sleep. She could afford to bide her time, knowing a man had to rest, had to, when he had not since . . . he had lost count how long it had been since he had dared even shut his eyes.

The ghost had shown him Bogdan—shown him his brother in goblin hands and he had not stayed to ask her whether that vision was true—he had had a sword by him in that cottage and he had clawed his way out the door and fled without even thinking of it, when, if he had been a man, he might have threatened her into telling him the truth, he might have learned enough to help them right there, and he might not then have needed Azdra'ik's rescue, or lost Lwi, or ended up where he was, running for his life with no notion even where he was going.

His footing failed him. He caught himself on Skory's saddle, or thought he had, except he came awake in the dark, flat on his back on cold stone, with a shadow leaning above him.

He was back in the troll's den, he had waked again and it was back—

"Tamas?" Ela said from out of that shadow. —Ela's hands were the hands touching his face. He had to recall where he was, and he almost longed for the troll, and the cellar, instead of the hillside, and the fires, and the flight.

"I haven't used the mirror," she said in a faint voice. "I'd rather not. Tamas, Tamas, are you all right?"

He had a bump on his head. He must have fallen when he reached for the horse—or he might have walked a ways blind and numb, for all that he knew. It was no matter. He was lying down and he had to get up and go on, but even a moment of rest was to cherish. He drifted, half-waking, aware of Ela, thinking that, except the lump on his head, he was more comfortable right now, and closer to sleep, than he had been in days.

"Tamas."

"I know. I know. I'm moving." But it was hard to move at all, and he lay there collecting breaths for the attempt, or however many attempts it might take. Then that tingling feeling began again, and a flickering glow like marshfire fluttered over Ela's arms, over her heart and throat and almost to her face—mirror-magic. She shouldn't do that, he thought, it's my fault she's doing that, I have to get up—

He tried. He began to rise on one arm, and got as far as one knee when he heard that faint sound of metal he had heard before. His heart sank. He snatched at Ela's hand, wanting no more magic, wanting quiet.

"It's a patrol. Quiet." He saw Skory's shadow, and got up as quickly and quietly as he could. Skory stood with head up and ears pricked—he caught her reins and put his hand above her soft muzzle, distracting her, cajoling her.

For a very long time there was nothing—only that sound, and Skory's alarm, and the soft, soft sound of Ela's cloak and skirts as she came near to wait.

Maybe the patrol was on the other side of the hill, he thought, maybe it was an echo from somewhere, and they were safe within their little cluster of scrub pine and brush.

Then, looking up the hill through the twisted pine boughs, he saw the flash of metal by starlight and the moving of shadows along the slope.

"Hobgoblins," Ela whispered, faint as breathing.

The small ones, he thought; the ones Azdra'ik compared to beasts. The ones that had taken the towers, and left them guarded by human heads when they abandoned the places they had taken, not even caring to occupy them. He kept his hand on Skory, felt her nostrils flare and her head toss in alarm as a wayward breeze carried goblin scent to her—it was not a greeting he had to fear from her, it was a sudden bolt for safety.

And thank whatever god watched them, the wind, that skirled so unpredictably in these cuts and crevices in the hills, was in their faces at the moment—goblin noses might be keen enough to smell them. Goblin hearing might pick up their least movement.

But for eyesight—the one in the cellar of Krukczy Tower had missed him, while these . . . these tramped down the hill and passed so close, so close to them at the worst moment that there was only a clump of brush between them and the goblin column, and they still did not see, nor smell, nor hear them. The foremost led the way downhill and the others followed, shadows sheened with figured steel and bristling with bows and spears, that diminished on the slope, and filed away into the dark approach to the valley.

Support for the siege of human towns, he thought, beset with a shiver now that the danger was past. He let go Skory's reins, wiped his hands on his sides, and felt he could breathe again.

"The hills must be full of their armies," he said in a hushed voice, and felt his knees trembling with exhaustion. For his part he would insist they keep going under cover of darkness, but Skory had had her own troubles at the last, had had to consider climbs carefully—Skory had had little rest herself, by day or by night, and, he thought distractedly, perhaps they should leave her and go afoot.

But she was goblin-bait for certain if they did that, and he was by no means certain they ought to go on in the haste they had been using.

(Go back, something whispered in him. Yes, go back. Bring the mirror back to the woods, Tamas. That's the only hiding place.)

He saw the ghost for the instant, white and drifting among the trees. He was not even sure he had had his eyes shut—he thought that they were open, but he could only see the dark, and that figure, and when a rock met his shin, he felt it over with his hand and sat down, propping his elbow on his knee and trying to rub sight back into his eyes, rubbed and rubbed and tried to banish that persisting vision in favor of the hillside, and Ela, and the ordinary rocks and shadows.

Stop it, he ordered the ghost, stop it, let me go, you swore to Azdra'ik—

A hand touched him and he flinched from it, thinking it was the ghost, but the rattle of pebbles agreed more with the hillside, and with the rock he had chosen as his anchor in the world, it felt more like Ela's touch, and he became sure of it when it slid to his hand and closed on his fingers—it was warm and fleshly, and it wanted his attention, sharply *insisted* on his attention.

(Two innocents, the voice within him said. Two damned *fools*.)

He jerked his head, thinking as forcefully as he could, Go away! And, beside him, Ela—

Ela slipped her hand from his and rose to her feet in silence. He could see her when he looked up—he saw her walk away from him as far as where Skory stood, and stand there, looking out into the dark. He felt a wall between them, as cold, as palpable as stone. He felt—a memory on his lips, that foolish moment he had thought to teach Ela a lesson. His mouth burned with it. It might have been an instant ago. Foolish, foolish exchange, with a witch . . . with the

witch of the Wood, no less with all that name seemed to
mean in this land, in this war—

He saw the pale edge of Ela's face appear from the
shadow of the cloak, like the moon from eclipse, felt her
eyes on him, a regard both intimate and dangerous, as if—
as if trust and mistrust and all she knew hovered only on
that moment.

He wanted to be nearer to her—he could not decide to get
up, and before he could persuade his weary legs to move,
Ela walked back to him, arms hugging the darkness of her
cloak tightly about her.

"Something happened to you," she said—as well say he
had committed every treason imaginable, it was that tone of
voice, it was that feeling in the air between them.

"I told you," he protested.

"I can *hear* you."

He was too weary for puzzles. But she meant more than
the words, she meant something dangerous, she meant
treachery and lies and the fragile hope that he was not lying.

He shook his head desperately. He did not understand, he
wanted her to know he did not understand even what she was
talking about.

"The way you hear magic," she said. "The way you—
know it. I *hear* you."

"Couldn't you always?" Nothing made sense to him. But
he was sure of things he did not know how he knew, he was
guessing things he could not possibly know, he remembered
her arms about him and how in the last few moments he had
felt her presence near him like a shadow in the wind, all in
the desperation and scatter-wittedness of the moment—he
was dreaming now. He had lost his sight or he had already
been dreaming then, and he was sitting on a real stone on a
real hillside looking up at her, but he was only dreaming of
Ela, as a man drowning in witchcraft might reach out to a
safer presence and a safer dream. Don't go away, he wished
her. The witch will come back. I can't shut my eyes but what
she comes back.

Ela turned her back on him, perversely left him prey to

the dream—but she stopped, then, and turned back and looked at him in such a way he knew she was not deserting him, he knew that she was angry at the ghost and not at him, and he could not remember if he or she had just said a word aloud—god, he prayed it was not a permanent condition, this listening, this—rawness of the soul that felt Ela's shadow, balanced dread of the ghost and fear of her own anger and her own impulses toward him, forbidden things, forbidden closeness—a witch did not care, a witch did not *this*, and did not *that*, mistress had always told her, and most of all a witch did not harbor such longings to be touched, or held, or to rest safe, with just someone, *anyone*, once in her life to hold her.

He would hold her—he would do anything she asked, anything but feel that lonely—he had never *been* alone, he had had brothers, he had had parents, he had had Karoly, he had never known such a feeling, except in the troll's den—but she turned abruptly away, and gave him her profile, pale as starlight. She stared into the night and her loneliness welcomed the shadows, the way mistress had taught her. Her presence cooled to ice.

"You didn't know," the child-woman said at last, the merest whisper. "Magic always had to be in you: the mirror knew. I know you didn't lie to me, but something's happened, somebody's made it happen—you're—hearing—me, aren't you?"

"I don't know what you mean," he said in frustration, but he already knew she meant the magic, and knew he knew—but he had no idea whether it was something that had broken out in him, or something someone had done to him, or it was good or it was bad, or whether it was the ghost's doing, some shameful mark of his near debauch and rescue—he was beyond his own understanding, utterly, afflicted with ghosts and with thoughts and feelings that were so certain and so utterly unproven to reason that he could not draw a line between what he had dreamed or what he had done. "I don't know what I'm hearing, I don't know what's going on in me."

His fear leapt to her like fire, and died, starved of substance, chilled to death while she gazed into the goblin-haunted dark—no, she did not want to be touched, now, to need that was weakness, and she was not weak—while he—he had meant no affection in laying hands on her or in kissing her lips, he had not come here to court some girl while his home was at risk, he was not so shallow as that, please the god, he was not such a fool, if only he knew whether it was his thought or hers that chilled his impulse to go to her and hold her. If he should touch her now, she would become more dangerous to the world than the ghost in the Wood; if he should want the things she wanted, he would never know his own thoughts again; if he should fly away to the ends of the earth this instant, it would make no difference: she would go on hearing him forever.

"Don't," Ela said faintly, still without looking at him—if she had looked at him just then her glance would have burned him like fire—Then the world jolted, thump! back to earth and rock, and Ela standing distant from him. After a moment more she did look at him, came back and sat down by him. Then he looked away, himself, not to start it all again. He felt precariously balanced, and he only wanted to lie down and sleep and wake out of the dream that had so many discordant parts in it—perhaps he *was* still sleeping, perhaps he was still in the troll's den, perhaps it would come back soon and he would not have to concern himself with solutions or escapes.

No, not asleep, yet. He caught himself from falling with a jerk of his head, which proved the case, and did the same thing again, thinking quite calmly that it was most unusual to fall asleep terrified, and that he was quite close to falling and adding another lump to his head, if that first one was real.

He simply could not open his eyes this time. He slid down sideways, with the whole night spinning, and tried to open his eyes, for fear of the ghost, but he felt the warmth of a cloak cast over him, and a living body next to him, and a weight on his arm. It seemed Ela was making a pillow of him, and hurting his bruises, but they were mostly numb: it was not that which he wanted to object to her—it was that it was no place and no time to rest, and that there was a ghost trying to find him in his dreams. She should magic them both awake . . .

But sleep was a weight he could not move this time, not even to lift his hand to wake her.

11

SUPPER SEEMED TO HELP. YURI THOUGHT TO HIMSELF THAT master Karoly must have been all day without food, and small wonder, then, he looked so vastly overcome: it was *not* all the ghosts, Yuri tried to convince himself. Fear was not the reason master Karoly's hands shook and rattled the knife against the pan. But Nikolai did not look cheerful in Karoly's arrival, and Zadny butted his head in Yuri's lap and tramped him with his huge paws, unwilling to be separated from him by so much as an arm's length—nor had the trolls come back, since the wind and the ghostly presence, and Yuri did not blame them: if he had not known Karoly, and known Nikolai, he might have run off, too.

"So what do we *do*?" Nikolai asked when Karoly set the plate aside. Yuri was very glad Nikolai asked questions like that. He had sat ever so long in his life waiting for grown-ups to ask questions like that.

"We see if we can get her back again," Karoly said.

"Who, your sister?" Nikolai asked.

"No telling. No telling what we'll get now. Ytresse was here. Ylysse was." Master Karoly took a stick and began stirring the fire around, sending up sparks in streams into the dark. "Ytresse was before Ylysse, Ylysse was the first of our time—Ysabel knew her. But Pavel—Pavel—*he* has to be one of the ones in the mix."

"What mix?" Yuri asked faintly, figuring everyone would tell him to shut up, they always did.

"The ghost," master Karoly muttered absently. "Ysabel's in pieces. Bits of her, bits of Pavel . . . Ytresse held this place after it fell, while Tajny Straz was building. And Ylysse. And Ylena. I wouldn't except any of them.''

"Who are they?" Yuri wanted to know, but Nikolai got up from the fireside and stood behind him, his hands on his shoulders. "The castelan. Dead witches," Nikolai said under his breath, not interrupting Karoly, whose meddling with the fire had not ceased.

"Attract her into a whole," Karoly muttered. "Ysabel's— diffuse right now. That's why you can't find ghosts." Sparks flew up. An ember snapped. "It takes passion to make a haunt. Murder, violent death, tragic death . . . that, oh, yes, yes, she had." More sparks. "Ysabel? Ysabel? Do you hear me, sister? It's Karoly calling you."

The sparks from the fire seemed to hang too long in the wind, to dance and swirl and come together like a congregation of fireflies.

"Then the obsessed ones," Karoly said, still stirring, still sending up stars, "the ones that can't turn loose of the world—that's Ysabel, too, that's certainly Pavel. I think that's Ylena."

Nikolai's fingers bit painfully into Yuri's shoulders and Yuri held his breath, unable to look away from that aggregation of sparks. He heard Zadny whining and growling, he felt the hair on the nape of his neck lifting and he wanted to run, except master Nikolai's fingers were bruising his shoulders.

A shadow rushed at them, a shadow shaggy with brown hair burst through the fire scattering embers, and turned and hissed and spat.

"Krukczy!" Yuri breathed, while Krukczy brushed at the singes to his coat, and spat and fussed, the other side of the fire, in the dark. Zadny barked, once and sharply, and Yuri hushed him.

But the magic had stopped. "Damned troll's right," Nikolai said in a low voice. Master Karoly had gotten to his feet, turning slowly to survey the woods, the ruined wall, the dark along the stream. The other troll had shown up, too. It huddled in the reeds.

"Damn," Karoly said, flinging out a gesture of disgust, and paced a wide circle. "Damn, and damn, Ysabel, don't be contrary, do you hear, don't be contrary! Do you want the goblins to get away with it? Is that what you want? To spite me, is the queen going to get away with what she did to you? With what they did to *Pavel*? He's dead. He's there with you. So are others, Ysabel, for the Lady's sake figure it out!"

Yuri flinched, because master Nikolai was hurting him—and it seemed to him now that the sparks were getting up on their own, that they were making a shape.

And the old man rounded on it. "Ysabel?"

The fire blew up and sparks showered and whirled in trails of glowing smoke, up and up and up, until it made a shape, or shapes, all rolling and twisting like snakes.

"Pavel," Karoly snapped, "get out of the way! Do you hear? You're not protecting her, you're in the way, do you hear me?"

A thread spun off, and snaked around and around the center shape.

"Ysabel!"

Sparks flew every which way, and of a sudden a great wind blasted through their midst. Sparks stung Yuri's face and hands, and Zadny barked and growled at something as Nikolai let go his hold and swore.

Trails of glowing smoke spiraled all about the stream bank, raced along the walls, wove among the trees, and spun faster and faster. Nikolai had his sword, but there was nothing a sword could fight, only the wind, and of Krukczy and his friend there was no sign at all.

Then came a voice that might be a woman's voice, Yuri could not tell. It was everywhere, and terrible, and a face loomed up right in his face, saying, "Who are *you*?"

He did not think he ought to answer. He stood still, while Zadny leaped and tried to bite it, but Karoly said sternly, "Ytresse! Is it Ytresse?"

The swirl broke apart and spun elsewhere, around and

around and around the circle of firelight, and suddenly rushed from everywhere at once, up and up, until it made a shape.

"Ytresse!" Karoly shouted. "You've no business here. Begone! *Ysabel! Urzula!*"

"That's gran's name," Yuri exclaimed, twisting to see what Nikolai might know. "What does gran have to do with it?"

"Maybe she wants her right name," Nikolai muttered, which made no sense. Nikolai was looking at the fire, over which, when he looked back, a shape hovered, and changed, until it was a woman's face, and another woman's, and a man's, Yuri could not tell which—they blurred one over the other and the features changed like pictures in glowing coals.

"To the queen," the image said, in its double voice, "to the queen, to the queen—the mirror of what is and may yet be—to the queen—the mirror of the moon, change fixed unchanging—" It said more than that, but more and more voices chimed in until nothing came clear.

Karoly ventured close to the fire—scarily close, Yuri thought: he would not have done that; close enough to pick up a burning stick and trace patterns in the air, patterns which stayed in the eye like the sun at noon. Letters, Yuri thought. Writing, all tied together in knots. The letters turned around and around the way the smoke did, and then streamed, *streamed*, large as they were, right to Karoly's open hand. The smoke followed the letters and the sparks followed the smoke.

Then there was just the fire, and Karoly leaned on his staff and sat down, plump! where he was, head hanging, in front of a tame, quiet campfire.

"So?" Nikolai wondered under his breath. "So? Did it *do* anything?"

Good question, Yuri thought. Excellent question, master Karoly would say. Nikolai gingerly let him go and walked over to where master Karoly was resting. Yuri followed, with Zadny crossing repeatedly in front of him and jumping at his hands. "Go away!" he told Zadny, and grabbed him before he bothered master Karoly, who did not look at all well.

"What was *that*?" Nikolai asked Karoly, and Karoly, with a deep breath:

"My sister. And Pavel. Together. Mostly. Ytresse. Ylysse. Lady Moon, what have I called?"

"So could you talk to her? Dammit, old man, could you find so much as where Tamas went? Did he go through the arch?"

"Oh, that they did," Karoly said, "that they most certainly did."

"Then let's go after them!" Yuri said. But no one listened. Nikolai muttered something about if Karoly had taken care of things the way he should, and Karoly said something about people needing to deal with what was instead of what could have been, and that sounded dangerously close to a fight.

"Stop arguing," Yuri cried, and to his surprise both of them stopped talking and looked at him. "My brother needs help," was all he could think to say. "If the ghosts won't help us, if magic won't, then we have to go there ourselves, don't we?"

"Not in the dark," Nikolai said.

"Not in the dark," Karoly agreed, and got up, leaning heavily on his staff, and began to draw a line in the dirt and in the grass.

Why? Yuri wondered. But it looked like what boys drew in the dirt when they were going to fight, or a line nobody was supposed to cross. And when master Karoly drew it, he thought, things had better think twice about crossing it. He went and brought Gracja closer, where she could be inside that line when it closed, and all the while Zadny kept at his heels.

All the way about a huge area, master Karoly went, drawing his line. And he came back and muttered something at the fire, which flared up and ran a tendril of smoke out and out and around and around them like a wall.

"We left the trolls outside," Nikolai said, "good riddance."

"They can come and go," Karoly said.

"Fine. Then what good is it? Trolls can come and go. Can ghosts?"

"Not if I can prevent it."

"Well, it's not damn much good at all, is it?"

"You didn't build it, master huntsman. Let's see your line, let's see you defend it."

"Don't fight!" Yuri cried, angry at both of them.

"Listen," Nikolai said, ignoring him, "one—*one* troll was useful. Two of them we don't need. Why are there suddenly two of them? What do we need with two?"

"Because Hasel had one," Karoly said. "Every civilized place has one."

"No place that I was," Nikolai said.

"Then you were never anywhere civilized! And they have them north of here, I have every authority for it."

"Bogles in the hayloft," Nikolai said.

"And the bath-house. And the grain-bins. And the fields and the milking-sheds and the cellars."

"Those aren't trolls."

"It's the same thing!"

"They haven't any tails! I never saw a polevik with a tail!"

"Have you ever seen a polevik?"

Evidently Nikolai had not. Nikolai sulked, and rubbed his arm and paced. Then he said, "So have we got any help from your sister, or what?"

"I don't know," Karoly said. "I don't damned well know, I'm not going to know until we go in there, it's not an ordinary woods."

"It's not an ordinary woods."

"It's not."

"Well, fine, what's not ordinary about it? Ghosts?"

"You might say," Karoly said, and Yuri sat down slowly and put his arms around Zadny. He had seen all of ghosts he wanted to see today. But if Tamas was the other side of that place, or lost in there, well, he was going, and he did not want to call attention to himself or raise any question between master Karoly and master Nikolai about him not going and one of them staying to watch him. There were times, if one was a boy, it was a good idea not to be noticed. So he let them quarrel with each other, and like Zadny, he just kept still.

Things went more than bump in the night, they moaned and they whispered, and they hissed in the leaves, they croaked and they creaked in the brook and the brush, and they trod on ghostly feet, disturbing the leaves around about the line master Karoly had drawn.

What do ghosts do when they get hold of you? Yuri wondered. But no one yet had said anything about taking him home, so he lay still, shivering in his blanket, and hoping that last noise was Gracja stirring about, *inside* their circle. Zadny was bedded down with him and Zadny was asleep. The trolls had not shown up again, and he wished he could think they were part of what was going on out there, but he feared that Krukczy had indeed found his brother, or whatever made his going worthwhile. He was glad for Krukczy if that was the case. He hoped that he would find Tamas tomorrow.

Hello, he would say, when they rode up on Tamas. Tamas would be surprised, and angry, but over all glad to see him. Tamas would be impressed with what he had done and his keeping his promise—no, truth, Tamas would be furious at him for leaving home and worrying their parents and losing Zadny in the first place; but Tamas would forgive him, because Tamas would be very glad he had brought master Karoly and master Nikolai, who were help Tamas must have given up on—whatever Tamas was doing, whatever he was into, running off with witches.

Probably he was looking for Bogdan. If Tamas had gotten out in one piece, he would be doing that. Or possibly Tamas was trying to do whatever master Karoly was supposed to be doing, that his sister had wanted of him; so master Karoly's sister should not mind helping them, if master Karoly could make her understand.

And what was that master Karoly had said, using gran's name? People said gran had come from over-mountain, and people said gran had been odd. The boys said gran had been a witch. And evidently she was.

So what did that make papa, and what did that make him? That was a scary thought, and one he kept skipping off of, like a stone going over a river—back to the rustlings in the brush and back to Tamas and skip-skip-skip, across that dark spot again that held things he knew for certain master Karoly was not going to tell him, or master Karoly would have before this.

Then—it was after a dark spot, so he thought he must have dozed off—Zadny brought his head up and jolted his arm, and he saw master Karoly down on his knees with his ear to the ground, listening, the way he would do at home. He wondered if master Karoly's sister was talking to him, and he moved his arm and put his own ear to the ground. He was not sure he wanted to hear what master Karoly was hearing, and he was not sure it was right to eavesdrop.

But he heard nothing, anyway, but the noise of the brook and the rustle of the wind, and Zadny's heavy sigh. For a long time master Karoly stayed the way he was, and sometimes after that he cupped his hand as if he were whispering to someone, and listened some more. Yuri's eyes were very heavy, and they kept drifting shut, since nothing was going to happen that he could hear. And finally he knew he was asleep, because he kept dreaming of the troll's cave, and the cellar at Tajny Tower, and about home, too, as if he could drift around the halls. He could see his father sitting late, late in the hall, with no one around him. He could see his mother, looking so worried and so unhappy. He wanted to say, We're all right. And ordinarily in his dreams he could do as he wanted to do, but this time he talked and they did not even turn their heads, as if in his dream he was not there at all. And he went to

Tamas' and Bogdan's room, but it was dark and no one was there; and he went to his, and everything was just the way he had walked away from it, even Tamas' box sitting on the bed, and everything dark, but he could see it. It was scary, as if he really was there, and his mother had not let the maids move anything, or even dust anything, because it had a musty, unused smell. He wished he were back with master Karoly and master Nikolai and he wished it would be morning soon.

Which it was, because he heard the birds starting up. And then he wanted to sleep, but master Karoly came and poked him with his staff and said they had to be moving.

Skory had snorted and moved, just a moment before Tamas knew that birds were singing—he had that vague, disturbing impression, and he opened his eyes on gray sky and the branches of pines, seeing nothing wrong: he was numb on his back from contact with the stone, he would ache if he moved, and Ela's weight on his shoulder was truly painful, but he would have been oh, so willing to shut his eyes just a moment more.

But they had at least to think through where they were going and what they were going to do. He moved his left arm to lean on and lifted his head, and saw the rocky nook by daylight, saw—

"Ela!"

Goblins, all about, armed and squatting on the rocks and the earth of the hillside, only waiting, spears angled over shoulders.

Ela waked. He gathered her to her feet in the sweep of his arm as he scrambled up, saw goblins reach for spears and rise to their feet. He reached and drew his sword in hope that goblins had some concept of honor, enough to bring them at him one at a time—enough that it was not a volley of spears they had to face.

But the goblins all about suddenly changed their expression and looked past him, to the sounds of a rider arriving among the rocks. He turned his head just enough to confirm the pale gray horse he suddenly, angrily, believed it was. The goblins stood waiting for the intruder as Azdra'ik took his own time, rode up on them at an easy pace, swung off and lit on both feet at once, with a clash of metal. Lwi shied, snorting in dislike, and Tamas brought the sword up, waiting.

But Azdra'ik waved at whatever was happening at his back. "Oh, put the damned thing down, man, I've brought your horse back, haven't I?"

For a very little he would have swung at Azdra'ik. He did not put the sword away, he held it, waiting for Azdra'ik's joke to play itself out how it would; but Azdra'ik came closer, Lwi's reins in hand, and, with the point a hand's span from him, pushed it delicately, carefully away with the back of his hand, offering Lwi's reins inside Tamas' guard, while all about them was silence and waiting.

"Tamas," Azdra'ik said, looking him straight in the face; and did a beast call a man by his name, or give him time to think how fatal a move it would be to kill the goblin they knew, in the face of so many they did not.

Ela was as much in doubt. He felt her behind him. He kept his eyes on Azdra'ik and everything within eyesight as he lowered the sword point and reached after Lwi's reins, expecting some goblin joke. But Azdra'ik gave up the reins, and grinned at him, for which he was not in good humor. Azdra'ik turned away and swept a grand gesture at his cohorts around them, beckoning them to join him.

"Come down," Azdra'ik said, "come down, pay your respects to the witch of the Wood and—" With a turn half about: "—What *are* you, Tamas, lad? *Have* you a title this morning? Witchly consort, or—"

"Be damned," he muttered, and knew what they had seen and what they thought, while Ela stood hearing this and there was nothing reasonable he could say to Azdra'ik's suppositions.

Goblins came from out of the rocks, two score of them at the least. Tall, these were—like Azdra'ik, with like armor, and like faces, and an elegance and grace about them that declared they were no rabble. They were every bit what he had seen in the cellar at Krukczy Tower, if it had not been Azdra'ik himself—that memory welled up with cold clarity. They *were* guilty of that butchery, one and all of them. He had Azdra'ik's word they were not the lesser sort. These— these, then, were the lords and masters, these were Az- dra'ik's kind; and he hoped for nothing different than his companions and Ela's mistress had gotten, seeing what he saw about them. He kept the sword in hand, he wanted to know Ela's mind—but perhaps he had dreamed last night: he felt nothing—nothing of her thoughts or her wishes or her intentions, only her presence. He saw the goblins going through the motions of courtesy toward her, but whether it was some mockery, or honest chivalry, their manner gave no clue. He felt cut off, bereft of that feeling he had dreamed he had last night, bereft of understanding friend or foe, or what Ela was, or where her allegiances lay: she had *been* at Kruk- czy Tower, she had escaped ambush, and he had thought when he first set out with her that she might be one of theirs. He did not want to think that there had never been any chance of his escape, that she served some goblin master,—oh, god, he did not want to think that.

Not an ordinary forest, the old man said, and Gracja objected to being saddled—smart horse, Nikolai thought, cinching up. There was no question which of them had to ride today. Their wind-blown wizard looked as if a breeze hereafter would carry him body from soul—his hands were shaking, his steps were wobbling: clearly the old man had had all he could bear, and one could give him credit for courage if not for success with his magicking.

If only the old man could have done something about the boys, or magicked Yuri home, or something useful, but there was no place to put the boy, that was the problem—no place to put the boy and meanwhile Tamas was going deeper and deeper into trouble, so far as the ghosts said anything useful to Karoly.

Even the dog was quiet this morning, pressing himself as close to Yuri as he could get. The dog knew there were things he could not get his teeth into, and things that could chill a body into shivers and haunt his sleep—if a body could get any, with skulkings and prowlings all about their circle last night. The little that Nikolai had slept, he had dreamed of ambush, and Krukczy Straz, and the hillside and the birds circling.

Prophetic, it might be.

Meanwhile the old man was sitting waving his hands at the fire and talking to it. If other old men did that, the neighbors gossiped.

"We'd better get moving," he said.

"He's doing magic," Yuri said.

"He's doing magic. He's been doing magic since yesterday morning." For his part he had as lief sit here and let the old man magic up an answer that would save them going through that gateway, but he had no trust that would ever happen, and no trust that matters were not getting worse for Tamas while they sat here. "Come on, old man, are you learning anything? Or should we douse the fire and be out of here?"

The fire went out. Gone to cold cinders. That was impressive.

"No need to waste your strength," he murmured, rethinking the old man's value and the old man's awareness of the situation. Karoly the pot-wizard he was no longer, and perhaps never had been, that much had been clear since yesterday. "Do you want to get up on the horse, or are we still going?" It had been rush and haste and hurry, before the old man had started meddling with the fire. Half an hour ago nothing would do but speed; and half an hour ago the old man had looked on his last legs.

Now Karoly leaned on the staff that had rested against his shoulder; and changed as he was, more lined in the face, whiter of hair, there was a force to Karoly as he rose that made Nikolai think twice about the dead embers and what a life and a fire had in common.

"War and famine," Karoly said in a low voice. "That's all I see. The cities of the plain are under siege. The world reflects the mirror now, not the other way around. God hope they don't lose it."

"Lose what?" Nikolai had to ask.

"The fragment. The one piece that still reflects this world."

"How do you know it does?"

"Because we're here, working against her."

"You mean—" Yuri asked the question. "If it reflects us not being here—"

"—we won't be here."

Enough to upset a man's stomach. "Then why in hell didn't we go last night?" Nikolai asked, and went and brought Gracja back for the old man to mount. "Wait around here with ghosts prowling around—what worse can the ghosts do to us? They can't lay hands on us . . ."

"Don't depend on it," Karoly said—the way Karoly said things and then held his silence, when a body most wanted to understand.

"Get up on the horse." Nikolai held the reins for him, turned the stirrup and helped him up—Gracja verged on horse-sized, a stout pony showing her ribs by now, wanting farrier's tools the boy had come away without: and she took the old man's armored weight with a laying-back of her ears and a stolid plod forward before Karoly took up the reins, as if she knew already they were bound for the gateway.

Or maybe it was like the fire just now, and Gracja had her orders.

Fire crackled. Goblins needing to make no secret of their presence, they were beginning breakfast. They spoke together in a language of lilt and necessary lisp, not without reference to the unwilling guests among them, Tamas was certain—good-natured reference, cheerful reference, oh, yes, of course. It was their fire and their breakfast.

They had not disarmed him. But then no one had, who

had ever had the choice. Evidently he did not look that much of a threat to anyone—which did not please him, but it was not, master Nikolai would say, an excuse to be the fool they took him for. He had gotten to unsaddle the horses and give them rest, he had brought their personal belongings to where Ela was sitting, next the fire-making, none of which the goblins prevented, but there was always one watching him, leaning lazily on a spear but never failing attention. He set down the baggage, sat down beside Ela, and darted a glance at Azdra'ik talking with one of his fellows.

From Ela there had not been a single word, not a supposition, not an opinion: counting the sharpness of goblin ears, discussing their choices probably was not wise. Ela had the mirror and Ela had chosen not to use it—Ela surely knew the danger they were in and knew the choices, but she was evidently no freer than he was, and he wished he dared advise her: she looked so young and so shattered in her confidence at the moment. Speak, he dared not; and as for knowing her mind—he could make no guess, only anxiously wonder what Azdra'ik was about—whether Azdra'ik thought that, having the witch of the Wood in his hands, *he* might have use of the mirror; or whether he expected some great reward of his queen for returning it to her.

Spits and forked sticks had gone into the fire, propped on stones, holding flesh black and shriveled already from some previous smoking: their owners set them to heat, each goblin to his own breakfast, as it seemed, no preparation of cakes or bread—and increasingly now his and Ela's place of warmth and refuge near the fire began to acquire companions.

A goblin settled on Ela's other side, and Azdra'ik himself sat one place removed on his side, with a stick on which he impaled something and propped it on the rocks that rimmed the fire, the same as the others had done. All about them now were goblin faces, jutting jaws and flat noses, ears not where ears ought to be. Not untidy creatures, Tamas had to admit: hair, manes, whatever one might call it, were cleanly, black and wavy, some, or straight; loose or in braids; some about the face, some in back. Most wore rings in the ears, and one—Tamas could not help but stare, amazed—had a ring in his right nostril, evidently no inconvenience to the goblin.

And he could not but wonder at the wealth in the armor, of every least goblin in the lot—the most of it was brown and black, plain leather, the sort that foresters might wear; but the knives, the swords, the armlets and other pieces that they wore were blued steel inlaid with brass and gold and silver, and the chain where it showed at sleeve-edges and tunic-hems shone brighter and finer than any he had seen. They were none of them impoverished, who managed ornament like that; nor they had the look of bandits: what they wore was well fitted. Lords indeed—arrogant lords, who laughed, and cast one another grins, with glances back at them.

"They say you're very brave," Azdra'ik remarked.

He did not in the least believe that was what they had said. Then Ela said, coldly: "Pahai'me. Shi ashtal i paseit."

Goblin eyes widened. Faces turned, conversation stopped, and Azdra'ik laughed in what sounded like surprise.

"Pase*ith*, ng'Ysabela."

Tamas cast a glance at Ela: he *heard* the name, constructed it with ng'Saeich, and saw the whiteness of Ela's face, cold, ever so cold and angry. "Spas'i *rai*, ng'Saeich. You are most grievously mistaken."

"Am I?"

"*Did* you kill her?"

Azdra'ik laid a hand upon his heart—if he had one. "I swear by Lady Moon."

"The Lady changes."

"No. She has moods, but she never changes. Nor I. Nor have I ever, young witch. I swear that, too."

Ela did not answer that, Ela only stared at him, and, oh, god, the stress of the question in the company. Tamas saw it in every face, every frozen motion.

"You should learn your friends, young witch."

"You'll let us go," Ela said coldly. "No three wishes this time, ng'Saeich."

Grins broke out among the goblins. One nudged Azdra'ik in the ribs, but Azdra'ik seemed not so amused. "Impudent child."

"You know who I am," Ela said coldly.

"Young," Azdra'ik retorted. "Very young. *Leave it alone*, young mistress. Yes, it has power. So does the queen, and she's well aware of you now, and of us, if you use it again."

Ela said nothing to that, only scowled. What side is she *on*? Tamas asked himself, but clearly it was not quite for or against Azdra'ik, who was not quite loyal to his queen.

Meanwhile the goblin next to Tamas had caught a stick back from the fire, snagged whatever black, ragged thing was sizzling there, cut it and leaned their direction to proffer a tidbit on the edge of his knife. "Our guests first?"

"No, thank you," Tamas said faintly: his stomach was upset enough with the debate and the company. He had rather not look at it, and now that he had, he had rather not imagine what it had come from. The goblin laughed as if it were a great joke, others laughed; Azdra'ik, too, who said, "Rabbit, man. It's rabbit."

"We have our own breakfast," Tamas retorted, which set off more of their laughter, but he got into their packs and unwrapped what they owned. He could not have eaten that bit of meat, or, on second thought, have used his borrowed goblin knife to eat with—he was glad to keep to bread and cheese, and he offered a portion to Ela.

"A slight of our hospitality," Azdra'ik said. "How are we to bear it?"

Ela said nothing. And so it went. They ate their separate breakfasts in silence. Azdra'ik and his company pieced out theirs on knife's-edge and spoke animatedly in their own tongue. But eventually Azdra'ik said,

"Not a word of thanks for your rescue."

"Rescue!" Ela said.

"Especially seeing young witches with more in their hands

than they can handle. That will not serve you in the least, mark me. You know *nothing* of it.''

"And you do," Ela said coldly.

The goblins thought this funny.

"Do you?" Ela wanted to know.

"Only," Azdra'ik said, "insofar as I betrayed its secret to the witches of the Wood, and counseled Ylena to make her mirror.'' Azdra'ik rested an arm on his knee and pointed a black-nailed forefinger at them both. "She was a fool. At the moment of the disaster, I was with the queen. I smuggled the fragment elsewhere and bided my time. Ytresse betrayed her maker.''

"Meaning Ylena," Ela said.

"Oh, no, meaning the queen. Ytresse was hers, in all senses but maternity. Ylysse—was her own. Likewise your predecessor—who was twice a fool. Now is the time, I said. Do something with the mirror, I said. But no, *she* was afraid. Now comes her apprentice to take her place, and what does her apprentice for a beginning? Her apprentice wanders the hills using the mirror for trifles and rattling the queen's own gates, then wonders that it attracts notice. Be *glad* that I found you, young witch. And show better manners.''

"To you."

"Ela," Tamas said. If there was a peaceful offer from the goblin lord, he was willing to hear it—he was desperate to hear it, considering it was himself Azdra'ik would slice in pieces first if Ela decided to provoke him.

"No, now, I have patience. You remember my patience, man." Azdra'ik nipped a bit of meat off the skewer with a small knife, and offered it. "*Rabbit*, I swear to you. Lady Moon, what a disgusting thought. —Will you?"

"No, thank you."

"The rabbit doesn't care. Not now. There are ways and ways to lose one's concerns. I'd listen to advice, man. I'd persuade the witchling to listen. There is something about her and you that cannot find the right way through the woods—that will never find it, because the magic weights you in one direction, do you understand?

The Wood is like that. You'll never meet a thing there but what you've already met, and I *wouldn't* advise going back in.''

"What do you advise?" he asked, since Ela was too proudly sullen.

Azdra'ik shrugged. "Why, rattle the queen's gate quite properly. A place of power, that's where to use that trinket. And the Wood is denied you. So—take it to the queen's gate to use it."

"That *would* suit you," Ela said.

"That *is* where you were going," Azdra'ik said, "isn't it? Else you could have circled full about and headed back to Tajny Wood—which I don't think you dared last night to do. The magic—the magic was bringing you toward the queen's own doorstep. And think of it—what better trap for your predecessor to lay, than to plot her magic right down the very course the queen wants most? Irresistible? The queen would not stop you. So who carries that fragment has to come this way. I only hoped to stop you so long as there were choices— to take that bauble back to hiding before you did yourself and us grievous harm."

"Oh, I am sure!" Ela cried.

"An effort foredoomed, I've no doubt now. You were set before birth to be where you are, and I couldn't prevent you. So—since you want to go to the queen, we'll take you to the queen."

"No," Ela said flatly.

"I assure you," Azdra'ik said, "you've no other choice. The world—has no other choice. You see in us a company that does not love the queen. But your obstinacy has put us in danger—has *damned* us to assist you now or die, and I assure you, young witch, we have our preference in the matter.''

"I'm sure I should believe you," Ela said, but it seemed to Tamas there was worse than listening, and a more dangerous course than asking why.

"So why," Tamas asked, "don't you just kill us, take the

mirror and do what you please? That seems the way goblins do things.''

A quiet settled at the fireside. Azdra'ik gave him a look that seemed to go on very long. ''Because, man, among other virtues I do possess—I am not a witch. None of us can use the mirror—worse, none of us can long resist the mirror—but the existence of that fragment of the great one is the only freedom we have.''

''You say,'' Ela retorted. But it seemed to Tamas that he had just heard a compelling reason, if it was in any sense true.

''I do say. The mirror shapes what is in this land—beyond this land, for all we know. But as long as there exists another mirror, as long as there exists a different vision in another such mirror, there is hope for us. No, we are not eager to contest with our queen. We'd be content to live as we have, in exile—because we *have* no great hope in opposing her and we have no wish to lose everything in hasty confrontation. But to work against the magic that draws these pieces together—that we cannot, and since we cannot, we attempt to persuade those who can. Unfortunately—'' Azdra'ik rose to his feet, towering above them. ''Unfortunately, considering who holds it, and who can and cannot use it, the fragment cannot go back into the Wood again. Everything indicates where it's going, and that, young witch, means the queen.''

A goblin said something to which Azdra'ik paid attention, something which brought frowns all about, and another and another spoke, in increasing heat.

''He points out,'' Azdra'ik said then, ''that there is no good for us in waiting for the outcome. If you fail, young witch, we will *be* the queen's loyal subjects—because there will *be* no other possibility once she gains the fragment. You see what's at stake for us.''

(The Wood is the only safe place,) something said in Tamas' heart, and he felt a great unease, as if that dreaded voice were giving him the only honest advice. (Azdra'ik is a liar, he's always been a liar, ahead *isn't* the only choice open to you. Everything he's done has been to his benefit and our harm. This is not the time to believe him, Tamas.)

But that was Ylena—he had Azdra'ik's word it was Ylena who haunted him, and Azdra'ik was standing in front of them in plain daylight, a goblin countenance which they had learned to tell apart from all other goblins, and which did not now appear to be lying.

"Are you going to let us go?" Ela asked.

"Go," Azdra'ik said, and waved his hand toward the horses. "Unless it occurs to you, as perhaps it will, that there are a great many hazards in the land, and that if you go back to the woods, you would fall into the worst hands that could hold the fragment, except the queen herself."

"And you," Ela said.

"Young witch, *I*, and my company, are as I said, yours to command, if you can command us. That's the nature of the mirror, and of any portion of it. Make us free of it."

Ela reached slowly to her throat, and drew the mirror from her collar. Goblins about the circle rose to their feet, and those nearest jostled for a look at it.

"Have a care!" Azdra'ik said, alarmed.

But Ela hurled it to the rocks at her feet. Tamas jumped back, expecting fragments, expecting—the god knew what. But it lay there whole, reflecting not the sky—but fire; and when he dived to retrieve it, his eye caught the roiling of dark images before his hand shut the sights away.

"Only magic can break it," Azdra'ik said. "Would not I have tried to have a piece of it to myself, when I had the chance? I tried the same. I tried stones and steel and curses, and it would not break."

Tamas gave it back to Ela—was glad to surrender it to Ela, because he only half-heard what Azdra'ik said: louder was the whisper of the wind in the trees, and keen and cold was the touch of a hand at his shoulder, an angry protest he could not altogether hear.

"Don't use it here," Azdra'ik said. "Wait. Be *wise*, young witch, put it away. And go where you please. But unless you use the mirror against us, and I do not for your sakes advise it—this company will go with you, this *company* will go with you against the queen, which is where you're bound, whether or not you know it—until you can no longer hold that portion of the mirror. We—come and we go with that. We rise and we fall with that. We will never betray the holder of the mirror. And that, young witch, comprehend exactly as you hear it, no more, no less.''

12

BEYOND THE ARCH WAS A TUMBLED RUIN, A WHOLE GREAT hall with hardly anything of it standing but the walls—a mysterious place, very old. Master Karoly said it was Hasel, but it was not at all what Yuri had heard regarding Hasel. Master Karoly rode behind them while Nikolai walked ahead with the bow in hand and he followed Nikolai—Zadny keeping right by him, sometimes crossing in front of him, sometimes trying to press up against his legs while he was walking.

It was hard to believe that these halls, open to the sky, had ever had a roof or held colors and voices. Nikolai had talked about wars and towers burning, they had seen the destruction at Tajny Straz, and seen the work of ghosts, but the spookiness about this place was unbearable—maybe, Yuri thought, that it had been dead longer or (he shuddered to think) that worse things had happened there. Constantly there was a hint of movement in the tail of one's eye. There was a chill in these stones that had nothing to do with early morning, and the echo any sound made lived on and on here, imitating voices, while they walked through what had been walls, and a horse went through what had been rooms, with a lonely clatter of hooves.

Yuri cast a glance over his shoulder, just to be sure—and something flitted in the edge of his vision. He felt a coldness at the back of his neck and swatted at it, but nothing was there. If he had been alone, he would have run for his life. But there was Nikolai, there was master Karoly, and he had to be brave. He had to figure master Karoly knew what he was doing and where he was leading them, and most of all that Tamas had gotten through here somehow—and if Tamas had gotten through, then he would.

He saw trees above the next wall, tall trees, and he looked to that as the end, the boundary where the ghosts tied to this place had to stop. He was ever so glad when they passed the farther gateway and leaf-strewn pavings gave way to earth.

"Keep together," Karoly said from behind him as they entered forest shade. "Nikolai, stay *with* us. This is no place to stray off. *Believe* me, master hunter."

Nikolai scowled and fell back to their pace. "I can't hear a damned thing with your clatter, master wizard. Ghosts are one thing—if it's goblins—"

"Not in this woods."

"Not in this woods," Nikolai echoed. And Yuri wished master Karoly would say more than that, too. "Not in this woods," Nikolai said again, and they walked, and the brush grew thicker. And darker with shadow. "Not in this woods, is it? Then what *is* in this woods, pray tell?"

"It's not always the same woods, master huntsman—and I don't know. It's not *been* the same woods since the mirror broke. By what Ylysse said—and that's all I know, the witches exist here, they spelled this place to protect them, and it did. Maybe for some it's random what woods you enter—but some of us—some of us some of *them* still have an interest in. I've brought Ysabel here."

A lady was walking far in front of them. A lady in black clothing. Yuri saw her of a sudden. And there was a shadowy figure of a man holding her hand.

"Thank the god," Karoly breathed. "Thank the god, she's *leading* us, and Pavel's sane. Don't lose sight of her."

She looked real enough. Yuri blinked as they walked, and blinked again, and the lady was still there, although one was not sure at times about the man.

They came to a sunlit spot and both of them faded, then came back again beyond it. Yuri wanted to tell *that* to the boys at home, if they would ever believe it. He forgot to be afraid, he was so fascinated by this going and coming.

Of a sudden he saw other figures standing in their path,

and he looked back at master Karoly, wondering should they stop or not, but master Karoly kept riding, without a change of expression, and Nikolai walked on the other side. Yuri gave Zadny a pat on the head as Zadny pressed close to him, and kept walking toward what he was sure were other ghosts—women, ladies, queens they looked to be; and he drew deep breaths trying to be calm and not act the fool in what he was sure was a very serious meeting.

"Damn," he heard Nikolai mutter. "Are they real?"

"As real as death," Karoly said.

"The trolls—" Nikolai said. And they were there, behind a shaft of milky daylight, at least two of them, no. . . .

"Three. There's three."

The lady in black kept walking, and so did her companion, slowly, slowly, dissolving in the light and reappearing faintly on its other side, while the trolls (three at least) sat like statues, like heraldic beasts, in the presence of the three queens.

Then the lady in black and her companion met with them, and turned and faced them as they came, with the man faint and gray behind her. Very solemnly they waited, until they had gotten into the daylight, with the trolls—one had to be Krukczy, Yuri was sure of it, but he dared not blurt out anything—it was too quiet, too dangerous.

"Karoly," one queen said.

And the lady in black: "Late, Karoly, damned late. Couldn't you hear me?"

"I came as quickly as I could," Karoly said, from Gracja's back. Zadny whined and wanted reassurance. Yuri ducked down and held his muzzle, for fear he would start barking—it was not the time for it, most assuredly not the time.

"I want their *heads*!" the lady said. "I want them to pay, Karoly."

"A matter of sovereignty," another said. "Do I know this boy, Karoly?"

"This is Yuri," Karoly said, and Yuri, feeling altogether too conspicuous, stood up, and made a respectful bow.

"And Nikolai," the same lady said. "Faithful Nikolai."

A wind began to blow, picking up leaves and rushing through the trees with a deep sigh.

The trolls leapt up and scattered, as Gracja backed and faced to the stinging gale—Zadny yelped and took out for the brush and Yuri grabbed for him, missed and grabbed a second time, afraid Zadny was going to disappear into the thicket forever.

"Yuri!" he heard Nikolai shout behind him. And: "Karoly, damn it!"

He made a frantic grab after the hound, sprawled full length in the leaves and scrambled up again with a glance over his shoulder.

But there was no sign of the ladies, no sign of Nikolai or Karoly and none of the trolls—it was just woods, just a lot of trees, and a leafy spot, and plain daylight.

He heard something coming across the leaves. He looked and saw Zadny waggling up to him, all humble and contrite, now that they were completely lost. He made a half-hearted snatch and caught Zadny's collar, knelt down by him to look around and try to get his bearings, and it was all just forest.

Zadny licked him on the ear, on the jaw. Damned dog, Nikolai would say. And he would not damn Zadny, but Zadny was not high in his favor at the moment.

That was stupid, he thought. Nikolai would call it stupid—losing himself for a dog, worrying everyone—making the ghosts angry at him. The woods did not feel as spooky as before, but there were ghosts. As real as death, master Karoly had said. As real as the fact he had had people with him, who were not with him now—or he was not with them.

"Stop it!" he said to Zadny's whining and washing of his face. "Stop it! You've got us both lost, you understand that? Stupid dog."

Zadny ran a few paces off from him as he got up, and ran back to him, and ran away again in the same direction, the same way Zadny had done on the mountain.

"Is it Tamas?" he asked, suddenly realizing what Zadny's behavior might mean. "Is it Tamas you're following? Do you know where he is, boy?"

Zadny went a little further, and circled back and out as he followed, faster and faster. Zadny had his nose to the ground now—he was on a scent, there was no question of it, and whatever had happened to separate him from the others, following Zadny before had never brought him to harm. So he trusted him this time.

A blast of dust in the eyes and a blink and there was nothing, no one, no sign of the boy or the dog—I knew it, Nikolai said to himself, casting about in every direction for something familiar. I knew it, I knew it, I should have had that dog for goblin bait . . .

"Yuri!" he shouted into the woods. "Karoly!" And furiously, desperately: "Krukczy, damn your hairy hide, find the boy!"

"Find the boy, is it?" said a quiet voice.

He spun about. It was the voice on the tower stairs. It was the voice out of his boyish nightmares, the voice drowned in thunder and in rain and sealed behind stone.

"And what about yourself, Nikolai?" the lady asked, drifting closer. Her hair was black. Her gown was black. "Have you no need to be found?"

He backed a pace without thinking about it, but she kept coming until she was as close to him as she had been that day. Wind stirred her gown and her silken sleeves and the dark veil of her hair. She was young and she was beautiful. And her eyes were bottomless.

"Faithful Nikolai. I asked you that day, were you faithful to Stani. And you said yes. Did you know then that was a promise?"

"I've never broken it," he said.

"You're here," she said. "Why?"

"For Stani's sons. For your grandsons." The ground rumbled underfoot. The wind began to blow. He flung up his arm to shield his eyes. "Witch, damn you, rescue the boys, can you do that?"

"But that's why I sent you, Nikolai."

"Sent me!"

"All those years ago. Yes. You climbed down from those stairs safe that night. You had a job to do for me. You've done part of it. But it's not done, Nikolai."

"Where's Yuri? What have you done with him?"

"Not I, Nikolai. Not I. All of us—the witches of the Wood, the goblins and their queen—and the young witch, Mirela. Tamas is my heir. Tamas . . . is my heir. And Urzula was not my name."

"Ysabel," he recalled.

"Karoly told you that. Yes, Ysabel, once upon a time. But Urzula is good enough a name for my son to know. Goodbye, and fare exceedingly well, Nikolai."

The lady leaned forward, and rested ghostly hands on his shoulders. He felt the chill even through armor. And touched ghostly lips to his ever so gently.

"I wanted to do that," the ghost said with a wicked wink, and was gone, in a whirl of shadow and pallor, and silence. "One thing more you will do," the voice lingered to say.

"What?" he called after it.

But it was gone, into daylight and ordinary woods.

"Damn!" he cried. "Damn! Lady! *What thing am I to do?*"

In its silence he walked straight ahead. He could think of no better direction. And if there was a ghost in the world that had reason to guide him to the boys, he believed in this one.

But all he found when he had come over the second leaf-paved hill was a bony old man in a gray cloak on an unlikely shaggy pony.

"Where's Yuri?" he asked the ghost. But it was master Karoly who called out from the bottom of the hillside.

"I don't know. I hoped he was with you."

Nikolai slid down the hill on slick leaves, caught his balance under Gracja's startled nose and snagged the bridle for a look up at the old man. "Not hide nor hair. Only the lady. Your lady. Ladislaw's wife."

"Urzula . . ."

"Urzula—Ysabel. You're the wizard, you *knew* what you were doing when you brought the boys here in the first place.

Don't lie to me, Karoly! They're caught up in something you know about. She said Tamas was her heir. She said he's with Mirela. What in *hell* did she mean?''

"Oh, god.''

"What did she mean, Karoly? You know, don't you, you damned well know!''

"She didn't say a thing about Tamas. She named *Yuri*, to me. But there's not a shred of magic in him, I couldn't find it in any of the boys and she never got a daughter—which she could have. Witches can do that.''

"I don't doubt it,'' Nikolai said glumly.

"Deception I can understand. Her whole life was deception. Krukczy Straz was the only guard on that border. But, god save us . . . Mirela? Are you sure that's what she said? That that's who Tamas is with?''

"The same name as you said. Mirela. I didn't forget it.''

Karoly said nothing more. Karoly climbed down from the saddle, and Gracja shied and pulled at the reins, nervous about something, ears flicking one way and another. Nikolai held fast to the reins and paid his attention to master Karoly, who seemed to have sudden interest in the treetops, or the weather.

"Tamas *isn't* a boy to set in a hard situation,'' Nikolai protested. "Nice boy—but he hasn't the toughness—god, Yuri's more resourceful than he is, the boy's shown it. Why did she settle on Tamas?''

"It's not settling, master huntsman. You don't *settle* on being a wizard. It's what you're born.''

"Then why didn't you see it?''

"You're not listening, master huntsman. *Urzula* may not have known. Magic has its ways of tricking everyone, most especially those next to it. I'd have bet on Yuri myself—but that's evidently not the way it is.''

"Tamas can't shoot a deer. What in hell is he going to do with the goblins?''

"Come again?''

"I said—'' God, he was off looking at the trees again. "Are you listening to me?''

"Ask your question again."

The question eluded him. "About Mirela?" That was the important one. But Karoly did not look at him. "I asked how he was going to shoot the goblins if he couldn't shoot a deer."

"He has nothing against the deer."

For some reason that sent a chill down his back. He did not know why—except . . . except he was used to Tamas the way he was: not a bad boy, nor a coward, now that he thought of it, nor anything he knew exactly to fault the lad on. The fact was—he liked Tamas better than Bogdan: he suddenly realized that for the truth—that if he could get two of Stani's sons back, he knew which two he would prefer. God, that worried him.

"Magic will out. Magic will out, do you understand, even after years. That Ladislaw fell off his horse and that Stani existed and that Urzula had sons and not daughters—these are all beyond us; and a lot of it was beyond Urzula herself. —Listen to me, Nikolai. Don't give me that frown. Understand me. Urzula sacrificed everything and everyone on the altar of her purpose. I make no excuses for her. That is sorcery. That was the way she chose. But Tamas—"

"The boy is not a killer. He hasn't the heart to be a killer. I wouldn't make him shoot the deer, Karoly. I talked to him, I reasoned with him—but I wouldn't shame him and I wouldn't force him. The boy's—" Reasons deserted him. The boy's expression that day came back to haunt him, the promise to try—the absolute surety in his mind that Tamas was lying to please him, that ultimately Tamas had rather the shame than the kill and the arrow would most certainly miss.

Lord Sun save the boy, he thought in despair, and, still holding Gracja's rein, beckoned Karoly to get up again.

"We can't find him here. We've got to do something. We've got Tamas going lord Sun knows where, we've got a boy lost out there following a damn dog who's following Tamas, if it makes any sense at all where Yuri's gone."

"Tamas," Karoly said, suddenly paying complete attention. "Tamas. That *would* be it, wouldn't it? That's where he *has* gone. No question."

* * *

They rode a faint footpath along the flanks of the hills, among pines and massive rocks. In the low places between hills gray haze stung the nose and the eyes, and made Lwi and Skory blow and shake their heads in disgust—while in front of them and behind them, dark goblin figures moved at an untiring pace, figures that flitted in and out among the rocks and sometimes, now and again, vanished along different tracks, to rejoin the trail at some further winding. Tamas wondered where they went—whether scouting for human ambush, or simply taking shortcuts they knew, paths the horses could not climb.

But at one such meeting came other goblins, in plainer armor, and after three of their own party had talked with them a moment, one returned and brought Azdra'ik forward to talk to them, the lot of them with chin-rubbing and fist on hip and downcast looks and language that, even when the chance breeze brought it to them, meant nothing but perplexity to a lad from Maggiar.

"Can you catch any of it?" he asked Ela. "Is it trouble?"

"Something about the way ahead," Ela said. "Something about a meeting, and horses."

He kept still in the chance that Ela could gather more of it.

"Something about the queen," she said. "Azdra'ik asked them something, I can't make it out. They say they don't know, they—"

Azdra'ik came back then in haste, passed all the way back down the column to speak to them. "We have horses. Around the hill and on. Yours may not care for them. Keep clear."

"Goblin horses," Ela said, as Azdra'ik went further back.

Tamas glanced back uncomfortably, wondering what they were, and suddenly heard movement on the road around the bend. He turned his head a second time to look, and the goblins behind him were moving to the rocks.

What came was shadow, shaggy maned, black, with a swiftness and silence on the stony path that made him think for a moment both riders and beasts were illusory, creatures of the mirror—but Lwi shied over and snorted as half the riders passed in strange quiet, and Skory shied further, until the rocks and witchery stopped her. It was a rattle and scrape of claws the goblin horses made, leaving white scratches on the rocks where their feet had touched. Their riders stopped them and slid down, both at the head of the column and behind them—Azdra'ik's company made a quick exchange with them, while Tamas kept a tight grip on Lwi's reins and kept seeing this and that view of the road as Lwi spun and backed, the old hunter snorting and laying back his ears. He caught an impression of long-tufted tails, abundant feather from hocks to heels, and when one goblin horse nearest turned profile, it yawned at the bit and showed fangs more formidable than its rider's—that, and a disposition to snap at its fellows. Eyes obscured in forelock and mane, nostrils less horse than cat . . . Tamas kept a tight hold on the reins and patted Lwi's neck; called him good horse and honest horse, and wished him back in his stall in Maggiar, where he might come to some better end—these creatures might well eat ordinary horses, for what he or Lwi could know.

And it was not fair that magic stilled honest fears, that first Skory and then Lwi quieted, and stood and sweated. Ela had done that, he was certain. "Good lad, good lad," Tamas said, patting Lwi and easing off on the bit, for the ease of the horse's mouth at least. "Just stay back, we won't put you near them."

The goblins began to move then, the ones that had brought the horses withdrawing up the hillside afoot, under what arrangement there was no guessing. It was only clear that their own party was going on and that the other band was staying—riders were behind them as well, and he no temptation to linger. Lwi jolted into a quicker pace, and Skory matched it, on the verge of bolting free.

"Watch her," Tamas said through his teeth, fearing not even magic would give Skory sanity, and all the while something kept saying to him, This is a mistake, Tamas. You have no place here, no earthly thing but breath in common with these creatures. And least of all believe ng'Saeich—

It began to be like a bad dream, their own horses too trail worn and weary now to keep the pace, and the goblin riders pressing them from behind, which distracted Lwi and made him lay back his ears and look askance. Worse, they entered a deep drift of stinging smoke, where the mountainside was afire—bright flame showed, and elsewhere the grass was blackened. Like the mountains, it was, like the descent to Krukczy Straz, like the way to ambush.

Smallish stout figures moved grayly through the smoke, pacing them on the hillside, figures that appeared and vanished like ghosts.

"Hobgoblins," Ela said. No rider before them had seemed to notice or remark them, and Tamas swung about in the saddle to see if the ones behind had seen.

But when he looked about again, there was not a one of the watchers on the hillside.

"I don't like this," he said. "I don't like this at all. —Don't touch it, Ela, don't."

Ela had her hand on the mirror below her collar, and cast a burning glance toward the goblins. "Those are the ones— *those* are the ones at Krukczy Straz."

"Get on!" he said. "They've looked us over. Let's close it up. Come on."

He put Lwi to a faster pace, and Ela kept with him, the goblins behind them following them or not, he was not sure until he cast an anxious glance over his shoulder and saw nothing behind him but gray haze and empty trail.

"Itra'hi," he said as they rode in among the riders ahead, and there were looks. Two and three and four riders reined back immediately and veered off to the rear before they even reached the foremost riders.

"Azdra'ik," he said to a goblin he passed in the haze.

"Gone," that one said. "Stay with us!"

"Gone after them?" He had not intended argument. It leapt out.

"Stay!" that one said sharply. Lwi and Skory were surrounded by goblin horses and he had his hands full with Lwi. He dared not break from the group and had nowhere to go if he should. Ela stayed beside him, clinging to the saddle, casting fearful looks behind, and with her hand reaching fitfully after the amulet she did not touch. Reassurance, he thought, the possibility of reinforcement . . . overwhelming temptation: (Take it, from her, something said to him. She won't refrain. Something will happen and she'll resort to it, and that's fatal, that's death, Tamas. . . .)

But before the horses had run out their wind, before they had even cleared the area of the brushfire, goblin riders came up from behind them through the smoke, and Azdra'ik was with them, frowning and angry.

"Keep going," Azdra'ik said, but Lwi and Skory could not stand the faster pace, and fell farther and farther behind as they went, as the trail climbed up and up among rocks likely for ambush. Tamas was not sure whether all the riders in their party had come forward with Azdra'ik, leaving no rear guard. For all he could tell enemies might be chasing after them and their group might be in full rout.

But at the crest of the hill and above the smoke, the goblins abruptly stopped, their horses milling about in confusion and turning and snapping at each other in the way of their kind.

Lwi slowed to a walk. Tamas let him. Ela rode beside him in silence as their winded horses climbed, up and up the loose earth that claws had scored before them. Something was wrong with the sky, that was—Tamas' first impression— some dreadful fire, far worse than the last, shadowing the eastern sky with a black pall of smoke.

But the higher they rode the darker it looked, until they came cautiously among the goblin riders and had a look over the ridge. The daylight stopped in the valley, simply stopped, and the rest was a wall of night, a division drawn in sun and shadow across the end of the valley, and across the hills. Looking into it, the sky was pitch black, the more stark for its touching the daylight where they were. Tamas blinked, and had an impulse to rub his eyes, although there was no wavering in the sight, no compromise with his outraged senses.

"Lord Sun," he breathed—but lord Sun did not rule yonder. Other powers did.

"Every day," Azdra'ik said, riding close to them, "it grows. Lately it has grown by valleys and hills. This is the queen's power advancing. This is what you attack, young witch, do you see it? Are you still confident, or will you retreat?"

"Retreat where?" Ela asked faintly. "Where could we go to escape this?"

"You might delay it. Go make young witches. Go make someone brave, or stronger, or wiser in choosing the hour."

Ela shot him a hard, pale-faced look. "It's *mine.*"

God, Tamas thought in despair: it sounded like the old, the unrepentant Ela, Ela who could do anything, and they were done, if that was her whole answer.

"Ela," he said.

"He *won't* have what he wants," Ela said. "He can't make up for stealing it, the queen won't forgive him—"

"That's not what I want, young fool! I want this thing taken away from here!"

"For how long, ng'Saeich? For how long do you think you can go on hiding in the hills and looking for charity?"

"No charity!" Azdra'ik declared, clearly offended.

"I remember a night," Ela said, and Azdra'ik glared.

"It was the collection of a debt. A favor done. There was no *charity*, ng'Ysabela."

"Mistress fed you. Mistress said to me later that you were harmless. I didn't believe it. I still don't."

Azdra'ik swept a bow from the saddle. "I'm ever so gratified, young witch." And with a cold stare: "But what *other* judgments are you fit for? Lady Moon, wait at least for your own maturity!"

Ela shook her head and shook it a second time. "That," she said, gazing out toward the dark, "is that waiting? Where is it going from here and how fast? Or is she content?"

The goblins murmured together; and Azdra'ik grimly nodded and slid down from the saddle. "Down and rest," he said, and said something to his people, some of whom rode back down the hill.

"Itra'hi," Azdra'ik said. "Sniffing about us. If you don't make the point with them, they'll not take you seriously. And one *cannot* trust them. —Get down, get down, take a rest. Closer than this—there's no safety."

"Should have let the forest have them," the one nearest muttered, and Azdra'ik:

"Worse will have them. They already belong to her."

"How long a rest?" Tamas asked. There was not a bone of him that did not ache, as he slid down and his feet touched the ground.

Azdra'ik's hand landed unwelcomely on his shoulder, and he looked the goblin full in the face, expecting some foul trick; but Azdra'ik's grip had no force this time.

"As long a rest as the queen affords us," Azdra'ik said in a low voice. "As long as that comes no closer. Personally, I don't expect a dawn."

He stared at the goblin, wondering—too many things to keep collected. His exhausted thoughts scattered, and beneath them a crawling of the flesh insisted, Don't trust him, don't believe in him, don't take his reassurances.

"Mind," Azdra'ik said, "the young witch holds all our lives." He did not know what Azdra'ik expected him to say. But Azdra'ik had not let him go. "A dangerous business," Azdra'ik said in a low voice. "Affections for a sorceress."

"She isn't," he said. And he heard the other word then. Absurd. "And she doesn't. She hasn't. She won't. Ela hasn't a shred of romance."

"Her opponent is darkest sorcery." Azdra'ik lifted the unwelcome hand on his shoulder, on the way to sitting on the rock beside him. "Sorcery that has less romance than you can imagine. Ask your guest."

"I've no wish to ask her anything! God . . . I want free of her!"

"She does devil you, then, does she?"

A breath. A difficult breath. Images and fears crowded him close. "Small freedom you won me."

"I bargained for your life, man. The bargain you made with the ghost was your own folly, and damn your prideful foolishness."

"I made no bargain with her!" But he thought of what he had done, paying the kiss the witch had asked, and of what he had been willing, then, to do. It was only from time to time and afterward that he had changed his mind and wanted his own life back.

"Listen. Long ago, *long* ago, man, when Ylena was in mortal flesh, she came to us. Granted, we have our moral faults—"

That was worth at least a bitter laugh.

"I say, our moral faults," Azdra'ik persisted. "Not far different from those of men. Among them contentiousness. And greed. And intolerance. We lost our place in the world— we were driven from it. If our queen took any means no matter how desperate to restore that to us, there were those who would do any work she required. Ask me tonight, when there's leisure for such things. But meanwhile—meanwhile . . . offer the young witch no choices, no distractions of your evidently potent charms—"

He started to object, but Azdra'ik's long-nailed finger lifted before his nose.

"Hear me," Azdra'ik said. "Hear me, or damn her and all of us. If the young witch with that fragment in her hands, with the queen at war with her, has one single thought of compromise, she will worse than die. If she spares a moment for interests other than her own, she will lose everything she has and might have, that is the war she was fitted to fight, that is the war she has undertaken, and that is the enemy she faces, do you comprehend? Sorcery cannot be half-hearted, it cannot *think* with a heart, it simply has to be the only answer she affords. If we are extremely fortunate, we may still be in possession of that fragment tomorrow and the sun may yet rise on this hill. But if you distract her young and eminently scatterable wits—"

Lwi was pulling at him at the other hand. Lwi jolted him with a butt of the head, one more irritance than he could abide in patience. "Her young and scatterable wits have out-witted you, m'lord goblin: *she* is where she chooses."

"Is she? Are you absolutely sure?"

Now that Azdra'ik said it—he was less so.

"There," Azdra'ik said, with a nod toward the horizon. "There is the most potent magic I know, that has moved events before now in the world. Whatever magic on this side and that may have done—the queen fences masterfully, feint and double feint and misdirect, press and provide the adversary the chance, do you see: the riposte and the waiting target, be it her heart, the queen has done everything on purpose. Disabuse yourself of all thoughts to the contrary."

"Are you her move—against the witches?"

"You might be. The young witch might be. You can't know. I can't. Even Ytresse betrayed her creator."

"The witch Ytresse."

"The witch Ytresse. My creation, the queen's . . . who's to know?"

"Your creation." Anger gathered out of that dark place in him, a muddle of desire and rage, regarding the creature that had its hand on him—he gave a shudder and knew at the same time it was the ghost, a woman's ghost, who had had a foolish, foolish knowledge of this creature. He could not move, he could hardly breathe collectedly.

"You might say," Azdra'ik said. "Surely Ylena remembers."

"Don't talk to her! Damn you, let me alone."

"So you understand what distraction can do to a witch. And how far this all reaches."

For a moment the sound of Azdra'ik's voice was faint to him. He gazed off into the darkness above the hills, and the valley where the fires of destruction still burned, faint pin-pricks of red light in the darkness.

"That I'm here is no accident either," he said.

"This close to the queen's domains, nothing comes by accident. You—and I. Your assumption that you are not the queen's may be true—or false."

"I know whose I am," he said, with a sudden thought of gran, like a breath of free air. "I know who sent me."

"Who?" Azdra'ik asked, curiosity quick and alive in his glance, but Azdra'ik surely hoped for no truthful answer from him.

"Ask me tomorrow." He jerked his shoulder free. "My horse is tired. I have work to do."

"Man," Azdra'ik said, as he began to lead Lwi away. He looked back. "It's good advice," Azdra'ik said.

"I don't doubt it, m'lord goblin. I'll keep it in mind."

He led Lwi over to where Ela was trying to care for Skory. "Here," he said, "rest, I'll tend to them."

"What did he argue?" Ela asked.

"Nothing," he said. "Nothing I regard. Go sit down. They're making a camp here."

"The lake is yonder," Ela said, looking off toward the east. "The lake that the queen bargained for. That's where I have to go tomorrow."

"We both have to go there," he said, and said it not for loyalty, but in argument to what in him loathed and feared the thought. I have to, he thought. If magic brought me here, if gran was what they say, gran had something to do with this.

And would she have told me so much about this land, the way it was—for no reason? That wasn't like gran. That wouldn't be like her. *Why* did she tell us—if she was a witch— if we weren't someday to be here?

Bogdan and I—both of us—here.

Zadny kept just ahead, constantly just ahead—the hound might at least have trusted him after all this time together, Yuri thought, especially given he had made not a single try to stop him. But for mile after mile through this endless woods, Zadny skittered away from him like a wild thing. Twilight came, and he stumbled blind and exhausted through the brush, shouting "Zadny, Zadny!" and sometimes calling after master Karoly or Nikolai in the hope they might hear him and follow him.

But it was not until he had fallen on his face and lacked the strength to get up again that the wretch showed up and licked him in the face.

"It's too late for that," he said, and struck at Zadny with his arm. But Zadny was too quick for him, and lay down with his chin on his paws, out of reach, watching him until he could get his breath and stop his side aching and get up to his hands and knees.

Then Zadny ran again, disappearing through the brush.

"Dog!" he yelled, hoarse and furious. "Zadny!"

He scrambled after, catching his sleeves on brambles, tearing his hair and his face and hands as he dived through the twilit brush—and onto an open, rocky hillside, where a shaggy lump sat, holding Zadny in his arms.

"Krukczy!" he cried, sitting up and nursing a skinned knee. It was not fair, it was supposed to be Tamas that Zadny was following, it was supposed to be his brother, and it was not.

Then another troll appeared among the rocks. And another one. They shuffled out and squatted down next the first one, and Yuri stared in dismay.

"Krukczy?" he asked, wondering now which was which, and the one holding Zadny bobbed as if he agreed.

"Come find brothers," the troll said, "find brothers."

It was a riddle. It was powerful and it was scary and the presence of the others made him sure he did not understand trolls, but they were all the help he had in front of him, and he thought he even might know their names.

"Hasel?" he asked, and the second bowed. The third was harder. But he said, "Tajny?" and the third bobbed in trollish courtesy. So he did understand the nature of them. And Krukczy had found what he had come for, Yuri guessed, but *he* had not.

"You've found your brothers," he said, "but I haven't. Let Zadny go. He can find Tamas. I *need* him."

The trolls drew closer together, until they were like one lump.

"Dangerous," said the one he was sure was Krukczy, and the others nodded.

"Wicked queen," said the one that answered to Tajny. And Hasel, whose tower was only ruined stones, said:

"Wicked, wicked, wicked."

"Long time ago," said Krukczy, "long time even for us— the goblins go below."

"Long time ago," said Tajny, "long, comes magic back to the land. The queen bargained with the witches. Foolish witches."

"Foolish witches," said Hasel. "Foolish queen."

"Wanted the lake," Krukczy said.

"Now we go there," said Tajny. "Mistress is dead. We go there."

"Go find brothers," said Krukczy, and rose with Zadny in his shaggy arms. "Find brothers. Make the queen pay."

"I think we ought to find Nikolai and Karoly first," Yuri protested, unwilling for Krukczy to carry Zadny away, or lead him anywhere without their advice. "Karoly would know what to do."

"Not theirs to do," Krukczy said, already shambling away, and the other two got up silently and went after him.

"Wait!" Yuri called after them, afraid to make over much noise on this open hillside. He ran, got in front of Krukczy and tried to block his path. "It's not that much to wait—we can find them first."

"Not theirs to do," Tajny said, and Krukczy lumbered past him and the other two followed, relentless as a landslide.

What did one do? What was right to do? If he went back into the woods, master Karoly had said it, he had no idea where or when the forest might let him out again, or what he might meet in that shadow, alone.

Zadny, let down to walk, skipped and leaped and went with the trolls, a willing companion.

So he saw nothing wiser to do, himself.

13

EVERY BRAMBLE, EVERY HEDGE, EVERY BRANCH IN THE FOR-
est reached out to stay them, Nikolai swore it: he was accustomed to pass through a woods as free as a deer's shadow,
but his eye could discover no path for himself, let alone for
an elderly wizard on an exhausted pony—while Gracja, in
Karoly's hands, had her own notion what was the easiest
route down a hill—not always the wise one. She fetched up
into a dead end, a narrow, leaf-walled wash barriered with a
windfallen tree, and Nikolai had to climb over the trunk to
reach her head.

But having sat down on the trunk in the process, he found
getting up harder than he had expected, and he rested there
to catch his breath.

"It's getting darker," Karoly said.

"I'm trying! This is a woods where we could use a dog,
never mind trying to track that fool hound!"

"I mean it's getting darker faster than it ought to."

Nikolai looked toward what he took for the west, and
glanced over his shoulder to what then must be the east, and
he could see no difference. It had gotten to that time of evening when all light was gray and equal in the woods, when
the trees and the canopy turned to their own woodland
monotones—and there was no knowing what sort of preda-
tors might go on the hunt for boys and dogs once night had
fallen.

That thought lent him strength to get up. He freed Gracja's
rein from the branch that had caught it and backed her out
of her predicament—poor pony, she was as blind-tired as

they were; and she made a powerful effort to get up the slope again. He patted her sweaty neck when they had gotten to the top of the rise, and swore to her that he would get her out of this woods.

"Get down," he said to Karoly. "Get down, she can't carry you anymore."

"We've got to keep going."

"Do it on your own legs. We may need her before this is done. Dammit, old man, just do what I say."

"Can't tell where you'll come out," Karoly muttered, trying to get down, entangled in his cloak, which was snagged on a branch. "Can't tell where he is, *Ysabel* can't get to us, we've just got to go on as we're going, as straight a line as we can hew, however long it takes."

"End up in some bear's belly," Nikolai said under his breath, and tugged the pony into motion so Karoly could get himself past the tree. "Some bear's late supper. Midnight snack. Probably already eaten the dog. Where in *hell* is the troll when you could use him?"

"Keep walking," Karoly said. Which was the only choice he saw.

It was a strange nightfall, a shadow that hung motionless in the east and then, slowly, in the dying of the sun, spread like a starry blight across the valley and the hills. The goblins built a great blazing bonfire, extravagant defiance against the night, and posted their sentries around about, whether against human armies from out of the valley or against others of their kind.

But their own light blinded them to all but each other.

"Join us at the fire," Azdra'ik said to Tamas. "I swear to you, I *swear* to you it's rabbit and venison, nothing else. Nor has ever been. Come."

There were scruples, and there was hunger, but truth to tell, they had little left in the way of provisions, besides that these goblins seemed fairer and more amiable than their smaller cousins, and one could slide toward believing their reassurances, even against experience. Tamas found himself looking toward the fire, beyond the goblin lord's retreating back, and telling himself he was a fool to have come thus far off his guard with the creatures, or to attribute any common decency to them.

But Ela got up, dusted off her skirts, and walked in that direction, which left him solitary and supperless, except a last little heel of stale bread. What they were cooking this time looked like rabbit and smelled like rabbit, for what he could tell. They had torn back the grass to afford safe room for the fire, a blaze thicketed with sticks and spits—each goblin being responsible, as before, for his own supper, which they collectively proposed to share with their prisoners, their—guests, their fellow fugitives from the night and the queen's displeasure: he had no clear idea what they were in the goblin camp, and that in itself made him equally uneasy with the invitation and with their own refusal. If there *were* overtures toward them and he refused, that could be foolish, too. Even if the goblins only offered a shred or two of understanding of what they faced or where they were going . . . it could make a difference in their living or dying tomorrow.

And if there was treachery and if the goblins intended betrayal, he would be more apt to discover it yonder in their company than sitting here alone.

So he got up and joined Ela in the firelight, easing his way in as goblins edged over to give him room. Goblins laughed with each other, albeit grimly, goblins spoke in low voices, and did their cooking, like any group of hunters. He watched the light as if it were the center of a black and unreasoning universe, until the voice within him said,

(Azdra'ik claims he's my servant. What do you think?)

He shrugged it off, watched as a goblin carved a small carcass in pieces, onto a square of leather, judging that that was the provision made for them, and sure enough, the goblin brought the packet to Ela and set it in her hands.

"Young madam," the goblin called her, bowing, and him: "Young sir."

Courtesy. Manners. There was too much puzzling about

Azdra'ik and the company about him, too much of contra-
dictions past unexplained. The ghost flared up all bones and
shreds of grave-clothes, and a shiver went through him, a
fear of believing anything.

But it was not bad rabbit. There was enough to eat, and
warmth from the fire. For a moment or two on end he could
shut his eyes and imagine he was back in his own woods, in
Maggiar. But the conversation around him was not conversation he understood, and the creak of leather and the jan-
gling of rings and ornaments was martial and strange.

He and Ela did not speak. There seemed nothing to say,
that they would say with strangers around them. She seemed
to drift very much as he did, remembering, perhaps, or
thinking.

But her hand rested over the mirror beneath her gown, and
her gaze turned toward the east.

He reached toward her arm. "Don't," he said. "Don't
touch it tonight. Wait." It seemed desperate to him that she
believe him, and he did not know why he should think so,
but what she was doing terrified him.

She let her hand to her lap, and laced her fingers together
and bowed her head.

(Inept, said the ghost. And thinking she knows. Damn
you, boy . . . listen to me. Listen before it's too late.)

He blinked, he looked distractedly at the fire. He reached
for Ela's hands and clenched them in his own, heedless of
goblin stares and nudges of elbows, thinking, God, how can
we survive till morning, how can we last the night, how if
there's not a dawn?

A goblin arrived out of the dark and whispered something
to one goblin, came to Azdra'ik's side and said something
into his ear. Azdra'ik made a gesture and sent off ten or so
of his company, who gathered up their weapons and followed
the messenger.

He was holding Ela's hands too tightly. He let go. But she
laced her right hand in his left and held on, only held on for
dear life.

"Nothing," Azdra'ik said with an airy motion of his fingers. "A maneuver. A movement. Possibly even some of ours."

"Are there others?" Tamas asked in Ela's silence.

"You saw them."

"Shadows in the smoke."

Azdra'ik said something to his company, and some few of them rose and left, gathering up their weapons from beside them. "Troublesome shadows. The queen's shadows. There will be a guard tonight, I assure you. Sleep with at least that confidence."

"In you," Ela challenged him.

"In us," Azdra'ik said. "In us who have not consented to the queen. No, now—" Azdra'ik forestalled her interruption. "Listen to me. For one night, only this night, will you listen to me, young witch, and let me tell you a story. Was a time we ruled this land, was a time we had the respect of men . . ."

"When," asked Ela, "when ever did you have our respect?"

"Oh, long ago. Long and long, when the old stones were young. Before the stone roads and the fences. Then sometimes men guested with us and we with them. But there was a falling out. Some say it was about the fences. Some say another thing. But however it was, a man died, a goblin was to blame, and bound as we were by a promise, and such as we are, and such as the promise was that bound us and men— we had no choice. We lost all the world. It was that absolute. It was that much trust we had placed in our virtue. We assumed too much, we believed in ourselves too implicitly. And we failed. So we left the world—and, young witch, let me tell you, to lose the sun and the moon was a dreadful thing. We would have promised anything for a foothold on this earth. Can you understand that?"

Tamas did. He would not have, before the troll, before the tower, before the woods, before he entertained a ghost within him. The firelight on the flat-nosed, jut-jawed profile lent it elegance, even comeliness—or the dreadful sights he had seen had made even a goblin face seem better to his eyes. He found himself glad of Azdra'ik talking to them, even longed to trust the voice, because it was alive, and in this world.

"After hundreds of years," Azdra'ik went on, in the soft crackle of the fire, "after so long a time, the witch Mirela read our stones and our signs and sought us out; and in exchange for a magic she could not do—one night a year we might see the world again. Of course we would agree. What would we not, for the smallest glimpse of moonlight? Then— you know the story—her daughter Ylena also found the way to us. Set me in my mother's place, Ylena begged us, and offered us a year to see the sun and the moon. For *that*, again—what would we not do? But it was an ugly bargain this witch wanted. We knew what she intended. Some of us spoke for and some against—but our queen in her cleverness said that any wrong Ylena did was a human's choice and a human's crime: that as the guilt of one goblin had damned us, the guilt of this woman was to free us. So she took the witch's bargain. We gained our year, and for all that year— can you imagine? We did everything, everything we had dreamed of since I was born—we walked in the sunlight, we saw the colors, we enjoyed every flavor and texture the world has to offer. We were happy . . . except one thing: that no matter our virtue or our fault, Ylena meant to send us back to exile."

(Virtue, the ghost laughed, and Tamas felt cold inside.)

"So the queen cast a spell, that Ylena should have a child Ylena did not want, despite all her magic—in which—" Azdra'ik made a small gesture. "I was an instrumentality."

"You," Ela said.

"I was," Azdra'ik said, with a downward glance, "in a position of trust. And it was not a position I cared for, let me say."

The anger, the darkness of the ghost was for a moment more than the firelight, more than the hillside and the earth and the presence around them. "Damn you!" burst from Tamas' lips, and he swallowed down the torrent that wanted to follow, stopped his own arm in mid-reach toward Ela and the mirror and knotted both hands together between his knees, where they were safe, where he could not reach after what Ela would not, not yield to him—

Not, not, not, he told himself, daring not shut his eyes, staring into the fire until the light hurt and burned and he could not see the darkness inside him.

". . . he's dreaming awake," Azdra'ik's voice was saying, and he became aware of Ela's hand on his arm, shaking him. "One simply shouldn't bed down with ghosts."

"I didn't," he said between his teeth, acutely aware of Ela's presence. "Don't listen to him."

"Or witches," Azdra'ik said, "but, after all, tomorrow things will be different—in one way or another."

"You were telling us," Tamas said, hands clenched, "what your own share of this is."

"Ah. That."

"Why should we believe anything you say?"

"Man, man, you prejudge us."

"What's the difference, you or the creatures that attacked the towers? What's the difference, you and the ones burning the cities down there?"

"Because we are *not* burning the cities down there. The queen tricked Ylena and held the land, *and* had a hold over Ylena's heir. Well enough if it had stopped there, if the queen or even Ylena could have been content—"

The things the goblin was saying roused echoes, memories of great halls, and goblin courtiers, and music, memories of a reflection that swam in liquid silver—a face that was his . . . or hers, or the queen's, he was not sure, he only knew he did not want to see it clearly. He bit his lip until it hurt.

"I betrayed the secrets of the mirror," Azdra'ik said, "for one reason: if Ylena could have ruled her mirror, the queen with hers could never have prevailed over the world entirely; Ylena's wickedness aside, if another mirror existed, there would be another power—and if one witch failed our measure . . . even if one witch *was* with the queen's, her *ambition* would have led her to wield her mirror for her own interests. Therefore any shaping the queen would cast on the great mirror would always have its rival and neither one could prevail. That was our plan.''

Anger grew and grew in him, the ghost troubling him so that he could scarcely sit still. He saw dark behind the fire, a great mirror swirling with baleful images—and he would not, *would* not consult the knowledge that lodged, screaming for attention, behind his teeth.

"The fragment," Azdra'ik said, "was our unexpected result. Ytresse ruled, then Ylysse, before Ysabel. Any of the three you might have met within the Wood: but when you were lost there, Tamas, my innocent, you strayed straight to the magic that had most claim on your presence. Of all ghosts in that wood, you met only Ylena. And that tells me there's more to this than a fledgling fool's bad luck.''

Thoughts tumbled one over the other. The goblin was half shadow, half light. "You," Azdra'ik said, "you—resound— of magic. Yet you're deaf to it. You come from over-mountain to Ylena's doorstep. And the witchling crosses your path, with the fragment. And . . . much against my advice," Azdra'ik said, looking at Ela, "you've looked into the mirror. What you see the queen can see, if she dares invoke your world within the great mirror. You've guessed that, surely. Tomorrow, you have to compel her to see—what you wish. That's the whole business of the mirror. It's so dreadfully simple.''

Ela said nothing.

"Do you understand?" Azdra'ik asked. "Do you want— perhaps—a year to think about it? To grow older? To bear children and pass this burden on? The i'bu okhthi can hide you—we *will* hide you, and set you away in safety where the queen may not reach you.''

"No," Ela said shortly.

"Pride," said Azdra'ik. "Pride is a deadly matter.''

"I don't believe," Ela said, "that there is anywhere safe.''

"What do you say, young Tamas?''

He thought of Maggiar this time. He thought of home and orchards and their woods and the mountain trails that led straight to the heart of this land, and he thought of gran, and

Karoly, and how gran had frightened them and Karoly had taken them over-mountain in full knowledge of where he was bringing them.

"There's no hiding," he said. "There's no hiding place even for a single year, that I know of."

A long time Azdra'ik looked at them, one and the other. Tamas thought—even began to hope—that Azdra'ik might know something he did not, and offer them a place.

"None that I would trust implicitly, no. No cradle for fools. No hiding place. Besides that we have no way off this hillside without more magic than we've yet seen, young witch. Make the sun come up. Make the day come. There's your first challenge."

"No," Ela said. "No. I won't fight her about that."

"What will you fight her for?" Azdra'ik asked, and the ghost in Tamas listened, oh, it listened, and he trembled.

Ela said, "I'd be a fool to say. Mistress said—never give that away to anyone. I think she meant anyone. And I won't."

Anger welled up, anger he hoped was not his, at her obstinacy, at her damning them to this encounter, at her refusal to argue or to listen . . . anger at Azdra'ik, who rose from beside them and walked away to the edge of the fire, a dark and martial figure that might have been human.

Not my anger, he told himself, struggling with the presence in him. Not my resentments, not my advice.

Shut up, he told the ghost, and feared it would find a way yet to harm them. It was vengeful. It had learned treachery at its mother's knee. He—had learned it from Azdra'ik . . . he had learned it from Karoly, if he knew how to recognize guile at all.

An unarmed babe, he told himself, a boy who should not have left his father's roof to be put where he was set, to fight a war where truth was bent and what one saw and what *was* were at war.

Why, gran? Why didn't you teach us more?

Stories about the fairies and green valleys and magic waterfalls? What kind of help was that? Was that all you could think to give your grandsons? They said you were wise. They said you were a great and dreadful witch. And, fairy-tales? Was that the limit of your magic?

Damn it, gran! What are we going to do tomorrow? If I've got one ghost, why not yours? Couldn't you manage *that*, if witches have the run of the forest?

Hate him, the voice came back, soft and bitter; and he was looking at Azdra'ik's back, thinking that he could never take the creature face to face, that somewhere in this Azdra'ik meant to betray them—that at some time he would have to take the creature, from this vantage if he could, preferably from this vantage, and with no one else to know—because he was not a fighter. And not, evidently, a wizard either, who could bend the creature to anything useful.

Be rid of him, echoed deep inside him. Protect *yourself*. You have too much value. Think of your own kind.

It left him a different feeling than the first ghost—less violent, more cold. Gran? he wondered. Is that gran? Or is it lying? Or is it something else altogether?

Many of the goblins had gone away from the fire, some to pallets spread about, some to the shadows. He saw them, he felt Ela's touch on his arm and felt her departure, he supposed for sleep. He watched her walk to where they had set their packs, near the horses, was aware as she wrapped her cloak about her, settled down and tucked up against the saddles and the packs. All the camp was settling, and oh, he wanted the idea of sleep—but he feared it, feared the ghost and its treacheries. He only wrapped himself in his cloak for comfort against the wind and decided at least to loose the buckles about his collar and his ribs, and find himself a comfortable way to prop himself, head on arms, simply to rest his smoke-stung eyes and armor-weary shoulders.

To his dim suspicion the ghost did not immediately trouble him. The dark within the shadow of his folded arms was empty and comfortable; he saw only—imagined—he was sure—a night clear and sparkling with stars. Not a bad dream, he decided, not a threatening dream. He heaved a sigh and imagined himself walking along boggy ground that seemed somehow familiar to him. He could not remember when he had acquired the memory, but he thought certainly he had seen it before, every detail of the reeds and the starlit water at their roots, at just this moment, on just this night.

The moon was a sliver of herself, embracing shadow. That, he saw, looking up, and then saw the whole lake, and the dark hills, like a blow to the heart.

No, he thought in fright, wanting escape, because he did know this shore, this lake—he had had this dream before, and it was a trick and a trap that had brought him here.

But before he could look away a movement drew his eye: came a troll past him in the dark, one troll, and another and another. That was enough: he did not want to see more than that. The dream was about to revert to the nightmare in the tunnel, and that might be preferable to this place, but he most wanted to wake up and have no dreams at all.

Then came a pale doglike shape down the hill. It looked for all the world like Zadny, and he could not understand why he would dream about that.

After the dog came a boy, so like Yuri in every way that his heart ached with homesickness. He stood perhaps a moment longer than he should have, watching Yuri chase after the hound who chased the trolls. It made no sense, it made absolutely no sense, except in his attempt to change this dreadful lake shore into something he knew, perhaps his dreams were going to be better disposed to him and show him something he longed to see. The three trolls—that was a bizarre touch, and there was enough of nightmare and of memory both about that apparition to disturb him; but seeing Yuri—cautions fell out of his mind. He even tried to call out to Yuri, reckless of the dark and the wild shore, but in the perverse way of dreams, he could not get a sound out, or run, when he tried—no matter what his effort he could travel no faster than a walk, as if the land resisted him, as if, in this dream, he could not recall the next bit of ground beneath his feet fast enough to enable him to go faster—he could not look down and look at Yuri at once, and he feared something else appearing, every time he took his eyes off his brother.

He walked and walked, while the trolls had gone farther

than was safe—there was a guard on the lake that he knew
was the goblins' lake, and the three trolls had gone past that
point, he was sure they had. He began to be afraid where
this dream was going, and told himself that it was of no
concern, his dream was powerless to harm anyone, and he
could withstand any fright it offered: Yuri was home safe in
bed. *He* was the one in real danger tomorrow. If he hoped
anything good would come from the dream, he hoped if Yuri
was dreaming, too, Yuri might hear him and wake up with
a memory of talking to him, and remember it. Maybe that
was what this dream was for. And, if that was the case, he
did not want to tell Yuri how afraid he was, or how dreadful
this place was, he simply wanted to say—Do what's right,
do what's wise, Yuri, mind papa and grow up, and if I don't
make it home—

No, he did not want to scare the boy. I've had adventures,
he would say, if he could. I've met this girl—

No, not that either: Yuri would make fun of him and girls.
And how could he explain Ela to his family?

—I don't think mother would like her.

But I think—where would I be without her? And where
would she be without me? She's very brave, Yuri. I don't
think she ever had a friend but Pavel and her mistress, and
that's no way to grow up. I think—

I think I needed someone like her. And you really would
like her. If she were your age she'd climb trees and run races.

God, he thought then, she *is* Yuri's age, isn't she? And in
his dream he said:

Yuri, if I get home I'll have the time to do things you
wanted to do. . . . I really mean to, this time . . .

All these things he made up in his mind to say, so perhaps
they were said. He walked along beside Yuri, chattering like
a fool about anything he could think to say. But after a time
he could go no further, he did not know why, he just stopped,
or Yuri was getting ahead of him; and Yuri just kept walking, farther and farther along the shore, where Zadny had
gone, where the trolls had.

Come back, he tried to say. Yuri! Come back!

But Yuri trudged along the boggy, reed-rimmed shore until he was part of the shadows.

Then came a slight shimmering of the lake, as if someone had shaken water in a goblet. Water lapped at the reeds. Metal clanged in that impenetrable darkness, like a gate gone shut, and he tried to go forward, but he could not take a step, could not call out, could not move.

And Zadny came running from out of that darkness, running for his very life.

Zadny! he cried silently, as the hound hurtled past him and up the hill. Halfway up, Zadny stopped and looked back, tail tucked, as if he had heard, after all, but he spun about and began to run again, to the top of the hill, where he vanished, as the lake did, as the shore, and the sky, the way dreams began to come apart when they had made their point.

He saw the drifting of a shape in this half-dream. He heard the ghostly voice saying, Fool, it's *not* a dream, never think things are only dreams, here.

He opened his eyes on dark that promised nothing of morning and gave not a hint of time passed or yet to come. He achieved a few moments of sleep and sleep left him with nothing but troubling images—did not purge his mind of nightmares or break off the chain of sleepless yesterdays and yesternights that ran unbroken through his awareness. His very bones felt now as if a force ran through him, insufficient to sustain him and too intense to make breathing easy. The movement of goblins about their watch, the flicker of the fire, all floated through his awareness, disjunct from every experience, every memory equally important: dreams of home, dreams of the ghost, with never a boundary of dark in which he could say, Asleep, or Awake, or know unequivocally past from future.

Ela understood the dark around them, and he knew that— intimately. Ela was awake and aware of his awareness. All of which was too much for him. He dropped his head into his hands and wished that whatever was happening would be over tomorrow so that he need not spend another night like this one, nor another day after it, never, ever another day like this, if he died.

Ela was angry at his despair, and something more than angry. He looked up from his hands to find her bending to him, reaching for his arm, and he flinched from her, thinking how the goblins were witness, the goblins had already laughed at their apparent dalliance, and now he was humiliated in her eyes, in the helpless trembling that came over his limbs, that he did not want her to discover, but she did. She hovered by him and he sat there wanting to scream, wanting to laugh, wanting to cry—but she *knew* what had happened to him, that it was magic that would not let him rest, would never let him rest until he had done what magic charged him do—that was what gnawed at him, she had not understood it before now, and she was afraid of it breaking out ungoverned in him . . .

"Mistress said," she whispered, as if that made enough sense, and gripped his hand with a force unlikely in so small a girl. Ela had not slept either, Ela had been thinking—as one did, on the brink of magic, as one must, when so much was pent up inside trying to find its way out. *She* was feeling it. And she had no doubt now that he felt the same force running through his bones.

"I'm not a wizard," he protested in their strange, half-spoken conversation. It horrified him to think of sorcery breaking out in him like some loathsome plague; to think of Ylena's ghost shedding him like some outworn skin and acting in ways he could not predict, maybe against Azdra'ik, maybe against Ela, he could not understand Ylena's motives or its presence, except he had given the ghost the chance it wanted to escape the woods.

"Dammit, it's not *me*, Ela, it's not me, it's the witch, it's somebody named Ylena that I don't know about, I don't know what she'll do, I don't know what she wants but what she wanted when I was in her house—"

But he could remember the mirror beginning to crack, the dark and bright lines running everywhere across its face, and the light breaking out through the seams of the world. He could remember Azdra'ik being her lover, and he could still *feel*, as if it had been a moment ago, Ylena's lips on his fingers, on his mouth. He could remember her walking up beside him, and seeing white bone through her flesh, when Azdra'ik had bargained him free.

"I won't go tomorrow for some dead woman, Ela! I won't do it! I don't even know what we're going to do."

But he was lying, he knew he would go, it was quivering in his bones and his brain, and he had no command over it.

"Hush," she said, "hush."

She had touched where the mirror rested beneath her gown and it was suddenly worse, overwhelmingly worse. He caught her hand, too hard, and tried to be gentle, but he was shaking beyond his power to master his own strength. He thought of taking the mirror from her—he *wanted* the mirror in his own hand, because he did know what to do, and she did not.

He flung himself to his feet instead and staggered for balance, while goblin sentries looked their way in alarm—incongruously unsure whether it was reason for weapons or not; while Ela—Ela rose slowly and was angry with him, with the ghost, he could not tell, he could not at the moment tell which he was.

"Ela, I can't—can't touch you again, I daren't, I daren't be close to you tomorrow, you understand? That's what it wants. When we can't deal with it, it's going to turn on us! Stay away from me, don't touch me!"

Ela shook her head, and a quiet confidence came around her, about her. "It's mine to carry," she said, so firmly he could not himself disbelieve it. "Sit down. Sit *down*."

He did. How could one do other than what Ela wanted? He fell onto the stone and sat down, dizzy and confused, and Ela sank down by him, and took his arm in hers and held on to him.

"Shut your eyes," she said. "Trust me."

It was not easy. The ghost protested, wailed and flinched from Ela's touch. (Fool! it cried.) But he made himself do it, and found himself after a moment drawing easier breaths, and then a great, deep one, that seemed to come from the bottom of his soul.

Dangerous, he thought. Deadly dangerous, this trust he let her impose on him. Or the ghost thought so. He shut his eyes, on a welcome, vacant dark, and heard Ela say—or was it Karoly? —Take your time, Tamas, *think*, Tamas . . .

They had their supper at least, from Gracja's pack, no thanks to their foresight. The two of them sat down to eat it in the tangle of woods that did not seem willing to give them up, and Nikolai for one had diminished appetite. "Not even a belt knife on the boy," Nikolai said to Karoly, over stale bread and sausage toasted on a stick. "I should have drowned that dog when I had a chance. —It's burning."

"Shhh," master Karoly said sharply, and sat staring fiercely at the fire while the sausage on his side of the fire caught fire and sizzled and popped and cindered. Nikolai watched the sausage, for want of other visible result— watched it turn to cinder, and the oil on the stick catch fire, and the stick burn, and the end fall off in the fire.

Curious, he thought. One wondered what wizards did. Or thought. Or thought they thought. Meanwhile the boy was still lost, *they* had to get up somehow and keep going, and he ached from head to foot. He had pulled the pony uphill and down, the pony having, reasonably enough, no driving interest in where they were going, until finally Karoly could not walk any further, and the god knew *he* could not carry the old man on his back.

So they sat and burned a sausage to the powers of the woods, or whatever forces Karoly was engaging.

Finally Karoly blinked and said, not to him, he thought, "No. No. Dammit."

The air was cold for a moment. For a moment Nikolai was certain he felt a breath on the side of his neck, and the fire went down flat and sprang up again.

"I know that!" Karoly objected.

Fine, Nikolai thought, fine, now we're talking to the air.

He looked around uneasily, afraid of what he might see, but he found nothing and felt nothing.

Then Karoly leapt to his feet. "Get the horse!"

"I'm not—" —your servant, was what was first to Nikolai's mouth, but before he could even get it out, the old man was wandering off into the woods, into the dark without a care in the world for his safety or their weapons or the supplies in their packs.

"Damn!" Nikolai hurled his aching body into motion and stuffed their belongings in the pack, threw the pack on the pony and buried the fire in the earnest desire not to have the forest burning down around them.

The old man was out of sight. It was a crashing in the brush he followed, tugging Gracja after him in the dark for fear of his head if he tried to ride her through the woods. It was a breathless hill later that he even caught sight of Karoly, and onto the other side of it and downhill again before he overtook the old man.

Karoly knew he was there. Karoly spared him a glance and said something about the boys and trouble, but he knew that already. Something had persuaded Karoly of the right direction: Nikolai most earnestly hoped that was the case. The old man talked to ghosts and one of them had finally come through for him, but *he* could not see it, he could not tell.

Then he spied a pale shape in the shadows ahead of them, a pale, dog-sized shape, going through the brush and circling and looking back, not as if he were following a trail, but in the manner of a dog desperate to be followed.

Something had happened to the boy. The dog was roughed from scratches, dark marks on the fur—he limped on one paw and the other and evaded every attempt to lay hands on him. There was nothing to assume now but the worst; and Nikolai hurried as best he could with the horse in tow. "Get on," he said to Karoly when they had gotten to a single spot of flat ground. "Ride after him, I'll follow!" Because he feared there was no time for a man afoot, no time for maybe and no time for consideration. He took the bow from the saddle and held the reins for Karoly.

But when he looked about he could have sworn a man stood near them—real enough that his first impulse was to reach for his sword: a man in armor, who paid no attention to mortal threats, Pavel, he thought, but young Pavel, who walked away through the trunks of trees. There seemed to be a woman ahead of him, and maybe a girl, he could not tell.

Something wet touched his hand. Claws raked his leg.

"Damn!" he cried, before he knew it was the hound: and the hound was bounding away from them, after the ghosts, as if they should follow.

"Follow them to hell," Nikolai muttered, because following ghosts and stupid dogs could well lead there. Karoly was trying to get his foot into the stirrup, the pony was moving about, uneasy with good reason as Nikolai saw it, but he shoved the old man for the saddle and led off, with the most queasy feeling they were not anywhere people could get to without magic involved; and without it there was no way back.

14

A SOFT HISS AND A SPUTTER OF SPARKS BROKE INTO HALF-dreams. Tamas suffered a moment of confusion, tucked into a stiff, foot-tingling knot next the fire, unable at the moment to recall what fireside of his life he was sitting at, or what was the warm and unaccustomed weight resting against his shoulder. But it proved disturbingly the latest place in memory, goblin-owned. The escaping sparks were a floating image in his vision, the night was still thick about them, smoke going up from a fire half smothered in earth, and the horses—goblin horses as well as their own—made uneasy sounds beyond the pale of the light.

"Good morning," Azdra'ik said somberly, "such as it is." Something else he added in his own tongue, exhorting his folk to wake and move, as seemed. Ela rested still against Tamas' shoulder, awake, but too weary to move and wondering (he was distressingly aware) whether there might be any breakfast, any warm cup of tea before they completely killed the fire. She wanted a hot drink very badly, astonishingly calm in her reckoning that there might be no more chances for such pleasures hereafter.

So she should have it, Tamas decided, excused himself to her and got up and told the goblin who was shoveling dirt onto the fire to desist.

That one scowled at him and he scowled back and interposed himself bodily until Azdra'ik intervened, asking what was the matter.

"Ela wants tea." That sounded foolish, but he felt exceedingly righteous in his insistence. Azdra'ik heaved a human sigh, shrugged and drew the other goblin aside for a word—which left untouched a single burning branch.

So Tamas fetched the wherewithal from their gear, and brewed a single cup of tea, with singed fingers, while camp was breaking.

"Thank you," Ela said when he brought it to her, seeming pleased that he had done that for her. It was indeed a silly thing to have done, he thought. But it lent a sense of their own pace in the morning which felt strangely necessary, in ways Ela herself might know, and it set him to quiet, unhurried recollection, as if, over the edge now, he had to pull pieces out of memory, as if—as if the pieces *were* there. . . .

He thought for no particular reason of master Karoly at home, taking matters at his own studied pace—Hurry, hurry! two rascal boys would shout, eager to be at the orchard or the brook or wherever they had convinced the old man to take them for their day's lessons. So what *is* the answer? two scoundrelly lads would ask, impatient to be away from their lessons and away from the smelly bottles and vessels in the tower room.

Master Karoly would say, In time, in time, hush, be still, nothing works but in its own time.

Even with magic? they had asked once.

And Karoly had said, in his close-mouthed way, Especially.

Especially this morning, Tamas thought, while the camp broke apart in martial order, while, under the final shovelful of earth, the fire went as dark as the heavens. Ela had her cup of tea and he had his moment to himself, recalling the tower study on a rainy morning when the old man had said, for at least the hundredth and maybe thousand and first time, Think about it, think about it, boy. Don't ask me the answer. Don't even ask yourself. The answer's not in either place.

What had they been talking about? What had he been asking, that morning?

Something about clouds and rain, or—?

"*If* our witchly guests are ready," Azdra'ik arrived to say, as goblins were going every which way into and out of the shadows. Behind Azdra'ik a goblin led up Lwi and Skory, saddled, without their leave; and Tamas frowned as he rose and took both sets of reins from the creature—angry at Azdra'ik's hurrying them, angry at the handling of their gear and their belongings and the lack of consultation when he was not, *not* hurrying this morning. He still did not know why. It was not the ghost. But he firmly made up his mind Azdra'ik should not be the one in their company to bid him do anything, or to require anything of him or her.

And most of all not to make him lose a thought.

"Don't hurry her," he said shortly. "Don't hurry *me*, master goblin, if you want our help."

"Ah," Azdra'ik said, hand on what ought to be a heart, extravagant as always. "And can you bid the queen wait? *That's* the question, isn't it?"

He stood sullenly telling himself he had had far and away enough of m'lord goblin in recent days; and telling himself that Azdra'ik was no different than he had ever been, and that it was fear he was feeling now: his body and his senses said that it was time for a sunrise and the stars were still bright—that was what had him short-tempered and jumping at every offense.

And if magic had sustained him through these sleepless days and nights—it had more to do now, and he felt nothing in himself like the currents of it that ran through Ela's fingers or the passionless confidence she had when that power worked—this girl that was hardly older than Yuri. He could not capture that confidence for himself this sunless morning.

Are we fools? he wanted to ask her. Are we fools to go ahead, or should I have given you better advice?

No, he thought then; she thought: even that distinction became muddled at unpredictible moments. He distressed her and distracted her and she wanted him quiet now, that was all. Shut *up*, she wished him, justifiably. So he asked nothing, tried to think nothing, and waited while Ela tucked the cup away and got to the saddle.

But as he was getting up on Lwi he suffered a lightning

stroke of overwhelming panic, asking himself what he was doing, why he believed Ela, what a lad from Maggiar was doing, riding with a pack of goblin rebels. It was mad. He was mad. The whole world was, this morning. He kept thinking: Stop, go back, this isn't where I planned to go when I left home, this isn't what I planned to be, I don't want to die today, in this dark.

But he settled into the saddle, while, in his moment of fear, the spiteful ghost stirred within him, saying things he could not grasp, something about choices and cowards, and showing him (but he would not look) the faces of goblin courtiers and the sound of goblin promises. He patted Lwi's neck, warmed cold fingers under Lwi's mane, and told himself Lwi had much rather other company than goblin horses, Lwi had much rather have the sun come up, and much, much rather his own stable. But Lwi, with a snort and a shaking of his neck, did what he had to, as the company began to move, as goblin riders surrounded them and swept them onto a starlit trail. And Lwi's rider did—what he had to—no way back now, everything in motion from very long ago. He had as much as gran and Karoly had given him, that was all; and as much as he had learned on this trail, of goblins and of the witches of the Wood . . .

He had a tenuous awareness of Ela riding beside him. Ela was not thinking about home. Ela was thinking about the dark, and the hills, and the lake in his dreams, the same lake, that had been the bargain, and the point of treachery, and the home of the goblins for hundreds of years.

There was the place where wizardry lay veined in the rocks and sown into the soil and mingled with the water and the air. And in that place there was all the magic and more that a mortal could draw on and use. That was where they were going. Ela believed in evil and believed that that evil was on the side of the possessor of that lake, in a long, long series of deceptions, goblins against the witches of the Wood, and in that place, with all of that to draw on, and the mirror in her hand, what was just and right had to count for something . . .

He wished it were so clear to him: evil and good had seemed so much more definable when he had thought all the evil came from goblins, and the ghost had done its best to urge that on him, but its reasoning was increasingly suspect; he wished he could recall something master Karoly had said on the matter of wickedness, but in all the years of teaching them, for the life of him, this dark morning, he could not recall a thing master Karoly had said on the subject, except that silly business of the frogs in the tackle-basket: It was not kind to *them*, boy. His mind fell into *that* memory for some reason he could not fathom. It was not kind to *them*.

And how did a man find his way on such thin and long-ago advice?

And what about the fish, that they had caught that very day for their supper?

Something about necessity, and doing what had to be done, and using no more of the earth than one needed . . .

Spookier and spookier, Yuri thought, worse than the troll's tunnel before he had known the troll. It was not a hallway, it was not a tunnel, it was just a place he could not get out of. There was the shimmer of water on the ground, everywhere the sound of water, and the chill and the smell of water. He had never imagined such a peculiar kind of tunnel, and as for trolls, he would give a great deal for the sight of Krukczy just now. But Zadny had run past him in such a terror he could not catch him.

All of which ought to tell a boy to go back—immediately. But when he had tried that, he had found himself up against a wall of—just nothing, that felt like an edge of some kind, where you could fall and fall forever if you got overbalanced; and Zadny might have run right off it, for all he knew. He hoped not. He hoped there was not another such edge ahead—though he thought not, because the trolls seemed to have gone on through; or they had just fallen off into the dark one after the other without a yell or a protest or anything, and that was not like trolls.

But he was truly scared, now, if anyone had asked him—

and ever so glad when he suddenly saw a light ahead, a hazy glow toward which he was walking.

And brighten, the pathway did, until there was a ceiling and there were walls as well as a floor—all rippling with water-patterns, and light beyond that watery surface, the way a pond might look if he was walking along the bottom, in some great bubble, and looking up at the sun.

It was water when he looked back, and when he went near the walls, they shimmered as if the bubble he was in might collapse. That scared him.

But he did not see any way to go but straight ahead, and if somebody like the goblin queen was doing this he did not want to give her any ideas about collapsing the bubble around him. And thinking about it might make it happen, if this place was like dreams, as it seemed to be. So he walked, quickly as he could.

Then—he could not be sure at first—there seemed to be someone standing in the watery uncertainties of the hallway, a long, long distance in front of him. He wondered if it was his own reflection he was seeing. Or it might be a goblin. But even when he stopped walking that figure looked as if it was moving closer. And when he blinked to be sure he saw it, it had moved closer still, seeming like someone he knew very well, who just should not be here. Whether he walked toward it or not, it just kept coming; and looked more and more—

Like Bogdan. It did look *exactly* like Bogdan; and he should have been ever, ever so glad—he would have been; but Bogdan did not smile, Bogdan did not meet him with open arms like a brother, or act astonished to see him, or even ask him how he had come here.

Bogdan only said, as if he were mildly disappointed:

"I expected Tamas."

Hour upon hour the stars stayed overhead, the same stars that shone down on Maggiar, as far as Tamas could tell; and the pole stars had not moved in all the time they had been riding. But he did not know how that could possibly be—unless the very sky was standing still even in Maggiar, and unless lord Sun himself had no power to break the witch's hold—in which case his own family and every farmer in Maggiar and lands clear to the great sea must have wakened in confusion this morning, must be huddling together, hour by hour of this darkness, looking up at the stars and wondering at the meaning of it and whether there would be another sunrise.

But Ela commented quietly, as they rode side by side among the goblins: "Nothing changes here. The stars don't move. It's the same hour. It's always the same hour. That's the spell she's cast. Until that changes, nothing can."

She need not have spoken aloud. He was hearing her thinking just then, and wishing he did not, because in her thoughts was something about this not being a part of the present world they were traveling in, and it not having been a part of the present world ever since they had entered the Wood.

He was not sure of that. He thought about what master Karoly had said, how one thing touches everything—and recalled the deer ravaging the woods, and the store rooms piled high with furs, and the spring failing to come . . . all this silent colloquy, while they rode above the fires in the valley, all this, while they rode in a serene high hills quiet. He thought, All this *is* there. What we do here, reflects there. Like the mirror . . . it's all one mirror, and which side is the reflection, and which is true?

Riders burst past, with that strange thump of pads and scraping of their horses' claws. The last reined back to ride by them, to Lwi's offense. "Itra'hi are out there," Azdra'ik said out of the shadows. "Sniffing around the hills. I don't think they'll dare come at us. We're going right where their mistress would have us. I don't know what she has to complain of."

Disquieting thought.

"Unless you'd like to change your minds," Azdra'ik added. "We can still retreat."

"I don't see we'd gain anything." Tamas felt constrained to give a civil answer while the ghost or his own fear clamored otherwise; and he *had* lost a thought, confound the creature, but for some reason he found himself adding: "Possibly the queen can make a mistake."

"Oh, the queen makes many mistakes. But so few can take advantage of them."

"Maybe we will."

"The night the mirror failed," Azdra'ik said lightly, "the morning failed. And for two days thereafter. Witches and wizards knew. But the world never did. Did it? Do your old men say?"

It cast his calculations into disorder and agreed with Ela's way of thinking. "You mean no one elsewhere even noticed?"

"Except within her power—as we clearly are. This is a night of her making. This is the goblin night. This is the goblin realm you've crossed into. And she rules it absolutely. To do other than she wills is a difficult matter. Will you still challenge her?"

You're wrong, he thought, forgetting the question. You're wrong, master goblin. One thing touches everything. The deer came to *our* woods. And the goblin queen doesn't rule everything.

"Here is your last chance," Azdra'ik said. "Hereafter— you have no retreat." With which, Azdra'ik moved off, with a suddenness that unnerved Lwi and made him jostle Skory.

In the next moment, round the shoulder of the hill a glistening horizon unfolded. He forgot what he was saying. He forgot everything he had had in mind to say, as he saw the starlit water cupped between the hills.

The lake, he thought, the place exactly, in every detail, that he had seen in his dreams.

The goblins in front of them rode down the steep incline toward the shore, fantastical shadows, they and their horses, against the star-sheen on the lake. They followed that lead, perforce, and other goblins rode down after them.

"The queen knows we're here," Ela said.

He felt nothing of the queen's presence. For a moment he

felt not even the wind around them, and doubted what a moment ago he had thought he understood.

"Then do something," he said. The sense of urgency was suddenly overwhelming.

"Not yet," Ela said.

"Not yet. Not yet. This is the place, Ela, this is the lake, this is where she lives. I saw it last night, I've seen it before . . ."

"Everything here is what she wishes," Ela said. "Even we are. We couldn't have come here, else."

"No! Don't believe that! *We're* here. We're here because *we* decided, don't think anything else."

But the hill was the very hill that Yuri and the trolls had descended in his dream—the very shore on which they had vanished, and Zadny had come back again, terrified and alone. . . .

Foolish fear. It was entirely unreasonable that Yuri or Zadny had been here. It was the sort of thing his own mind might conjure, out of his homesickness, that was all, and the goblin queen had nothing to do with it.

But that meant his vision of Bogdan might be no different, and that there was no hope of finding him. Or—the thought came to him, and now he was not sure it was his own—if the mirror could make anything happen, if the queen could learn anything of his family none of them was safe . . .

His confidence ebbed away from him as they drew rein on the very shore of the goblins' lake, and the horses, disrespectful of haunted places, dipped their heads to drink. He was terrified for his family, for his brother, for his land—

But Ela's thoughts slipped in again, calm as the lake in front of them, on which the horses' intrusion sent out an irreverent ripple far across the mirrorlike surface—Ela had no attachments to anyone or anything, except, remotely, him—the goblin queen herself had seen to that; but not alone the queen. Her mistress *Ysabel* had left her no certainty, even about her own identity, but she had no one the goblin queen could threaten: everything she owned was hers. She stared into the dark, her hand above the mirror beneath her gown, he could feel it as if it rested against *his* heart, and said, so faintly he could scarcely hear:

"When I wish. That's my choice. When *I* wish. And no one can change that."

The lake reflected the sky and the sliver of moon so perfectly the mind grew dizzy searching for the seam of substance and image. One was the other. Up was down. Down was up. And the juncture between the two was the very heart of illusion. There, something said to him, there is the place.

It might have been the ghost that spoke. It might have been Ela. But the fear that stirred when Azdra'ik climbed down and walked along that reedy edge—that was most surely the ghost.

Treachery, it said. Treachery. Watch him. This is a potent place.

Treachery? he thought. Azdra'ik serves his own kind. Is that treacherous in him?

He slid down from Lwi's saddle and intended to lead Lwi with him; but a goblin offered to take the reins. He gave them into the creature's hand, thinking if there was duplicity now, if there was ill intent, it needed little violence to achieve its purpose. Either Azdra'ik's folk were rebels against their queen or they were the queen's most loyal subjects. And no goblin had moved against them yet.

Then he thought of what Azdra'ik had said, that his kind would be whatever the mirror made them—whatever the mirror could make them; and something about the fragment . . . that as long as it existed . . .

Ela had said and he had not understood until now. They were in the queen's realm, as close to the queen's absolute will as she could compel them or lure them. They were her enemies. They bore what the queen most dearly wanted—without wanting them to succeed. And in the goblin queen's sight, they were here with her permission, walking into her hands, himself, Ela, Azdra'ik and all of them . . .

Delicate, oh, so delicate, to be here within the queen's will in her view of the mirror, and not to be *as* the queen willed in their own. The whole world poised on the knife's edge of that distinction, precarious as a next and necessary breath, two reflections nearly identical—Ela with her hand poised above the mirror, and himself—

Himself, walking along the lake shore in Azdra'ik's tracks, with his sword at his side and intent against the queen in his heart.

He trod on bog. One boot leaked. He looked down before he thought, at water among cat-tail roots, reflecting his presence, and the dark reeds; and he had seen this exact thing before, so small and ridiculous a detail, but he had dreamed it, the exact same sight; and when he had looked up, in his dream . . .

—He beheld the face of the watcher on the shore, the armored figure whose face shifted with the changing moon. In his dream he had not recognized him—but of course it was Azdra'ik who faced him on the shore, Azdra'ik who, in that very image of his dream and this moment, turned his face from him, folded his arms and stood looking philosophically across the lake.

"Don't believe the quiet," Azdra'ik said. "The queen isn't waiting. This is her spell. This is her mirror. We're standing in it. The question is—will there be anything else? So far, our fledgling witch accepts what she sees."

"I've dreamed this," he said. "I saw my brother in the mirror. I saw him in the company of goblins like you. Is he possibly alive?"

"I'm sure I don't know."

"*Don't* you."

"Are we back to lies and liar?" Azdra'ik faced him, the exact figure of his nightmares, of his prophetic visions, he had no idea. "Not I, not I, lord human. Do you suppose I dealt with your ghostly tenant all those years ago . . . for my queen's welfare?"

The ghost he had thought might be gone moved in him like the striking of a snake—there was blinding anger. He walked away without thinking about it, along the boggy edge, and on a saner uncertainty and a steadier breath, looked back, in possession of himself again, forewarned of its presence and sure, now, that the ripples he sent into the still lake were of his own making.

"Where will I find her?" he asked Azdra'ik.

"Find whom?"

"The queen, of course."

"You're quite mad. With that sword, with my dagger, will you attack her?"

"Yes."

Azdra'ik grinned, as if he had been waiting for that very thing, as if the dream were still proceeding, in the way of dreams, with a sense of necessity. "I'll take you there," Azdra'ik said, and, splashing across the boggy ground, gave orders to one and the other of his people.

Tamas looked toward Ela. She sat on Skory's back, Skory still as a painted image. Her hand was where it had been, above the mirror she wore beneath her gown; and he thought then—

Perhaps I should tell her what I'm doing.

But she's aware. And as for where I am in her mirror— I'm either, aren't I? I'm in the queen's mirror and I'm in Ela's, and when she looks, I'll be there—

(Don't rely on it, the ghost said. Young fool. Her fears can overwhelm her. Fears for *you*, young fool. She's blind and deaf to what her mistress taught. It's disaster . . .)

Azdra'ik's hand landed on his shoulder, startling him, making him look more closely than he liked into Azdra'ik's face.

"Come with me," Azdra'ik said. "I'll show you the way."

"To her?"

"As close as we can, as close as ever you'll wish."

Fear for *me*? he asked himself, disquieted. When did she ever care for *me*?

Am I doing the right thing?

They walked along the lake rim, the same path he had dreamed of Yuri taking, following the trolls. And they were not alone. Four of Azdra'ik's company were behind them— he discovered that as he glanced back.

The lake shimmered as it had in his dream, a watery flash of reflection, all around them, and above them. The stars vanished, and a gate clanged shut behind them.

15

IT WAS NOT AS IF THERE WAS ANYWHERE TO GO, IT WAS NOT
as if he had tried to get away and not as if he had done
anything wrong except be where his brother had not expected
him, but Bogdan insisted on holding Yuri's arm as they
walked the tunnel. "That hurts," Yuri cried, trying to twist
loose. It did hurt. And Bogdan jerked him hard.

"Behave," Bogdan said harshly.

"I am! But where are we going? We need to find Tamas!"

"We need to find Tamas," Bogdan mocked him, and
swung him around to look him in the face. "Do you know
where he is? *Where* is he?"

"I don't know." It happened to be the truth, but the way
Bogdan asked him he would not have told anything he knew.
"Let me go!"

"What are you doing here?"

"I don't know." That sounded stupid. "I just decided to
follow you, that's all!"

"Decided to follow us." Bogdan gave him a shake.
"You're lying, Yuri. Where is he?"

"I don't know! You're hurting me! Let go!"

"Let me tell you something. They don't play games here.
They don't understand boys here, they don't have any, and if
you keep on like that they won't have *you*, do you hear what
I'm saying? Don't play these people for fools. It doesn't work,
here. They'll kill you, do you understand, they'll kill our
mother, our father, every single one of us, if you try to play
them for fools —*do you understand me, little brother?*"

"I don't know what you're doing with them! Why don't we run away?"

"There is no running away, get that through your head. These are dangerous people. Offend them and they'll go against us. Accommodate them and there's nothing that can stand in our way. Maggiar can rule everything from the mountains west to the river and beyond that. The goblins have no interest in ruling men. *We* can do that for them. *We* can be the power, our little Maggiar can become an important place in the world, *the* important place, and there's nothing in the way of that. They actually *want* us to succeed, do you hear?"

Maggiar being a power and the goblins keeping promises did not sound reasonable to him. He could not think what to say to Bogdan. He knew he was waiting too long to think of it; and Bogdan lost patience with talking to a mere boy and spun him about and haled him down the tunnel.

Then of a sudden—it was more a change in the place around them than the opening of a door or a gate—they were in a hall blazing with lights, and those lights floating about in arches of green stone that itself rippled with water shadows. Yuri gawked, he could not help it, he was still thinking about how they had gotten into this place, and he had never seen lights floating in the air before, or stone the color of old summer leaves, or a place as rich and powerful as this.

But he stopped gawking then, because goblins came walking toward them from all sides, some no taller than he was, some taller than Bogdan, which few people were, and all of them bristling with spiny armor and with weapons. He was ready for Bogdan to draw his sword and defend their lives from these creatures, but evidently not. Evidently these were the friends Bogdan was talking about. Bogdan only said,

"This is my younger brother. He's mine. Keep your hands off him. Understand?"

Yuri did *not* like the look in the goblins' eyes. Least of all did he trust the whispering behind them as Bogdan hurried him on along the fantastical hall. He had heard that kind of thing from bullies and wicked boys like his sometime friends back home. He pulled to free himself from Bogdan's grip, wanting to find the tunnel again and get out of here, because Bogdan was being stupid if he thought these were friends. But next to a carving that might have been real lily roots and lily stem, towering up and up, Bogdan set him against the wall.

"Listen," Bogdan said, bending to look him in the face and giving him a shake. "You're safe if you do what I say. Do you hear me? We can be safe here, you and I, and Tamas can be safe here. There's an army out there burning Albaz, and Burdigen, and all the towns in the valley to the ground— because those people were stupid. That's not going to happen to Maggiar. It's not going to happen to *us*. . . . because you're not going to make trouble, you're not going to offend these people! Remember that before you act the fool in this place!"

He saw nothing in the way of bad things happening to him or anyone the goblins could catch, except his brother was giving orders to goblins instead of being a prisoner, and his brother was talking about goblins burning towns their gran had told stories about, stories Tamas had handed down to him after she died. He thought he should be happy that Bogdan was alive—but he had far rather know that Bogdan was the brother he remembered.

"Do you understand me?"

"Yes," he said, because he did not want his arm broken.

"Come on," Bogdan said, and pulled him along a hallway. "I want you with me. I don't want any misunderstandings."

"What happened to Jerzy and everybody?" he asked, hoping Bogdan would at least remember that something bad had happened at Krukczy Tower.

Bogdan jerked his arm so hard it brought tears to his eyes, paying no attention to his question, and Yuri suddenly had no inclination whatsoever to tell Bogdan about Karoly and Nikolai having escaped the goblins at Krukczy Straz. He was scared, really scared, since Bogdan had chosen not to answer his question about Jerzy and the rest, who had been Bogdan's friends, and the men he was leading. Bogdan had not been his favorite brother, but Bogdan had never, ever acted like this, or talked about being safe with goblins who had shot Nikolai and tried to kill Tamas and master Karoly.

Bogdan took him down one hall and into another, with the floating lights and goblins coming and going. Bogdan gave him to a goblin to watch, while Bogdan went over and talked urgently to a handful of tall goblins that looked more important than the rest, all in armor, all bristling with weapons.

Yuri calculated the chances of kicking his goblin guard in the shins and making a break for a door, but Bogdan had said don't be stupid, and that, in this place where halls happened without ordinary doors, seemed good advice, except not the way Bogdan had meant it: as he saw it, it was a question of biding his time.

So he watched the disgusting sight of his brother talking with his goblin friends, while another goblin was holding his arm, and he (he could not help it) looked up at him to get an undersided view of a goblin face, while the lights were floating around them like fireflies and congregating where Bogdan and the others were talking.

A strange sight, that face was. But he did not like it when the goblin realized what he was doing and glared down at him.

He heard the group with Bogdan say something about other goblins; and he heard Bogdan say something about promising to let him deal with Tamas himself.

So he crossed his eyes at the goblin who was glaring at him and made a face, for good measure. And the goblin clearly had his orders not to bite his head off, and did nothing. A light floated right around the goblin's shoulder and drifted off to join the others bobbing around Bogdan and the rest, where the center of interest was.

So Yuri straightened around and kept a calm face, watching his brother betray Tamas, and Maggiar, and everything and everyone he knew.

Which hurt—hurt worse than anything anybody had ever done to him. It was not a thing boys did. It was something a man did, and that man was a brother of his—which made him somehow dirty, too, and responsible, and completely desperate to find a way out of this trap to warn the people he cared about.

Like finding Tamas, he thought. Tamas was older. Tamas would know what to do first and where to go.

He stood there in a goblin's keeping until Bogdan decided to take him back. Bogdan took him down the hall, past the fantastical lilies and the carved fish and the monsters that lurked in the stone, while a trail of excited lights tried to keep up with them.

"We've got to find Tamas before he undoes everything," Bogdan said as they went. "He's around here somewhere. Come on! Fool!"

They walked a corridor of strange watery darkness, and Tamas asked himself, alone with goblins and the consequences of his confusion, whether he was entirely sane. The ghost had ceased to trouble him, inside, for the moment—Ylena was visible now, apart from him, walking ahead of them—at least he fancied he could see her from time to time, at the instant the eye had to blink: most horrible in aspect, a tattered figure of a woman, all bones and gauze.

"Ylena," he said to Azdra'ik, as the only one who might understand his distress. "I can't be rid of her."

"I see her," Azdra'ik said. "The pretentious baggage. A tag-along."

"More than that, damn it." Azdra'ik had a way of provoking the ghost, and he flinched, expecting its spite.

Azdra'ik said, close by his ear, grasping his arm. "She fears dying—and die she will, if ever goblins leave the earth again. That was the term of her long life. You should be wary of that. Promise her you don't intend to banish us."

He heard that, and his heart gave a thump, as if he were being threatened into an agreement more important than his distracted wits could surround at the moment.

What does he want of me?

"Ask that favor of Ela," he said. "What have I to do with it?"

"As the residence of a power that can damn us? As Ylena's means into the queen's hall? A great deal. I gave her the secret of the mirror and the woman blames me that she was a fool—not *my* fault, I say."

He was trying to understand Azdra'ik's position. But the witch hovered near him, there at the edge of every blink, a shadowy swirl of living anger. "Let be. Don't quarrel with her."

"Oh, not with her, man, with her successors. Given the choice, your young witch out there—"

A shiver went through the floor—but the tremor was more than in the earth, it was a shock within his heart. A desire that was Ela's. A solitude that was Ela's, overwhelming the ghost's faded spite. This was now. This was imminent danger.

"Someone," Azdra'ik said, "just gained the queen's attention."

"Ela!" He jerked his arm away from Azdra'ik's grip and at once felt an edge near his foot.

"Fool!" Azdra'ik caught him as another tremor ran through the tunnel, making the reflections shimmer—and he did not fall, only by the intervention of Azdra'ik's hand.

And the silence that followed the shaking was smothering. He tried to free himself.

"Be calm, be calm." Azdra'ik released his arm slowly. "You can so easily fall here, man, you can fall to something like death—you can drown in the queen's imagination. Or in the queen's all-demanding will, which I personally count worse."

"Ela's under attack."

"Did you expect not? I asked you—take the mirror. I pleaded with you, take the mirror. Now—*now* you have second thoughts. The war is launched, man. There is no disengagement. And for good or ill, the mirror shard belongs to the fledgling."

"The witch with a wizard consort," another said, close

at hand—which startled him: few of the goblins seemed to have human speech.

"With a wizard consort," Azdra'ik agreed. "That's true. That's never been. It may make a difference, that she wants him more than the queen does."

"She has no consort! Don't assume—"

"Man, you echo of it. The whole mirror does. Do you think we're deaf?"

He was surrounded by goblins, and Ela's presence ran through him like hammer-blows, shock after shock to his bones. He saw only fierce, expectant faces in the dim, watery light, and suddenly—suddenly a sense of that presence so vivid there was no difference between him and her, no housing left for the ghost that clamored outside. He *saw* into somewhere he could not see with his eyes, into a hall . . . but he could not make it clear. It shimmered—

The lake . . . god, the *lake*, Ela!

One thing touches everything. One thing affects everything. They wanted the *lake*, Ela, everything for the lake—that *is* the mirror, in our realm—

"Man!" Azdra'ik cautioned him. "Man, listen to me."

There was light, watery reflections glancing and bouncing off the floor. The way ahead looked like a bubble in the sun. He rubbed his eyes, and started walking with Azdra'ik and his companions about him.

Came a cold touch at his shoulder. Too late for recriminations, he said to the ghost's nagging at him. We're here, madam. We've no chance to be anywhere else. Shut up!

It did not *like* to be addressed that way. He felt its anger.

And will you die? he flung back at it. We all can die. Easier than not, at this point.

It did not want to be here. The *queen* wanted it to be here, it believed that beyond a doubt, now. It had touched him, it had tried to hold him and it had gotten swept up in the current of spells—

—of spells ages old and more powerful than she understood. The ghost had kissed an innocent to steal his life and found something far from innocent; she blamed him for that, she railed on him for that, she suspected him of wizardly complicities she could not find . . .

Consort, the goblins had said. The witches of the Wood had no such thing. There had been no wizards in Ylena's time . . .

But in gran's, he thought distractedly, there was Karoly. . . .

Fear broke forth in Ela, then a regathered collectedness, as the air in their very faces began to shimmer like the air above a forge: the water-patterns shimmered violently, and then stopped. They faced a man and a band of goblins that reached instantly for swords.

But it was himself, his own startlement, their own reflections, that dissolved into ripples of light and pattern, as if someone had cast a stone into water.

"Tamas?" a boy's voice called out—a boy's shape was the new image it was taking. Yuri's image looked out at him— touched the invisible surface, and made it ripple, but no more than that, and, for a boy Tamas knew beyond a doubt was home and safe—lord Sun, it looked and sounded so very real.

"Tamas!"

"Is it a lie?" he asked Azdra'ik. "He's not here! He's safe over-mountain!"

Yuri's reflection shook its head, remarkable in the likeness that pulled at his heart. "Zadny got away. I followed him and I got here—Bogdan's here. —*But don't believe*—"

The mirror shimmered violently and something snatched Yuri out of his sight.

Goblin hands snatched Tamas back, on his side, or he would have followed.

"Let me go!"

"Don't," Azdra'ik said, "don't be a fool. It's the mirror that governs such things. Make it give the vision back!"

"I don't know if I want it!"

"Then know!" Azdra'ik shouted at him. "Know once and for all, man, you've few other chances. Will you face it? Yes or no!"

"I want it back!" he cried.

The shimmering steadied, and Yuri came bursting through it, sprawled flat and looked up, still as a fawn before the hunters, his expression all dismay and desperation.

"It's *me*," Tamas said. But the mirror showed another image before him—: Bogdan, in every detail it was Bogdan.

"Come across," Bogdan said, beckoning him. "Tamas, bring Yuri, and come here."

"No," Azdra'ik said under his breath. "That's the queen's work. Pass through that surface and he can touch you."

"Tamas."

He thought how his company must look to Bogdan, and he had the thought to explain to Bogdan it was safe and he was not a prisoner, but suddenly there were goblins at Bogdan's back, too, a good many of them, a hall, bright with lights, and it was himself who stood in shadow, with his younger brother dazed and trying to choose what was real. It was the look on Yuri's face he could not bear, the doubt between the two of them.

"Yuri," he said. "Yuri, can you answer me?"

"Yes," Yuri's image said, sounding like Yuri's very self if Yuri were frightened out of good sense. "I hear you."

"What should I do, Yuri? Should I listen to him?"

"No," Yuri said definitely enough.

"The boy doesn't understand," Bogdan said. "Tamas, I want you to take Yuri and bring him with you. I've a guarantee of your safety."

"The queen's promises," Azdra'ik said.

"Shut up!" he hissed at Azdra'ik. "Bogdan. Are you free to come to this side?"

"Free," Bogdan said. "Free, yes. But I want you to come to me. You'll be safe. I promise you."

The rippling surface belled outward and gained a portion of the hall. "Tamas!" Yuri yelled in dismay as the mirror snatched him back, and Tamas made a desperate reach for him, but goblin hands held him back.

"Come on!" Bogdan said. But Yuri was not pleased with

where he was. Tamas saw the shake of Yuri's head and stopped struggling with the goblins' hold on him.

"Back up," Azdra'ik said, laying a hand on his shoulder. "We're losing, back up. We can't press it yet."

"No," he said. Backing up and leaving Yuri and Bogdan there—even the illusion of his brothers—he could not risk losing them. He tried to feel Ela's presence. He reached for magic, and intended the wall to waver the other way and give up his brothers, by the god, it would.

He held steady, at least—the surface shook one way and the other, as if a stone had struck it.

"What are you doing?" Bogdan asked.

"Wizardry," said a lisping, soft voice from somewhere among the goblins, at Bogdan's back. "Grandson of Karoly Magus—the gift you don't own, your brother Tamas clearly does. He has magic enough to make him a power in the world. Did he tell you that on the other side of the mountains, or did he keep it secret from you? Clearly we have the lesser brother on our side."

Tamas heard it, angry at its insinuations, he heard it and he saw Bogdan half-turn to cast a look behind him, and, in the same moment, knew the way he knew his brother's character what that cursed voice had done to them, what a soreness it had touched, the same that he had protected in Bogdan with every duck of his head, every taunt turned and every provocation declined that his brother had offered him.

Damn you, he thought on the instant, a lifetime's evasions all come to this.

"You're no wizard," Bogdan said, angrily. "*You're* no wizard."

"Bogdan—"

"—I want you to come here," Bogdan said.

"He didn't tell you," the insidious voice said. "But certain ones had to have known. And lay odds that your brother knew—and Karoly Magus. Probably even the servants—"

"I didn't," Tamas said. "That's rubbish, Bogdan, for the god's sake, what are we talking about? Get out of there. Walk out. Give me your hand and hold on to Yuri."

"To do what? To have Maggiar burn? But maybe you don't care about things like that—Tamas Magus."

"Oh, for the god's sake, Bogdan, I never hid anything from you. I don't even know what they say is true, I don't know to this day that it's true—don't listen to them, this is family, this is our *family*, Bogdan, not some strangers' word on it—"

"Then come over here. Do what I tell you. They're willing to have us rule Maggiar, to have us rule over all the world on our side of the mountains. They'll let us do as we please, Tamas, one kingdom after another—"

He shook his head. "You. Over here."

"Am I the oldest, Tamas?"

"You're the oldest."

"Do I know better than you do? I'm telling you what to do, little brother."

"No. Bogdan, don't listen to them. We don't have to take their terms. We can beat them. Get Yuri out of there."

"He's very confident," the voice said, thick with fangs—and it began to sound feminine to his ears. "Isn't he?"

"Shut up," Tamas said to the queen—he was sure it was the queen—and the mirror shook.

"Wizard," the goblin queen said. "Come across. You can be with your brothers. You can have any reward you like."

"No."

"Tamas," Bogdan said.

"He won't listen to you," the goblin queen said. "He knows everything."

"He'll listen," Bogdan said, in his no-nonsense way, his side of the mirror advanced as he strode forward, and Tamas backed a pace: he had learned when he was five to back up when Bogdan sounded like that and came in his direction. But his back met a wall of armored goblins—and Yuri was held by goblins on the other side.

"Get hold of him," Tamas said, turning to Azdra'ik, trying to avoid the fight Bogdan was pressing. "Hold on to him."

But that was the wrong thing to have said. Bogdan drew his sword with a rasp of metal that made the mirror shiver.

"Put it away," Tamas said, turning again. "Bogdan. Put it—"

Bogdan sliced through the mirror surface between them and Tamas jumped back as goblin steel rang out. Swords cleared their scabbards on either side, and Tamas was still trying to evade Bogdan's attack, empty-handed.

"No, Bogdan!" A second close pass, the wind of which passed his cheek: he flinched back again, hard against a goblin arm—parry him, was his desperate thought, he drew on the retreat, brought the sword up and Bogdan's blade clanged against it with a shock that jolted his wrists.

"Bogdan, quit it!" he cried, but there was the queen's laughter from beyond the barrier, there was Yuri shouting to watch out. "Bogdan! They want this, stop it!"

Blow after blow came at him and he kept turning them. No one else was fighting. They all were watching, one side and the other of the mirror surface, and jeers came from Bogdan's side. "Go on," the goblins shouted, and Yuri shouted at them to stop it—but he could not drop his guard without Bogdan cleaving him in two, and Bogdan's strokes were growing wild and desperate, ringing through the blade to his bones. The clangor filled his ears, rang over the wailing protests of the ghost, rang over the goblin voices and into the watery walls that shook to the sound of blades.

Stroke met and next stroke met: he was unwilling to back up, but he had no choice. Azdra'ik was shouting advice at him he could not hear, Yuri was yelling and his arms and his wrists were buckling under the clanging and hammering. Get the sword away from him, was what his good sense screamed at him, but doing that to Bogdan was no easier than reasoning with him when Bogdan's pride was at stake.

"They want this!" he shouted, in the hope that Bogdan was wearing down enough to hear him. "Bogdan, they've got Yuri."

"I'm not a fool!" Bogdan shouted. His face was suffused with anger, his eyes were crazed with it. "You're so damned

smug, you're so damned clever, don't you think I know
what you were doing getting into our company, you and Karoly—?''

He hardly had the wind to argue. Get it away from him,
was all he could think of, trying to wield a goblin sword in
a wearying defense, with Azdra'ik's company yelling in his
ear and Azdra'ik himself shouting advice he could not con-
sciously hear over the ringing in his ears. He made an over-
reach with the blade, tried to hang Bogdan's blade with the
quillon-spine on his and almost succeeded; but Bogdan's
strength jerked the blade half out of his grip before the im-
perfect hold raked free. He made a desperate recovery. The
goblins yelled advice. A familiar hand landed momentarily
on his shoulder and shoved him. Azdra'ik shouted, ''Attack,
fool!''

''Shut up!'' he yelled at Azdra'ik, and dodged Bogdan's
attack.

''They're coming at Ela, man! We can't hold them forever—''

This as he trod on someone's foot trying to back up, and
Bogdan's sword grated and sliced along his shoulder.

''Get out of my way,'' he panted. ''Bogdan, stop it! You're
wrong, for the god's sake, Bogdan—'' He gave up trying
to coddle Bogdan's sense of righteousness. ''Papa would
say—''

''What? That we're all wizard bastards?'' A downstroke
beat his blade down. But Bogdan was tiring, too. Bogdan
could not take advantage on the recovery: Tamas shoved him
back with his shoulder and tried bashing him with the hilt.

The barked quillon drew blood across Bogdan's hand.
''Damn you!'' Bogdan yelled, looking at it, and launched a
crazed attack, blow after blow.

''The edge!'' Azdra'ik yelled. ''Watch your feet, man!''

He had no more room. A goblin's shove at his back flung
him within Bogdan's guard and he used the hilt and the side
of the blade, to batter himself free. Sweat was running in his
eyes. The goblins were all shouting, both sides at once. He
made a second desperate try to trap Bogdan's guard, and

trapped himself, the swords bound together, the tines piercing Bogdan's hand—he *had* him, if he did not let go, he could keep from killing Bogdan or being killed, if he did not let Bogdan get free, but Bogdan was grabbing at his throat and forcing him backward in a frenzy of pain and outrage, step by resisting step—he knew the edge was behind him.

"You'll take us over!" he yelled at Bogdan. "You'll take us over the edge, dammit, don't!"

His foot hit nothingness. He felt himself going, he felt the drop beginning and he let go the sword—he had made up his mind to that—rather than kill them both.

But a hand snagged him by one arm as he let go the sword. Bogdan spun past him with all his weight and both swords—into empty space past his reaching hand. The pull on his left sleeve was hauling him back to solid ground breathless and cold and shaking from head to foot—

"Bogdan!" he shouted into that gulf, in hope that if it was a magical place he might yet find him.

"He's gone!" Azdra'ik shouted into his ear, with his arms around him. "You're *here*, man. Do you hear me? They won't stop us. *Man!*" Azdra'ik shook at him. "Listen to me! You've got the power to do something—do it! Use the mirror! Break through the wall!"

One thing touches everything, he thought, for no reason. And: for less reason and with a sudden unreasoning hope: Master Karoly!

Nikolai tried not to think about the stars above the tangle of woods, but he was sure that it was at least rightfully noon, that something magical was in progress, and that if their two ghostly guides were at all reliable they should have found the boy long since.

"They're not getting us anywhere!" he protested to Karoly.

"We're not where we were," Karoly snapped. "And it's not that easy, master huntsman, it's not a deer we're tracking."

"What does that mean?"

"That it's not a deer!"

That was what one got for arguing with a man who thought in circles and heard things when he set his ear against the earth. But from the beginning Ysabel and Pavel had seemed on the track of something the hound was interested in following: Karoly's murdered sister and her soldier lover drifted effortlessly in the lead as they slogged through thicket and up and down hills, Nikolai leading the old man on the pony— with the hound out in front of all of them, running with his nose to the ground, immune to the dark that impeded a human hunter and probably tracking better than both ghosts together, in Nikolai's estimation.

Then of a sudden Nikolai smelled apples, when no apple tree should be in fruit—and that made him think, oddly enough, of the courtyard in Maggiar, an overset basket by the kitchen door, and Michal's horse.

The dog barked, letting every goblin in ten leagues about know where they were.

"Quiet!" Nikolai hissed. "Dog, hush!"

In the same instant he felt a tweak at his hair, which might have been a twig raking him. A slight breeze had started up, a whispering in the brush.

Good lad, someone said. He was sure it was not master Karoly—Karoly did not call him good and no one called him lad these days. It sounded like a woman's voice. He could not be certain.

Loyal to Stani, indeed, the voice said next his ear—no one could fault you that.

"Urzula?" Karoly asked of a sudden. "Urzula, is that you?"

"Just the wind," Nikolai said, wanting to believe in anything but the lady gran next his ear.

But in the self-same moment, on a trick of the wind, he heard a sound he had not heard since his wandering youth: the clash of swords and the sounds of warfare echoing through the woods. Gracja brought her head up, pulled at the reins he was holding, and Nikolai scrambled aside as a shadow of a rider passed right through the brush without disturbing any of it, and passed right through Gracja and Karoly to boot.

A second rider passed, and a third, all shadows, and Nikolai began to shiver in a way nothing had made him do since he was a boy hiding from the soldiers.

But he had the impression he knew who they were without clear sight of any of them: Michal, and Filip, and Jerzy and all his dead comrades, all riding toward the sounds of combat. Zadny barked at them and set up a sudden howl.

That was the only thing that brought him to his senses, because for a moment he felt so light-headed, so slightly connected to his body, that it would have been so much easier to let go and run after them.

He reached out for Karoly's knee, fearing for the old man's life. But: "Follow them," Karoly said urgently. "God, give me up the reins. The boy's in deep trouble!"

The dog crashed off into the woods ahead of them. He handed Karoly up the reins, Karoly flailed at Gracja with his heels and the pony started moving, stolidly, relentlessly forward, while the ghosts went before them with a sighing in the branches, and ghosts of every sort poured in from left and from right of them, drifting shadows in the starlight, afoot, ahorse, some on creatures an honest man did not want to see—those might be goblin dead.

There was a brilliance ahead, some sort of light cast up from the valley below on the thinning screen of trees, and came a howl from ahead of them that Nikolai had heard only once before in his life, at Krukczy Straz when the arrows had begun to fly—goblins leapt up ahead from ambush, with shrieks and waving of swords that glittered in the eerie light.

But that howling changed abruptly when the shadows in their lead poured into their midst. Goblins broke from cover and turned in flight; Nikolai ran, gasping for breath, to add whatever solid force he could to the ghosts, shielded his eyes with his arm and broke through a screen of brush onto a barren hillside, beneath which something shone like a star brought to earth. Shadows flowed down that hill like a river of darkness behind the fleeing goblins, a river on which the light still picked out detail like a helmet or an arm or a mailed shoulder—shadows flowed over the goblins and left them still—except a few that scattered shrieking and gibbering to the four winds, and a handful of stragglers from the ambush that tried to regroup in Nikolai's path.

Nikolai did not stop to think: he laid with blind desperation into what resistance he found, clearing a path, because an old fool on a pony was coming behind him, and there was the light down there, the only relief from the night around them. That was where they had to go and he did not even question the idea, he was only aware as he sliced his way through that Karoly and the pony had flanked him, headed downward past him.

Somewhere he found the wind to take out running after the old man, with a stitch in his side and the light blurring and blinding him. Wizardry for certain, he thought, a white glare unlike sun or fire—centering somewhere about a girl on a motionless horse.

And surrounded by goblins.

"Karoly!" he yelled, half doubled with pain—and ran the faster to overtake Karoly, having the only sword, and seeing the old man going on as if he saw nothing at all but the light.

But these were different goblins, taller, surrounding the girl on the horse as if they stood guard—the goblin queen, Nikolai thought it might be—but if she was, her guard was trusting her magic and not shooting at them or lifting a sword.

Then the girl did move—Nikolai saw it in the jolts of his running: she looked toward them and Karoly stopped the pony as the light in her hand flared like the lightning. He could see everything, the detail of goblin armor, more than those he had seen—hopeless odds, even discounting magic.

Karoly lifted his staff, that thing that had encumbered him through the woods, waved it overhead; and Nikolai fetched up against Gracja's sweating rump for support, unable to run another step; while *something* happened. The fire grew brighter and brighter and sheeted out across a lake he had not even seen so dark it was—one blaze and another and another until it seemed from where he stood that he could see moving shapes above its still surface.

And came the belling of a hound, off along the lake shore, a pale shape running as if he had taken leave of his senses—"Follow the dog!" Karoly shouted at Nikolai.

"What?" He hardly *had* a voice.

"You're no damn use here—*follow the dog!*"

Nikolai caught a breath, shoved off from the pony's side, and started running, only then realizing that the dog would be after the boy, and that the old man might have a reason. He ran limping and splashing through shallow water, his side shot with pain—he hoped no goblins saw him; but some did and ran after him . . . and he had no cover and no strength to turn and fight: he only hoped to stay ahead of them and find some cover to duck behind and lose them before he led them onto the boy's trail.

Dark surrounded him of a sudden—he thought he might have lost a moment or passed out still running, because around him was suddenly confined, and dank and cold, lit by a watery light just enough to see—and with the dog's barking echoing in far distance, the armored clatter of pursuit immediately behind him—he kept going, he did not know how, thinking if Karoly wanted him alive Karoly should do something—but he could not keep ahead of them. When they were on him he pulled a staggering halt and spun about to meet them, but they swarmed him, grabbed his left arm and his sword arm, and held on, a solid mass of them, glittering with metal in the watery reflections.

He fought to free himself. They fought to hold on, with no reason in the world they should not swipe his head off and be done.

Which finally persuaded him they did not intend to. He stopped fighting to get a breath, and they let up their hold somewhat.

"Man," one panted, displaying dreadful fangs. And clapped him on the shoulder and pointed down the way he had been going.

It took him a moment to sort his wits out—in the realization they were offering their services at dog-chasing. The heart of hell and the queen of the goblins, Karoly had said about this place . . . but in his travels he had found more than one band of discontents.

They let him go, he found the breath to keep going, and he went with an escort with only one human word in their speech. But either they were taking him to their queen or they were going with him to their queen, and either way, that got him in reach of the goblin responsible for this devastation.

That was agreeable to him.

Nothing moved the other side of the barrier, not the goblins, not Yuri, not for the small moments Tamas could press the mirror surface: holding everything stone still was the best that he could do. But it was not an effort only with the hands—the instant his thoughts scattered to any other object, changes began to happen, and figures frozen so long as he could hold them, began to move beyond the barrier. He had no idea whether it was any good to try to stop it, he was not sure whether it was winning or not or had any hope, but he tried, and kept trying, although he knew something was dreadfully wrong outside. He had lost any sense of where Ela was, or what had happened—he might be the last hope left; and he had no knowledge to replace her—had no understanding what he was doing or had to do, he only persevered in blind attacks, willing to entreat the ghost, the goblins with him, any ally he would take if he could rescue Yuri from the hands that held him.

Yuri tried not to admit that he was afraid—Yuri scowled in slow movement, Yuri drew back his foot and, god, he knew what Yuri was going to do, he did not want him to do it, for his life he did not, and he held everything still as long as he could—but he felt something slip, then, some vast disturbance that made the barrier change—and of a sudden he lost all purchase. Yuri's foot swung, the goblin winced and doubled, and he—

—he was able now only to shout at the enemies who had

his brother. He struck the barrier with his bare hands: but breach it he still could not, could not even feel solidity in what took and took his strength.

The goblins with him added their force—Azdra'ik's was far more than his; Azdra'ik was face to face with him, shoulder to the barrier, and it was the face of a beast he saw, a fear no less than his—Azdra'ik was near to losing himself and all he hoped to win back, and he, of losing Yuri—

Suddenly the surface gave way—dissolved in front of them. An image of an image of an image froze within his eyes, and they sprawled in a heap in the further hall, lights fleeing and bobbing like living things, himself and a handful of exhausted goblins . . .

Facing a sheet of glass or water—he could not tell, it shimmered so—but Yuri was there, in the hands of enemies; and most of all, most of all the goblin queen, the face in the mirror, that of a sudden blotted everything out. He got up. Azdra'ik did, and the others, facing the queen on her throne.

"Over-confidence," the queen said, "is a deadly flaw. Do you want the young one?"

"Yes," he began to say, but Azdra'ik stepped in front of him and shouted something he had no idea what, but it was enough to make the queen's nostrils flare with rage, and her cheeks suffuse with color. The queen shouted and stood up with a clatter of bracelets and pointed toward the goblin lord.

No, Tamas thought, *no*—and saw that small darkness next the queen's arm, that darkness that was the shape of Ela's mirror; and *that* was what he looked at—dared not take his eyes from that single patch, that single place on the mirror where he had a hope of seeing what he wanted, instead of what the queen wished. When he saw light on that spot, exactly the shape of Ela's mirror, the mirror was whole.

Then—he did not want it; he did not sense that the queen did—something of shadow and of bone and malice slipped into his vision to take everything from him. He saw the woods, the night, the tangled brush, the scattered bones . . .

"Stop her!" Azdra'ik shouted at him, shaking his shoulder.

Of a sudden the whole mirror shifted backward, and became a wall of dreadful colors, a rush of goblins toward them with spears and swords.

He took a step back, among Azdra'ik's few, and sought his single spot on the great mirror—and saw the shard rippling with uncertainty. Lights streamed and bobbed about them as goblins fought goblins, as steel blades flashed between him and the mirror. Without taking his eyes from that haziness he drew the dagger he had, Azdra'ik's gift, held it ready to defend himself, as he heard Yuri call out desperately for him.

But in the same moment he heard a hound baying and barking at his back—shadows poured about him in a wave of inky chill, about him and past him, as a yellow hound came skidding onto the marble floors, skidding and yelping in startlement as he skidded through the battle, against the very mirror.

It shimmered—and the queen's image shook.

"Zadny!" Yuri yelled from somewhere, and the startled dog was on his feet in the melee of shadows and goblins— but how that issue was, Tamas did not take two blinks to see. In the whole mirror he saw Ela by the lake.

He saw, around the mirror, Azdra'ik and a band of goblins pounding one another on the shoulders and shouting at each other like human boys . . .

He saw Nikolai, leaning on a goblin arm, limping and breathless, and suddenly Yuri running for him—through the very substance of the mirror. Zadny put himself in his path and dog and boy somehow navigated the battle-ground to reach him.

"Tamas!" Yuri was yelling, trying to hug him. Zadny was jumping at him, trying to get his attention.

But it was not done. It was not done until the mirror was entirely still and until he could see Ela, nothing but Ela's face against the night, completely occupying the mirror.

Master Karoly was in that image. He knew that without seeing him. He knew the presence of ghosts, that warred within the mirror, quarreling, in shouts and shrieks, and

Jerzy, lord Sun, Jerzy complaining it was dark and unpleasant—

He caught a breath, on his knees with both arms full of boy and dog. He could not move, else. He dared not move or think or wonder, so long as the image remained what it was.

Something was terribly wrong, even if things had gone right for a moment. Yuri took hold of Zadny's collar, not knowing whether to let Zadny try to wake Tamas up or whether he ought not—but when his lap was free, Tamas got slowly to his feet and went on staring at the mirror, regardless of a room full of excited goblins, or anything. "Tamas?" he said, and when he had no answer from Tamas, he looked over at Nikolai and saw Nikolai limping toward him, covered in sweat and hardly able to keep his feet—so he kept Zadny tightly in hand.

Nikolai set his hand on his shoulder, hugged him against his side, and told him they were taking Tamas out of here—

"If we have to carry him," Nikolai said.

But a tall goblin said, soberly, "No. It's not over. He hasn't won."

"What's not over?" Nikolai said hotly. "What's to win?"

He did not want Nikolai starting a fight with them, not when Tamas was the way he was. He tugged at master Nikolai's sleeve to stop him.

"The young wizard has his way," the goblin said, "and our people have the hall for the moment. But nothing's certain." Nikolai made a move to defy him and the goblin interposed his hand. "Fatally uncertain. He might die."

"Don't." Zadny was trying to get away, and Yuri held on to his collar with all his might.

"I'm going after Karoly."

"Wizard enough is here," the goblin said, and he meant Tamas, plain as plain. "Let him finish his work."

It needed a while, simply to gain a little breath. Ela was there, as shocked, as weary, as desperate. Master Karoly was there. Karoly was the one who said, or thought, "The whole place is hanging by a thread. Don't look away, boy. Well done. *Well* done."

There were others present. Jerzy was indignant: I've business to take care of. I've no time for this nonsense, damn them, I've a horse in foal—

I'd care for it, Tamas thought, if I were there myself, back in Maggiar.

And Filip: What about my father? He's old. Who's to take care of him?

I won't forget, Tamas said.

Bogdan showed up in that company. But Bogdan was not speaking to him. Tamas was not surprised. He was immensely glad that Bogdan had found his friends again.

Then he heard gran speaking, shooing the other dead away too soon—but she banished one other that he felt lurking in the shadows.

Be off! You're not dead! Don't whine at me, you fool! You made your own mistakes! Leave my grandsons alone!

He was afraid for the outcome. He was not sure gran was a strong enough witch, to deal with Ylena. But he dared not all the while look away from Ela's face. He let all these things go on and he refused to give way to any diversion or trick or to look away from the only sight he was sure of.

Mirela, gran said severely.

No one calls me that, Ela protested, gazing fixedly at him, the same, holding on, only holding on, but afraid.

No one should, gran said sharply. —And you *are* Pavel's. And descended from Ytresse and Ylysse. That should make you cautious in your tempers, *and* your wants; if nothing else does. For the rest . . . grandson?

"Gran?"

Remember the stories.

"Gran!"

Remember the stories, gran said again, and he could not help it, he was so startled: he began to remember exactly the way gran had told them, the woods and the waterfalls, the cities in the plain—

* * *

The lights began bobbing crazily, flitting around the watery walls and bouncing off them like housebound birds, the whole mirror began shaking, Zadny started barking, trying to get loose, but with all of that confusion going on, Yuri held on to him for dear life.

"What's going on?" Nikolai shouted at the goblins, but they looked to have no answers, either, just—

"Look at the mirror!" Yuri cried. It was changing, the reflection within it leaping from shadowy forests to starlit waterfalls, to courtyards and fountains and fields and beautiful places. Lights flitted above woodland pools, and wandered through the wood. Fairies, he realized. "Just like gran's stories!" he exclaimed, his arms wrapped about Zadny's neck and shoulders. "Tamas is doing it! *He's* doing it!"

Because Tamas had told him the stories, just the way, Tamas had sworn, the very words that gran had told them to him.

Doors banged open, and a wind blew through the hall, fresh and clean, direct from the outdoors.

Then Tamas turned away from the mirror, and Yuri flinched, seeing—he was not sure what he saw in Tamas' face, he only knew Tamas was still gazing off into thoughts that wanted no stupid boy interrupting, or rowdy dog jumping at him, in front of all these dangerous folk.

"Karoly's outside," Tamas said quietly. "Go and wait for me, master Nikolai. Bogdan's gone. Yuri needs to go home."

"Boy," Nikolai began to say. But Tamas only stood there, not angry, not impatient, just—that no argument was going to win with Tamas, even if Yuri had a question of his own— like, What about *you* going home?

But Nikolai gave him a shove, meaning they should do what Tamas wanted, and Yuri held onto Zadny and made him come away, with Zadny looking back and whining in confusion, because Zadny could not understand. That was what made Yuri saddest, because Zadny was more honest than he could let himself be.

The doors led straight out under the stars. If so many odder things had not happened, Yuri would have blinked at that; but he hardly asked himself where the tunnel had gone. Master Karoly was there, exactly the way Tamas had said. And there was the witch, hardly older than he was, on a horse, among a handful of goblin guards. But the lake was not dark and dreadful now. Fairies darted and flitted above the water. It was all very beautiful.

But it was dark and cold, all the same, walking along the shore. He was glad to see Karoly and Gracja; and master Nikolai met a surprise, too, because there was Lwi, being held by goblins. It was only three words Nikolai spent on Karoly once he saw that: he went and put his arms about Lwi's neck.

And Yuri was glad about Lwi, too. But seeing the witch sitting on horseback looking just the same as his brother did, and, staring off like that, upset his stomach.

"What are they doing?" he asked master Karoly, scared, because Karoly had something of that look, too—looking at things he could not see, listening to things he could not hear, and murmuring answers to them, what was worse.

But at least Karoly seemed not to forbid him asking. And Karoly slid down from Gracja's back and put an arm about him, dog in tow and all. Yuri set his jaw, because it made him feel a lump in his throat, and brought him very close to tears. He wished Karoly would just answer his question and not do that to him.

Karoly still did not answer his question. He only said, "I have him. He's all right. He's very worried about you."

It was Tamas he was talking to, Yuri understood that of a sudden. It made him feel both better and worse.

"I know," Karoly said, but he was still talking to Tamas. "I will. I understand." Karoly gave his arm a hug. "He'll be here."

"Who?" Yuri asked quietly, trying not to interrupt something. But it must have been him that Karoly was talking about this time, because Karoly did not answer him.

* * *

Deeper and deeper the change had to go, then, down into the earth, and into realms where strange things moved, old things, that ages of the earth had cast aside. And gran had talked about dragons and such, and said how they were cold and proud, and how one should never promise them anything, so he did not. Gran had said about the creatures of stone and ice, how they were not to trust, but, slow-moving and deliberate, they came above in winters, to howl in the mountain heights, and they had their place in faery.

The greatest and the lesser, and latest the things that could not change: it was only a matter of knitting those things together, one thing touching everything, as it had been.

And last it was a matter of letting go of things that seemed to have grown into one's soul.

And doing justice that had not been done.

He shut off seeing. It was a moment before he could knit Tamas back together, and be different from Ela, or the earth. It was self-blinding. It felt like darkness and smothering. But he endured it, and held himself to it, and eventually flesh and bone grew easier to wear and less heavy. He could open his eyes and move his hand and turn his head toward the goblins that stood watching and waiting for their banishment.

The goblin queen was already below, with every one else of her half-goblin creatures: he had seen to that, among the first things. But he looked at Azdra'ik, at nameless others, and set his hand on the dagger that was Azdra'ik's gift.

"Nothing from you," he said, "comes without attachments. And what did this come with?"

"My help," Azdra'ik said, without flinching. "When you were a young and weaponless fool."

He laughed. He could not help it. And probably there was a spell on the gift. There was when he drew it and gave it back, and caught Azdra'ik's arm in his and said he should come outside.

"Are we dispossessed?" Azdra'ik insisted to know as they walked. "Is that part of this bargain?"

"I named no bargain."

"There has to be one."

"No, no, no, master goblin. There *is* no bargain. You're in my debt, is what you are. From now on."

"No more than you're in mine! Who bought you free? Who carried you out of the woods? Who—?"

But they were at the doors, and what he had seen in the mirror, Azdra'ik could see for himself, and Azdra'ik freed himself and stood gazing at the lake, with its flitting and gliding lights.

"Oh, man," Azdra'ik said. "This is what our eldest saw. This is what our legends say. Who could know, but us?"

"My grandmother," he said, wondering suddenly about gran's sources.

But something broke the mirror stillness of the lake, and disturbed the skimming lights, something large and dark, that surfaced and dived again.

"What's that?" Yuri exclaimed. But in a moment more he knew for himself, as a trollish head broke the surface. And vanished again.

"Careful!" Karoly said, but Zadny set up a frantic barking, straining to get free, such a lunge he slipped Yuri's grip and evaded Yuri's dive after him.

Straight into the water Zadny ran, splashing and barking, and one and another huge head broke the surface.

"Krukczy!" Yuri shouted.

One splashed. But they kept surfacing and diving so quickly, swimming in a circle, that it was impossible to tell.

"What are they doing?" he asked master Karoly; but Nikolai had come to see, too, and Nikolai muttered,

"Lost their minds. Happy, one supposes."

The witch came, with her cloak wrapped about her, walking along the shore. The goblins gathered to watch. And from up the shore—

"Tamas!" Yuri said. "It's Tamas, with the goblins!"

"Four of them!" Nikolai exclaimed, but he was not counting goblins. There were four dark heads in the lake, and Zadny, running back and forth along the shore and barking as if he had lost his wits.

"Krukczy," said the witch, "and Tajny, and Hasel."

"And Ali'inel," Karoly added. "This place."

Their circle had grown tighter and tighter. And a bright spot grew in the water, bright as the sun. Their circle widened and it grew and grew. They dived all at once, in the middle of it.

But the light kept going, until it lit all the lake, bright as day; and then it brightened the ground right under their feet, and crept up their legs and up the sides of the hills and up the foundations of a beautiful tower just past where Tamas and the goblins were.

The light kept going until it had topped the tallest trees on the tops of the hills, and then it went right up into the sky, on all sides at once. And where it began to meet, in the height of heaven, the bright edges came together in a glare the eyes could not look at. It was noon, that was all. The night might never have been.

But Zadny stood looking at the lake, with now and again a bewildered bark, then ran, wet as he was, straight for Tamas.

Yuri ran after him: he could only think of Zadny making some trouble for Tamas. But he stopped in confusion when he saw the goblins, that seemed somehow—different. Not vastly changed. But maybe sunlight favored them—lent them a touch of mystery and magic, a touch of mischief, a touch of merriment. He would not have been afraid of these goblins—in awe of them, oh, yes. He was.

But not Zadny. Zadny jumped up on Tamas while he had stopped to stare and had his dusty armor all wet and muddy.

But it *was* his brother, because Tamas laughed, weary as he was, caught the hound in one arm and held out the other for him.

"Come here," Tamas called to him. "Yuri, come meet a goblin lord."

At such a chance, how could anyone hesitate?

But all the same, Yuri thought, the night of the third day on the lake shore, watching Tamas walk hand in hand with Ela, and the two of them talking that way wizards talked with each other, that no one but a wizard could hear—all the same, he did not want Tamas to have magic. It was all very fine to have supper with goblins and have trolls living at the bottom of the lake, and fine, he supposed, to have the occasional ghost straying in from the mysterious Wood, where things did not just go away in the ordinary fashion (Ylena's spell, master Karoly said, something about preserving her own life)—but Tamas was very preoccupied, very sad, sometimes, Yuri thought, about Bogdan, and it was clear to him that he was going home and Tamas would not.

I don't know why *I* have to explain to our parents why, Yuri thought bitterly. I don't know why Bogdan acted like that, except he never could stand to be second to anybody, and I don't know why Tamas and that girl are both like that, Tamas isn't ready to get married yet, and mama certainly wouldn't approve of her. I don't think papa would.

She was brave, though, and a witch (a sorceress, Karoly said) and she was looking right at him right now, giving him the most uncomfortable notion that she and Tamas were talking about him.

He glared at her, and turned his head and glared at the fairy-lights on the lake, and thought about Krukczy.

Tamas was going to keep Zadny. Tamas said wizards might understand Zadny, but the houndsmaster never could, and if he went home with him, he would only get in trouble. And that was all right. Zadny knew who he wanted.

But he did *not* want to talk to Ela, and Tamas was bringing her in his direction. He watched the fairy-lights instead, and told himself they were very pretty. Seeing gran's land was very well, too, but it was going to be better to see Maggiar.

That, if Tamas happened to be listening to him.

"Yes," Tamas said, disconcertingly. "I know. But I can't help it."

"Don't *do* that!" Yuri said.

"I'm sorry," Tamas said. But Yuri looked at Ela, all pale and pretty beside him. Master Karoly said she was Azdra'ik's great-grand-daughter and his niece, and gran's cousin. So master Karoly was going to stay behind a year or two, master Karoly said, and see Tamas stayed out of trouble. So he and Nikolai were riding home tomorrow, on Lwi and Gracja. And he did not plan to sleep tonight.

Ela reached out and tousled his hair. That did not endear her to him. But being a witch, and overhearing people, she stopped immediately, and looked unhappy.

He imagined, for some reason, she had never seen a boy. She was curious. She thought he was very clever.

It was very hard to go on being mad at someone who really believed that—which was probably a spell she was casting, who could ever know? A lot of people had been scared of gran. Probably with good reason.

Which was why, Tamas had said, it really was not a good idea for him and for Ela to come back over-mountain just yet. Neither of us knows anything, Tamas had said. We had a lot of help, that's all. And there's an immense lot we have to learn.

Stupid girl, he had said back to Tamas, being surly. Lord Sun, he did not want to remember that now, when Ela was listening. She was not a stupid girl. Not, at least, stupid.

One had to look hard to see if Ela was amused. But he thought she was. He knew Tamas was.

He decided that, on the whole, Tamas would be all right. And Tamas had promised to send him word across the mountains, how he was, how he was getting along.

He did not think, somehow, that Tamas meant writing letters.

YVGENIE
by
C. J. CHERRYH

Eveshka thought she had protected her daughter from the forces of dark magic, until the day she discovered her daughter with a ghostly boy who was none other than the evil wizard Chernevog.

A Del Rey Book